TYCHE'S DECEIT

A SPACE OPERA ADVENTURE EPIC

EZEROC WARS
BOOK 2

RICHARD PARRY

CONTENTS

TYCHE'S CROWN

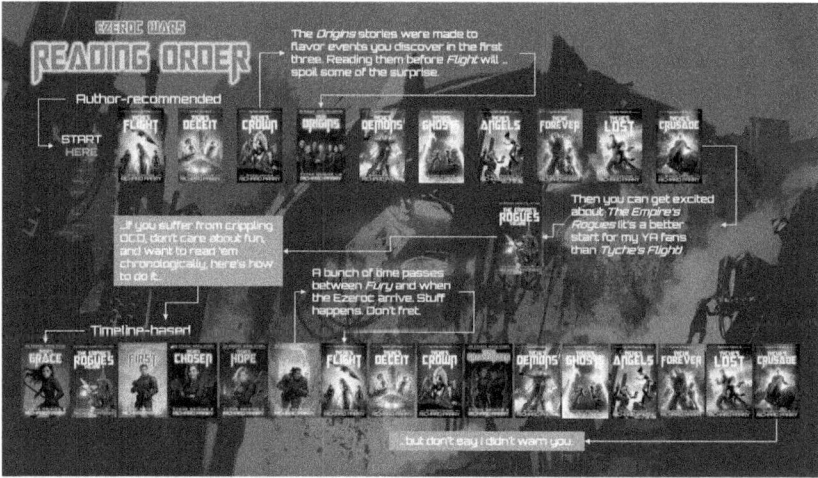

TYCHE'S DECEIT
THE ENEMY ISN'T COMING. THEY'RE ALREADY HERE.

After barely escaping Absalom Delta, **Grace Gushiken and Nathan Chevell have a mission: warn humanity.** The insect-like Ezeroc are real. **And they've already infiltrated Earth.**

The crew of the free trader *Tyche* is being hunted. **Men in black—fearsome fighters with inhuman abilities—will do anything to silence them.** When *Tyche* lands, the ship is locked down, her crew scattered and on the run. **Without their ship or each other, there's no escape.**

The Republic is compromised. The Ezeroc's influence runs deep. And time is running out.

Hope arrives from an unlikely source: the abhorrent espers of the Old Empire, **humanity's outcasts and monsters.** Their offer is simple: **join us, or die.**

Five souls. A battered heavy lifter. **The last chance to stop an enemy already entrenched in humanity's homeworld.**

If Grace and Nate fail, **there won't be a war. There will only be a harvest.**

Tyche's Deceit is the second book in Richard Parry's gripping *Ezeroc Wars* series. If you love **page-turning space opera** with sharp dialogue, heart-pounding action, and the fight for humanity's future, **grab your copy today!**

YOU'RE AWESOME

You could have picked any book, but you chose this one. That means a lot.

Your support keeps independent authors like me forging ahead, writing the stories we love (and hopefully, the ones you love too). Whether you're here for the characters, the worldbuilding, or just a little escapism, thank you for being part of this journey.

You. Kick. Ass.

ROLL FOR NARRATIVE
WHERE WORLDBUILDING AND OVERTHINKING COLLIDE

Love stories that linger in your brain long after The End? Ever wonder why some books hit like a natural 20 and others critically fail their way into the 1-star abyss?

Join *Roll for Narrative*, my hub for sci-fi and fantasy lovers. I explore storytelling like a rogue casing a dungeon, review movies, books, and games, and dish out writing tips like a chaotic-good bard with a grudge against bad prose. No spam, just good stuff.

Join the quest:
https://rollfornarrative.parrydox.com

For Anthony. This probably doesn't make up for all the therapy sessions, but you've got to start somewhere.

ONE GOOD LEAD

"IT ALL LEADS BACK TO EVANS." Nate had his arms crossed, blaster at his side, murder in his heart. The *Tyche* was adrift, holding in the hard black somewhere between Pluto and Neptune. Nothing out here to mine. Nothing out here to salvage. Not even rich folk came out here to see the sights anymore. It was a perfect opportunity to run silent, watching for danger. Things like: huge asteroids that were in fact alien ships that launched rocks down gravity wells. Nothing so far. Just the usual susurration of radio chatter from ten billion human souls shouting into the void, hoping someone would pay attention for a second. Nate was sure of one thing: attention was coming.

"That little shitwipe? I should have glassed that motherfucker back on Enia Alpha," said Kohl. "I don't know why you stopped me."

"Technically," said Grace, "he was hiring us at the time. If you'd ... what did you call it?"

"Glassed," said Kohl.

"Like, nukes?" said Hope. She was floating off the floor a couple centimeters, just within reach for her magboots for when it became go-time.

"Glassed," said Kohl, "like with a bottle. You smash it over the head of someone who deserves it, and if they don't go down like a sack of drowned puppies, you poke 'em with the sharp end."

"That a foreign term?" said El. "Sounds like you imported that one from off-world."

"Used to run with a Glaswegian," said Kohl. "Real asshole, used to say it a lot. Thing is—"

"Thing is," said Grace, "he was paying us good Republic coin. Or promising to. If you'd 'glassed that motherfucker,' we wouldn't have been paid."

"Still," said Kohl. "Would have saved us and ours a bunch of hurtin'." He paced on the worn deck plates, his magboots clunking with each step. "We should have—"

"Generally," said Nate, "I'm not into agreeing with Kohl wholesale. But bearing in mind that taking Evans' coin led us off a short plank with a long drop, well. Here we are. Thinking Kohl is right."

"I haven't been here in a long time," said Hope, meaning the solar system, not Kohl's point of view. Or, at least, that's what Nate's mental math tallied to. Her voice was low. "A *long* time."

"You haven't been alive a long time," said El.

"It's all relative," said Hope. "I don't know why we came here for him. We should be on Enia Alpha."

"Enia Alpha," said Nate, "is where he won't be. No way he was a local boy. No way he was there by random chance of fate." He put a hand on the butt of his blaster. "I think we should encourage him to tell us a little more. About the mission. About ... why us. Our crew." He met Grace's eyes across the ready room, the hum of the *Tyche* quiet for a moment. "Our family."

"Okay," said El. "This is all very touching, but where to first? You think he's batting here for the home team. Nine planets. Which one do we touch base with first?"

"The only one that counts," said Nate. "We're going home."

"Great," said Kohl. "Just great."

"I haven't been there in a long time too," said Grace, looking down at the deck. Then she looked at Kohl. "Wait. Why don't you want to be here? Got a warrant out on you or something?"

"Me? No," said Kohl. "Just, I guess I'm more of a burning bridges kind of guy."

"Me too," said Hope. "The fires help light the way."

"Anyway," said Nate. *This is getting real maudlin, real fast.* "We need a plan. If we open a comm up, say, 'Yo, this here's the *Tyche*, and we're hunting assholes,' we won't get a warm welcome."

"Or we'll get a really warm welcome," said El. "Lasers and plasma, couple of torpedoes, that kind of thing."

"Exactly my concern," said Nate. "So, I have this plan."

"Oh God, oh God, why," said Hope.

"Uh," said Nate.

"Your plans do suck a little," said El. "I'm trying to be honest. What do they call it? Three-sixty something?"

"Three-sixty-degree reviews," said Grace. "You give feedback on your boss. It's where—"

"We can give feedback on the captain?" said Kohl. "I'm in."

"*The plan,*" said Nate, "involves an old buddy of mine. He'll know where we can look for Evans. He'll want a favor in return. Most like? We'll have to lift something heavy—"

"Fuck," said Kohl.

"But Harlow? He'll do us right," said Nate. "Leastwise, he has in the past. Most of the time."

"Most of the time?" said Grace.

CHAPTER ONE

THE RAIN WAS the best part of this place. It sure as hell wasn't the people.

Now, the rain: it smelled clean. It tasted clean. It washed away grime and sweat and the smell of being on a ship for weeks. It carried the smell of the sea, even though the sea was klicks away. It was cooling in the heat, although in twenty minutes when it stopped raining the air would turn into a kind of cloying miasma of humidity. Nate planned to be inside somewhere air-conditioned, preferably a place that served alcohol, by the time that happened. Odds were against him, because his contact wasn't here yet. Which led to...

The people: they were everywhere. Underfoot, like rats, if rats could be big, selfish, and loud. Actually, nothing at all like rats, because rats didn't try and sell you knock-off holos or umbrellas that didn't work. Nate eyeballed the man in front of him. The guy was trying to sell Nate ... well, what *was* that thing? "Hey," said Nate, interrupting the man's mishmash of Cantonese, Tamil, and Russian. "What the fuck is that?"

"*Elektroshokovyy pistolet,*" said the man. "Taser. *Mikavum nallatu,* yes?"

Nate looked at the man, then at the bicycle the man had. It was laden with knick-knacks, odds and ends; some of it might have been garbage for a recycler. Hard to tell. Nate would have called the collection *souvenirs* if it wasn't for the thing the man kept trying to shove in his face. "A taser, huh?" said Nate. He patted the blaster at his hip. "Now why would I need one of those?"

"*Fēi zhìmìng*," said the man. "Sometimes you don't want kill."

"Ah," said Nate. "For those times, I use my charm."

"We're all going to die," said Grace. She'd worked her way back to Nate through the steady throng of humanity he was neck-deep in. He hadn't even seen her coming. There were so many people here it was hard to check all the corners. *I already miss having a deck under my feet and no one for a million klicks in any direction.* "But it'll be a clean death." She handed him an ice cream. Nate took it without comment, testing the flavor. *Butter pecan.* Could be a lot worse. And — being fair to their current location — getting a decent ice cream on the *Tyche* was out of the question. Hope couldn't magic one up in her fab. The galley served food lookalikes. But at least there weren't this many people.

The man with the souvenirs gave Grace a withering glance and then pushed his way off into the crowd. "How much luck you suppose he has?" said Nate. "You know. Selling worthless shit." He had to raise his voice over the noise of the throng around them. He gestured with his ice cream, which was getting wet. An excuse to eat it fast, if ever there was one.

"A taser can be useful," said Grace. She had her own ice cream, something green with flecks of black. Mint and chocolate chip, maybe?

"Not in our line of work," said Nate. "We live on the binary edge, Grace. Hot and cold. Yin and yang. Black and white. Dead or alive." He shook his butter pecan cone for emphasis.

She pushed a few wet strands of black hair out of her eyes. "Dead or alive, huh? You trying to channel Kohl or something?"

"Speaking of whom," said Nate, "where is he?"

"Said he was running errands," she said. "Can we go inside?"

"Harlow's not here yet," said Nate. "Harlow is our key to not living on the wrong side of the binary edge."

"The death side?" she said.

Nate frowned, playing the conversation back in his head. "Did you say," he said after a moment, "Kohl was running *errands*?"

"It's what he said," said Grace, looking over the crowd. "Hey. That your guy?" She used her ice cream as a pointer, drops of water and mint-chip falling to the road.

Nate followed the direction of her gesture. Yeah, that was Harlow all right. He was being man-handled inside a building by two larger humans, one on each arm as they hustled him in. The building, in this case, was Harlow's bar. Harlow ran a friendly place; welcomed spacers and grounders alike, served whiskey that wasn't too watered down, and handed jobs to people like Nate when they were of interest. Nate and Harlow went back a few years, been through some shit, and in all that time Nate had never seen Harlow taken into his own bar against his will. Nate sighed. "Yeah, that's Harlow."

Grace nodded. "You know those guys with him?"

"I don't," said Nate. "I guess this explains why he's late."

She looked at him. "Do we go in there and ... I don't know. You said he was a friend of yours. We going to help him out?"

"'Friend,'" said Nate. "That's an interesting word."

"It was your word this morning, when you said we should come down to this particular rock and get some information. A lead."

Nate gave her a sour look. "I did say that, didn't I?"

"Yeah, you did, Cap," she said.

Nate patted his blaster pistol, then tossed the remains of his cone in a trash can. "Well, let's go get that information, Assessor."

"WHICH ONE OF you assholes wants it first?" Nate pointed his blaster in the general direction of Harlow, the two guys holding him down, and the man who wore a surprised expression above a black suit. Grace ghosted off to Nate's right, lithe form moving in the gloom of the bar. Nate felt a momentary pang of worry — she was still carrying injuries from her run-in with Kohl, when the Ezeroc had been using the big man like a puppet theatre — but she seemed focused. Silent. A night killer. Unlike Nate, who had a metal leg that creaked in the rain.

Creak, creak. That was the only sound — his damn leg. That, and water dripping from somewhere. The bar — dark for the moment, empty of patrons — was silent as the grave. *Perhaps not the best analogy, Nate.*

"Nate," said Harlow, through bloody lips. "Sorry I was late for our meeting."

Nate shrugged, waving the blaster in a manner he hoped was both casual and threatening. *A hard sea to sail, that one.* "I can see your previous appointment ran over." He tried to catch Grace's position out of the corner of his eye, but failed — she'd vanished, like smoke in the wind. "I'm not interrupting, am I?"

The man in black ... *reanimated*, like he was waiting for a cue. "Who are you?"

"I'm Harlow's eleven o'clock," said Nate. "Who are you?"

"His ten o'clock," said the man.

"This isn't helping either of us," said Nate. "Look, I'm just here for some information." He gestured with the blaster again. "I mean, I can just take it and go if you like. You look like you're busy."

"Nate?" said Harlow. "What are you doing?" He spat blood onto the floor.

"Excuse me," said the man in black. He pulled black gloves tighter onto his hands. "I ... this is very confusing. You're not trying to ... *rescue* our mutual acquaintance? Lend assistance to Harlow?"

"Does it look," said Nate, "like I'm crazy?" He frowned at his blaster. "Although I guess I have given a bad first impression."

"Nate?" said Harlow. "A little help."

"Yes," said the man in black. "It does, at first blush, look like you are pointing a weapon with intent at me."

"Hell," said Nate, "that's just to ensure no one does anything rash. If you can give me your assurance you'll do ... well, something just not plain stupid, I can put it away."

The man in black looked over at the two other men holding Harlow. He gestured, palms down, at them. Nate figured that for a *calm down* kind of motion, so he holstered his blaster. "There."

"There," agreed the man. "What is it you want to know from Harlow?"

"Nate?" said Harlow. "Look, if this is about the ship, I don't even care anymore. You hear me? I don't care. You can take it. On the house! Just get me out of here."

"What ship?" said the man in black. He turned back to Harlow. "*What ship?*"

"The *Ty*—" started Harlow.

"Well, I think we're getting ahead of ourselves," said Nate, walking forward. *This whole thing will get a lot worse.* "My question is quick. To the point. Brief, almost. I'll ask it, then be on my way."

"What of your accomplice?" asked the man in black. "The one with the sword."

"Her?" said Nate, careful not to use Grace's name. "She's out back, checking for surprises."

"There are no surprises," said the man in black.

There was a short scream, then a sound like two halves of a watermelon hitting the ground right next to each other, a *thunk-chunk* sound. "No," said Nate, "I expect not."

The man in black winced. "She's quite good."

"She's borderline average," said Nate, "but that's not the point. I feel like we've got off to a distrustful start. Two people like us, in a place like this? We need a few rules, so accidents don't happen."

"Hm," said the man in black. "You look like a spacefaring man."

"What specifically," said Nate, "makes one man look spacefaring and another seafaring? One man a beachfront dweller and the other a gutter rat? One man a—"

"You walk like the world is heavy," said the man in black, "and you are accustomed to low light. This bar," he gestured around the room, "is dark, and yet you are having no trouble seeing."

"Fair enough," said Nate.

"Also, you are wearing a ship suit under your long jacket."

Nate looked down at himself, then back up. "That is another clue," he said. "What of it?"

"Would you happen to be Captain Nathan Chevell?" said the man in black, taking a step closer to Nate. "Of the *Tyche*? Former military heavy lifter, sold to the land merchant Harlow, and used in the Absalom system?"

Nate flexed his metal fingers. "You know?" He frowned. "That is a super-specific set of questions."

"What I've been trying to say," said Harlow. "Nate— " He hissed in pain as one man holding his arms twisted.

"I'll take that as a *yes*," said the man in black, tugging at his suit jacket. He turned back to his thugs. "If you would be so kind?"

The thugs looked at each other, gave each other the universal *whatever-the-fuck-but-this-guy-is-paying-the-bills* look, and let Harlow go. Harlow didn't run, just kind of sagged in his chair, still trying to suck air in through a few broken teeth.

"There's one small problem," said Nate. He hadn't reached for his blaster. The thugs paused, looking at the man in black, because this was the point where people would scream, or run, or shoot at them. Nate didn't figure them for the intellectual persuasion, so they still had to spend compute cycles wondering: *what the fuck is going on.*

The man in black was a step ahead. "You do not seem concerned by your predicament," he said. "That sounds like the Nathan Chevell we are looking for."

Nate winced. "Captain."

"I'm sorry?"

"It's *Captain* Nathan Chevell," said Nate. "I've got a Guild license and everything."

"*Captain* Chevell," said the man in black, "it is now time for you to die."

"Now," said Nate.

"Yes, now," said the man in black.

"*Now*," said Nate.

"That is what I am saying," said the man in black, a single eyebrow raised in puzzlement.

"*NOW!*" said Nate. There was a short whine, then the window behind Nate ruptured in a shower of glass. Red light cascaded over one thug, his entire body painted in ochre, then the man exploded into wet chunks, the pieces on fire as they sprayed across the room. Nate covered his face with an arm, already rolling to the side, as the remaining thug pulled out a sidearm and fired at where he'd been standing. Plasma cracks tore hunks out of tables, the wall, random passers-by outside. Nate kicked over a table, huddling in the lee it provided. No real safety, not against blaster fire, but not being able to see their target would make those fuckers *work for it*. He pulled his blaster out, firing wild over the top.

"Captain," said the man in black from somewhere deeper in the bar. "It doesn't have to be like this. Your crew can make it out alive."

There was another short whine, and the *pop-splat* of meat falling somewhere, coupled with a background sizzle. Screaming came to Nate before the smell of barbecue. A big shape looked in through the window, led by a heavy laser carbine. "Cap," said Kohl. "You good?" He paused, looking at something behind Nate. Nate spared a look over the top of the table, taking in the second thug — trying to scream again, eyes wide, but no sound coming out. His left arm was gone, the flesh there smoldering. Harlow was nowhere in sight, having vacated his chair for some safer location. Kohl hefted the carbine, sighted, and pulled the trigger. The thug was colored red before he erupted in a shower of meat and fire.

Nate stood up, his metal leg *creaking* with the motion. "What part of 'now' do you not understand?"

"Aw, Cap," said Kohl. "Dramatic effect, you know?" The big man frowned, moving his torso sideways a fraction. The snap of a blaster spat plasma past Kohl into the street behind him. More screaming. Kohl squeezed the carbine's trigger again, and red light lazed across the bar.

Silence.

"You get him?" said Nate.

"Don't think so," said Kohl. "Slippery fucker, isn't he?" Kohl swung a leg through the shattered remains of the window, stomping inside in a crunch of glass. "Lemme go find him."

"I've got him," called Grace, from the back of the bar. "Also, asshole, watch where you're firing that thing." Nate watched as she walked the man in black towards them, her sword at his throat.

"Gracie," said Kohl. "I figured you would, you know."

"You figured I could dodge light?" she said. "I'm flattered, but ... how?"

"You're just so ... talented," said Kohl.

"Anyway," said Nate, to no one in particular, "here we are." He considered the blaster in his hand, then the man in black. "You've found me. Nathan Chevell. Captain of the free trader *Tyche*. How can I help?"

The man in black gave a thin smile. "Could you die?"

"Not my preference," said Nate. "I'm kind of curious about why you're so hot and sweaty about that particular outcome."

"Cap," said Kohl. "We should take this outside."

"Where all the screaming people are?" said Grace. The sword against the man in black's neck hadn't moved a millimeter. "Clever."

"Please do take this outside," said the man in black. "My people will see you with me, and cut you down like the traitor to humanity you are."

"You what now?" said Nate. He tossed a nervous glance out the broken window. The thing about Earth was, with this many damn people, there were as many people running *towards* you as *away* from you. Outside that window? Chaos. Even with drone support, they had a few moments. *Unless these assholes have backup close by.*

"Oh, *please*, Captain," said the man in black. "This is not the time for false modesty! You, the downfall of the human race. Treating with aliens. We know all about it."

"Cap," said Kohl. "You want me to waste this lying motherfucker?" The big man held his carbine like it weighed nothing. "There wouldn't be enough teeth left to identify him, you know what I'm saying?"

"Blood," said Grace. "They can always use his blood."

Kohl gave her a hard look. "You do kind of take the joy out of a day's work."

"You know," said Nate, "I've been accused of being a lot of things. I've been called — I believe unfairly — a lousy lover. All manner of players say I cheat at cards. There is a city on Gala Nine where there is a warrant out for my arrest for falsifying my identity on port paperwork. That one," Nate shook his finger at the man in black, "is at least a little bit true. But the downfall of humanity? That's a tall order. I'm more of a short order cook. Could you, uh, help me out? It'd help. You know. I'd like to learn — specifically — *why* you think I'm the downfall of humans."

The man in black gave an expression that was half surprise, half disgust. "The last messages from Absalom were quite clear," he said. "You set them up to die."

"Huh," said Nate. "*That's* how this will play?"

"What?" said the man in black.

"If you *had* the actual messages from Absalom — the ones that were 'quite clear' — you would have a few more details," said Nate. "Still. The Republic's never one to let facts get in the way of a good ol' fashioned witch hunt."

Nate's comm chirped. "Cap," said El, "I'm getting some distressing radio chatter. The kind that indicates you've done a little more than run out on your check."

"How distressing?" said Nate.

"I think there's some kind of party coming your way," said El. "Hope's having trouble breaking into their comm lines, even with Penn's codes."

The man in black was smiling large now. "Ah," was all he said.

"Can you come get us?" said Nate.

"You want me to fly the *Tyche* into an area of hostile action on *the* core Republic world?" said El. "Don't be stupid."

"Worth a shot," said Nate, flicking the comm off. "Where the hell is Harlow?"

"Went out the back," said Grace.

"He'll be dead by now," said the man in black.

"You sure?" said Nate.

"I gave the order myself," said the man in black.

"Okay," said Nate. "Best you be off now."

"I ... what?" said the man in black.

"Go. Shoo." Nate waved his blaster.

"You're not going to kill me?"

"Not yet," said Nate. "Could always change my mind."

The man in black gave him a cautious look as Grace lowered her sword. He took a quick couple of steps sideways, waiting for the rain of death. No rain of death came. He turned, scuttling for the back of the bar.

"You know that'll come back on you," said Kohl.

"I hate to agree with Kohl," said Grace, "but that wasn't wise."

"I can't shoot a man in cold blood," said Nate. He was watching the man in black's exit. "My moral compass isn't that flexible. I need ... a really good reason."

"Like what?" said Grace.

The man in black had made it to one of the fallen thugs. He reached down, grabbing a fallen sidearm. Nate could see it all play out, the spin, the shot, either getting him, or Kohl, or — and here, he felt a peculiar twinge — Grace, or some poor fool bystander outside. *Hell.* "Like that," said Nate, leveling his blaster. He fired, plasma bolts tearing the man apart, sending his body backward in a rain of burning chum. "Let's get moving. But first..." He moved towards the fallen body, searching the remains.

"Where to, Cap?" said Kohl. "Could try and blend in outside."

"I think we need Harlow," said Nate. A few good Republic coins on the body, a small comm device, and not much else.

"But he's dead," said Grace.

"Harlow?" said Nate. "Nah. Harlow's not dead."

"But the ... guy," said Grace. "He said."

"The guy was Republic black ops," said Nate. "They lie. It's like their default setting."

"How do you know?" said Kohl.

"You don't hire black ops people to broadcast the truth," said Nate.

"No," said Kohl. "I mean how do you know he's black ops?"

"No ID," said Nate. "Let's go find Harlow." He wiped his hands on the man in black's suit, standing up, his metal leg giving another *creak*. He held a hand out — *that way* — offering Grace a smile. "After you."

CHAPTER TWO

EARTH.

Grace hadn't been to Earth in a long, long time. Last time she was here, she'd walked out on her so-called family. Grace left them hunting her. She knew it wasn't *Grace* they were hunting, but rather their *asset*. Mongrel she may be, but she was still cursed with amazing gifts by the standards of norms.

If only they knew what it was like to have everyone shouting at you all the time.

That's what it felt like. Being on Earth was like being surrounded by a thousand DJs at the world's biggest party, except they all had bad taste in music.

When she'd left her family's house in Ise, it had been dark and quiet. She'd had the snapping fangs of the Republic at her heels ever since. They didn't know her, but they also didn't know what her father was capable of. Hopefully they never would. If they found out, humanity would have a worse enemy than the Ezeroc.

"You good?" It was Nate, calm voice at her ear, touch on her elbow.

"Yeah," she said. "It helps having just one guy to focus on. With the noise."

"Harlow's still alive?" said Nate. "You're sure?"

"Looks like a duck, walks like a duck," said Grace. Since Harlow had run out of his bar, sprinting away as fast as his bartender's physique would allow — which wasn't fast at all — she'd been watching him with her mind. It took focus to keep his feelings — *run/fear/betrayal/fear/panic/fear* — in her head, but that focus helped to drown out the thousand or more mouth-breathers around her. Grace kept Harlow's fear in her mind, watching it like a beacon. She could see it, if that was the right word, through walls. It was so bright that the usual tapering of distance kept it fresh. It was so *loud*.

She missed space. The hard black was ... quiet.

"But, like, *alive* alive," said Nate. "Not—"

"There's only one kind of alive," said Grace. "He's not dead. Although he'll give himself a heart attack. We should get after him."

"Probably didn't help," said Kohl, "that you made him think you were selling him out."

"That?" said Nate. "Naw. Harlow knew I was playing with them. Right?"

"Right," said Grace. "That's why he's terrified."

"Shit," said Nate. "We best be off then. Lead on."

"Best bloodhound money can buy, is our Gracie," said Kohl.

Grace eyed the thug. "Asshole."

"Sure," said Kohl. But he said it with a grin, not a leer, and she caught nothing hostile coming off him. *Maybe people can change.* People like her father? When it was a cold and frosty day in hell, *maybe.* Kohl, by comparison, was wet clay, ready for shaping.

Grace sheathed her sword, the blade whispering back into the scabbard. She held it low and ready. Being armed was a Republic right, but walking through city streets with a naked blade would cause more than a little concern. She led Nate and Kohl out the back of the bar. Grace hadn't caught the name of it on the way in, not that it mattered. They left by way of a kitchen empty of workers, none of the induction surfaces bright and ready to cook. No food smells, just the faint odor of another person's fear. The alley door opened to her touch, swinging free. The lock hadn't been set, just more evidence that Harlow was running blind.

People who ran didn't think right. Grace knew this from her own experience — it was only when she'd stopped running she'd found this small family to call her own. A family where only one person — Kohl — had tried to kill her. Her luck was improving.

Tyche. Their ship, their home, named after the Goddess of Luck. Maybe names had power.

She squinted at the light of the alley. Despite the gray clouds threatening to rain again, the sky glared at her. Grace paused, turning left and right. *Definitely left.* Not that Harlow had left breadcrumbs, but there were more people that way, panicking and screaming, that would be useful for them to hide among while they moved. Just three more people in a crowd. The Republic's survey drones would be less likely to mark them as *of interest* if they were just more stray human chaff in the wake of a random shooting. Say what you will about Kohl, but the man had a way of making a situation ... *more* impressive.

Grace paused, but didn't turn. "Kohl?"

"What's on your mind?" he said. "Harlow still ahead?"

"Yes," she said. "But I've been thinking. About being conspicuous."

"I'm big, I know," said Kohl. "I can't do much about that."

She gave him a look over her shoulder. "What about the gun?"

He blinked, then looked at the laser carbine. "This?"

"You carrying another gun?"

"Well, actually—"

"I mean, another huge gun that's big enough to see from space?" She waved at the sky. "Drones."

"Lots of people have personal protection," said Kohl. "Republic made it law that a person could carry something to defend themselves. We live in dangerous times. Hell, someone just shot the ass out of a bar. Goddamn, you know what I'm saying?"

"I think what Grace is driving at here is that it's a little ... *too* defensive," said Nate.

Kohl eyed Grace's sword. "And that thing's not?"

"This thing," said Grace, holding the scabbarded sword up — blade ever sharp, since Hope had recast it for her in the heart of the *Tyche*, "hasn't been used to blow the windows out of a perfectly good bar."

"I'm not sure Harlow's place is good," allowed Nate. "I mean, I'm on your side here Grace, but I think we need to be honest about Harlow. He's—"

"Nate," said Grace, "I've got this." She looked back at Kohl. "Could you maybe compromise? Meet us half-way?"

"Like what now?" said Kohl. She was picking up genuine *confusion/confusion* from him, but the look on his face mirrored that. You didn't need to be an esper to see he was having trouble processing the conversation.

"If you didn't point it at everyone, you wouldn't look like you were about to shoot them," she offered.

"Oh," said Kohl. "Right. I get you." He let the gun fall on its sling, slipping it behind him. It dangled off his shoulder, barrel towards the ground. "Better?"

"Better," she said. "Now don't shoot yourself in the back of the leg." She turned back towards the mouth of the alley, street panic ahead. Grace tried to ignore the drunk passed out under a pile of trash. The glare of daylight above the gloom around her made her want to squint. *Just focus on Harlow.* The man's scent was getting fainter as he put some distance between them, but it was still out there, bright as a shiny new Republic coin.

They breached the alley mouth and hit the crowd, people still moving, shouting, cursing, and milling about. *Perfect.* An air car blasted overhead, rounding the corner to the front of the bar. That worked — they were headed in the opposite direction — but it also suggested the man in black hadn't lied. He'd been connected, he'd asked for backup, and — lo! — here was the backup. Grace lowered her head, wishing for something to hide her face, but they hadn't come here expecting to start a war.

Although: Kohl might have.

The tide of humanity was ebbing back out to sea, away from the Republic air car and the troops that implied. People weren't stupid. Even tax-paying normals knew it was just a bad idea to be caught in the affairs of the powerful, even if you were a card-carrying sympathizer. There would be at least ten shock troopers coming out of that air car, primed to ask questions in a way that encouraged honesty. No matter how honest you were, they'd ask a couple more times just to be sure. Grace hadn't been caught by them, not yet, and today would not be that day.

She set off at a steady walk, not hurried, but with a purpose. You hurry, they see that. You stop, they see that too. The trick was to move somewhere in the middle, not be one of the aberrant movement patterns that drew the eye of a careful watcher. A man ran past her from behind, jostling her shoulder, and she stumbled. If she hadn't been so focused on Harlow, she might have felt that one coming. She'd need to be more aware, more alert.

Her head hurt. It did that sometimes when she had a lot going on. Her father had said it was all in her mind, and she would have laughed at the unintended irony if it wouldn't have resulted in repercussions. Her father wasn't a man with a shred of humor in him. She paused, closing her eyes. *Just breathe.*

"Hey." It was Nate, his hand on her arm. She felt her shoulders relax at his presence, and wondered if this was how the rest of the crew saw him. Someone safe. Someone who stood with them against the terrors of the night. "You okay?"

Grace nodded. She looked out at him through a curtain of her hair, offering him what she hoped was an easy smile. "It's ... a lot."

"Huh," he said. The noise of it was lost in the crowd, but she took the meaning plain enough. *I get that. It's cool.* "Want me to go up front?"

"You don't know the way," said Grace.

"I'll chart by the stars," said Nate, "and you can tell me if I get it wrong."

"Okay," she said. She pointed ahead, a corner lit brightly by holos advertising prismatic hair replacement. "He went that way."

"Kohl," said Nate.

"What up?" said Kohl.

"See all those people?" said Nate.

"Hard to miss," said Kohl.

"Make a path," said Nate. He stood by Grace's side as Kohl shrugged, then bulldozed ahead. A person dressed in a street leather yelled at Kohl, and the big man brought his fist down on the other's head, dropping him like a stone. "It's kind of marvelous," said Nate. "Like watching a hurricane."

"I thought you were going to make the path?" said Grace.

"Delegation," said Nate. "Important skill for a captain."

Grace gave him a grin. Not that her head wasn't hurting anymore; it was that Nate made it seem like it didn't matter. She set off after Kohl, the man's wake an easy path to tread. He might trigger warnings from observing drones, but time was becoming a bigger issue. Harlow's ... signal? ... was getting weaker. Almost impossible to see through everything around them.

Another air car buzzed overhead, this one stopping not far from them in the direction they were going. *Uh oh.* Kohl saw it, watched the troops ready to pour out the side of it, and raised his carbine in one smooth motion. There was a brief whine, a stab of red light, and one thruster on the air car exploded in a boiling cloud of flame. The air car's remaining thrusters took on an urgent whine as the machine tried to right itself, and it started a slow spiral towards the street. More people screamed, ran, shouted, turned on each other. The air car hit the ground around the corner, and there was a *whumf* as something coughed into flame.

"Kohl!" said Nate. "You trying to get us killed? That's Republic troops there!"

"They know we're here," said Kohl. "Now instead of ten fuckers with guns, we've got a little more time."

Hard to argue with that. Grace nudged Kohl. "We need to hurry."

"Got it," he said, shouldering ahead once more. Faster this time, almost at a run, the crowd not slowing him down quite as much. Grace tried to keep up, Nate at her side, but it was hard, so many people now pushing at them, shoving against them. Grace could feel their *fear/fear/fear/run* battering against her, and it made her feel like she was drowning in their distress.

She slowed to a stop. She couldn't help it. "We've got to … get off the street." She wasn't sure if anyone heard her. Grace wasn't sure if she'd said it out loud.

Nate had kept going for a bit, but when he realized she wasn't at his side, he turned back to her. "Grace!"

"I…" she said, sagging a little.

She watched as he fought his way back to her. He made it to her side. "We've got to move!" he said. Kohl's path in the crowd was distant now, the top of his head sometimes visible. He may as well have been on Mars.

"I can't breathe," she gasped.

"Kohl!" said Nate. But the big man was gone now, lost in the crowd ahead of them. Another air car blasted overhead, but it didn't stop. It was heading in the same direction they were going. Probably after Harlow.

It'd get to Harlow, and they'd snatch him away. Take him to somewhere blacker than space, colder, and they'd extract from the man everything he knew about Nate, about the *Tyche*, and about the esper that crewed on the ship. Then they'd kill him, if not during, then after. And he'd have died without ever knowing *her*, still fearing espers, not knowing who he was dying *for*.

Grace gripped her sword tighter. *Fuck that. Fuck these assholes.*

Fuck the Republic. She gritted her teeth. "We've ... got to get off the street."

Nate nodded, and they pushed — *together* — towards an underground shopping entrance, bright lights highlighting the stairs leading down. The people around them were pouring down the stairs like water down a drain; after entering they let themselves be carried with the flow. As they broke away from the street, the noise of panic faded into the noise of people moving with a purpose. Grace grabbed onto Nate's arm so they wouldn't get separated. They passed holo lit entrances to stores selling everything from body-mapped clothes through to baby needs — *Everything your new family will love!*

But it was okay. People weren't so *afraid* down here.

Grace pulled Nate to the side in the shallows of the flow, a natural eddy of people created by a stall selling noodles. They smelled good, and that touch of normal helped her feel less desperate. She leaned close to Nate's ear. "I've lost him."

"Kohl?"

"Harlow," said Grace. "I can't see him anymore."

"Well, shit," said Nate. "That's not ideal. But it's probably okay."

"How so?" said Grace.

"That last Republic air car," said Nate, "was heading in the general direction of a, let's call it a general place of unstructured business."

"A black market," said Grace.

Nate winced. "Let's agree to call it a free market."

"Would there be people with guns there?" said Grace.

Nate thought about that. "You're concerned that someone'll start some shit."

"It had crossed my mind," said Grace. "The Republic want something, Nate, and they won't take no for an answer."

"Yeah," said Nate. "Maybe we could wait it out?"

"Would other people there know you?" said Grace. "Would they hold grudges?"

"I don't think I like where this is going," said Nate. "Whose side are you on?"

"I don't have a horse in this race," said Grace. "All I'm saying is, well. You know."

"You think I'm a smuggler who cheats at cards," said Nate.

"I *know* you're a smuggler who cheats at cards," said Grace. "The question is whether anyone you've swindled will be at this free market of yours." She watched the people around them for signs of interest in anything other than the noodle cart, but people were just doing people things. Buying stuff they didn't need and eating things when they weren't hungry. She turned back to Nate. "Well?"

"Hey," said Nate. "It's not *my* free market."

"I'll take that as a yes," said Grace.

"That's fair," said Nate with a sigh. "Let's go get Harlow."

"Where is this place?" said Grace, following Nate back out into the stream of humanity.

"It's underneath an all-day club," said Nate. "The kind of place you'd call a nightclub if it was only open at night."

"I get it," said Grace. Talking to Nate helped keep her calm. To buffer against the adrenaline still going through her body from other peoples' *fear/fear*. "Nightclub, but in the daytime."

"Underneath, though," said Nate. "You got to know the way in. Republic's unlikely to shoot their way in because they don't know where to go."

"But you do," said Grace.

"I do," said Nate. He gave her a smile. "I know people."

NATE BANGED on the closed door in front of them again. "Hey!" he said. "I know people!"

"Fuck off," said the voice from behind the door. Despite the *thud thud thud* of the bass above them, the voice was clear, angry, and not going to let them in. Grace wasn't getting a warm, rosy glow of calm.

They'd entered what looked like a dark, dismal janitorial access bay under the club. The club itself was loud, full of *lust/want/hunger/want/want/want*, bodies moving together, the air misted with sweat and drugs and people in heat. At another time, it might have been a release. Now, it was a source of friction. Nate had led them down here, a winning smile and the right words getting them past the expected back-room guards, gruff men hell-bent on stopping those under the influence from stumbling where they weren't wanted. *Here* was at the bottom of ceramicrete steps, chipped and pitted with time. Lights were infrequent, the comm signal blocked. The door they were in front of was metal and ceramicrete, the kind of thing that would take a lot of time and dedication to get through without the right passphrase. A passphrase that Nate seemed to no longer have.

Grace touched Nate's arm. "Want me to try?"

Nate sighed. "Help yourself."

Grace knocked on the door. "Hey," she said. She focused for a second, feeling for the person on the other side. Grace felt their *fear/fear*. "I know you're scared," she said.

"You know you can *fuck off*," said the voice, louder this time, but Grace still felt the *fear/fear*. Louder, if that was even the right term for something you felt inside you, that came through a sense no one else had.

"I know you've got a man in there," said Grace. She leaned her head closer to the door, lips almost brushing it. "I know his name is Harlow. I know that he has a story about Republic soldiers and being sold out."

There was a pause. "How you know that?" Still anger in the voice, like it was demanding to see the waiter for a bungled restaurant order.

"We're the ones who sold him out," said Grace.

This time there was a long pause. "What?"

"Of course, we didn't," said Grace. "But it looked like it. Would we be here — just two of us — if we were with the Republic? They do not knock."

"Let's say I buy your story," said the voice. "What do you want?"

"I want to come in," said Grace, "because I don't want to die. I'd also like it if we could talk to Harlow. Get him out of here, so a power of hurt and pain doesn't descend on this location."

Nate touched her sleeve. "It won't work," he said. "They don't—"

The door *clanked*, bolts pulling back, and there was a small hiss of air as it opened. The face that stood by the door wasn't what Grace had expected. She'd thought about a huge man, imagined tattoos, a big gun held in a threatening manner. The gun she got right, and the man she got right, and that was it. The rest was ... different. This guy? Short. Like, *real* short, up to her shoulder short. No ink of any kind, just a pale face over a fearful expression. "He's gone," said the man.

"Harlow?" said Grace.

"Yeah," said the man. "But you'd best come in anyway. We sent Harlow out the back."

"There's a back?" said Nate. "I've been here fifty times, and I never saw a back way."

"Ah," said the pale man. "Not a VIP, then."

"I ... don't know what to say to that," said Nate.

"Get in," said Grace. "We're burning daylight."

They slipped inside, a tunnel dug into the rock under the city. Lighting strips lined the walls, banishing what could have been an oppressive air with something more clinical, like a hospital waiting room. If hospitals sold illegal firearms, mods, and ship parts.

Nate was checking his comm. "Still down," he said. "I can't raise the *Tyche*."

"They'll be fine," said Grace. But she knew it wasn't true. The Republic would work out where the *Tyche* was, and they'd close their iron fist around the crew's only way off Earth. But that was a fear for another time. Right now? They needed to get Harlow, find Kohl, and unpick who was setting them up to die.

CHAPTER THREE

THE PROBLEM with people was that they were people.

Kohl had always thought this, back when his mom's pimp used to beat him, through to his first gang when the team he was running with tried to shaft him. Then a bigger gang found him, seemed to appreciate his talents, then fucked him over for a percentage on a drop. Set him up against Old Empire, the big bad coming down the line for him, and there was no one at his back and an empty weapon at his side. He'd almost gone down on that one, but he'd been saved by the bell. Timing was more important than people: the Republic coup had seen the Old Empire crumble, Kohl left in a jail where no one cared. A couple of hard hits against a warden or two and he was free on the wind again, running small-time enforcement for a local dealer until Nate found him.

Found might not be the right word. The Republic assholes in front of him right now had *found* him. Nate had just bought him off, sold him some line about nobody ever appreciating his talents. The man had a ship and a crew and promised Kohl that *people* wouldn't be trying to kill him quite as often. It'd been true, too, right until that fucking esper Grace Gushiken had slipped aboard, the justice of the

Republic on her heels. The very Man himself was after her, all resources of the Republic bent trying to scrape her out of the crack she'd crawled into, and the only thing that stopped her being taken to a dungeon so dark even space looked bright and cheery was that they'd come up against aliens.

Fucking *aliens*.

Not aliens like migrants from Europa, trying to get back to a crust with proper daylight, but actual aliens, ones that looked like giant insects. Giant angry insects, and they'd stabbed Kohl through the shoulder, planting some fucking thing in him that used his body like a sock puppet. It would have eaten his brain like a snack, just calories for the hive, except that fucking esper Grace Gushiken had stabbed him in the back, killed the bug, and here they were. Under a bright and sunny sky, boots on dirt. Except the sky wasn't sunny, and there was nothing under his boots except ceramicrete, pavement bubblegum, and trash.

Speaking of trash: back to the Republic. These guys had had their sense of humor beaten out of them, all black armor underneath black visors. They came looking for trouble with large plasma weapons. No problem. They wanted trouble? October Kohl knew all about trouble. Trouble was his stock-in-trade.

An air car blasted overhead, the fifth one he'd seen in about fifteen seconds, which didn't promise good things for anyone. Not good things for Kohl, not good things for the cap, and not good things for Gracie. Despite stabbing him in the back, that girl had fire in her belly, and she went up against Kohl with nothing but a sword. That encounter should have ended with her bleeding out against the metal decking of the *Tyche*, but instead here Kohl was, feeling like he owed her one. He hated owing people anything. That's how people turned into problems.

Kohl turned his head around. "Cap." And then blinked, because the street, while far from empty, wasn't full of captains or espers. Nate had turned into mist, blown away on a breeze, and taken Gracie with him. Not that Kohl blamed them: when things turned to shit, you needed to look after yourself. Find a hole to crawl into if you weren't able to tough it out. If you could muscle through, you needed a big gun in your hands. If Kohl hadn't been so intent on barging through all these fucking people, he might have noticed them drifting off to safer places. Truth be told, he was just angry that he hadn't thought of it first. Here he was, sticking his neck out for a captain who wanted to throw him out an airlock and a ... a goddamn *esper* who'd stabbed him in the back. October Kohl didn't stick his neck out for anyone, unless there was a good percentage in it.

"DROP THE RIFLE," said a woman's voice, amplified to be far louder than it needed to be. It certainly drew Kohl's attention. There in the street, in the direction he'd been headed, was one of those Republic soldiers. She wore the standard black-on-black, with a black blaster pointed at Kohl.

Kohl looked down at his carbine, still slung from its sling. "I'm not holding a rifle," he said.

The Republic soldier turned her head to the side, as if looking for support, but she was alone. Which might have been a mistake, but Kohl could see how it would look from her perspective: a lone gunman in the street, no weapon in his hands, and she had the drop on him. Easy bag, and some sort of completion bonus. Hell, she bagged the great October Kohl, and she'd be drinking for free on stories of this for a month at least. It was an approach to life Kohl himself had used on occasion.

"THE LASER," she said. "DROP IT."

"Oh," said Kohl. "I see what you mean. It's a carbine, not a rifle. Shorter barrel. Makes it easier to swing around, you know?"

"I DON'T GIVE A FUCK IF IT'S AN UMBRELLA. DROP IT, ASSHOLE." She hefted her blaster, a short ugly thing, for emphasis.

Kohl sighed. Thing here was to make a show of it, like he would comply. And then *not* comply. At that point, the shooting would start, and her having the drop on him was an important factor in any future actions he would take. There were still about a thousand people around, and any of those would probably do for a distraction. With one hand held high, Kohl reached around and down for the carbine. He could see her helmet move incrementally as she followed his hand, which was what he was waiting for. A man dashed between them, trying for the safety of the other side of the street — *like any side of the street is safer than any other, asshole* — and Kohl whipped his hand out, faster than a snake, collaring the man. He took in an expensive suit and a startled expression as he hauled the man in front of him.

What was *supposed* to happen next was that he would say something like *now I'm just going to back away* and she'd keep the blaster trained on him, but eventually he'd get to some cover, and at that point he could run, or shoot, but probably run, because the numbers wouldn't be on his side in about thirty seconds. Kohl figured in an unfair fight he'd be good for five or more of these Republic clowns, because soldiers learned to fight for money, but Kohl had learned to fight for two reasons. First, because it was necessary. Second, because it was fun.

What happened was a surprise to Kohl, and more of a surprise — briefly — to the man he held. The soldier opened fire with her blaster, plasma impacting the man's body with bright actinic splashes of fire. The man Kohl held turned into pieces of burning flesh quickly, reducing Kohl's makeshift cover to zero. Kohl didn't pause: his hand that had been reaching for his carbine just kept on going, raised the weapon, and fired. The soldier was painted head to toe in red light for a heartbeat before her body erupted into a steaming cloud of meat. Kohl's armor took the blaster residue from her shot like it wasn't anything to be worried about.

Kohl let the remains of the man's suit jacket fall to the ground to lie among the smoking flesh, and considered his carbine for a moment. When he'd been *running errands* earlier, what he'd meant was *buying a better gun*. After the run-in with those damn Ezeroc assholes, he'd seen some of them handled plasma fire pretty well. The smaller ones, sure, they burned like kindling, but the larger ones that looked like crabs, if crabs could be angry and twice as tall as a human, had big armor plates that coped fine with small arms fire. The laser carbine was a weapon designed to focus light, but it did it across an entire body at once, a tiny computer inside mapping the target, finding its shape, direction, and velocity. It then delivered microbursts of laser light to the target over the entire surface, like the world's most violent laser lighting display. The fluid inside the body expanded fast — *damn* fast. Deliver enough energy into a body of water, you turned it into a rapidly expanding cloud of water vapor and, with a little luck, anything left behind would catch on fire. When Kohl had explained that he wanted things to *pop* to the arms merchant, the merchant had concluded Kohl was a professional and just directed him at a range of lasers and masers. Kohl wasn't sure if a laser — or microwave — would work better or worse against Ezeroc chitin, but he'd figured a different approach couldn't hurt.

The carbine had won, because it looked like a gun. Its emitter looked down a barrel-like lens array. The masers had looked like toys; they might have *worked* fine, but first impressions were important in Kohl's line of work. He eyed the patch of steaming remains where the soldier had been standing, and then considered the carbine again. Impressions were important, but results were king. He did not feel like he had buyer's remorse on this one.

Time to move.

Kohl kept the carbine ready as he ran to the side of the street. Right side, because why not? He tried to hide his frame behind an abandoned holo cart promising the *LATEST HOT REELZ*. If he'd had a memory sliver he could have downloaded a couple new items for his collection, but he didn't have one and now wasn't the time. Kohl peeked around the edge of the cart, checking out the street. The soldier had come from up the street, because she hadn't come from behind Kohl, or she'd have just rapped him on the back of the head, lights out — and, like nuns, they didn't travel solo. Another one was coming out of a store that printed clothes on demand, moving at speed. No doubt because he'd been on comm with his partner before she tried to shoot Kohl.

Think. He could start some shit, sure, and that might be fun for a while. But the smart play was to get out of here. No one was paying him to shoot people, and Kohl did nothing he was good at for free. Also, even Republic soldiers got lucky; Kohl didn't have Ezeroc armor, and a stray blaster round could turn him into a street barbecue. Okay, so: time to move. Back the way he came, since all the resistance was up ahead. He turned back, poked his head out from the other side of the holo cart. *Well, shit.* Wouldn't you know it, the Republic were sweeping from the rear too. Three soldiers, blasters high. Looking for something. Probably Kohl, although it could have been Gracie. Time to go.

Thing was, he had nowhere to go. Back, front, both looked bad. He could blast his way out, but the numbers weren't looking good. Or just sneak out, blend in with the crowd. He turned, and felt the hard snub nose of a blaster against his armored stomach, eyes level with the black helmet of a soldier. The moment stretched until it felt too thin.

"Uh," said Kohl. "Is this where you speak first, or I speak first?"

"SHUT IT," said the soldier.

Kohl winced. "Can you ... turn that down? It's just, I don't know. You've got the gun on me, and that means you should—"

"I SAID SHUT IT." The soldier emphasized this with a press of the blaster into Kohl's armor.

"Okay," said Kohl, and then slapped the blaster aside with the hand not holding his carbine. The blaster went off, incinerating a wall of the holo stand, hot pieces of plastic and metal spraying through the air. Kohl used his free hand to grab the soldier's wrist — *control the weapon, don't get cocky* — and tried to bring his carbine up. There wasn't enough room between him and the soldier, so Kohl let it fall. The soldier tried to wrestle his hand free to bring his blaster to bear on Kohl, but he wasn't having much luck. Kohl might not have been smart, or pretty, but he was strong, and that helped. Keeping hold of the soldier's wrist, he used his other hand to grab the side of the soldier's body armor and — with a quick heave — slammed the other man into the holo cart. The blaster fired again, someone screaming from that direction. Kohl pulled him back off the cart, then slammed him into it a few more times, until the blaster tumbled from his wrist. Hard to knock a man out when they had a helmet on, but Kohl had learned that if you did enough damage to the body they'll turn a little boneless. Kohl pulled the man towards him again, stepped to the side, and clotheslined him to the ceramicrete sidewalk. There was a crack as the solder's helmet hit the ground, and that sound was loud enough to promise Kohl a little getaway time.

He turned, meaning to run, but stopped short at the three soldiers facing him.

"DROP THE RIFLE," said one. Hard to tell which one, they all sounded pretty much the same.

"Like I said to the other one, it's not a rifle," said Kohl. But this time — three on one? Not good odds — he unslung the carbine and let it clatter to the sidewalk, then raised his hands behind his head. Hell, he was a professional, he knew this music.

One of the soldiers walked towards him, holding out a set of rigid solid bar handcuffs. Those things were bad news; once on, they weren't coming off. Kohl waited for the man to get close; what he couldn't work out was why they hadn't just blown him into pieces, but he wasn't one to look a gift horse in the mouth. He felt the cuffs go on one wrist, heard the click of the lock, and then jerked his arm down. The soldier cuffing him was pulled off balance, and Kohl grabbed the man, pushing him towards his comrades. One of them fired their blaster but the shot hit nothing but air, wild and wide. Kohl caught movement off to his side, turned to see a soldier coming at him with a stun rod. He let the soldier come, ducked under the swing, and heaved the man over a hip and down onto ceramicrete.

Another one rushed at him, stun rod tip leading the way, and Kohl snaked in around it. Held the soldier close, almost like a lover, hands gripping the arm holding the stun rod. They pivoted together

— although the soldier was by no means willing as Kohl twisted his arm — and Kohl stuck the tip of the stun rod into another soldier. There was a flash of blue light as the rod discharged, the faint smell of ozone, and the stunned soldier dropped like a sack of puppies into a river.

Kohl's entire world lit on fire, his teeth clenching together, his eyes frozen open. He would have screamed except his chest was locked tight, like it was in a vice, except it was the vice and lock all in one. He felt himself tipping sideways and crashed onto the sidewalk. A soldier's visor — black, expressionless — looked down on him, the tip of a shock rod held in her hand still smoking. "GOT HIM," she said.

"Uur," said Kohl, because that was about all he was good for after a big dose of volts. His eyes weren't working right, and he was having trouble focusing, but one thing he could pick out was a set of black shoes. Black, underneath a black suit. Kohl tried to get up, but his arms didn't move right, or his neck, or any other part of him. The best he managed was to roll from his sideways angle on to his back.

A face — no visor, no helmet, an actual human face — looked down on him. The face was blurry, like he'd been drinking. The after-effects of the stun rod made Kohl feel like that, without alcohol's funhouse ride to get there — and he blinked a couple times to clear his sight. Craning his neck forward, he tried to bring the face into focus.

"October Kohl," said a man's voice. "We have a proposition for you. One, I think, you will appreciate."

The man crouched down, bringing his face closer — and into focus — for Kohl. "Im...possible," Kohl managed to get out.

"There are a great many things possible in this world, and beyond it," said the man in black. "Let's go somewhere a little more private for our conversation, hmm?"

CHAPTER FOUR

HONOR AMONG THIEVES WAS BULLSHIT.

Nate knew it, these assholes knew it, and Harlow knew it. Thing with Harlow was he wasn't just another thief, he was a friend. Or Nate had counted him as one, despite that little thing over the *Tyche*. She hadn't been called the *Tyche* back then. Harlow hadn't loved her like Nate did. Harlow? He hadn't even seen the ship's potential. Despite his lack of vision, he'd still asked an extortionate sum of money for the ship. Tried to explain that Old Empire ships like the *Tyche* were collector's items, going to bidders well above typical rates.

So Nate had cheated him at cards, and when Harlow hadn't wanted to give over the transponder codes, Nate had taken them. But all that was ancient history.

Ancient.

Nate followed Grace down the sterile corridor, the lights more blue-shifted than was normal on a crust. Nate didn't mind, because it reminded him of home — the artificial lighting inside the *Tyche* that pushed the dark away wasn't warm like a yellow star, despite doing its job of keeping the dark at bay. The sooner they sorted out what appeared to be Republic G Men trying to capture or kill him and his associates — and put a collar on whomever was trying to sell humans up the line to a bunch of insects, he'd be back in space, shipping cargo of questionable origin to destinations of questionable providence.

He frowned, pausing in the corridor for a second. The pale man who'd opened the door kept walking, but Grace slowed, looking back at him. "You good?" she said.

"I'm good," said Nate, hand on his blaster. "It's just ... never mind."

"You know you can't lie to me," said Grace. "Right? You've worked that out?"

"Yeah," he said. "It's just ... I liked being a pirate, Grace."

She laughed, then sobered as she saw his expression. She stepped closer to him, putting a hand on the side of his face. "Oh, Nate," she said. "You can't lie to me, but you keep trying to lie to yourself."

He liked the feel of her hand on his skin. His metal fingers flexed, but he held himself still. "I'm not lying," he said. "The life out there? It's less complicated."

"There's a long distance from pirate to privateer," said Grace. "And a longer one from privateer to—"

"Hey," said the pale man. He'd come back to them. "No fucking around down here, you know? Go in the wrong doorway, you might never come back out."

Grace's hand dropped from Nate's face, and the set of her shoulders as she turned back to the pale man was all business. "Just comparing notes," she said. "Not trying to go off the charts. There are dragons at the edge of the map."

"You know the life," said the pale man. He eyed Nate. "Better than him, anyway."

"Uh," said Nate. "This is what irony feels like." But it was okay, having Grace here. Great, even, because she knew people. She knew how to push their buttons, and how to get them to react in certain ways. Nate figured he might have learned those talents too, even without the esper bit, if he'd had the full might of the Republic on his heels for ten years or more.

"Harlow," said the pale man, as he led them down a set of stairs, "is concerned about your loyalties."

Nate hadn't been down the stairs in any of his previous visits. Hell, he hadn't even known they were here. He hoped there wasn't an illegal kidney harvesting operation at the bottom. "Harlow was about to sell me out to the Republic. I ... liberated him."

"Liberated," said the man. "Funny word for it. What's the percentage in that?"

The stairs didn't go down that far, ending on a gray concrete floor — old tech, not new ceramicrete. The genuine original bones of the city. He scuffed his boot against it. "You guys are really going for the vintage look, aren't you?"

"Excavation," said the pale man. "We always need to expand away from ... curious eyes. You understand how these things are."

"I get you," said Nate. "I haul for you."

"You used to," said the man. "Whether you still do remains to be seen."

"This like a job interview?" said Nate. "Last job I had, I sucked at it."

The pale man paused before a vaulted door set in the wall of the corridor. He gave Nate an appraising glance. "That's not what we heard." He pushed the door open and walked through.

Grace gave Nate a glance. He shrugged. *No fucking clue.* He walked ahead of her through the doorway, taking in the scene. First, there was Harlow, on a chair like before, but instead of being beaten bloody there was a medtech putting him back together. Harlow had his shirt open, which wasn't a pretty sight, not just because his body was a reclamation case, but because the man in black's thugs had done a number on him. The medtech had a shiny tray of equipment, analgesic spray and skin weld being the popular choices of the moment. The room was a little bigger than the ready room on the *Tyche*, and — aside from the pale man, Harlow, and the medtech — had one other person in it: a woman, holding a blaster, pointed in no particular direction. She was chipped around the edges like old porcelain, handled poorly by time, as faded as the walls.

Nate stopped in the doorway, Grace behind him. "Hi," he said. He looked at the blaster the woman carried.

"Nathan Chevell," she said. "Do I kill you or do I help you?"

"Nate," said Grace, from behind him. "Something's not right here."

"I'd prefer help, to be honest," said Nate, not moving. He tried on a smile. "I'm not sure it's such a binary decision though. I mean, we could have a few drinks upstairs."

She laughed, but didn't holster her blaster. "I think it's pretty ... *binary*. You see, Harlow here has told me quite the story."

"Quite the short story," said Nate. "Because he didn't have that much of a lead on us."

"Nate," said Grace, her voice clipped tight. "We need to *go*."

"Harlow has spun me a great tale. Adventure on the high seas," said the woman. "A man, dressed in black, murder in his eyes and his heart. But lo! The dashing captain enters his bar, but instead of acting like a friend, offers to look the other way."

"It's a little more nuanced than that," said Nate. "Because if we'd said, 'Hey, asshole, stop hitting my friend,' then we'd all have got shot."

"Sometimes getting shot is what it takes to show you're not a traitor," said the woman.

"She's not there," hissed Grace. "Nate? She's not *there*."

"Traitor," said Nate. He saw, with no particular surprise, that the pale man had produced a blaster. "What kind of traitor? A traitor against the Republic? Maybe. A sell-out? Hanging my friends out to dry? Not my usual play."

The woman's eyes flicked to Harlow. Harlow coughed, wiped his mouth. "Kinda true," he said. "But the ship? Always been that lying between us."

"Hey now, Harlow. I won that ship fair and square," said Nate.

"You cheated at cards," said Harlow. "I know, because I was trying to cheat as well. And you double-cheated me!"

"You shouldn't have marked the aces," said Nate. "It's an easy tell." He looked back at Grace. She was still there, fear in her eyes, hand on her sword. But she was still there. Hadn't run. He had precious few people in his life who wouldn't run, and that made him feel better. Not — *hah* — that they were about to get shot. But if they *were* going to get shot, it was standing beside someone who mattered. He looked back at Harlow. "That what this is about? You got some revenge kick going on because you think I took the *Tyche* from you?"

"She's not the *Tyche*," said Harlow. "That's not her name!"

"Is now," said Nate. He sighed, putting a hand on his blaster. The pale man tightened up at that, coiling like a spring, but no one fired. The medtech looked at Nate, then back at Harlow, then kept doing his thing. Which boded well: if the medtech screamed and cowered in a corner, shit was about to get real. "You have no idea what a new transponder costs."

"I have some idea," said Harlow, looking down. The medtech tipped his chin up so he could keep working the cuts on Harlow's face. "I want my ship back."

"Not your ship," said Nate. "Never play a player, never cheat a cheater, and never steal from a thief."

"Still," grumbled Harlow. He looked disappointed, but like the expression was for show. Almost like he was trying to convince himself he still had a right to put his boots on the *Tyche's* deck.

"Look," said Nate, turning to the woman. "You seem to be in charge here."

"How you figure that?" she asked.

"Because you're doing all the talking that doesn't make sense," said Nate. "Usual providence of cryptic overlords."

She blinked, then laughed again. "I think things'll get a lot worse for you. Before they get better."

"That's the typical path," agreed Nate, keeping himself in the doorway. Between this woman and Grace. "So. How's this play out?"

"I can tell that you're not with the Republic," said the woman, "because they're not stupid enough to come in here with just two people."

"I could have a whole backup plan going on," said Nate.

"You could," she agreed, "but they wouldn't have captured your crew mate in such a spectacular gun show."

"Which crew mate?" said Nate.

"Big guy," she said.

"He'll be fine," said Nate.

"Be as may," said the woman, "the remains of that team will come down here and try and extract you, like an oyster from its shell. Do you want that, Nathan Chevell?"

"Not especially," he said.

"Do you want to know all the dirty secrets of this world?" she said.

"Not especially," he said again, but slower this time.

"Sometimes we don't get what we want," she said, holstering her blaster in a smooth motion. Practiced, like she was used to shooting fools six times before breakfast. "They call me Amedea."

"Why's that?" said Nate.

"Because it's my name," said Amedea. "And I specialize in giving the Republic what they deserve."

CHAPTER FIVE

GOT STUFF TO DO. *Don't wait up.*

El looked at the message on her console, read it a second time, then a third. It was odd, not because Hope had sent a message. Hope was the kind of soul who preferred engines to people. But if people had to be involved, it would be through messages, or fogged by the haze of alcohol or something harder. No, messages from Hope were a staple of shipboard life on the *Tyche*. The odd part here was Hope had left the ship.

She was wanted for — what was that term the Republic beaks used? *Financial Obligation Avoidance.* It was a charge that carried time, with labor. If Hope was snared in someone's net, she'd go somewhere with chains on her wrists and a debt on her life that would last out her natural span. Fringe worlds out along the edge of Republic influence gave a little more leeway, letting you buy them off before they tossed you to the wolves. Here on Earth? Hope couldn't put a foot out the airlock without covering her face. Since her rig had been destroyed out in the Absalom system, that was an easy option removed. Hope would need something to cover her eyes against retinal scanning, and her face for systems that could know who you were by how you held your mouth. Something to mask her voice too. Yeah, the rig would have been perfect, if it wasn't space junk.

El sighed, leaned forward in her acceleration couch, and stretched. Something in her back popped, then something followed in her shoulder. *Too many hard Gs, El. You'll give yourself a stroke if you're not careful.* She read Hope's note one more time. "Hope Baedeker, what are you up to?"

Sitting here wouldn't answer the question. El pushed herself upright, snared her beer from the console, and walked back through the *Tyche's* ready room. The usual things were absent — none of Kohl's bad coffee, or Grace's even worse coffee. No food smells, just a couple empty beer cans from El's earlier efforts. Nate had said she should get some shore leave, and she would. Soon. Right now, she wanted to make sure her ship was okay. El wanted to spend a little time alone with the *Tyche*, because the ship had been through worse situations in the last week than she had in her entire service in the brief war between the Old Empire and the Republic.

Rubbing her face, El sighed again. The beer was making her maudlin, but it also made her realize the *Tyche* didn't need her. It's not like she was an Engineer, and if the Engineer had left the ship, the only things El would test were the lights, showers, and toilets. She sniffed her ship suit: she could stand to test the showers a little more. El grabbed her empties from the bench in the small galley, tossed them in the recycler, and looked at her faint reflection in the door of the convection oven. Hair, a mess. Lines, all over her face. Sneer, firmly in place. Nothing there made her proud, and she wondered who this person was looking back at her. When she was a kid, she'd expected to grow up and see an adult staring back at her. Now that time was here — had been here for more years than she wanted to admit to at the birthday parties Nate insisted on — she wasn't pleased with what she saw.

Fuck it. El turned on her heel, heading back to the supply room. There'd be beer and, if she was right about Kohl's *special hiding place*, something a lot stronger. Food that wasn't good to eat, the stuff you ate when you weren't hungry.

Got stuff to do.

What stuff did Hope have to do that would have put her out in the streets to get caught up in the Republic's net?

Don't wait up.

"Oh, damn. Hope, what are you up to?" El paused at the airlock between the ready room to the rest of the ship. "Elspeth, you need to get out more." Kohl's single malt could wait. A shower couldn't.

BRIGHT. The goddamn sky was bright. It was full of fire and the righteous fury of angels.

If it feels like that when it's raining, you'll have a rough time when the clouds clear.

El pushed her visor up her face, the tints cutting out some of the glare. You spend too much time on a ship, lights at a cool low burn, you lost the taste for real sun. Earth's warm yellow sun was a balm to the soul. It was supposed to give your heart something to hold onto out in the hard black. Right now, it felt like the sky was judging El for her earlier mistakes in life. It wasn't even trying to reach too far back. It wasn't saying, *El, you're a coward who'll run out on your friends*, because that wasn't true. Not anymore, or at least, not most of the time. When she had the sticks under her fingertips, El knew she could fight with the best of them. It was more ... *personal* conflict she shied away from.

No, the sun was judging her for too many beers before lunch. Plain and simple, the ball of fire was trying to sear away the clouds, so's to better touch her ship-softened retinas.

Despite her time in the shower, she could still smell said beer on herself. At least it'd get her a little personal space. El didn't mind people so much, she was used to cramped quarters, cramped galleys, cramped toilets from her time in the Navy, but after a long stretch on a ship with just a handful of people, she could use a bit of time to acclimate to the busy nature of things.

The docks were like docks the universe over. Ships facing the sky. Dock hands yelling at each other. Cargo lifters carrying things from place to place, some automated, a few manual. Ships blasting by overhead, streams of fusion fire pushing them towards the stars. El paused, taking it in. She had a few Republic coins in her pocket, her sidearm — because Earth wasn't the safest place in the universe, despite the sun's judgment of people on the crust — at her hip, and her visor over her face. No particular destination in mind. The big question for the fans at home was: *where had Hope gone?*

El clicked her comm, the *Tyche's* cargo bay closing under a groan of servos behind her. The ship was locking down, waiting for someone who cared about her to open her back up again. Until then, she'd stand quiet, alone, and vigilant. El watched the bay doors until they clanged shut, bolts sliding into place, lock seals firm. She pursed her lips at the scar in the hull that came from over the top and down to the back. It was patched with shiny new metal, but that scar was because El hadn't been good enough on the sticks. Sure, there had been aliens after them, and she'd been trying to fly close to a Republic destroyer under full thrust, but all those things sounded like excuses. That scar was how close El had come to getting them all killed. The scar said she wasn't as good as she thought she was. The *Tyche's* face, a woman painted on the side of the ship, winked down at El.

Time to pay back a little broken trust.

She found her way across the ceramicrete to a group of dock workers. Greasy, rough, laughing a little too loud. Normally just her type of people. But they quietened as she drew closer, which wasn't the expected reaction. The eyes swiveled her way — nothing too unusual about that — but then the eyes swiveled towards the *Tyche*. The *Tyche* had no cargo to unload, no business drawing attention from dock hands. *Be cool, El. Be cool.* "Hey," she said.

One of them, a woman trying to look like dock trash with her overalls and smudged skin, but who failed to hide the physique given to her by long hours of physical training, took a step forward. The hardness about her might have been military service, or police work, or rubbing shoulders with an underground enforcer squad. It wasn't lifting crates. Her hands were too soft, her eyes too hard. "Hey yourself."

"Looking for a beer," said El. "Just put boots down."

"Expensive beer or cheap beer?" said the woman.

"I'm not proud," said El.

"You want to get yourself to *The Merchant's Daughter*," said the woman. "Cheap beer. Earth-made, too."

"Thanks," said El. "Be seeing you."

"Sure," said the woman, turning back to the other dock hands.

Now here's what we call 'a pickle.' Hope will have found a rough bar to get another rig from someone who won't ask too many questions. Somewhere like The Merchant's Daughter *would be perfect, if the beer's cheap enough for an easy crowd. Problem is, these assholes will try and tag and bag me when I get there.* They might want to ask questions. They might want to find any one of the reprobates El crewed with. Kohl was an easy target, he'd killed too many of the wrong people to avoid notice. Nate admitted to a little smuggling, which meant *quite a lot* of smuggling. Grace Gushiken was an esper, the same type of person who'd caused the Old Empire to fall. The Republic wanted to burn them all out, get to the bottom of their coven, and even a faulty unit like Grace was on their shopping list. Hope was wanted for a debt she could never pay, given to her by a wife who cared too much about gambling and not enough about the people close to her.

Hell. The only person on the *Tyche* who wasn't at least a little dirty was El herself. For someone who hated danger, she wasn't sure how surrounding herself with criminals had come to pass. Most of the time the people trying to kill the rest of the crew missed her, which was fine, but this time? It felt like this time, they were all in the wrong place at the wrong time. El would get killed, by the Republic, and if not them, one gang or another.

El sniffed at the clean Earth air. At least the atmosphere wasn't trying to kill her. Not yet.

HER HEART WAS POUNDING.

Could have been the booze in her system, sugars making her jittery. Since she'd said goodbye to her early thirties and stopped answering questions about whether she was late thirties or early forties, El couldn't handle the booze like her younger self had. Her younger self would sling back enough rum to cripple an old man with gout, sleep it off, or just ignore her bunk and go on shift.

Her older self? Not so much. She tilted her visored face at the gray cloud, glaring at the brighter area the sun hid behind. It glared right back.

The booze was a convenient excuse, except for two things.

First thing, she hadn't had that much. She'd tossed four dead soldiers into the recycler. Or maybe it was five. Whatever, that was barely getting started when you were on shore leave.

Second? She felt terror. Bubbling up from somewhere behind her rib cage, tapping her heart up those few notches, making her tense her shoulders. Tense, because after she'd walked away from the dock hands, she'd paused at a holo with guided maps of the city, showing places to eat, sleep, and fuck. Everything a spacer would need. Reflected in a piece of metal, she'd seen those dock hands coming after her.

El had pushed her visor up on her nose again, put her feet to the ceramicrete, and walked with a purpose. She'd made it into a crowd, jostling people left and right, and without thinking about it, hit a taxi. She'd dropped coins into the slot, asked the automated system to take her to *The Merchant's Daughter*, and leaned back. The car, tinted windows hiding her from view, had pulled away from the busy front of the spaceport, leaving the dock hands outside. They were definitely looking for her.

What got her palms sweaty was the Republic air cars that landed out the front as she was leaving, black armored figures running inside. The dock hands had pointed, talked, and generally been helpful, which put those assholes in the *Republic military* or *police* camp. El didn't have much against the Republic, but she didn't have anything for it either. And military and police were much the same thing with the Republic these days.

The taxi had spat her out alongside the front of a dingy spacer bar, no sign outside, just a cheap flickering holo with what was, if you were a thirteen-year-old heterosexual male, a sexy girl-next-door type dancing on the stage. No bouncer at the door, just a ... let's call it *rustic* door, complete with dents and rusty rivets, atop steps leading to an underground bar. The holo beckoned El inside. Far be it from her to argue with advice like that; she needed more beer in her system for what was coming. A lot more beer, or a lot less, and since she was half-way there already she would start with a top-up and see how that sat with her. She gave the glaring clouds another glance, rain flecking on her visor, and stepped inside.

THE BARTENDER WAS AUTOMATED, which meant it wasn't so much of a bartender as a collection of interfaces that took your coins and gave you something in return. That was, with a little luck, what you ordered. El scrolled through the list of drinks it knew how to make, rang up a French Connection, and watched as it rattled ice into a glass, a warm-colored liquid that could have been actual cognac following the cubes. El pushed her visor up on top of her head, because the bar's interior was shrouded in a comfortable gloom. Warm, low lighting, like the owner knew the kinds of things likely to happen if given opportunity and a comfortable corner.

"Hey," said a voice at her elbow. El turned, taking in a man sporting impressive muscles, with faux tribal tattoos on just about every piece of visible skin, including his face. Could be nice if you were into that kind of thing. If you had the time to be interested.

"Hey," said El, voice guarded. "It's, you know. Opportunistic."

"Y'all..." started the man, then looked at her drink, then back to her. "What?"

"I just got here," said El, snaring her drink from the autobar. "I mean, usually you'd let a girl take a sip of her drink before you fired those thrusters. Bit strong, you know?"

"The drink?" said the man.

El took a taste from her glass, winced. At least it wasn't watered down, but she was sure some types of ship fuel would have a better aftertaste. "Yeah, but I meant you."

The man laughed, big chest shaking with it. "Yeah, okay. You a pilot?"

"Sometimes," said El. She leaned against the bar. "Sometimes I just drink. You?"

"Naw," said the man. He reached out a hand. "Moses Schloss."

"Moses, huh?" El shook his hand. Firm. Warm. Not clammy at all. *Nice.* "El."

"Like the letter?"

"Exactly like it." El looked around the bar. A little early for an evening crowd, and it wasn't the place that was going to attract a lunch rush. "You come here often?"

"That's supposed to be my line," said Moses.

"You can use it on me later," said El. "Promise."

"I come here more than I don't," said Moses. "Why?"

"I'm looking for someone," said El. She caught his frown. "Hell, Moses. Don't get all maudlin on me. She's a friend of mine."

"Friend, huh?" said Moses, hope returning.

"Yeah," said El. "You'd have struck out with her in about thirty-eight seconds, though. You're playing for the wrong team."

"Ah!" said Moses. "I know who you're talking about. Engineer?"

"She is," allowed El. "How'd you know?"

"Grease," said Moses. "Done my time inside a hull. Gets under your fingernails. Pink hair?"

"That's Hope," said El.

"Yeah, she came in here." Moses frowned. "Left too."

"I figured," said El. "She would have been after some parts."

Moses snapped his fingers. "Altman Razor."

El looked between Moses and the autobar. "That a drink?"

"It's a dude," said Moses. "I mean, it might be a drink as well. But it's a dude. Sells shit. Parts, machinery, other kinds of junk."

"Sounds like the right match." El twirled her empty glass, curious about how it got so empty, so fast. "Hell, Moses. My glass is empty."

"They do that," said Moses. "One of the annoying things about the universe." He shifted his frame, biceps flexing. "I'd guess you could use a refill."

"I could," said El. "What are you having?"

"Flaming Jesus," said Moses.

She gave him a look, shrugged, and used the autobar's console. *Yep, there it is.* More coins in the slot, and the machine hummed to itself. On a whim, she ordered one for herself. The autobar whirred, clicked twice, and ignited their drinks. She handed one to Moses. He took it with a nod, slapped his hand over the top to put it out, then took a hit. "Thanks."

"Least I could do," said El. "Since you've been so helpful." She slapped a hand over the top of her drink, taking a cautious sip. *Tastes like rum. Earth assholes always got to give a simple drink a hard name.* She eyed Moses' biceps again. "So."

"So," agreed Moses. He tossed her a grin. "You come here often?"

"Not often enough," said El, leaning closer to him. No harm seeing where this conversation went. She'd forgotten, right until that moment, how she'd come to be at this particular bar, and *who* had told her to come here.

But she was reminded by the sound of boots. She whipped her head around. Black armored troops were clattering down the stairs into the bar, blasters held high. El's mouth was open, drink half-way to her lips. Moses burst into action, screaming something that sounded like *DIE MOTHERFUCKERS* as he threw his glass at them, then pulled out a blaster — *now where the hell had he been hiding that?* — and firing at the Republic soldiers.

El didn't think, didn't draw her own sidearm, she just dropped to the ground. Kohl? He'd be good at solving this kind of problem. Her? She needed to get the fuck out.

Plasma erupted from around the bar as patrons returned fire at the Republic soldiers. Wood laminate and glass and burning alcohol rained down on El as she crawled on her elbows across the floor. She heard a scream, then another, then the *whoomf* as something caught fire. She spared a glance over her shoulder, saw Moses drawing a bead on a soldier, his blaster flashing blue-white fire. A moment later, Moses was gone, burning clods of what used to be a person raining down after the hail of return blaster fire from the Republic soldiers.

El found a service door, pushing her shoulder against it. She had to get the *fuck* out of here, back up to daylight. She didn't care how much the sun glared at her; at least it wasn't trying to shoot her. She kept on her hands and knees as she made her way across what was, in a more prosperous time, a kitchen. It was now a storeroom for cheap alcohol. But there, at the back: another door. El got up, giving a glance behind her at the service door. The sound of blaster shots still came from out there, a lot of anger in the room yet to be spent. She tried to open the exterior door but found it locked. The lock was an old mechanical one, and she had no key.

You've got a key. She pulled out her sidearm, got herself on an angle so the pellets wouldn't bounce back on her, and fired. The shotgun round took out the lock and a chunk of the door. El kicked it open, finding an alley filled with rats and rotting boxes but — *thank God, thank God* — no Republic soldiers. She broke into a run but tripped on a box, falling. That was what saved her as the back of the bar exploded in a shower of fire and ceramicrete, pieces of burning wood and red-hot metal flying about the alley.

El coughed, dragged herself to her feet. Her shoulder throbbed, and she noted with almost absent surprise that a jagged piece of metal was sticking out of it. She reached a hand to yank it free, and almost passed out from the pain.

No way that the Republic brought all that noise for little ol' Elspeth Roussel. No, they were hunting bears. Could be Moses, as the man had gone off like he'd been locked and loaded already. Could be any one of the people in that bar. Didn't matter. Nothing mattered, except finding Altman Razor before the Republic did.

CHAPTER SIX

FINDING people wasn't hard for Hope. It was the keeping them that always sucked, and sucked hard.

The street outside the tenement was full of trash. With that came the smell, rust and organic rot mixed like a stew. There were plastic bags, the kind supposed to biodegrade but never did. At least, not before getting stuck in doorways, wrapped around legs, or blown in your face a few thousand times. There was the odd paper bag, sodden, dingy with the recent rain, rendering back to pulp, leaving brown lumps around drains. This much trash meant no one came down here to clean the streets. Sure, the city would have crews on the job, or at least taking the coin, but because doing the actual work was dangerous, they stopped before that crucial step.

Hope could feel that danger, the eyes that watched her, taking in her spacer clothes and her shiny new rig. Those eyes were hard and bright, and she could almost feel the thoughts going through their heads. *Does she have anything worth taking?* Or, something like, *Let's try shaking that tree and see what falls out.*

A woman stepped in front of her. Her eyes had been rimed with black makeup, the rain having made dirty smears of them down her face. Like a raccoon crying. Not like Hope hadn't seen her, like she was invisible or wearing some kind of chameleotech. She'd been hanging with some friends, or maybe not-friends, by a wall. The woman had detached herself like a shuttle departing a bay, full thrust in zero G, to arrive in front of Hope. A hand out, touching the chest plate of Hope's rig, right over her heart.

Hope looked out through the rig's visor. She squinted, as if it would help make sense of the situation. "Hi, I guess?"

"Give us the rig. And your coins," said the woman.

"Uh, no," said Hope.

The woman blinked at her. "What?"

"No," Hope repeated. "I mean, I can see." She waved a hand at the others of the pack, also detached from the wall, circling her like she was a planet, and they were small, fast satellites. "You've got backup. Some people to take from me what's mine. I get that. But I need it, see? I need it more."

There were three of them, all men, which in Hope's math — and she was good, like *great* at math — made four all up. Four on one would have been easy for Kohl, the kind of thing not worth getting out of bed for, and not more than a hard workout for Grace. Even the cap would have been able to hose the place with blaster fire, leaving pools of bubbling organic matter, and do it with cocked hips and a smirk, even with that metal leg making his movements stiff and cranky. Hope wasn't like that. She was just an Engineer. Or she had been, before ... what had happened, had happened.

"I think that *we* need it more," said the woman, a knife appearing from under her vest, like a magic trick. "We're not spacers. Got no ship. Got no home. Just got a knife and a will to use it. You get me?"

Hope looked at the woman again, really *looked* this time. Took in that tatty vest, the shirtless chest underneath. Sagging breasts, dirty skin, too young to look like that, but there it was. The only thing of value she had was the knife. A common vibroblade, the edge less about being sharp and more about moving fast. It would cut through most things, given enough time. Metal, sure, it'd go through metal about a centimeter a second. Wood faster, but last time Hope had tried that the air had filled with dust and left her coughing, and regretting that she'd cut up something that used to be alive and had done nothing to her. Those knives could cut ceramicrete too, no problem at all, just a lot slower. Where this was all going in Hope's mind was that knife wouldn't have any trouble cutting through Hope's flesh. An accidental wave of the weapon and it'd part her skin like it was torn paper. The woman wouldn't feel any resistance through the handle, and Hope would feel a lot of pain, and scream.

That wouldn't do, because just a building down was Hope's destination.

The cap was good with people. He understood them, what made them tick. He might have talked his way out of this one, or showered coins on the ground, enough time to get a head start, and that'd be that. Hope wasn't like that, but she had one advantage. She studied. Looked at the angles. Sweated the odds. Did the reading.

She *planned*. And her planning had included something like this.

Back when she'd dropped more coins than was comfortable for her to part with on the counter where she'd bought her new rig — she'd looked at that pile, and thought, *man, you know, Rei-Rei could use that* — she'd figured the money well-spent. Not because she wasn't getting stiffed a silence fee — she was — but because this new rig was state of the art. It was better than her last one. That rig, she'd had to cobble together herself from broken parts supplemented by a few patterns courtesy of the *Tyche's* fab. It was all memory work, things she'd done before, and it was good enough for a little ship like the *Tyche*. But getting across Earth, in a city where there was a price on her head, took some serious tech. So she'd paid the coin, and bit her lip while the man counted the coins to make sure it was enough.

Once she had the rig, she'd done what any good Engineer would have done: she dumped all the standard programs and put in some of her own. One of those programs she selected now. It was a little something she'd learned back from when people had first chased her with weapons. They'd pointed guns at her, and if it hadn't been for the cap, drinking at that bar, then getting his fool ass tossed next to her in jail, Hope would have been in a box forever. *Never again* she'd thought, and so she'd cranked out a program or two.

She let one fly free, like a baby sparrow. It fluttered from her rig, across the comm, and — *God oh God please let me have got it right* — landed in the vibroblade. The knife was chattering and humming and coming towards Hope, propelled by a hand with mean purpose, and then the blade *clanked*, made a *zzzz zzzzt* sound, and stopped.

The woman looked at the blade in her hand, now useless tech. Sure, it'd hurt if you tried to poke someone with it, but it wouldn't part the meat from their bones like a cutting laser. Those raccoon eyes narrowed, flicked back up to Hope's visor. "What did you do?"

"Me?" said Hope. "No, no. You've got it wrong. I'm just trying to get somewhere. Looks like your knife is out of charge."

"No," said Raccoon, face bunching like she was shoring up for a storm.

"You charged it this morning," said one man, their orbits halted. He was leaning in to look at the knife. "You paid Lorenzo good coin to use his station."

"Yeah," said Raccoon, looking back up at Hope. "I paid—"

"You know," said Hope, "that sometimes people can steal, right?"

Raccoon blinked at her, still holding the knife between them. "What about it?" Because it was obvious, people stole all the time. That's why Raccoon had the knife, after all, and it's what had led Hope to be standing here, with a price on her head, and fear in her heart.

"Lorenzo, I don't know, might have, you know, taken your coins. Just taken them, and only given you a little juice," said Hope.

"Not enough," said Raccoon.

"Not nearly enough," said the man. He was shifting from foot to foot, like he wanted to run. Or he needed to pee. "Lorenzo—"

"Lorenzo's always done right by us," said Raccoon. *Smarter than the average bear, but about as pretty*, thought Hope. "Always."

"Yeah, so," said Hope. "I tell you what." Her visor was still down, and she knew her voice was coming out of a speaker, sounding like a machine. These people couldn't see her eyes, couldn't see her fear. "I could fix your knife."

"Fix," said Raccoon, "like break it?"

"That's one option," said Hope.

"We'd kill you," said Raccoon.

"I figured," said Hope, "so I've got another option. You see my rig."

"We're taking it," said Raccoon. "After we take your coins."

"That's one option," said Hope again, pressing her lips together behind the rig's visor. "The other option is I fix your knife, and you let me go, with all my coins."

"Why would we do that?" said Raccoon. "We could just take all your stuff. There's four of us."

"I get the math," said Hope. "There's one thing. It's tiny, but I figure I should put it out there."

"What's that?" said Raccoon, an eyebrow raised at half-mast, the bastard child of suspicion and curiosity.

"No one else here," said Hope, gesturing at the street, "will help you fix the knife. Lorenzo might, but he'd charge you for it. More coins you don't have, right?"

"That motherfucker," said the man. "We should fuck up Lorenzo next. Always taking our coin."

"Sure," said Hope. "If that works, do it. You'll need a knife, though."

Raccoon was still eying up Hope. "You could use the knife against us."

"Could," agreed Hope, "but there's four of you. Right? I mean, four on one, even with a knife? I don't like those odds."

"Me either," said the man. "Try it, and we'll cut you up."

"Sure," said Hope again. "After you get the knife back. That I fix. But you know ... I'll need something."

"What's that?" said Raccoon.

"Your promise you'll let me go," said Hope. "Got places to be. People to see. You know how it is on the streets."

"I know it," said Raccoon. She looked at the knife she held, then spun the hilt towards Hope. "I promise," she said, her tone exasperated, "that if you fix the knife we won't cut you up with it."

"Cool story," said Hope, taking the knife. She keyed up another program in her rig. The thing with anything — marriage just as easy as a fusion drive — is that it's always easier to fuck something than to unfuck it. *Unfucking* something took a special charm with equipment, which Hope had. Less so with people, but one thing at a time. The program she'd fed into the knife had high-grade fuck all the way to the core, and she needed to clean it out, like de-worming an apple. Not that Hope had ever done that, but it struck her as about as annoying.

She sighed. If her Guild could see her now, repairing a knife for some street thugs, they'd kick her out. If they hadn't already stripped her Shingle from her.

A couple of extra clicks from her rig, and the knife gave a *zzzz-click*. Not there, but close. Hope raised her eyes, taking in Raccoon and the man leaning in to see what she was doing. Like there was something to see. There wasn't, but even if there was, they wouldn't understand it. Not likely, anyway, any more than a dog would understand how a sausage was made. Your basic sausage would still taste fine to the dog, but a little mystery went a long way. While Hope worked on the knife, removing the program that had crawled right to the core of the knife, she prepared another program. She could see two of the thugs — Raccoon plus the wordy guy — right in front of her, which meant two were still behind her. Like a ship's tugs nosing you in for salvage. Hope didn't want to be salvage. That meant new programs, and a little guesswork. To buy a little more time, Hope pulled a cord from the back of her rig, a small charging lead. The knife didn't need a charge, but it would give a little more credibility to the situation. Hope figured most people didn't like being lied to, but if they never knew they were being lied to, it made the whole thing frictionless, like a good bearing.

There. The whole thing had taken a couple minutes, but those two minutes felt like a long time. The man was agitating from foot to foot, almost like he was a vibroblade shivering in the air. Raccoon looked angrier as the time wore on, like time was a rough surface and her whole body was a callous she was building against it.

"Is it—" started Raccoon.

"Hold up," said Hope, holding up a hand.

"I—"

"Almost done," said Hope, looking up through her visor. Which Raccoon couldn't see, but whatever. Hope clicked the stud on the vibroblade, the knife giving a comfortable buzz in her hand, then turned it off. She unclipped the charging cord, handing it back to Raccoon. "Here. Look, the charge is low, but it's back up."

"Great," said Raccoon, hefting it. She spun it, then clicked the stud, holding it back up. "Now, give us your rig, and all your coins."

Hope sighed. "No."

"I—"

"No," said Hope. "Got things to do."

"Like dying?" Raccoon's eyes were harder, her lips crueler. "Like bleeding to death, and hurting the whole time?"

Hope felt her arms grabbed by the two men behind her. Raccoon was laughing, enjoying her joke over a gullible child, and the man at her side was laughing along like this was the greatest show on Earth. The vibroblade came at Hope like a diving falcon, straight at her heart. A blow like that would have gone in, cutting through the shiny new rig. Reduced its value a lot, and coupled with the blood that would be everywhere — Hope's blood — it would make it worth just a handful of coins. But a handful was worth more than nothing, and you took what you could get on the street.

So, Hope took what she could get. The programs she'd loaded kicked in.

First, the vibroblade: the knife spent its entire charge in the time it would take a fly to beat its wings just once. The vibroblade had a maximum rate of movement, which it went right by — a reactor in the red — in that same breadth of time. The blade heated past tolerance, pieces crumbling to the ceramicrete sidewalk. But the real deal happened next, after the blade was no longer moving. With nowhere left to go, the charge in the handle looped in on itself, a crackle and spark of blue-white curling from hilt to pommel. It was like a ball of lightning, and it hit Raccoon like the world's angriest taser. The woman's body was rigid like steel, eyes pinned wide, teeth clenching so hard they'd surely crack. As pieces of the blade fell to the ground, Raccoon's momentum carried her forward into Hope. The movement jarred Hope, and the two men holding her arms. Hope's shoulder wrenched, and if she'd had time she might have cried out. It was fortunate her programs had been queued up, ready to go.

Which led to the second thing, her rig: the articulating arms unleashed from the back, all four coming out and around. The rig knew Hope's shape, the heft of her body, where she stood in space and time. It knew where her arms were, and her chest and her legs, and like a sort of bonus, her head. It needed to know things like this because ship engineering was dangerous work. An Engineer could get caught in the rigging, snared between the spars. Metal or cerami-crete could pin you to the deck like the weight of your life's guilt. In space, you could be held fast against the hull by broken parts, and without a ship's skin to save you, radiation or fusion fire could end you in a heartbeat. With this in mind, rigs knew their keepers, held them close, and were ready to save them from entrapment. The arms of the rig whipped out, and noted the hands holding her as artificial constraints, and thus dangerous. Hope's program told them to free her. On Hope's left, two waldos grabbed the man's arms, twisting them away in a *crrrrunch* of bone. Human elbows and shoulders were not designed to go through those planes of movement. On her right, the man holding her was more — or, depending on your point of view, less — canny; he shifted his grip on Hope's in response to the manipu-lator arms coming for him, tightening his grip. The rig processed this in microseconds, and brought an arc cutter to bear. In a shower of steam, the man was shorn free from Hope in less time than it took to blink.

Hope sagged, the sudden release from her arms startling. Raccoon tumbled to the ceramicrete at Hope's feet, teeth still clicking together. Hope looked at the remaining man through her visor. Everything had happened so fast, the man was looking at his three friends, his expression turning from *let's see what this bitch is carrying* to *what the actual fuck just happened* in short order. He was turning his head, looking first at Raccoon, then at the two men lying at Hope's side. The man who'd had his hands sheared off was making a keening noise; the one whose arms were broken was making a noise that sounded like coughing. Hope realized the man was trying to cry and breathe at the same time.

The rig's arms whirred and slid back into the panels at her back. She wanted to run, to hide, but neither of those things would help. "Uh, hi," she said, her shaking voice cloaked by the rig's external speakers.

The remaining man looked at her, finally *looked* at her, gave a short, high-pitched scream, and ran down the street. His feet *splat-splatted* in puddles as he went, little splashes of water flying in his wake. Hope noticed that his shoes were tatty and worn, one of his soles flapping as he sprinted away. Whether he would find more friends, or Lorenzo, or a beer — all good options — Hope didn't care. She cared about getting off the street.

She raised her visor, took in the street, which was suddenly, conveniently empty of people. No one wanted to get involved, not in a part of the city like this. No one wanted to help. They'd come crawling back when Hope was gone, pawing over the remains she'd left behind, like hyenas, scavenging for the remains of the kill. Hope almost sank to her knees, because she wasn't a killer. She hadn't been one before, and didn't want to start now. And these three *would* survive, but whether it was a good life in the shadow of injuries like that was a hard question to answer. Hope looked at the bodies groaning, crying, and moaning at her feet, then set off. It would all be worth it.

It'd all be worth it once she found Rei-Rei.

THE ELEVATOR WAS OUT.

Hope stood in front of it, her eyes scanning around through the visor. She took in security cameras, their electronic eyes looking for people just like her, but unable to get a match through the visor. Not a *real* match; if she'd just blanked out her eyes, made it impossible to read, that would have ignited the Republic's interest, had them swarming in here like flies to honey. She'd programmed the rig's visor, got the surface — designed to deal with the glowing radiation of a fusion drive, the scan of harsh space, the fire and fury of burning machinery — to accept the gentle touch of the cameras. Take the retina scanning, hold it close, and give an image back. She didn't know whose eyes she was using; she'd grabbed a quick scan of a woman on the street, clean clothes, a business jacket — and put that in play. As far as these cameras knew — for as long as Hope's visor was down — Hope was a woman in the wrong part of town, nothing more. It wasn't a crime, and as long as she didn't become a part of the problem rather than the solution, she figured they'd leave her alone. If the Guild hadn't killed all the AIs hundreds of years ago, something behind those cameras might have worked out something was amiss, but as it was? Nothing but humans and dumb logic gates were watching her. Which were kind of the same thing, in Hope's experience.

The Republic was one thing, but this elevator was quite another. Her intel said Rei-Rei was sixty flights of stairs closer to the sky than the lobby where Hope stood.

Of *course* the elevator was out. The machine was old, prehistoric. The power was still on to the building — the rig confirmed it, glowing lines appearing in her visor's HUD, where live conduit lay behind walls. She followed the lines, some of them going to apartments, others crawling into the elevator shaft. The buttons were broken, smashed by a previous hand that had been frustrated with the idea of climbing five or fifty flights. Hope sighed — at least the lobby's lights worked, no gangs waiting here to take from her the things she needed for what was to come — as she fired up the rig's manipulators. *Time to go to work.*

The rig pulled the panel off the elevator's controls — an old-style touch interface, its capacitive surface cracked and marred. The rig exposed the circuits behind the panel, a brief shower of sparks falling to the floor. Its manipulators were quick, their movements faster than Hope's hands would ever be. They shucked corroded wiring, spat solvents at dirty metal and glass, curled metal fingers around components that needed to be straightened, teased back into alignment. There was a click from the panel, then something in the elevator shaft groaned. Lights in the lobby flickered as power breathed back into the elevator system.

Hope allowed herself a small smile behind her visor. She had fixed the elevator. She could fix anything.

Except, perhaps, what had fallen between her and Reiko. That was a dark shadow, something that blotted out the sun itself. It felt bigger than Hope, bigger than the whole world. It wasn't a machine, and she didn't understand it very well. But she had to try.

There was a chime, and the elevator doors shuddered open in front of her. The floor of the car was dirty but otherwise empty. No angry youths holding angry weapons, although they'd have been angry *and* hungry, having been stuck in a broken elevator for a couple weeks. Hope took a step inside, feeling the car shift with her weight, cables above more elastic than metal should be. That'd need fixing too, but fixing it would take supplies, materials she didn't have, so some other Engineer would have to do it. Which meant no one would, and Reiko's apartment's elevator would be dangerous. But it wouldn't be Reiko's apartment for too much longer, not if Hope could fix all the things that were broken.

Hope reached out a trembling finger, touching the elevator controls. There was an off-tone chime, the car's speakers damaged, but it accepted her entry and shrugged the doors closed in front of her. With a jerk, Hope rose.

BODIES IN THE HALLWAY. Just four, and not — at least, not as far as the rig could tell — dead. But bodies, high on stims or down on liquor, whatever they could afford. One person had been nestled against the doors of the elevator, a mumbled *go fuck yourself* teased free as they opened. Hope stepped over the body, doors closing behind her. The light from the elevator car was cut off, leaving the gloom of the hallway — maybe one in four lights was still working here.

It didn't matter to the rig, the visor capable of working in the hard black of space that seeped into every corner out between the stars. It chattered happily to her, her display adjusting lighting to show her the way. She counted off the doors as she passed, arriving at the one she wanted.

The one she needed.

There wasn't a panel to press, no camera to speak to. Hope curled her hand, rapped fingers against the door, the wood hard and cruel against her skin.

"Fuck off," said a voice from behind the door. The voice she knew; it was more familiar than breathing. It was the best part of her, and she'd left that voice behind.

"Rei-Rei," said Hope. "It's me." She wondered if she should add, *Hope, the lover who left you.* She wanted to know if Rei-Rei remembered her. Whether her wife remembered the smell of her, like she remembered Reiko's. But if she said those things, she'd never know, so she bit her lip again, held her breath like she held her hands to her sides.

There was silence for a few more seconds, then the pinpoint of light over the door's spyglass was blocked. Reiko would look out into the hallway, would see Hope's rig, and figure someone was screwing with her. And then she'd tell Hope to go away.

"Take off the visor," said Reiko. "I need to know it's you. I need—"

"I ... can't," said Hope. "Not here."

"Cameras are out in the hallway," said Reiko.

Hope reached a hand up, pressing the controls at the base of her visor. The rig shuddered, the helmet pulling back away from her face. Her pink hair fell across her face in sweaty clumps, and she brushed it away. The air of the hallway smelled of old mildew and pain, and without the visor on her face she felt blind. Like maybe she didn't want to see. Still, the air was cooling, like a gentle hand telling her it would be okay.

"Rei-Rei," said Hope. "Reiko. It's me."

The sound of bolts and chains being drawn sounded from behind the door, then it was yanked open. Light streamed out, blinding Hope for a second. She held a hand in front of her eyes, squinting against the brightness of it, her face turning away. Hope didn't want to see. She shouldn't be here. She shouldn't have come back. Reiko would be in danger, Reiko would hate her, Reiko would turn her away—

Hope felt strong hands against her arms, felt Reiko shake her. Fingers pushed into her arms, urgent. Hope made herself open her eyes, saw Reiko's face inches from hers. That face she'd never thought to see again. She wanted to cry, to run, but she was held there by Reiko's strong hands. Hope's wife had always been the strong one. "I'm sorry, I shouldn't have come. I—"

Reiko Crous-Povilaitis pulled Hope close, kissed her hard on the lips. Reiko was crying, and Hope was crying. Then they kissed again, and tumbled back into Reiko's apartment, the door closing behind them like a bible closing on the sins of the past.

CHAPTER SEVEN

KOHL DIDN'T much like being interrogated. It brought back the bad memories, reminding him of the first gang he'd run with. Never a good moment to be had, always somebody's bitch.

The trick was to claw your way to the top, fast and mean. Using people's eye sockets as finger holds if need be. Kohl wasn't fussy how it happened, but it *needed* to happen. Here, it wasn't happening. This whole deal in front of him? Not his thing.

The man in black was watching him, eyes hooded, expression closed. There was a standard Republic officer at his side, generic type, all minted from the same factory as near as Kohl could tell. Same uniforms, same equipment, same damn haircut over the same damn clean-shaven face. That whole shtick made Kohl want to go over there and punch the Republic officer in his perfect, clean mouth. Bloody it up some.

"I guess one of you needs to say something," said Kohl. "You ain't here for the quiet, and you ain't here to ask me what happened to these chumps." *These chumps* were the five men sprawled at Kohl's feet in various stages of *out for the count* through to *will need coma care and six months in rehab.* That last guy had just been mean with his fists, and Kohl didn't like mean when he was chained to a wall. He gave his chains a tug; good strong steel, running through eyelets set above him. Enough play to swing his arms, not enough play to get to the man in black or his piano monkey Republic officer. More than enough for Kohl to lay about like a lumberjack when the now-unconscious five had come for him, all quiet intent and hard eyes.

"Many of these men will need intensive medical care," said Piano Monkey.

"Okay, got it," said Kohl. "You're bad cop. He," he jerked his chin at the man in black, "is the good cop. You know what, though?"

Kohl could see the officer fighting with the urge to not respond, and watched him lose that internal battle. "What, prisoner?"

"You're both total assholes," said Kohl. "Tremendous assholes. Giant, Jupiter-sized—"

"I get where you're going with this," said the man in black, "but it's all beside the point."

A little puddle of quiet settled between the three of them, broken by one man on the ground groaning. Kohl sniffed, wiped blood from his nose across his arm with a jangle of chains, and coughed. "Okay, so you're both bad cops. Still assholes, near as I can figure."

"Depending on your point of view, we could be angels from the heavens," said the man in black. "Do you like angels, October Kohl?"

"Dunno," said Kohl. "Never had the pleasure. I know one thing, though." He jerked at his chains. "Angels do not chain a man."

"Do they not?" said the man in black. "I have seen all humankind tethered to rocky crusts, unable to fly free."

"The *Tyche* flies pretty good," said Kohl.

"The *Tyche* flies where we want, when we want, and only when it pleases us," said the man in black.

Kohl gave that a little bit of thought. "Okay, I get you," he said. "Help me with one thing."

"What's that?" said Piano Monkey, as if he remembered having a voice. Like someone had just wound up his gears, put in a new battery, and set him to the *GO* position.

"Y'all giving me this speech about being angels, and about being the very boot on our necks." Kohl worked his tongue around his mouth, wiggled a fragment of tooth free, and spat it to the ground. "Your story ain't very consistent."

"You're lucky to be alive," said Piano Monkey. "You're lucky we didn't exercise our legal rights of summary execution."

"Legal's one word for it," said Kohl.

"You've got another word?"

Kohl looked at him, then to the man in black. "Your piano monkey is wearing the uniform, but you're the one in charge. So, bossman, why are we having this conversation? Angels, whatever. I don't give a shit. Honestly. You got a thing you want to do, you *do* it. That's my motto. You don't need the hard sell on October Kohl. You got to speak plain."

The officer took a step forward. "You'll show respect to your betters."

"If I saw any of these betters, which — and I'm trying to be clear — are as likely to walk in here as his mythical angels," said Kohl, "I'd show 'em respect. All I see are two assholes. *Giant* assholes."

The Republic officer's face twitched, and before the thought had cleared High Command in his brain, he'd dropped the shock rod from his belt, took two steps forward towards Kohl, and swung.

Perfect. Kohl let it come, then jerked aside, the shock rod sparking against the ceramicrete wall where his face had been. Kohl brought his knee up into Piano Monkey's stomach — not groin, because it hadn't got personal yet — and as the officer sagged forward, Kohl slammed his forehead into the other man's face. Piano Monkey dropped to the floor, joining the other five bodies, his shock rod tumbling free. It sparked a few times as it rolled across the ground, coming to rest against the man in black's shiny leather shoes.

The man in black hadn't moved before, and he looked like he didn't want to start now. Heaving a sigh, he leaned forward, picking up the fallen shock rod. He stood, holding it in front of his face, turning it this way and that. "Ah," was all he said.

"Yeah," said Kohl.

"I think that you are just the man we need."

"I'm the man everyone needs," said Kohl. "When the fucking sun goes dark, you'll still need someone to do the dirty things that need doing."

"Someone to do the heavy lifting," said the man in black.

Kohl cocked his head sideways at that one. "Huh," he said.

"What is it?"

"Well, you're not the first person I've known to use that turn of phrase," said Kohl.

"If the shoe fits," said the man in black. "Or, should I say, boot."

"Huh," said Kohl again.

"If you're wondering about the theatrics," said the man in black, "there's a reason."

"A reason," said Kohl. "I figured as much. You could have had me ... what'd he call it?"

"Legal summary execution."

"That thing," said Kohl. "You didn't need five of your boys to come in here and try and work me over."

"No," agreed the other man. "It's more fun this way though."

"I thought so," said Kohl, showing his teeth in something that could have, under a certain light, been called a grin. "Guns and shit like that? They get the job done. But fists and harsh language, that's more my speed."

"You want it to be personal," said the man in black.

"Fuck, I just wanna get mad," said Kohl. "I went to this anger management class once. My probie said I had to. You know what those fools wanted me to do? *Reduce* my anger. As if you can put the brakes on awesome, you know?"

"Indeed," said the man in black. "What we were trying to find out is just how far you'd go. How skilled you were at doing ... how did you put it? Doing the dirty things that need doing."

"You want to pay me to hurt someone," said Kohl.

"Yes."

"You want to pay me to hurt someone I know," said Kohl.

"Two for two."

"I ain't gonna hurt the captain," said Kohl.

The man in black pursed his lips. "Why is that?" He held up a hand. "Not that it's required, in this instance. But I'm curious."

"Well," said Kohl. He thought *maybe I couldn't*, followed by *maybe I shouldn't*. "He's already paying me. Gives a bad rep, you know, if you take a man's coin and then space him."

"Good enough for me," said the man in black. "We will pay you two hundred thousand Republic coins to bring us to Grace Gushiken."

"Gracie?" said Kohl. His surprise level went from a steady zero right to eleven.

"Is there a problem?" said the man in black.

"Naw," said Kohl, but his brain said *yes, big fucking problem*, and then it said, *there's no problem*. His brain was swinging back and forth between those two compass points, trying to work out which one was north. It was confusing, so he tried running his mouth for a while. "It's just ... well, you've made the offer now, so no take-backs, right? But I'd have done that for free."

"A fair day's work for a fair day's pay. Isn't that what our great Republic is built on?"

"I'm not a politics kind of guy," said Kohl. Still, the man had a point. The Republic's whole deal was being fair all around. He jerked his chains. "I'm more of a let-me-go kind of guy."

"You must have a view," said the man in black. "You must feel the might of the Republic."

"Yeah, I kinda like it," said Kohl.

"You 'kinda like it?'"

"That's right," said Kohl. "The Old Empire was run by assholes." He shrugged. "There are still assholes." He nudged the Republic officer with the toe of his boot. "But they're more my speed."

"Hmm." The other man shook his head. "I guess we'll take what we can get." He made no obvious gesture, but the clamps holding

Kohl's wrists released with a *clink*, the chains falling back against the wall.

"Let me get this right," said Kohl, rubbing his wrists. "You want me to bring you to Gracie? You don't want me to hurt her? Not even a little?"

"No," said the man in black. "We want Grace Gushiken, alive, and unharmed. So, rather than ask you to get her — something we don't have great confidence in you being able to achieve — we'd like you to find her, and make sure she doesn't get away while we come to you."

"That's it?"

"That's it," agreed the man in black.

"Just one more thing," said Kohl. "I'm gonna need my carbine back." He stretched, rolled one of his shoulders, winced, and then started forward. "That was a fine gun, and I'm expecting to need it."

THE WAY out was like any way out. Full of assholes, howlers, and deadbeats.

When the man in black had unlocked the cell — opaque glass walls turning clear, giving Kohl a view of his surroundings, and allowing the cameras outside a view of what occurred inside — Kohl had relaxed. He was sure that the man in black was playing a straight game. Why else would he be snatched off the street after axing a bunch of Republic soldiers? Activities like that had garnered many a gang runner a death sentence before the day was done. Hell, they could have just shot him in the street. They were going to a lot of trouble to keep him alive.

He'd been perplexed when the glass box they'd put him in turned opaque. Prisoners didn't get privacy, that was the whole deal. But then the door had slid open with a hiss, five men had come in with evil in their hearts, and Kohl had understood. It was a test. Hell, the cap would have tried to talk his way out. Kohl had seen the way Nate moved, knew in his prime he'd have been a fearsome opponent, but that leg and arm bound him up. So, the cap would have talked.

Not Kohl. The talking route was boring, and he'd always figured that wasting words where fists could do all the talking you'd need was a bad principle to follow.

Anyway, he'd beat on those boys like they were a collection of dirty rugs. Test passed. After that, the Republic officer — looking like he was in charge on account of the uniform, but actually being the man in black's bitch — had come in. Events had unfolded, and now October Kohl was leaving, about to do a little more heavy lifting for a heavier load of coin.

No elevators out of this dungeon, though. Elevators were risky for officers. Basically a kill box: you needed a prisoner sedated or dead to use 'em right, which was just too much like hard work, which is why they were walking up a ramp. Ceramicrete floor, walls, and roof. Kohl hadn't got a good look on the way in because he'd had a bag over his head, but he figured he hadn't missed much. Not much at all. *Green* was the color, kind of a puce shade, but that might have been the lighting strips.

Back to the assholes: there were a lot of guards. Like, a lot. More than might be expected in a prison. Kohl had seen the inside of a few jails in his time, because he wasn't one for following rules, especially if those rules got in the way of a good time. Uniforms everywhere made his skin crawl, and the scar on his back shoulder started to itch. The same scar where that damn bug had been under his skin, burrowing up his spine. The same bug Gracie had cut out of him. He still didn't understand why she'd done that, but it was nice of her. It helped him live to see another day, and earn good coin.

A guard took in the look on his face, and said, "Prisoner. Don't eyeball me, son."

Assholes. Fucking *assholes.* "I ain't a prisoner, and you sure as hell ain't my dad," said Kohl.

The guard's jaw clenched, muscles in his neck bunching. He saw the man in black, like he'd just noticed him, and then saw Kohl wasn't wearing prisoner restraints, and said, "My mistake."

"Yeah," said Kohl. "You boys sure make a lot of those." And then ignored the guard, because nothing else would happen. Sure, he could have swung at the guy, but it wouldn't have done anything but slowed him down getting outside. And he wanted to be outside, because these places smelled the same: bad. Antiseptic over vomit and blood.

Bringing Gracie down, now that was a thing. He'd told the man in black — the guy was still walking at Kohl's side, like he wasn't afraid of anything — that he'd do it for free, and there was a time that would have been true. But the scar, and the itch, reminded Kohl he had debts to pay. A little more red ink, right alongside the marks he carried in the ledger when the cap pulled him out of a shit situation in a shit town, working for shit people.

Howlers: down the ramp, four guards were dragging another prisoner. Standard orange suit, mask on the guy's face to stop him biting, long poles attached to a metal collar on his neck. Kohl had been strapped to a chair as he was wheeled in, but this other guy was getting the star treatment. Kohl almost felt jealous, right until the prisoner screamed something about *let me go you fucking pigs or I'll rape your daughters*, and one of guards had stepped in with a shock rod and lit the guy up.

Gracie could have found a shock rod on the *Tyche*, brought it to the hold, and made Kohl dance at the end of strings made of burning blue light. Gracie hadn't; she'd come with a sword, because that's who she was, but she hadn't meant to use it on him, because that's also who she was. Until Kohl had made her, because of the fucking *bug*, the Ezeroc thing inside him. And then Gracie, she'd fought the good fight, right until Kohl had beaten it out of her. And when she was broken, she'd still got the drop on him. She could have cut his head right off with that sword. Even Kohl agreed she'd earned the right. But she hadn't. She'd cut the Ezeroc out of him, took the risk she'd miss, and Kohl would finish her, and that perplexed Kohl. He wasn't used to giving people a second chance, or a third, or however many she'd given him in those few minutes in the *Tyche's* hold.

More assholes: there were always *more*. Like the man in black, walking at Kohl's side. The weird thing about the man was he wore no uniform. Just that plain black suit. Nice shoes, a belt of real leather, which would have been expensive, and borderline contraband, but once you were high enough up people stopped looking at things like that. The problem with this particular asshole was Kohl had already killed him. He'd used his laser carbine on the man and turned him into a shower of exploding meat.

About that. Kohl cleared his throat as they came to a vaulted door, all manner of locks and seals designed to keep *bad* on this side, away from the *less bad* on the other. "So," he said. "I figure we've got a conversation between us due."

"How's that?" said the man in black. There was a rhythmic beeping, and the door clanged as bolts drew back. It hinged open.

"Well," said Kohl. *Better to be direct.* "There was that time I killed you."

"Best left in the past, don't you think?" He held a hand out, palm up, in an *after you* gesture.

Ahead of them was another puce-green corridor, but there were fewer assholes and no howlers. Kohl walked through. "I guess," he said. "It's just that it's been my general experience that once you reduce a man to his component parts, that's it. There's no do-overs. No come-backs. It's a set of guidelines that have served me well. It's what I *do*."

"Learning new things is a part of living a fulfilling life." He kept pace with Kohl, not acknowledging any of the people they passed. They — assholes all — stood aside to let them pass. Eyes down, sometimes a hushed intake of breath.

Interesting. Kohl looked at the man in black, then kept walking. Nothing unique about this asshole, apart from him not wearing a uniform inside Asshole HQ. "I figure you're not really a person."

The man in black thought about that for a few moments, brow furrowing. "If it walks like a duck," he said.

"What?" said Kohl.

"It's an expression," said the man in black. "'If it walks like a duck, and talks like a duck, it must be a duck.'"

"Ducks don't talk," said Kohl. "That's stupid."

"It's ... a metaphor," said the man in black. "Do you understand what I'm saying?"

"You're not a duck, that's for sure," said Kohl. They arrived at another door, this one a little less like a vault, and a little more like a security door. It slid open with a few beeps. "I figure you're a clone. From a clone army."

"If that works for you," said the man in black, "you have my permission to go with it."

"There's another thing," said Kohl.

"What's that?"

"Y'all got a name?" said Kohl. "Like, what do I call you?"

"Sir would suffice." The man in black paused before a door. "Here we are."

"I don't even call the cap, 'Sir,'" said Kohl. "Leastways not often. So let's pretend that's not going to fly. What's in here?" He looked at the door suspiciously. It was closed, sure, but it had no markings, signs, or other leading indicators of what was inside. In Kohl's experience, there were two types of door like that: the first was a janitorial closet, and the second was a place that harvested organs.

"Why don't you call me Abel?" he suggested. *Abel, huh?* "It's a back way out. Your equipment is here, along with your clothes."

"Back way?" said Kohl.

"Back way," agreed Abel. "If we take you out the front, there will be questions. Questions need answers, and answers take time and energy away from the real purpose of our glorious Republic."

"I get you," said Kohl. "Silence is golden."

"Silence can be bought," said Abel.

"Whatever," said Kohl. "I just want my gun." With a click, the door opened. Not an organ chop shop, not a janitorial closet either. So, Abel wasn't a bald-faced liar. That was worth bearing in mind.

CHAPTER EIGHT

AMEDEA WAS STRANGE. That was the feeling Grace got from
her; not *angry/mad/rage*, or *confused/fear/fear*, just *strange*. Like
there was a hole where her mind should be. Not a hole, but a blank
space, a white wall, perfect, not a blemish on it.

Grace could almost always tell what people were feeling. Her ...
gifts were of questionable providence. She couldn't pluck the
thoughts from people's minds like her father. He'd had to work at it,
but with concentration he could hear people, or so he said, and sometimes influence them. Grace didn't have to work at it; feelings came
off people, emotions showering her like a summer storm.

Also strange was Nate had drawn on Amedea, blaster in his
hand. He'd put a hand behind him, pushing Grace back, like she
needed protecting, the nose of his blaster hungry for targets. Off
Nate, Grace was getting *fear/fear/anger*. The odd thing wasn't that
he felt that for *himself*.

If she had more time to unpick that, she might have been flattered. As it was, it was annoying, because she couldn't draw steel
down on this room of Republic sympathizers. "Nate," she said.

"Back up," he said, not looking behind him. Blaster still moving between Amedea, and the pale man, the medtech, and — almost reluctantly — Harlow. "We've got to leave."

"Nate," she said. She wanted to say *these Republic assholes can be made to talk, just give me one, any one, and I'll cut it out of them*, but there wasn't time. "We've got to stay."

"Say what?" he said, the cant of his shoulders suggesting confusion louder than the *confusion/confusion* coming from him.

"Listen to her," said Amedea.

"There are noises coming from you," said Nate, waving his blaster at Amedea. "I'd suggest you stop that for the moment."

"You're not going to shoot me, Nathan Chevell," said Amedea. "I know it like water's wet. I know—"

Nathan fired his blaster, a bright arc of plasma going past Amedea, gouging the brickwork behind her. She stopped talking, eyes wide. "Hey," said Nate. "Sorry. What were you saying?"

Grace took a careful step forward, put her hand on Nate's shoulder, gentle like a small bird. She leaned her lips close to his ears. *Hear me.* "Nate, if these assholes set us up, it gives us an opportunity."

"Spell it out," said Nate. "I'm itching to just lay down cleansing fire in this room."

"Uh," said Harlow. "Nate?"

"Not now, Harlow," said Nate. *Frustration/confusion.* "I've got a lot of inputs going on, you get me?"

"Sure," said Harlow. "It'll keep."

"The opportunities are like this," said Grace, lips almost touching Nate's ear, body close to his. "They can tell us *how* they know about us. They can take us to whichever part of the Republic sent 'em here. It could be the same part that's selling out entire colonies for bug food." While she was talking, Grace kept scanning the room. Amedea's eyes went wide when Grace said *selling out entire colonies* and Harlow seeped *anger/betrayal* when she'd talked about the Republic sending them here. Neither of which was conclusive, but ... "Not everything here is what it seems."

"Listen to her," said Amedea. "Listen to your Assessor. You pay her to Assess things. *Things you do not understand.* This is one of those things."

"Sister?" said Grace, pulling away from Nate and the comfort of his closeness. She was getting herself ready to do what needed to be done. "I'll come over there and cut on you myself if you don't shut the hell up. We're having a moment here."

But Nate relaxed, the tension leaving his gun arm. He didn't lower his blaster, but it seemed from his *hesitation/caution* he wasn't about to spray the room with plasma. "Okay," he said. "Okay. So, Assessor, what's your take?"

Grace closed her eyes for a moment, feeling the room, the people in it — the medtech, who was all *terror/fear/run/flight*, Harlow's *sullen/smoldering anger/betrayal/friend/foe*, the pale man who was *opportunity/patience/excitement*, and Amedea's emptiness. Grace breathed, then opened her eyes. "Harlow is your friend, and you need to work out what's going on with him over a beer."

"That's what I was going to say," said Harlow. "It's just—"

"Not yet, Harlow," said Nate. "I'll let you know when shit's not quite so real on this side of the room."

"Got it," said Harlow, and looked at his feet.

"Amedea is *something different.* She's not *here*," said Grace.

"She's right there, Grace," said Nate, pointing with his blaster.

"You know how we've had our little talk about the things I can do," said Grace.

"Oh," said Nate. "*Oh.*"

"Your Assessor has the right of it," said Amedea. "You need to—"

"Haven't finished," said Grace, giving her a glare. "Medtech's just a medtech. He doesn't want to be here. We don't want to be here, so maybe we get him and Harlow in the same bar later. The guy there? The one who needs a tan."

"Hey," said the pale man. "I spend a lot of time down here."

"I see him." Nate swung the blaster to point at the pale man. "What about it?"

"He'll sell us out," said Grace. "He's a liar and a thief. I'm a liar, and I know those. You're a thief, you know what they look like."

"Hey—" started the pale man. He didn't get to finish — faster than Grace could track, Amedea's blaster cleared its holster and fired. She shot him three times, although after the first shot the need for the next two was questionable. The pale man was thrown back by plasma fire, his torso coming apart in flaming pieces of meat.

Nate swung his blaster towards Amedea, then back at the remains of the pale man, then back to Amedea. She ignored him, examining the burning remains of the pale man, then holstered her blaster. Grace took in the medtech, who was cowering on the floor, body in a fetal position, and Harlow, who's eyes were wide, his mouth wider, but with no noise coming out. He seemed epoxied to his chair, which was the safest way to be in this sort of situation.

"Thanks," said Amedea. "I haven't been able to get a read on that guy. Had my suspicions, but ... well, when you spoke his guard came down. Got a glimpse."

Grace swallowed. "Nate, we should go."

"Uh," said Nate. "Look, I'm confused. You said we should work on these guys until they spilled intel. Now we should go? What's changed?"

"What's changed is I know what Amedea is," said Grace.

"What's that?" said Nate.

"Nathan Chevell," said Amedea, leaning forward, eyes hard, "I'm the devil. I'm the evil that brought down your precious Old Empire. People like you call us espers. But as with so many things in life, all is not what it seems. The question you need to ask is whether you want to find out where the Bridge goes. How far this jump is. Whether what's on the other side of space is something you can bear to see. Or, you can leave. I won't stop you. You can get back in your ship and fly far away, as far as you can before the end finds you, like it will find us all."

"Huh," said Harlow. *Surprised/surprised.*

"Harlow," warned Nate. *Surprised/confused/conflicted.*

"I know," said Harlow. "Not yet?"

"Not yet," said Nate, looking at his blaster. He said something that sounded like *hell with it* and holstered it. Then he looked at Amedea. "Is Amedea even your real name?"

"It's the name I gave myself when I broke free of my chains," she said. "It's the realest name I have."

Grace's fingers found Nate's arm, squeezed. "We shouldn't trust her," she said. "I can't get a read on her."

Nate turned, looked at Grace, and put his hand — flesh and blood, warmth and comfort — over hers. "Grace? I can't get a read on you. It's how we work, all of us. I ain't saying we should trust her. Hell, if you've seen what I've seen? Seen what espers do? You'd want to run."

"Why aren't we running?" said Grace. Because she wanted to run. The only other esper she'd known was her father. She'd felt his dark soul, his desire for dominion over people, felt his *I'm better than you* leaking out no matter who he looked at. But like everyone else, she'd heard the stories. About how espers had cored the Old Empire, tore it down from the inside. The Republic had risen against them, a response to fight the good fight. Humans vowed to rid the universe of people who could see into your mind and into your heart. Bounties were set to keep humanity clean. The bounties weren't high enough. Not yet. But high enough to keep Grace hiding, flawed diamond that she was.

Nate gave her a crooked smile. "I gave you a shot, didn't I? Best damn call I made." Grace swallowed. She didn't know what to say about that. Nate curled his fingers around hers, gave them a squeeze, then turned back to Amedea. "Okay. Let's say I want to make this jump. Kick in the Endless Drive, see what's on the other side of those stars. Where do your charts take us?"

"To hell," said Amedea. "To the broken, crippled heart of the Republic."

"Cool," said Nate. He looked at Harlow. "Harlow? Now's your moment."

"I was going to say I think we need a beer," said Harlow. "We should have a talk, you and I. About who owns the *Tyche*. About how friends don't let friends get worked over by Republic assholes. And about how you should get to know the people I work for a little closer."

Nate nodded, and Grace could feel *chagrin/regret/regret* coming off him. "Well, hey now," he said. "I expect we should have that talk. And that beer. Know any good bars?"

"I do," said Harlow. He gave Amedea a look. "We taking them on the tour?"

"We're taking them on the tour," Amedea said.

THE TOUR WAS MORE impressive than Grace would have thought. She was expecting Amedea and Harlow to lead them into a few dingy tunnels, emerging out at some hole in the wall where a seedy bartender would offer them watered down liquor. Grace expected rats, and she expected three-day-old bar snacks, if there were bar snacks at all.

They saw nothing like that.

"The place above," said Amedea, leading them further down into tunnels carved from raw rock, the smooth surfaces shiny from the lasers used to cut through, "is a front. It's designed to be raided. Let the Republic come in here. Let them take a few knick-knacks. A little contraband. They think they're solving the problem. The real deals happen down here."

Down here was well-lit. Men and women walked with purposeful efficiency, nodding to Amedea as she passed, occasionally nodding to Harlow. Grace felt none of the *rancor/bile* she might get from lesser people, just a little bit of *respect/acceptance*. Like Harlow was used to this music, could dance the dance, liked his place on the floor. It made sense; he was a dealer. He wasn't a leader and wasn't trying to be. But Grace hadn't picked him as a revolutionary either. Maybe times had got hard, extruding revolutionaries from common people like sausage from a machine.

These people seemed to have it all. They were led through barracks, bunks racked on top of each other, with clean and folded blankets. They were shown training rooms, equipped with shooting ranges, sparring rooms, holo sims for training. Amedea had asked them if they'd wanted to try their luck, and Nate had held up his metal hand saying *doesn't seem fair now, does it*, and Grace had smiled behind her hand. Amedea had turned to Grace, taking in the sword slung on her back, and raised an eyebrow. Grace had just shaken her head, because she didn't fight for money, or fame, or to impress people. She fought from fear, to survive, because it was necessary. And just recently, she'd learned to fight for love.

Maybe that was too strong. Love was for fools. But she'd learned to fight for something good, and it was enough. It was everything.

Nate and Amedea had been talking back and forth, Grace ignoring them for the most part. Captain's business, and she knew he'd get the job done. But one thing caught her ear. Nate said, "So now you've shown us this, what happens if we don't want to join the party?" Grace didn't pick up on this because of his words, rather the *caution/anxious* coming from him. He was worried — not enough to draw or run, but enough that the vibe made her tune back in to the conversation.

Amedea stopped before the double doors to a mess hall, soldiers moving back and forth with their food. Grace could tell they were soldiers because of how they moved, all oiled efficiency. You couldn't tell from their clothes — streetwear, designed for the ceramicrete above. Shopkeepers, bartenders, beggars, students, company people. All of them were ... conscripts in something big. Amedea said, "You're a man of the world, Nate."

"A man of the universe," said Nate. "I don't like my boots on a crust. Ties you down."

"As a man of the universe, you should know what happens."

Amedea held her arm out towards the soldiers in the mess hall — not an invitation, but a display.

"You'd erase us," said Nate. "Leave us in a dumpster."

"There wouldn't be enough left to put in a dumpster," said Amedea, hand resting on her blaster. "Do we have an under-standing?"

Nate gave Harlow a look like he was sucking a lemon. "You didn't say your friends were assholes."

"Hey," said Harlow. "I know you, don't I?"

Grace cleared her throat. She felt three sets of eyes swivel towards her. "You must have known we'd take the job."

"What job?" said Nate and Harlow, at about the same time, with the same expression on their faces. Mouth open a little, eyes wider than usual.

"I did, because you're here, Grace. *Captain* Chevell won't take the job. But *Nathan* Chevell might take the job, because his esper — sorry, Assessor — tells him too," said Amedea.

"What job?" said Nate, again. But with a little less of the *I am stupid* and more of the *I am angry* on his face. Because he was the captain, and the captain took the jobs. Not a lowly grifter who had conned her way on his ship.

Grace pushed a strand of black hair away from her eyes. "You can't run an operation like this with one esper," she said. Amedea's expression was neutral, like she was waiting. Harlow was looking between Grace and Amedea, back and forth like he was seeing something new for the first time. Nate just sighed, so Grace pushed on. "Takes one to know one. You're down here under the city, living a good life, building a, what, an army. An army, now that takes time, and effort, and a little inside knowledge. The Republic is notorious for not giving away inside knowl-edge. I know, because getting knowledge out of them is how I stay *alive*."

"Superb," said Amedea. "Let's see how well you've ... *assessed* the rest of the situation."

"What job?" said Nate, louder this time.

"She wants us to get them back," said Grace.

"Who?" said Nate. "Where?"

"All of them," said Grace. "Everyone. My guess? They're in a Republic reprogramming facility. Brains being strung out on a wire, and when the wires don't work, the drugs go in. Doesn't matter how long you've been trained, or what kind of special snowflake you are. Eventually? You'll crack." She swallowed. "You'll crack and then all your friends will die."

"Specifics are important," said Nate.

"How much do you know about the Old Empire's Intelligencers?" said Amedea.

"Everything," said Nate. "I know that they corrupted the Empire from within." Grace could see his hands clenching, metal and flesh both. The metal hand was whining with the force of it. "They plotted and planned. Wanted all the power. They wanted ... they killed my friend." This last was said through clenched teeth. "They all deserve to die."

"Hmm," said Amedea. "Your intel is a little rusty."

"Rusty?" said Nate. "I was *there*."

"So was I," said Amedea, "on the other side. I was there as our Emperor was cast down. Emperor Prirene IV, last of his line, and his sister, both fell."

"Dominic and Annemarie," said Nate, his eyes hard. "Dom was a friend."

"Emperors don't have friends," said Amedea. "The Emperor had his Black." Her gaze went to Nate's metal hand, then to his leg, hidden by his ship suit, but metal nonetheless. "His Black stood in the path of fire, until all was lost."

"This one was a little different," said Nate.

Grace watched them, feeling the emotions boil off Nate like steam from a ruptured pipe. She reached out a hand, laid fingers on his arm. "No wonder you got such a princely gift," she said.

Nate barked a laugh, turning away from the doors to the mess hall. He walked away, his metal leg catching at his stride. "Sure. Early retirement. A broken arm, a broken leg. A broken body."

Grace hurried after him, caught his arm. Made him turn. *Listen. Hear me.* "No," she said.

"The sword," said Nate.

"No," she said again. "Nate? Dom gave you the only gift he could. He gave you your life."

"What's left of it, anyway." His eyes searched hers. "He ... said he couldn't have me on the Black. Not anymore."

"Because that was the only way to stop you from dying." She touched his metal hand. "Here. See? You'd already tried to die for him once already."

"Yes," said Amedea, coming up behind them. "And no."

Nate turned to her. "This better not be more cryptic overlord shit," he said.

Amedea gave him a tired smile. "Not today, Captain. I had to kill a man earlier, and I'm trying to work out if I need to kill another. Dominic Fergelic knew the end was coming. He was going to die. That was never in any doubt."

"He knew?" said Nate. "How did he know?"

"Because I told him," said Amedea. "He had a chance. One chance, to fire a perfect arrow through the heart of his enemy. A shot, fired far into the future. The feathered shaft would strike through time and space with the fury of his fallen line."

"How did he know?" said Nate. "Specifically. The specifics are always important."

"Because I told him," said Amedea, but her words were softer, like there was something behind them. Grace couldn't read this woman, not in the usual way, but she could tell when someone was hurting. "I gave him the arrow. I said he could avenge his name, his family. Make them pay for what would happen to his sister." She looked at Nate's hand. "For what had already happened to his friends."

"*How*," said Nate. "Did. He. Know?"

Something inside Amedea seemed to break, her shoulders slumping. "Nate? I was one of the Empire's Intelligencers. I knew the plot. I knew the plans. I knew them for a long, long time."

Nate's blaster cleared its holster faster than Grace could blink, the muzzle up against Amedea's throat. Amedea swallowed, closed her eyes, like she was ready for it. "Please," she said, and Grace couldn't tell whether she wanted to die or wanted to live.

"Nate," said Grace. "Not like this. Not here." She jerked her eyes at the people flowing in and out of the mess hall behind them. At Harlow, whose look of astonishment looked more like a permanent fixture.

"She said I was a perfect arrow," said Nate. "Fired right into the heart of those who'd betrayed him. Well, here I am. And here she is."

"Nate," said Harlow.

"Not now," said Nate.

"Yeah, now," said Harlow. "Look, we need that beer. We need it now like we've needed nothing else. It doesn't have to be a fancy off-world beer. It has to be cold and wet. And then we can talk this out."

"Nothing to talk out," said Nate.

"Don't you want to know why Dom was happy to lay down his life? Why he didn't run?" Amedea swallowed again, her throat moving against the muzzle of Nate's blaster.

"We'll take the job," said Grace. Three pairs of eyes went to her. "We'll get your espers back, Amedea."

"The fuck we will," said Nate.

"Fine," said Grace. "*I'll* take the job."

Nate's expression was hard, but Grace could feel the *pain/betrayal/anger* he wore like a cloak. Or a cape. "I never ... I never thought *you* would turn."

"I'm not turning," said Grace. "Not from you. Not ever."

"Feels like it," said Nate.

"Nate," said Grace, eyes flicking to the blaster at Amedea's throat. "Think. *Think.* Doesn't all of this feel ... weird? Like a song you've heard the first time, but felt you've known your whole life?" Grace pointed at Harlow. "Your old friend, back in your life. Easily found on this planet of ten billion souls. We've just escaped from aliens. We came here to find out how deep the corruption goes. And now we find it's not deep, not at all. That's the wrong word. It's from *before*. The corruption? It's old, Nate. It threw down the Old Empire. It killed the Emperor ... your friend. Dom. It killed him. And there's one person who says they know why. Don't you want to know *how*?"

"How?" said Nate, but his arm was relaxing. "Don't you mean why?"

"No," said Grace. "We know why. Power. Control. The usual reasons assholes have."

"I guess I'd prefer to kill 'em all."

"And not know?"

"I don't ... *need* to know." But Nate lowered his blaster, *curiosity/caution* coming off him, and Amedea closed her eyes. Grace couldn't tell whether it was because she was relieved or disappointed. Grace pushed her hair back from her eyes again, and said, "Amedea. You claim to be one of the Intelligencers."

"I am," said Amedea, "or, I was."

"Then show a little intelligence," said Grace. "Start talking."

"Okay," said Amedea, then she paused. "What..." Her voice trailed off, and she looked down the corridor.

"What is it?" said Harlow.

"We need to move," said Amedea. "We need to get out."

"Time for a beer?" said Harlow, almost hopefully.

"No," said Amedea.

Grace could feel the floor shake, just a tremor, and she stooped down to put her fingers against it. A shake, building up in frequency. "Something big is coming."

"Let's go," said Amedea.

"Hold up," said Nate. "We haven't finished."

Amedea hurried down the corridor. She was talking into her comm, orders to units, teams, squads, numbers, deployments. Things Grace couldn't follow, and didn't care about, because there was only one thing to worry about. Something was coming, and it couldn't be good.

The light strips flickered, then cascaded into darkness. Someone shouted from back towards the mess hall, half-joke, half-fear. The people around Grace let their *concern/fear/anxiety* out, a ripple spreading towards her from the way they'd come. She clicked the lamp on her suit, bathing the area around her in light. She grabbed Nate's arm. "Time to go."

"I think you're right," he said. "I think—"

He was cut off by an explosion, something that rocked the world around them. Grace fell against him, and he fell to the ground. The rumble of the explosion seemed distant, like the memory of thunder, like the promise of rain. Grace tasted dust and fear.

"They've found us," said Amedea, reaching a hand out in the darkness towards Grace. "Sister. Will you stand with us?"

Grace pushed her hand away. "I'll stand by myself." She got up, realized that she and Nate were helping each other as naturally as breathing. "I'll stand with my captain."

"Good enough," said Amedea. "Now *run*. Harlow knows the way."

"I do?" said Harlow. There was another explosion, and the glimmer of fire from far back down the corridor. "Oh," he said. "I definitely do."

CHAPTER NINE

FINDING ALTMAN RAZOR was easier than El had expected it to be. She had imagined a crime lord, in a vast and unassailable lair. He'd have thugs inside and out, and he would kill El if she ever found him.

That was her cowardice talking, an old friend that always knew the wrong things to say at parties. Altman Razor was short, dirty, and worked alone. His tiny store was tucked in behind a haberdashery, and if that was all the cover he had, it wasn't good enough. Not because the customers of a haberdashery didn't need illicit electronics — some of them did — but because of the sign.

A massive holo, taller than El, sprayed light into the alley. *RAZORS WAREZ* it said, and underneath that, in smaller type, *ALTMAN KNOWS BEST*.

Subtle.

El pushed her way through the door. It was an autodoor, but the auto part had failed at some point in the past, leaving it stuck on the runners, and her first thought was the store was closed. But Altman — the only person inside, a rig of familiar style covering his face — had waved her in. So, El leaned into it and forced the door open with a squeal of metal on metal.

"Hi," said Altman, from her chest height. The guy was short. He flipped up the visor on his rig, gave her a quick up-and-down, then decided on a second pass, up-and-down. "This a business, or, uh, social call?" He sounded hopeful.

El took in the sweaty hair — like any Engineer, they lived in their rigs. Never got enough sun, or enough air, and always seemed to have grease on their faces or under their nails. Hope was the same, but she pulled it off better. His question caught her off balance. She wasn't here to buy something, so... "It might be a social call," offered El.

Altman wiped his hands on a pleather apron, held his hand out. "Altman Razor, at your service."

She reached out to take his hand, and he curled his fingers in hers, bent over, and kissed the back of her hand. El watched this with a horrified fascination, pulling her hand back as an afterthought. "Elspeth Roussel," she said, and it felt like it was the wrong thing to do. Like breaking a priceless vase, it was a thing you couldn't take back, but you could say with honesty to your friends later that it was an accident.

"Elspeth," said Altman. "I like that."

"Uh," said El, then tried again. "I'm looking for someone."

"And you have *found* someone," said Altman, a big smile coming out across his face. It was a nice smile, just a little closer to the ground than El preferred. Add soap, and ... *no*. She'd been on a ship for too damn long. "I could close the shop for lunch." He stepped closer.

"Uh. No."

"No?"

"Look, Mr. Razor—"

"Altman, please."

"Mr. Razor," said El, feeling like an idiot, and looking like one too, "here's the thing. I don't want to have sex with you." There. It was out, done, that problem cleared up.

"Of course not," said Altman.

"Great," said El, breathing out air she hadn't known she was holding.

"You want to have lunch *then* have sex with me," said Altman. He had a hand on her elbow, and she wasn't sure how it had got there.

"Uh," said El, shaking off his hand. "No."

"You're sure?" said Altman, pulling off his rig. It folded up just like Hope's did — or like her old one did. Most Engineers' rigs worked in similar ways, but they all looked a little different. Altman's was no exception; he'd tied feathers to the manipulator arms, maybe going for a mystic vibe. It wasn't working.

"I'm sure," said El. "I'm after a woman who bought a rig from you."

"I don't sell rigs," said Altman. "I sell fine, illicit electronics."

"Is that legal?"

"It is if they're sold in less than working order," said Altman, putting the hand back on her arm, just a gentle touch. "If I also sell instructions on how to make them work, well, I ask you: does that make me a criminal?"

"It ... might," said El. She removed his hand. Again.

"What are you, some kind of lawyer?"

"No," said El. "I'm a Helm. On a starship." *Duh.* Like there was another kind of Helm.

"Flygirl?" said Altman, his smile — which had never seemed to leave his face — widening.

"Isn't that ... uh, like a dancer?"

Altman smoothed his hair back. "If you want to be a dancer, who am I to stop you?" He worked his wrist console, and music with a low, slow beat played from farther back in the shop. El couldn't tell from where, stacked piles of machinery and components hiding any hope of line of sight to a target. "You could dance here, if you like."

"I don't like," said El. She smoothed her hands down the front of her flight suit, brushed her hair back, and squared her shoulders. "She was about this high," and El held her hand out, "pink hair, Engineer. Like you."

Altman laughed, the tone deprecating. "Oh, you flatter me. But, of course you do. I'm no Guild member. Not really, well, it's political. I never got my Shingle. The exams, they're rigged—"

"She would have been in here this morning," said El, teeth gritted. "She would have paid in coins. Hard currency. For a rig. Like yours."

"I'm sure I would have remembered a woman—" said Altman, then stopped when he saw El's gun. His hand, *again* on her arm, slithered away of its own accord this time.

She hadn't remembered drawing it. It'd been a long day, and the liquor she'd had earlier had more than worn off, leaving the sky bright and painful above her. Finding Altman had felt like the end of the trail, and now the man turned out to be a *player*, had some sort of *idea* about what would happen. "So," said El. She pressed the gun into Altman's stomach, but not too hard. Just enough for some motivation.

"She got my last rig, paid, and left," said Altman, words tumbling out of his mouth. He scrabbled on his console, and the music cut off. "Pink hair, right?"

"That's right," said El. "Did she say where she was going?"

"Client confidentiality," said Altman.

"You some kind of fucking doctor?" said El.

"Uh—"

"Because this," El waved her pistol around the shop, "doesn't look like a surgery."

"Well—"

"An illegal chop shop isn't a surgery," said El. She pointed the gun at Altman for emphasis. "Where'd she go?"

"Uh," said Altman, and wound down like an old ship's drive, too much asked of it all at once.

El rubbed her free hand over her face. *For fuck's sake.* She sighed, holstered her pistol, and cleared her throat. This guy? Just a small-time operator. Just like any weasel sitting at dock control, hard on the comm, low on principle. Lazy in thought. She knew how to fly these skies. "Mr. Razor."

"Hi," he said, brightening a little now El's sidearm was back in the safety of her holster.

"Would it help if I bought something?" El gestured around her. "Look, I get the whole I'm-an-illegal-trader thing. I *get* it. A guy like you? He's got a reputation to maintain." Altman was nodding along, not even realizing it. "But it's just that, a rep. You've got a sign out the front the size of a skyscraper saying you're doing illegal shit in here. If it was *true*, then the Republic enforcers would be down here stretching you out like an old sock. Since they're not, you know, and I know by proxy, that this is a sham."

"A ... *what?*" said Altman.

"Sham," said El. "Oh, hell. I don't mean nothing by that. But selling a rig in hard coin? Hardly a crime. Selling a few gizmos that don't work? Also not a crime. Give a few rich kids something to dream about, think they're skirting the hard line of the law? I'd bet the Republic thinks you're doing them a favor."

"Uh—"

"Which is fine," said El. "I got nothing against the fine Republic, under whose flag we all sail. I used to Helm for the other side. But I meant nothing by it. You know what I mean?"

"No," said Altman.

"Of course not, we've only just met," said El. "Here's the thing. My sidearm," she cleared the pistol from her hip almost absently, pointing it at Altman, "is conspicuous."

He swallowed. "I can see why people might think that. I, personally, find it charming—"

"It's got a huge barrel," said El. "Do you know why?"

"No," said Altman. But he leaned forward, all Engineer curiosity. Even if he didn't have his Guild Shingle, these people were all cut from the same cloth. "It looks like it ... by the stars. Does that wonderful device fire kinetic rounds?"

"You what?" said El.

"Physical objects," said Altman.

"Yeah, it's a shotgun," said El. "Single shot." She put the sidearm away, pulled out a cartridge. "See?"

"My," said Altman. "It's an antique."

"Kinda not," said El. "Shoots pretty good."

"Well, *obviously*," and the way he said the word made El's teeth clench, her shoulders rising towards her ears, "that specific unit is not an antique. Machined within the last fifty years, I'd say. But the design? Prehistoric."

"Yeah, it's conspicuous," said El, "like I said. So something less conspicuous would help."

"If you didn't point it at people—"

"That's just not a line of thought we want to go down," said El. "I don't like pointing it at people. You need to believe me, Mr. Razor. It's just sometimes people get the wrong idea. You understand."

Altman swallowed. "I guess that could happen."

"So. Whatcha got? Something a little less conspicuous."

"Energy weapon? Well, I'm not licensed to sell weapons—"

"Mr. Razor, I thought we were getting along so well."

He raised his hands in surrender. "Elspeth, wait. I can't sell you one that works. But I can sell you one that *almost* works."

"That sounds good enough for me," said El, "as long as it comes with instructions on how to find my friend."

"Don't you mean instructions on how to make it work?" Altman sounded confused.

"I don't give a shit," said El. "If I find my friend, she can make it work."

"Okay," said Altman. "Have you ever used a maser before?"

WELL, shit. This wasn't good.

It wasn't good because the broken maser had cost more than a maser should *ever* cost, but she had to admit the weapon had a certain style to it. Altman had said — when it worked — it would boil people from the inside out, which sounded effective. El hadn't heard of personal masers before; the ones she'd used were mounted on hulls, used to cook machinery, electronics, and hundreds of people at a time on enemy ships.

It also wasn't good because of where Hope had gone. Downtown. Which meant *poor*town. In any city there was a seedy underside, where people with no money and even fewer prospects lived. Because everyone needed somewhere to bunk, a shell around them to shield them from the harsh universe. The roughest of them would live downtown.

El used her wrist console, flicking through a city map. She was better among the stars, but a 2D map she could handle no problem. *There.* Altman had said Hope had asked him for the fastest way to get to that spot, meaning a specific building, and so that's where El needed to go.

Because if El was right, Hope was going to find Reiko Crous-Povilaitis. Reiko, Hope's wife, was a liar and a thief.

El knew the story from Hope. That Hope had screwed up, gained a debt, and then run, with the Republic burning hard after her for justice. Now Hope had to live on board a ship and never feel the sun on her face again. Price of mistakes. Price of failure. Etcetera.

It had sounded like bullshit. Hope didn't make mistakes.

No, the story was simpler, or so Nate said. Reiko had a gambling problem, and had tagged Hope with the debt of it, and let her wife take the fall. It wasn't hard to believe, because some people were just mean. Especially if they called downtown *home*. Hope's home was on the *Tyche*, and El just needed to remind her of that.

CHAPTER TEN

GETTING BACK to the *Tyche* took some doing. There were few autotaxis willing to take him. It wasn't the carbine. Laws on Earth allowed Republic citizens to protect themselves most any way they saw fit. It was the change from the Old Empire to the Republic that Kohl liked most. There were others, like how the Republic put down miscreants that sucked the life from the system, like that debt-runner Hope. But carrying shooting irons in the street, bars, and brothels? That worked for Kohl.

No, it was the remains of other people all over his stuff. Blood, mostly, but some other components of Republic troops that had adhered to him. The screws hadn't bothered to launder his clothes, just left 'em in a box for him. It figured, because the box could either be given back to Kohl — let's call that option A — or incinerated to remove any evidence (option B).

It'd been a few years since Kohl had slummed it on a subway. There was a time when the underground was a natural home — a dark place that allowed for dark deals. A place where violence wasn't so monitored. But those days were aways back, and besides he had coin in his pockets. Good Republic coin that let him buy whatever he wanted, except when the autotaxis refused him entry.

Assholes. Even the electronics are assholes these days.

But he made it. The spaceport was like he'd left it, but the *Tyche* wasn't.

As he approached the ship, there were a few crucial — El might call 'em *key* — differences. The first was that the *Tyche* was dark. None of the usual hiss of steam as the cooling systems vented. No umbilicals connecting to fueling ports in the dock.

Kohl remembered how El and Hope were supposed to be on board, keeping the home fires burning. Ready for a quick getaway. He'd expected Gracie to come back here, Kohl to use the fancy transponder in his pocket to call the Republic, and be two hundred thousand coins richer. But the ship wasn't ready. The cargo bay doors had been sealed, the ship locked down. There were people home, and none of them were named Nate, El, Hope, or Grace. They were strangers and they'd cut into the skin of the *Tyche's* cargo bay airlock, breaching the ship.

Nate would be *pissed off*.

There were a couple of ways this could go. First, Kohl could just turn the fuck around and leave. Find Gracie some other way. Problem with that was that this was a big, busy city and he didn't know Grace Gushiken well. The second way was that Kohl could get on the *Tyche*, coax the ship back into life, and ask her where her crew was. The *Tyche* was used to it; she kept tabs on wayward crew that made planetfall on a hostile crust. Which made that approach the preferred option, but Kohl had to get in, around the people inside, and get to the flight deck.

He sighed, checked the charge on his carbine, and walked towards the *Tyche*.

There were two people — one man, one woman — outside the breached cargo hold. They were dressed like dock workers, but nothing else about them looked like dock workers. The grease under their nails was too perfect, and they walked like soldiers. There was a dirty plasma rifle propped against the *Tyche's* hull next to the man. Both were leaning against the ship like they owned her. Kohl clumped forward in his boots, carbine held low, in what he hoped was a non-threatening manner. "Excuse me," he said.

They'd both been watching him approach, but the man spoke first. "Help you?"

"Might be able to," said Kohl. He pointed at the *Tyche*. "You looking to sell your ship?"

"What makes you think that?" said the man.

"Well, simple," said Kohl. He pointed to the breach in the side. "Y'all don't carve a hole in your hull when you're looking to grab some sky. So I figure, you're stripping her. Seems the thing most folks do before they sell a hull."

"You looking to buy?" said the man, taking a step closer. A step away from his rifle. The woman hadn't moved, just watched Kohl under heavy brows.

"Might be," said Kohl. "What's the price like?"

"A million coins, even," said the man.

Kohl whistled. "Seems steep for an old hauler like this."

"This?" said the man. "She might be old, but she knows the stars." *Like he'd know. Asshole.* "Got an Endless Drive. There. See? Twinned fusion pipes with enough thrust to put your spine through an acceleration couch easy. One of the old milspec ships from the war. She'll keep you and yours safe. Right 'till the end. Oh, and the reactor's been upgraded."

Interesting. So these clowns had been on the *Tyche* long enough to know most of the things about her. About the *Ravana's* reactor. About her basic layout. And they were also willing to sell her, which meant they were willing to kill the crew. They were Republic forces, looking to scrap and salvage after a legal seizure — which didn't sound right to Kohl, because the cap had done nothing wrong, not yet leastways — or they were mercs, working for some dock gang, looking to make a quick buck on a ship. He knew how those kinds of people worked, because he used to *be* those kinds of people.

"Hmm," offered Kohl. "Still. She's old. You done a refit inside? Could I take a look?"

The woman stiffened at that. Kohl almost sighed, but that would have given too much away. The man looked at him suspiciously. "You don't trust us, friend?"

"No," said Kohl. "I don't trust anyone until I see the color of their coin, or they see the color of mine. You could be junkers—"

"We ain't junkers," said the woman, her tone abrupt, a little pride leaking out. Which was a shame, because it meant that they weren't a dock gang. Sure, a dock gang would have said the same thing, but without the pride. A dock gang would be a little sullener about it, because it would have been true. No, these were Republic, which was all kinds of wrong.

"Okay," said Kohl. "I got one more question."

"You are full of questions," said the woman. Her hand reached behind her to the small of her back, right to where the grip of a blaster would have been.

"I am," said Kohl. "Here's the question. Do you guys talk to each other at all? You know, at Republic High Command."

The man turned away, rushing towards his rifle. The woman drew a blaster. Damn, but it hurt being right all the time. Kohl had already raised the carbine, clicked the stud, and the cascade of red bathed the woman for a split second before she exploded into barbecue. The blaster she'd held popped like a cork out of a bottle as the cartridge inside hit three thousand degrees in a microsecond. Kohl swiveled towards the man, who'd made his rifle. Kohl squeezed the trigger as the man turned, and in a fraction of a second he was turned into chunks of meat and red mist. The red mist drifted on the light breeze to stain the side of the *Tyche*.

Where there's two, there's more. Kohl looked into the dark of the hold, put a boot up, and hoisted himself inside. He ducked to the side, giving himself a little time to adjust to the dimness of the hold. While the Republic clowns had said they had uncovered a few things, they hadn't found out how to turn the lights on. El might have put the reactor into safe shutdown, but starting it up was just the click of a few buttons. Even Kohl could do it, no need for an Engineer on hand unless something went wrong.

The remains of the airlock door were laid out on the cargo bay floor, the metal burred and rounded at the edges where they'd cut on the *Tyche*. The old girl had been in the wars over the last couple weeks.

No point in putting this off anymore. His eyes were fine in the gloom, so Kohl walked forward. Past the remains of the door, and into the middle of the bay. He paused, but couldn't put his finger on why. He bent down to examine the metal floor. There was a small scar in the decking, about an inch or two long. *Ah.* This was where Gracie's sword had stood when he'd stabbed it in place. When he'd tried to kill her.

It wasn't you, it was those damn Ezeroc.

Still, the thought wouldn't leave him, because she'd taken the sword and *hadn't* killed him. And here he was, trying to sell her out for a few coins. Well, okay, not a *few* coins, quite a lot of coins, but the principle was the same. Kohl stood, shrugged, and set off towards the metal ladder leading up to the crew deck. Didn't matter if it was a few coins or a lot of coins. Coins were coins, and he'd agreed to take someone's money and do a job.

He scaled the ladder, easy as pie, and listened. There were rustling noises coming from his cabin, which was close to the ladder. Captain had said it was the best place for him, on account of it being close to where the action happened, but Kohl had always harbored a sneaking suspicion he'd been given this cabin because it was the farthest from Nate's. *Whatever.* Kohl moved slow and easy, putting his boots down on the metal deck with care. No need to spook whoever was in his cabin before it was necessary.

Kohl poked his head around the corner of the room, taking in someone going through his stuff. Some of his best rifles were laid out on his bunk, and the innards of his small console had been taken apart, data slivers scattered everywhere. There was a man, head down in the console, blaster holstered at his side. Kohl looked at the blaster, thought about the pop of the woman's weapon outside, and leaned forward. A small, quick step took him close to the man, and he pulled the blaster from its holster. The man gave a shrill cry — *let's call it what it is, the guy just screamed* — and stood up. Or tried to, because he collided with Kohl's bulk, stumbled, and fell back, knocking his head against the side of Kohl's bunk. The sound of it, the meaty, rolling crunch like when you tore a drumstick from a thigh, made Kohl wince. The man went down and stayed down. Red leaked from the back of his head all over the floor.

Kohl turned in time to take in a woman — from across the gantry, where Gracie's cabin was — pointing a carbine at him. Kohl ducked to the side of his door as plasma, bright and loud, sparked past him, hitting the bunk and a part of the wall. Kohl didn't stick his head out to see, he instead poked the carbine out from around the door and squeezed the trigger. His carbine clicked, mapped the target — he could see the backscatter of red against the doorway — and with a whine, fired. There was the sound of someone emptying a bucket of water, then silence. Kohl risked a look around the doorway, saw the remains of the woman across the gantry steaming in the chill air of the *Tyche.*

Gracie's room, huh? He stepped out of his own cabin, the need for stealth well past. He made to walk towards the opposite end of the crew deck as a man poked a head out over the railing leading to the ready room. *Blaster or carbine, blaster or carbine.* It was the choices that defined the nature of a man. Use the carbine, and be showered with red? Or use the blaster, and risk another man's weapon being poorly maintained? Still, the blaster needed to be tested at some point, and now was as good a time as any. Kohl whipped the blaster up and fired. He was rewarded — *it worked!* — with a bright blue flash and the bark of plasma. The man lost his head and the top part of his torso in the blast, the remains of the body falling to sizzle on the deck plates.

"Brodie?" said a man's voice from above, in the ready room.

"Brodie's dead, I think," said Kohl. He looked at the smoking corpse. "Was he a guy about medium build with a falcon tattoo on his forearm?"

"Who the fuck are you?" said the voice.

"Guy who shot Brodie," said Kohl.

"I'll kill you!" screamed the voice.

"Come get some," said Kohl. He flexed his shoulders, readied the carbine, and waited. He expected a blind rush, some anger for a lost comrade, but what he got was a grenade. It tumbled down the ladder, clanked on the deck of the *Tyche*, and rolled with a metallic rumble in a small circle. Kohl watched it for a second, then threw himself over the side of the crew deck down into the hold below. The grenade went off when he was still in the air, the shockwave grabbing him, shaking him like a dog with a fresh kill, and tossed him against the inside hull of the *Tyche*.

He lay on the ground for a few heartbeats, feeling stunned. *Get up, October Kohl. There's killing that needs doing.* Kohl could hear feet on metal, the sound of someone descending from the flight deck to the cargo bay. And here he was, laying on the carbine, which was uncomfortable as hell what with his fingers still wrapped around the handle. The weapon was *click-click-clicking*, trying to find a target, because his finger was mashed against the firing stud. Kohl groaned, got himself to one elbow, and the carbine spat red light across the hold. It mapped the face leaning out from the crew deck, then turned that face into water vapor and fire.

"Huh," said Kohl. The carbine was working out better than expected. Hell knew why people still used blasters, this thing did all the hard work for you. A little slower on the firing, maybe, but you didn't need to be accurate worth a damn.

Kohl coughed as he stood, feeling a little singed, but otherwise fine. He climbed the ladder back up to the crew deck, the rungs still warm from the grenade. There could still be people on the *Tyche*, people with murder in their hearts, and Kohl still felt in a killing mood. Odds were low, though, because the blast of the grenade should have flushed 'em out. Better to be safe rather than sorry. He stomped around the crew deck, checking out all the cabins, saving Gracie's for last. The cabins all looked similar to his — tossed in a hurry, a quick check for valuables. Gracie's was a different story. Everything — every last thing, from her bedding and pillow, through to her small chest of items — was open, cut, torn, broken, or otherwise ruined. The personal console here was in pieces, and the pieces were in pieces. They were looking for Gracie, and they were looking *hard*.

You know what, Kohl? No one else should do this to your crew. No one 'cept you. He sighed, making the trip to Engineering. No one home, Hope having fled, or some such thing. Kohl could worry about what the hell was happening with Hope after he'd found Gracie. Because, you know, two hundred *thousand* coins. He made his way back to Grace's cabin, hoping to find a clue about where she might be. Nothing obvious, so time to get the *Tyche* to look for her instead.

"Even the big man," said Gracie.

Kohl paused, one foot out the door from her cabin. He turned, slow and casual, because if someone was behind you with a weapon of appropriate size, the last thing you wanted to do was spook that motherfucker. Kohl kept the carbine ready, but low, like it wasn't a thing worth worrying about. He'd learned a while ago that keeping a gun out of an eyeline did wonders for calming people the fuck down.

No one there.

"Even the big man," repeated Gracie. It was her voice, alright. Loud, and proud, but coming from underneath her bedding. Kohl took a step forward, tossing caution aside like a used rag, and pulled the pillow away. It was synthetic, smelled a little like her. Blankets, the rustle of the plastic the only noise, no poison vipers lying in there. He kept going after he hit the mattress, a thin sheet of foam that couldn't be called comfortable except by the tired. Kohl found his mattress provided all the protection for his bulk as a piece of paper, and he'd been on at Nate about replacing 'em, and Nate had said *sure, after we fix the drives* or whatever else Hope had been whining about at that particular moment.

"Even the big man," said Gracie. *There.* Kohl's fingers found the recorder, an expensive unit by the looks of it. He'd bet a sizable portion of his inbound two hundred thousand — *two hundred thousand!* — coins it was not off-the-shelf equipment. It had no logos, no brands visible to the naked eye, just a sleek little holoprojector and a couple buttons. The unit was cracked, though, a harsh crease in the plastic stretching across the input console, long enough for him to trace his thumb over while holding it, but not big enough to show any sensitive electronics inside.

If Hope were here, she'd be able to fix it. She wasn't, though, so that left percussive maintenance. Kohl shook it once or twice, listened to pieces on the inside rattle about as he held it up to his ear, and sighed. He glanced at the doorway to the cabin — *could get the power on first, could get that message to whoever the hell is still on comm* — and then sighed again. He gave the device a cautionary rap against the bunk railing, and when that produced nothing of interest, he hit it harder with his hand, once, twice, and then—

"Hi, Mom," said Gracie, as she shimmered into space in the small space of the cabin. "Hi Mom," she said again, the recording looping, so Kohl hit it again, the holo flickering in the air before settling into the clean lines of Grace Gushiken, her ship suit rumpled and worn, like she'd done a hard day's work. Kohl couldn't be sure, but it looked like it was dirty. It might well have been when they'd done that last piece of nastiness on Absalom Delta. Right after they'd had words in the hold, except they didn't use words so much as fists and teeth and her damn *sword*.

Recorded Grace didn't care about any of that, just keeping on speaking. "I know you worry, and I know Father will see this too, so I can't tell you anything fun. But, I've ... people, Mom. I've met some people. They're not like other people." Her face turned away from the recorder, perhaps looking to make sure she wasn't being observed while she was recording. Face back to the camera, tired lines around her eyes, Recorded Grace leaned forward. "There is a woman who flies this ship and who cares about it like it's her daughter. And I see in her heart, and it's not the ship, but the people on it. Can you believe it? She is not flying it for a," and here the holo stuttered, looped, and started again. "There is a woman—"

Kohl slammed the holo-recorder against the side of the bunk, because there was no need to wear out his hand.

Recorded Grace shimmered, part of the holoprojector cutting out, but there was still enough to see her eyes. "...Ship's Engineer. I think we're friends, but I'm not sure. She is young, like I was, until I wasn't. You know what I mean. I think she is Hope." Kohl didn't know what the hell that meant, but hitting the device wouldn't make more sense, so he left it alone. "The captain is," and the eyes projected in front of Kohl became unfocused, looking away. "He is the captain, but he is something more. Something else. I like him. No, that's not it. I trust—"

Kohl gave the device a slap for good measure, because it was getting boring. It chattered angrily at him, Grace's form shifting in a haze of static, then it stabilized. "They accept me, Mom. All of them. Even though I lied to get on this ship. I told them that I was just like them, but I'm broken. You know that part. But the thug? Kohl. Everyone calls him by his last name, like they're afraid of waking something from the other side by using his first name. They all accept me, even the big man," said Recorded Grace. "Because there's something in him that's just like me. Boxed up and beaten by someone else, until the thing that's left is ugly. But he's beautiful, because he could have killed me, but the ship would have died, so he didn't. He didn't want to do something that would have hurt his friends." She looked down. "I've got to go, Mom. They'll miss me if I take too long. Would you believe it? *They* will *miss* me. *Me.* No one's missed me before. Not even, I think, you." Recorded Grace looked over her shoulder again, then leaned forward — no doubt turning off the recording — and the holo shimmered away.

"I don't have friends," said October Kohl to the empty room. "I got me a contract."

The walls around him said nothing, because Recorded Grace was gone. And there wasn't anyone else here, because they'd all gone some other damn place. And he would find one of them, for two hundred thousand credits.

Two.

Hundred.

Thousand.

"Fuck!" screamed Kohl, throwing the recorder against the wall. It exploded into at least fifty pieces, data slivers and holo lenses and encryption silicon all falling to the deck with a clatter that sounded like machinery crying. "Fuck, fuck, *fucking* fuck." He turned towards the door, paused, and swiveled back to the remains of the recorder. He pointed a finger at them. "Why'd you have to say that? Huh? I ain't got no friends!" He pounded his chest. "It's just *me*, Gracie. October Kohl. Nobody else. And I'll get my two hundred grand."

The recorder sat, in pieces, on the ground. After a moment, something inside it arced, and there was a smell of burning ozone. "Even," said Recorded Grace. "Even."

"Oh, you *cunt*," said Kohl. "You cunt!" He slammed a fist against the wall of the cabin, and then did it again, and then one more time, so hard that he heard a crack, but it didn't hurt. It didn't hurt, because there was something in his chest that hurt more, but he couldn't work it out.

Maybe if he got the damn *reactor* back online, things would seem clearer. Maybe if he did his *fucking job*, things would make more sense.

Only problem so far? October Kohl wasn't sure what his job was anymore.

He massaged his hand, then turned away from Grace Gushiken's cabin, her recorded memories, and her judgment. Time to find Hope's room. Not her cabin, because she didn't spend time there. No, Kohl needed to get up to Engineering and fire up the *Tyche*. He needed to find the crew.

But it would have hurt his friends, he heard, and snarled. "Two hundred thousand, Gracie!"

TURNING on the reactor was easy. Like drinking cold beer on a hot day. Kohl pressed a button, and the reactor lights went from amber — not a good color — to green — a far better color. There was a hum, a low vibration, and then the reactor was live. Power flooded back into the *Tyche*, her heart beating again, systems coming online. The *hush* of air through the cyclers as life support breathed once more. The bass of the Endless Drive doing automated checks.

"If you're listening to this," said Hope, "I've locked the drives. Because you're not me, and you're not El, and you ain't the cap, which means you're not supposed to be here."

Kohl whirled, carbine out, because *fuck* not startling people anymore. Again, no one there. Just a blinking light on Hope's console. He stomped over, clicked the console, and waited.

Nothing.

"Fuck you," he said. Because he didn't need to go anywhere. Just needed the comm back online. He ran a hand over his face, then stomped out of Engineering. Flight deck. Just get to the flight deck, press a few buttons, and everything will be *fine*.

"YEAH, SO," said Kohl, feeling uncomfortable. He was in the captain's chair, because sitting in El's didn't seem right. Sitting in Nate's didn't seem right either, but it was the better choice, because at least the cap was closer to his size, and he wouldn't feel like he was being extruded like meat substitute into a shape he was never meant to hold. He leaned towards the comm. "It's Kohl."

There was a hiss, and then the comm did nothing else.

"I say again," said Kohl.

"Don't," said El, voice coming loud and clear over the comm.

"Thank God," said Kohl. "I was beginning to think that, well."

"Think what?" There was a pause while they both thought about the nature of that question, then El said, "Look, it doesn't matter. You're on the *Tyche*?"

"Yeah," said Kohl. "Hope's done something to it. Locked the drives or something."

"Of course she did," said El. "Because only the cap and I can fly her, and if you tried it would all end in a huge, and I mean colossal, fireball."

"That's fair," said Kohl. "How do I get to you? Everything's fucked."

"It is," agreed El. "I'm on my way to Hope. The situation there is fluid."

"Define 'fluid,'" said Kohl.

"Completely fucked," said El. "I'm pretty sure her wife will betray her *again*, which will be bad."

"Yeah," said Kohl. "We'll need another Engineer." He stared at the comm for a second or two, then tapped it. "Hello?"

"I'm here, Kohl," said El. "I'm just ... I guess I shouldn't be surprised at that. Give me a second, I'm thinking." Kohl leaned back in the cap's acceleration couch, waiting. "Okay. Here's what we'll do. We'll meet at Reiko's apartment—"

"Who the fuck is Reiko?" said Kohl.

"Hope's wife," said El. "You knew that."

"I did?"

"And when we're there, we'll get Hope, because we all need a little more of that, and then we'll find the cap."

"And Gracie," said Kohl.

"Of course," said El. "Those two are never far apart."

He is the captain, but he is something more. "Sure," said Kohl. "I get you."

"And when we find the cap," said El, "he'll know what to do."

"Wait," said Kohl. "I was with you for most of that, right until you said the cap would know what to do."

"Yeah," said El.

"He *never* knows what to do," said Kohl. "That's why he pays me."

"But damn," said El, "he looks so *good* while he's flailing about, don't he?"

"He does," agreed Kohl, wondering why no one ever said things like that about him.

"Kohl, I'm not going to ask you to shut down the *Tyche's* reactor, because you can't make coffee right even with instructions. Can you get to these coordinates?" The comm spat out GPS numbers, which looked easy enough to find on a map.

"Yeah."

"Okay, get yourself there. Bring a gun."

"Always have a gun," said Kohl.

"Oh, hey. You're on the flight deck?"

"Yeah," he said.

"You in my chair?" she said, suspicion in her voice.

"Nope," said Kohl. "Wouldn't fit."

"Thank God," said El. "I need you to bring up the *Tyche's* watchdog protocol. Do you know how to do that?"

Kohl looked at the console in front of him. "There are buttons," he offered. "Look, why do I want to do this anyway? Sounds hard and unnecessary."

"It'll let the *Tyche* do her job," said El. "It'll let the *Tyche* find us, wherever we are. And Kohl? We're a rudderless ship on a stormy sea right now. We need all the finding we can get."

Kohl thought about it. He would turn the ... watchdog thing on anyway. He hadn't known it had a name. *They will miss me.* Recorded Grace, telling the truth like it cost nothing to do so. And he thought about his two. Hundred. *Thousand.* Coins, an easy pot of gold at the end of a rainbow. A rainbow that the *Tyche* could lay out for him in something called a watchdog protocol. He clicked the comm. "Okay," he said.

CHAPTER ELEVEN

"HARLOW," said Nate, "if this is how you're punishing me for some imagined past sin, you're doing a great job!" He sucked in more air, his metal leg clipping along beside the meat one, catching a little at his stride as he ran.

"Don't," gasped Harlow, "talk. Run." The man was gasping, his bartender's physique not lending itself to the situation at all well.

Grace loped along at Nate's side — *always there, always* — making it look easy, one hand holding her sword so it wouldn't bounce against her back, eyes forward. An explosion rocked the tunnel, a chunk of rock falling before them from the ceiling like the hand of God, and Grace didn't even slow, just put a hand on the top and flowed over like water in a river.

Nate hit the same chunk of rock and scrambled up, metal hand scraping against the stone, leaving chalky marks where the fingers scoured the stone. His feet scrabbled, nothing about it feeling easy, and then her hand was on his arm, pulling him over. "Got you," she said.

"Hey," he said. "I should be helping *you*."

She gave him a look, half a smile visible in the gloom. "You are," she said, and then she was running ahead again.

Nate turned, offered a hand to Harlow, and pulled his friend over the rock. "You could stand to lose a few kilos," he said.

"You could stand to shut the hell up," said Harlow. He wheezed, hands on his knees. "Not much farther."

"Where are we going?" said Nate, starting after Grace.

"Topside," said Harlow. "We've got an escape route all planned. Hey!" he called after Grace.

She stopped, turning in the gloom, dust swirling around her. "Yeah?"

"Don't run off," he said. "Might be soldiers."

"I'd know," she said, eyes reflecting the light from Nate's ship suit.

"Also," said Harlow, "we're not going that way anymore." He jerked a thumb at a side door, lights out on the controls, a sign bolted to it saying *DANGER CONSTRUCTION ZONE.*

"Uh," said Nate. "Sounds super safe."

"Relax," said Harlow. "It's a piece of shim sham." He pressed the controls on the door.

Nothing happened.

"That was unexpected," said Harlow. "Let me see your blaster." He held a hand out to Nate. Nate pulled the blaster out, spun it, and offered the weapon to Harlow grip-first. Harlow took a step back, pointed the weapon at the controls, and fired. Bright blue-white light flashed as plasma spat into the control box. There was a moment of silence, then the door rumbled, a blast shield dropping in front of it, slicing the sign clean off.

"Let me guess," said Nate. "Also unexpected." He retrieved his blaster. "Where to?"

"Uh," said Harlow.

There was a flash of fire from back the way they'd come, the corridor lighting up with the ambers and ochres of destruction. Nate watched the blast die down, the wind of it pushing at him — *they're getting closer* — and turned back to Harlow. "I vote we keep going the way Grace was going."

"I'm good with that," said Harlow, nodding. "I'm great with that. Just, uh, a little slower. Because." He patted his stomach.

Grace was already moving, feet whispering over the rubble and dust falling from the ceiling. They ran after her. Nate turned to Harlow as they jogged. "What was behind that door?"

"Safety," said Harlow. "Supplies. An air car."

"What's this way?" said Nate.

"Another way out," said Harlow. "Probably a hundred Republic soldiers. If we're lucky, none. Hard to tell if they know about this way in."

"We're not that lucky," said Nate. "We've left our luck at the spaceport."

"My ship?" said Harlow.

Nate grinned at him. "Not anymore, Harlow."

"I guess not," said Harlow. "She would never fly true for me anyway. Not ever."

"She only flies for pirates," said Nate.

Ahead, the gloom gave way to an elevator, all lights out. Beside it, a doorway led to the stairs. "I got this," said Nate. He pulled out his blaster.

Grace gave him a look, then turned the handle. The door opened. "Not locked," she said.

"Oh, I mean, of course. I meant, *naturally*, that I would go first, on account of a blaster being a better weapon for stairs," said Nate.

"Naturally," she said, eyeing him suspiciously. She held a hand out, palm up — *after you*. "Be my guest."

Nate wiped sweat from his face. "Why, thank you, Grace Gushiken."

"My pleasure, Nathan Chevell." Grace gave a tiny bow, a smile hinting at her lips.

"Get the fuck moving, both of you," said Harlow.

Another explosion rocked the floor, the sound closer than before. The walls around them shook with it. Nate got moving.

THE WAY back up to the world felt like a long climb, although in reality it was only ten or so flights. Nate hated stairs; he'd hated them before he had a metal leg, and he hated them more now. The techs had said his leg was fine, *just like a real one*, except for the obvious things like it being made of metal, and not working right. Had some machine learning in it — *but not AI*, they added with a little too much effort for it to sound like the truth — which meant as near as Nate could tell it had a mind of its own. Nate didn't like tech that thought it was smarter than him.

They made the top without seeing anyone or anything. The 'top' was a landing of sorts, cluttered with old cleaning supplies. A floor polishing robot's casing was in front of the door, innards lying next to it. An old-style mop was beside it, because *why the hell not*, everything else was crazy today. There were buckets. There were bags of coffee. There were big plastic containers of water. All of it was between them and the door; the stairs came up behind it all. A small skylight let the overcast light from outside into the room, highlighting a haze of dust in the air.

"What the hell is all this?" said Nate, gesturing with his blaster.

"Cover," said Harlow. "Someone opens the door, all they see is a bunch of supplies."

"I get it," said Nate. "It's a great idea except for one tiny detail. So small, I hesitate to mention it."

"What's that?" said Harlow, eyes narrowing in suspicion.

"We've got to move all this shit to get out," said Nate.

"Look out—" started Grace, as the door leading outside opened. A soldier stood there — Nate took in the black helmet, visor, compact gun, and raised his blaster. He squeezed off three shots for good measure; not one of them hit as near as he could tell, plasma splashing against walls, pieces of polishing robot, and the last shot scoring the side of a water barrel, steam exploding into the small space.

The three of them ducked down, huddling against the walls, behind shelves, whatever they could find. The soldier outside poked his gun back inside, squeezing the trigger and holding it down. Plasma roared around Nate, and he huddled down, hands over his head, a steady fusillade of broken materials, pieces of robot, and burnt coffee coating him.

Silence.

Nate wiped his eyes, pointed his blaster, and waited. He didn't have to wait long; the soldier — might be a different one, they all dressed the same — poked a head back in, so Nate shot him. The soldier spun out of the way, helmet shattering, uniform on fire as the plasma bolt hit home. Nate gave a glance at Grace, still huddling beside a metal shelving unit. "How many?" he said.

"One more," she said. "He's confused."

"Why's he confused?" said Harlow.

"What am I, a mind reader?" said Grace.

"Uh," said Harlow.

"Don't," said Nate, putting a hand on his friend's shoulder. "It's complicated."

"You want to find out why he's confused you ask him," said Grace.

"I'm good," said Harlow. "Hey. There's an upside." He pointed to the detritus in front of them. "We don't need to move anything out of the way."

Nate stood up, checking himself — yep, everything still in place, still working, nothing on fire. The cabinet he'd been hiding behind was slag, the metal still glowing from plasma fire. He walked nice and slow, boots crunching over broken items, metal leg *whining* as he went. The floor polisher had started up, sparks coming off it, and its voice — smooth, cultured, like a British butler — said, "Please advise maintenance crews I am in need of repair."

Nate considered the polisher, then looked at his metal hand. "You get used to it, trust me." He reached the wall beside the doorway outside, pushed it open a span or two, and yelled, "Hey out there!" He pointed at the skylight, then at Grace. She nodded to him, tapped Harlow on the shoulders. She whispered something to him that could have been *give me a boost*, and Harlow nodded, lacing his fingers. He helped Grace up, and she levered the skylight open.

There was a moment of silence, then a woman's voice answered. "Come out with your hands held high!"

"Not gonna happen!" said Nate. He wiped his mouth, spitting out pieces of wood or something like it. "We want to get the hell out of here. Came in to do a deal, and what the hell, you know? People shooting, explosions, the works."

"What kind of deal?" said the woman's voice.

Nate looked at the floor around him. "Columbian dark," he said. "Four thousand kilograms, short haul to Triton. They're out, usual supply lines down, you know how it is." There was a pause, the voice saying nothing, so Nate continued. "Like, can you imagine what it's like being stationed out by Neptune? Dark, cold, and the holos are all weeks out of date. Triton Station's a shithole, the geosynch is iffy at the best of times. They keep firing the damn boosters but that number four is shoddy. Can't get an Engineer worth a damn to stay out there—"

"I get it," said the voice. "How are we going to resolve this?"

"You've been to Triton?" said Harlow. Grace had slipped out onto the roof like an eel, the whisper of her ship suit a memory of her passing.

"Once or twice," said Nate. "It really is a shithole." He pitched his voice again. "I tell you what. Why don't you back up some. We'll come on out. Just be on our way."

"You shot my partner," said the voice.

"Your partner was an asshole," said Nate. "I mean, he drew down on us first."

"I can't just let you—" said the voice, then cut off with a squawk.

Nate grinned at Harlow, pushed open the door, and stepped out into a light rain. He frowned at that, but refused to let it get him down. Grace was behind the Republic soldier, sword held to the other woman's neck. Grace had already disarmed her, holding the blaster high and clear.

"That's quite something," said Harlow. He looked at Grace with an appreciative gaze.

"Not your ship, not your crew either," said Nate, feeling something that *couldn't* have been jealousy stir inside him. Because you didn't get involved with your crew, and Grace was her own woman, plus Harlow didn't shop in that aisle. And she could do better, all three of them could see that, so he pushed down that series of emotions. "What I mean is—"

"Which car is it?" said Grace. There were three; one was a Republic air car, so not that one, but there were two others. Both nondescript, paint chipped in places, one black, one white.

"Both," said Harlow. "Which would you prefer?"

"Always bet on black," said Nate. He walked over to the Republic soldier. "Off with the helmet."

The helmet tipped sideways, considering him, then she unclipped the seals, shucking it. Sweaty hair, angry eyes. "What now?" she said.

Nate sighed. "Look, what we'll do is take that car," he said, and as she followed his eyes, he clocked her over the head with the back of his blaster. He caught her as she slumped, propping her against the Republic vehicle.

"That's not a permanently solved problem," said Grace. But she didn't look unhappy about it.

"No," said Nate, "but it's solved enough. I call shotgun." He stepped towards the black car, Harlow already in and behind the controls, Grace at his heels. He keyed his comm. "This is the captain."

Nada. Just a hiss. He tried again. "This is Captain Nathan

Chevell of the free trader *Tyche*. Calling all my lazy, layabout, wayward crew—"

"This is El," said El's voice. "We've got a situation."

"What kind of situation?" said Nate, slipping into the air car.

"A Reiko situation."

"Sweet and merciful Christ," said Nate. "I thought she was on Triton?"

"Was," agreed El. "She's now here." Some coordinates clicked across his comm.

"On my way," said Nate.

"Cap," said Kohl, cutting in to the comm channel. "Cap, it's me. It's Kohl. I mean, October. Sir."

'Sir,' huh. Kohl never *calls me sir.* "I know who you are, Kohl. What's up?"

"It's the *Tyche*," said Kohl. "She's got a huge hole in her side. Which, unless I miss my guess, will stop us getting outside an atmosphere. I didn't study much, you know me, not one for books—"

"I didn't hire you for your brains, nor looks either," said Nate, thinking, *man, he's weird today. How the hell big is that hole?*

"Right. So. We're going to. Uh." Kohl trailed off.

"We'll *need Hope*," said El. "Isn't that right, Kohl?"

"Uh. That's not how I would have put it," said Kohl, sounding as reluctant as a man about to dive into a pit of alligators.

"How would you have put it?" she asked. "Just curious."

"Well, we *do* need an Engineer," said Kohl. "We're on Earth. We could hire one."

Grace laughed from behind Nate. She leaned forward. "C'mon, Kohl. You know we need our Hope."

There was a pause, the hiss of static coming across the comm brighter than words. "Gracie?"

"Asshole," she agreed.

"I tell you what," said Kohl. "Why don't we all just, I don't know. Relax. Think it through."

Think? Kohl? "Kohl," said Nate, "what's going on?"

"Nothin', Cap," said Kohl. "I'm just nervous on account of the huge hole in our hull. I'll meet you at Hope's location, yeah? You and Gracie."

Nate sighed. Kohl was being Kohl, except he wasn't, which wasn't too unusual. He might have been high on something, the man had a tendency to unwind at an extreme volume when he was dockside. "Copy that, Kohl. See y'all there."

"Copy," said El.

"On it," said Kohl. The comm hissed and clicked, the connection dropping.

"When you say, 'on my way,'" said Harlow, "you mean, by way of the people we've got to meet. The bar. The *drinking*, Nate. And then the rescuing of people of immense power and influence. People who can read and change minds."

"I mean by way of my crew," said Nate.

"I think what's going on here is a little more important," said Harlow.

Nate turned and looked his old friend in the eyes. "Harlow," he said. "You know me better than that."

"You've got a plan," said Harlow.

"He's got friends," said Grace, leaning back, looking out the window. "Harlow? We've all got friends. Our friends are just ... higher up the list right now."

"Also," said Nate, before Harlow could speak, "we'll need the *Tyche*. For the *Tyche*, we need my Engineer, and my Helm. To get them both, I need my deckhand."

"Huh," said Harlow, looking at Nate, then his gaze sliding out the window of the air car. "I should get my own ride."

An explosion ruptured the skyline, a massive vermillion ball of flame stretching into the sky. Debris, at this distance looking like ants, were tossed into the air. The shock of it shook the air car even at this distance. Nate looked at it for a minute, then said, "What do you think that was?"

Harlow looked sour. Sour, and pale, and a little lost. "That looked like my other ride options. That was about where our super-secret underground spaceport was. Those *fuckers*." This last had iron in it, like he was trying to talk his spine straight.

Grace leaned forward, her hand on Harlow's shoulder, her head next to his ear. She spoke low, but Nate had no trouble hearing what she said. "Harlow. You have friends *here*. And *these* friends will help you save the rest of your friends. The captain and I, well. We'll get them." She looked at Nate, a stray strand of pitch black hair covering her eyes. "Right, Nate?"

"That's right," said Nate, offering a grin. "Harlow, I'm a pirate. And running a blockade of Republic troops to rescue a bunch of political hostages? It's not gold doubloons, but it's honest pirating if ever I saw it."

Grace was still looking at him. "You're no pirate, Nate."

"Privateer, then," he offered.

"You'll be something so much more before we're done," she said. "You'll have to be."

He didn't know what she meant, but he nodded to Harlow. Harlow sighed, grumbling something, and started the air car. The vehicle shuddered, in need of a decent Engineer itself, but clambered towards the sky. It wasn't the *Tyche*. It wasn't freedom. But it reminded him of what that might feel like.

CHAPTER TWELVE

WHEN HOPE WOKE UP, it was with the lazy stretch of a fed lioness. She gave a growl, low in her throat, reached out a hand for Rei-Rei, and came up with nothing but empty blankets. Her eyes opened, taking in the room.

Tired, dirty even, but that didn't matter. Hope lived in oil and grease. The rooms she frequented had stacks of radioactive fission-ables used to fuel giant machines towards the stars; a little grime wasn't a thing that registered at anything more than a superficial level. The walls: uneven gray plaster and paint, a little drywall showing through. Some of the worst looked to be covered up by some picture panels, three of them studded around the room. One panel was broken, lines of signal compression and mismatched color crossing an image of Reiko and Hope, arms around each other. They were laughing in that photo, but that was all that showed — the corruption of the image had eaten everything else. Hope frowned at it, thinking, *I should fix that*, and then thinking, *I don't remember that picture being taken*. It might have been Triton, because Triton was where everything had started and ended with them.

Hope closed her eyes, giving herself a mental shake. *Not worth thinking about right now. Plenty of time for worrying about the unfix-able later.* She opened her eyes again, this time looking at the ceiling. A single ship's lamp was attached to the roof, alongside the regular light strip that — presumably — didn't work anymore. Another thing to fix? She smiled, thinking about how she could right this place for Reiko. Make it all functional again, and how that would let them talk about the things that mattered. A small favor here or there, leading to the undoing of Hope's great crime.

Was it too much to pray for? Hope hadn't ever prayed before. She didn't know how. Hope didn't know who you prayed to, or whether they'd answer, or how much it would cost.

She pushed aside the thin blanket — worn, tattered, but it had covered them both as they'd remembered each other's bodies. Reiko's had been a little gaunter, a little less the ripe form Hope had remembered. Hope wished she'd thought to bring food, or liquor, but Reiko's kisses told her it didn't matter. Reiko's hand on her arm, her breast, her stomach had made her shiver and yearn. Reiko's kisses had silenced her, quietened her doubt.

After, Hope had slept like she'd not slept in five years.

There was the sound of voices from the small living area. Reiko, talking quiet and low, so as not to wake Hope. Hope smiled. That was Reiko, thinking of Hope. Hope pulled the blanket around her shoulders and pushed the curtain between the sleeping cube and the living space. She didn't even notice the smell of mildew, Reiko's scent all around her on the rough and worn fabric. There she was: Reiko, proud, strong Reiko. Leaning next to a small console against the wall. She turned as Hope entered, her face opening into a smile. That smile was like the sun coming around the edge of a planet, all bright-ness and warmth. A signal that the universe wasn't just made up of the hard black. "Hey, you," said Reiko.

"Hey," said Hope, enjoying this feeling. She didn't deserve it, but she let it in anyway. "Who you talking to?"

Reiko looked at the console for a second. "Oh, just breakfast," she said. "Except it's almost evening, so breakfast will be pizza."

"Best kind of breakfast," said Hope. "Best kind ever. I've got coins."

"No need," said Reiko. She stood, walking towards Hope, pulling her close. Tasting her lips.

"But..." said Hope. She pulled away. She looked at the room, looking for a place to sit.

"What's wrong?" said Reiko. Looking where Hope was looking, at the tattered couch, the bare kitchenette, the old console against the wall. "What's wrong, baby?"

Hope felt her strength leaving, along with all the warmth. The hard black felt like it was everywhere. Outside, a gray sky faded into an ochre sunset, but it was all a lie. Behind it was black, an airless void that wanted to suck the life from everything it touched. Engineers could hold it back for a span, maybe two, their hard work keeping a hull between the souls aboard and the shoals outside. A well-maintained reactor was enough to stave off death for another haul between the stars. But Hope wasn't an Engineer, not anymore: she'd lost that and more when she ran. She sank down to the floor. "I..." she said. Then she started to cry.

Reiko squatted down next to her. "Hope, baby," she said. "What is it?"

"How can you ever forgive me?" Hope asked, tears tracing lines down her cheeks.

Reiko's face was soft in the evening light, a question hovering behind her eyes. "For what?"

"Everything," said Hope, an arm under the blanket pointing at the walls, the worn couch, the universe. It was all the same thing. "I left you. On Triton."

"It was that captain of yours," said Reiko. "Hush. It wasn't you."

That captain of yours. "Nate?"

"It's Nate now?" There was something hard in Reiko's tone, like a wire inside its insulating sheath.

"I mean," said Hope. "He pulled me out of jail."

"That's right," said Reiko. Her Rei-Rei. "If we'd stayed—"

"They'd have put us away for life," said Hope.

"This look like being put away?" said Reiko. She tipped her head at the window, the orange bloom of the fading sun. "There's no cages here."

"You don't..." said Hope, winding down. She rubbed her eyes, her nose, and tried again. "You must blame me."

"It doesn't matter," said Reiko. "This will all work out. I promise. I've made sure of it."

That pricked up Hope's ears a little. "How, Rei-Rei?"

"You'll see," said Reiko. "It'll be fine. And that captain of yours won't come between us again."

There was a knock at the door. They were both startled, and Hope laughed at the absurdity of it. "Sorry," she said. "I've ... been running for a while."

"You won't need to run anymore," said Reiko. "Not after today. Let's eat, yeah?" She stood, walking away from Hope. The thought of pizza — real dough, meat that might have come from a vat rather than a synthesizer, tomatoes that could have been grown in sunlight — made Hope's stomach growl. She hadn't eaten, not since leaving the *Tyche*, and it had been a long day. She'd found a trail here through people sometimes willing to help, sometimes not. There had been a barrier or two. But here she was, about to eat dinner with her wife. For the first time in five years. And Rei-Rei said it would be *okay*. That there was nothing to forgive. Reiko had a hand on the door, pulled it open. Said, "Hi..." and then her voice trailed off. "Who the hell are you?"

Hope turned at her tone, that old adrenaline *you've-got-to-run* kicking in, until she saw who it was. "Oh, hey. El." She frowned. "El? What are you doing here?"

Elspeth Roussel stood in the doorway, looking pissed off. She had her pistol strapped to her waist and carried two boxes. One was a rectangle of a size and shape that might hold a bottle of wine. The other was also a rectangle, with the writing *LITTLE LUIGI'S* on the side. "Hey," she said to Reiko. "Can I come in?"

"Uh," said Reiko.

"I've got your pizza," said El. "It smells good. I haven't had actual flour in a long time."

"Sure," said Reiko.

El handed the pizza box to Reiko as she entered, Hope picking up something in her glance. Something that said, *Oh,* you. *We'll get to* you *in a second.* But she said nothing, just navigating the short distance to Hope's huddled form like she owned the place. El crouched down, handed Hope the other box. "I got you something."

"What is it?" said Hope, taking the box.

"Something broken," said El. "Also, what the *fuck* are you *doing,* Hope Baedeker? Do you *know* how hard it was to find you?"

"Hey!" said Reiko.

El stood up, fury snapping her frame straight like a rod ready to channel the lightning. "Was I fucking talking to *you,* Reiko?"

Reiko bridled, simmered, boiled over. "Who are you to come in here? Into *my* home, *my* family—"

El laughed. Clear and loud, like it hurt to hold it in, the sound cascading out of her like champagne shaken, the cork popped. "You aren't Hope's *family,*" she said. "She's *got* a family, Reiko. And you know what? Her *real* family didn't lie, cheat, and get in debt. Her *real* family didn't make it look like her gambling debts were mismanaged finances from a station job. We know how you did it, Reiko. Me and the cap. Called in a few favors. We found the trail. Because she's *our* family."

"I—"

"Did I fucking *look* like I was finished?" El shook her head. "Christ, it's easier dealing with dock control. At least they've got *reasons* for trying to fuck you over. Why'd you do it, Reiko? Did you figure Hope would say, 'Oh golly, I must have screwed up the project management on this job,' and soak up the extra funds for you? That was a lot of coin, Reiko. A lot of good Republic coin they wanted accounting for."

"El!" said Hope. "This is my *wife!*"

El ignored her, like she wasn't even there. "Maybe you bribed the cartel. Maybe you convinced them that a family debt was easier to claim than your solo one. But you lied, and you hung a yoke around Hope's neck. It's been there for five years. She went to fucking jail. The best damn Engineer I've ever known — and I've known them all. I've known the drunk ones. I've known the ones with forty years of experience. I've known the high fliers, the politicos. The speakers, the shakers. The inventors. The ones that can make a broken drive run like it's a newborn colt. Put 'em all together, and they still wouldn't be as good."

"You don't know what you're saying," said Reiko, but her face was ashen, her shoulders crooked. "You don't know ... they said they would kill her. If I didn't. Was it worse for her to live or die?"

"Rei-Rei?" said Hope. She felt like she was teetering on the edge of a massive pit, darkness and spiders below her. "Reiko?"

"I—"

"Don't say it," said El. "Don't tell her another lie. *Not one more lie, Reiko.* I don't care that you broke her heart. That's for kids. I care that you broke her insides. You made Hope one of the hopeless." Hope watched El's fingers twitch and tremble, her hand next to her sidearm.

"What are you saying?" Hope wanted to understand what this meant. There had to be a reason. Circuits made sense. Fusion reactors made sense. The gravitational pull and yaw of planets made sense. None of the words in the last moments made any sense at all.

El turned to Hope. "The cap's a sucker," she said. "Collects lost puppies, shit like that. He is the *worst* pirate I've ever met."

"Nate's not a pirate," said Hope. "Nate's..."

"Your precious *captain*," Reiko snapped. "I get it. Well, it won't matter. I've solved this problem for all of us."

El looked like she was thinking about that comment more than she should. "Reiko, I'll ask a simple question. Deserves a simple answer. What did you do?"

Reiko wore that lopsided snarl like a smile. "Enough," she said. "We'll be happy."

"Because," said El, "if you called the Republic debt controllers, hoping to square things away, well. That will happen. But not how you think."

"They said—"

"The thing about the Republic is that they say a thing, and often do another," said El. "Hey. It's just the way the system works. I flew against them before the Old Empire fell. Before it didn't work out anymore. Then I paid my taxes. I ironed and folded up my uniform. I did what I was told, and everything's worked out okay. Have you paid your taxes, Reiko?" El took a step forward. "Have you done any fucking *ironing*?" She gave a sound of disgust, turned back to Hope. Made the short journey back across the mottled carpet like it was easy, like reaching out to a friend was simple and painless. She reached a hand down to Hope. "Come on, Hope. Let's get you out of here."

"I don't want to go," said Hope, her voice small in her own ears. Like it was coming from far away. She didn't mean it, and she did, all at the same time.

"That's as may be," said El, face still taught with anger or frustration or an amalgam of them both. "But—"

There was a crash, a spray of glass showering out from behind El's head, the shards forming a brief halo. El's eyes rolled back in her head and she crumpled to the ground. Behind her stood Reiko, the broken end of a bottle in her hand. "You listen," she said to Hope. "You listen to me, Hope."

But Hope was scrambling across to El's side. Hands on El's face, fingers feeling the back of the skull. *Humans are just complicated machines, nothing hard about this, nothing at all. Keep repeating that. Keep moving.* Her fingers found the break in the skin at the back of El's skull, the warm wet of her blood. Hope pulled red fingers back, held them up to the light. Looked at Reiko, her stance, her raised bottle, the jagged ends full of promise. "Rei-Rei," she said. "What have you done?"

"I'm going to *fix* this," said Reiko. "You don't need *them.*"

The moment held, stretched, Hope looking at the jagged ends of that bottle, her Helm — the other side of the *Tyche's* operations crew, more than just a friend, her *partner* — on the floor beside her. "But I do," said Hope. "I need you all."

"It's nice to want things," said Reiko. "It's nice to walk free with coin in your pocket and hope in your heart. I haven't had my Hope for five years. Do you know what that's like?"

"I do," said Hope. "It's like being lost and alone and not having anyone to talk to about the things that matter."

Reiko's arm lowered, the steam ebbing out of her pipes, the over-load dropping below the redline. "They've all lied to you. You're *my* Hope. Mine." There was another knock at the door. Strong, almost a banging, but right on the verge of it. Reiko seemed to get smaller for a second. "It doesn't matter. That'll be them." She turned to the door, seeming to forget about the jagged end of the bottle she held. As she turned away, Hope turned back to El. Her movements were on autopilot as she put her friend onto her side, checking her breathing. *Shallow, but still there. Hadn't thrown up. Hadn't bled out.* Good start. Hope looked up as the door clicked open, her heart giving a couple of kicks in anticipation, then stalling outright when she saw who it was.

October Kohl stood in the doorway, his eyes going to El, then to Hope, eyes widening a little in appreciation at her partially naked body, then to Reiko, and to the broken bottle in Reiko's hand. "Hey, Hope," he said. "How you doin'?"

"I'm not good," said Hope. "I'm bad."

"Figures," said Kohl. He seemed to reach a crossroads. "Here's what'll happen."

"Who the hell are you?" said Reiko.

"First thing," said Kohl, pulling his arm back, then forward like a logging train. His fist caught Reiko on the side of the head, her body tumbling back into the room, the jagged end of the bottle falling free. "First thing is, we do not glass our Helm." He stepped into the room, shutting the door behind him. Reiko tried to get to her feet, but her legs kept slipping out from under her.

"Kohl!" said Hope, her voice returning at last. "Stop!"

His gaze lingered on Reiko for a moment, as if he was seeing if she needed another interrupt or two. His eyes slid sideways to find Hope's. "In another time and place, this would be a treat. What with you half-naked, and your wife here." He shook himself. "Problem is there's a whole squad of Republic assholes coming down this way. They're a block back, wasting time and air talking to each other." He looked at Reiko. "You got any idea why there'd be a squad of Republic officers on their way here, Reiko? You are Hope's wife, right?" He looked doubtful for a second. "Did I hit the wrong person?"

El groaned. "Kohl, you hit the right person."

"Figured," said Kohl. "Get dressed, Hope. We've got to move. Cap's coming."

"Cap's here," said Nate, from the doorway. There was another man beside him that Hope didn't know, but he had a friendly face, like he'd listen to your problems over a beer. Nate looked at El. "I need to shoot someone?"

"That problem's been stowed for the moment, Cap," said Kohl.

Grace pushed into the room from behind Nate, and Hope's heart lifted at the sight of her. Someone she could talk to about all this, someone who didn't know what was going on either. Grace's eyes were warm as she kneeled beside Hope. "Hope," she said.

"Hey," said El, from beside them. "Why is Hope getting all the love?"

Grace looked at El, took one of the Helm's hands, gave it a squeeze. "You're okay, El."

"I feel like three-day old shit," said El. "Help me up. Someone I need to shoot."

Kohl grabbed a hold of Reiko, hauled her to her feet, and then tossed her onto the dusty couch. Reiko's head knocked against the wall, the woman's eyes rolling back into her head. "Present for you," he said to El.

"Hey!" said Hope. "That's my wife!"

Nate held his hands up, the gold of his metal fingers catching the last rays of the setting sun. "Everyone? Take a moment. What we have here is a volatile situation. You go to sea in a squall like this, you'll be as like to lose someone overboard." He paused, frowning. "Hope?"

"Yes, Cap'n." Hope shivered, with fear or pain, or just the overflow of adrenaline and fatigue, she didn't know.

"Put some clothes on," said Nate. "A storm's coming."

CHAPTER THIRTEEN

PAIN/PAIN/PAIN/CONFUSION/PAIN.

It was coming off Hope like radiation off a blown reactor, cascading out around the room. Grace bit her lip, trying to push it to the side. Trying to not *be* Hope, but be *with* her. The young woman's eyes were wide, stunned, like she'd been hit in the head with a bat. Or like she'd just had her world pulled inside out, the whole thing put through a mincer. All the ugly, hidden things inside a body were ground up, extruded, put in a familiar shape like a burger you were supposed to eat. And Hope didn't look hungry. Not at all.

Pain/pain/pain.

It didn't help that El was borderline for a coma call, her brain sparking in the air, pushing fingers of disrupted signal, incoherent noise that underlaid Hope's cries for help. A hissing like arcing pylons, making the air bright and deadly. To be caught in the storm was to be drowned by it.

Grace breathed in, out. In, and out again. One more time, she drew breath, holding this one, and then sighed it out.

"Are you," said Hope, "okay?"

Grace almost laughed, the absurdity of the young woman's question in the face of all she'd seen. "I'm fine, Hope."

"Everyone's fine," said Kohl, slinging Hope's rig to the floor between them. "Suit up."

"Kohl," warned Nate.

"Cap, you know how I like to be gentle and kind when I've got the time. But we ain't got the time." said Kohl.

"Kohl—" started Grace.

"He's right," said Hope, reaching for the rig. Grace watched Hope press the power stud on the unit, and it gave a jerk of simulated life, the front and back flexing. As she held it in front of her, the arms reticulated from the back, flexed, and then the unit crawled up her arm like a metal insect, hugging her body, settling in. The clamps that held front and back armor together *snicked* out around Hope's torso, locking into place. The visor slid over her face, the machine chiming its readiness, a synthesized voice saying *Hope's Alive!* in cheery tones.

"That is some creepy shit," said Nate. "I have never seen one of those things do that."

"That's because you haven't seen one of mine," said Hope. Her voice took on the hard tint of the external speaker, muting the pain of it. But Grace could still feel the *pain/pain/pain/confusion/pain* coming off her.

"I don't know, Cap," said El, her voice the slur of someone trying to remember how words worked. "Looked like it wanted a hug. Like a big fluffy bear."

Kohl walked towards El, held her chin in one hand. She tried to push him away, but the movement was weak, like her heart wasn't in it. Kohl stared into her eyes. "Can you fly?"

"Course," said El, then staggered back. Kohl grabbed her, held her up. "Can fly anything with a stick," she offered. "Walking's hard though."

"What we've got is a situation," said Nate. "Our car's downstairs. There's a bunch of debt collectors downstairs. They're looking to make good on Hope's bounty." He paused, taking a look out the window. "Yeah, okay, so there's a small ray of sunshine in this otherwise dark and miserable day."

"I'm sorry," said Hope.

Nate cast a glance at her, and Grace could feel his *surprise/apology*. "You're good," he said. "This isn't on you."

"You mentioned a ray of sunshine," said Grace, wanting to feel some of that light on her face.

"I did," said Nate, flashing a grin at the room and whomever in it was interested. Finding no takers, he let it slide into a frown. "Those guys downstairs aren't real Republic."

"Got uniforms," said Kohl.

"Oh, sure," said Nate. "It's all a part of the sham. They're bounty hunters, plain and simple. A debt this old? It's been farmed off, handed to an agency. I'd guarantee it."

"You're saying that like it's a certainty," said Grace. "But you also sound like you're guessing."

"It's a little of each column," said Nate. "But mostly it's a certainty. Almost positive. Nearly."

"Groovy," sang El. She pulled out her sidearm, waving it around the room. Kohl and Nate ducked as it passed through where they were standing. El laughed, winced, and then looked surprised when the gun tumbled from her fingers to hit the ground.

"Which means what?" said Grace. "Like, it's a piece of information, but it doesn't have a home to go to."

"There is that," acknowledged Nate. He rubbed his chin. "If only we had some *real* Republic."

"Why's that?" said Kohl, looking out the window, then back at Nate. "What's *real* Republic, Cap?"

"The ones where the uniform's not just for show," said Nate. He pulled out his blaster, sighting along the barrel, then spun it back into its holster.

"I've got an idea," said Kohl, glancing at Grace. Grace could feel *uncertainty/guilt* coming off him.

She took a step forward. "Kohl. What did you do?"

"Why's it got to be something I did?" said the big man.

"Because it's you," she said.

"That's a little unkind," said Nate.

"I guess," she said. "Doesn't stop it being true."

"Well," said Kohl. "Let's say I *did* something. But there was a way I could *undo* it. Like it never happened. That'd be the same thing as not doing it, wouldn't it?" And there it was, *uncertainty/guilt,* but the guilt was stronger this time when his eyes met hers.

"I could go," said Hope, her small frame seeming stronger inside her rig. "If I go, they won't try and come for the rest of you." She shrugged in her rig, then picked up a small box, turning it over in her hands.

"What?" said Nate. "No." Hope continued to fiddle with the box, pulling out a small sidearm. Energy weapon by Grace's guess. The rig around Hope hummed to life, arms reaching out to open the weapon up. Because that's what Hope did: she fixed things, even when everything seemed pointless. Maybe that's why Grace liked her. Because she had a heart bigger than the world deserved.

"I think it's a good plan," said Kohl. *Relief/escape.* "Solid. Worth putting on the table."

"Definitely not," said Grace. *Push it. What's going on here?* "There's no way that plan goes on the table."

"Do I get a vote?" said Harlow.

"This the asshole from the bar?" said Kohl. "No way he gets a vote. He's not crew."

"He's not just the asshole from the bar. Harlow sold me the *Tyche,*" said Nate. "Old friend. But no, he doesn't get a vote."

"Hey," said Harlow, hands splayed, an eyebrow raised. "We should at least turn over all the stones. See what's underneath."

"I'm with you," said Kohl, slapping Harlow on the shoulder. "Let's talk this out."

Talk. This. Out. From Kohl? "October Kohl, what did you do?" said Grace.

"*No one* gets a vote," said Nate, "because this ship doesn't run under a committee."

"We ain't on the ship," said Kohl.

Nate eyeballed him. "You want to go, Kohl?"

"I'm just saying—"

"Because you could go. Down through those debt collectors. Try your luck, just you against all of them." Nate took a step forward. "You think you could take them all?"

"Maybe," said Kohl, looking doubtful. He counted off on his fingers, lips moving. After a moment, he said, "Probably not."

"Then it's not a committee," said Nate.

"What did you *do*, Kohl?" said Grace.

All the air seemed to leave Kohl in a rush, the big man deflating. He was still bigger, taller than anyone else in the room, but in that moment Grace thought he looked smaller than a child. "I might have agreed to sell you out to the Republic."

"You *what?*" said Nate.

"It was for two hundred thousand coins, Cap," said Kohl, hands up. "Two. Hundred. *Thousand.*" He looked at the rest of them. Harlow first, because they didn't know each other, but Harlow still knowing enough rough details to put an expression of disgust on his face. Hope, her face hidden by her visor, but her hands now cocked on her hips. El, who looked at Kohl, then held up a hand, and lumbered to the small kitchenette, retching into the sink. Eyes wary now, Kohl looked at Nate, took in the captain's hand on the butt of his blaster. Then, to Grace. "It was a good deal," he said. "It seemed like a great deal."

Grace felt sick, but it wasn't the first time she'd been betrayed. Maybe this crew wasn't for her. "Don't sweat it, Kohl," she said. "It makes you like everyone else."

"But," he said. "I *didn't*. I didn't call them. Cap," he said, turning to Nate. "You wanted real Republic? I call 'em, and we'll be balls-deep in assholes." Nate's fingers twitched over his blaster, then he turned to the wall, jaw clenched, eyes wild. *Disappointment/angst* came off him like spray from the sea.

"How would you call them?" said Harlow. He continued in a rush, as if not wanting his intent to be mistaken. "Is it a snatch and grab?"

Kohl fished a small device from a pocket, holding it up. "I press this button," said Kohl, "when I'm next to Gracie. They'll come and do the rest." He offered it to Grace. "Here."

"Two hundred grand," said Grace. "You sure you don't want a taste of that action?" But she took the device, considering it.

"Well," said Nate, turning back. "We don't push that button. And we don't send Hope out." He ran his hand — the flesh and blood one — through his hair. "Where's that leave us?"

Grace sighed. "It leaves us out of options," she said. It was a good crew. Maybe the best. Her eyes went to Kohl — sure, they'd made mistakes. They'd made big mistakes. But even when everything was stacked against them, they did the right thing in the end. They were too good for a grifter like her. Having a home might have been too much to hope for. Her eyes went to Hope, the young woman fixing the energy weapon. El, who'd come here against all odds to scoop Hope up against the might of a Republic that would crush them all. Then to Nate, the captain who played at being a pirate because he thought it's what the world wanted of him.

Except he wasn't a pirate. He wasn't built that way.

There was one thing Grace could do for this crew. Whether the Republic got her was a matter of debate; she was good at running, and better at hiding. But she knew these people deserved more than to be scooped up alongside her. If the Republic got her *now*, while Kohl was under contract to apprehend Grace? The boot of justice might not press on them at all. Grace could choose the manner of her passing, and the rest of them would be left to chart a new course into the hard black. They wouldn't be taken up: she could protect them from that at least.

Grace pressed the button.

HER SWORD ITCHED at her hand, like it wanted to be drawn. Like it was thirsty.

There was a *crump* of an explosive charge, the walls vibrating a little with it. Dust and plaster fell from the ceiling around Grace, and she looked up, hand shielding her eyes. "What was that?"

"Whoring and coring," said Kohl. He had Reiko slung over his shoulder like a sack of laundry, her arms bouncing against his back. "They get to the roof and just burn holes down through the floors."

"At least we've got their attention," said Nate, leading the way down the corridor. "Bounty hunters coming up from below, Republic from on high. This will be a wild ride."

"We need to get out of here," said Harlow. "And by here, I mean this hallway."

"Good idea. Lemme use my boot key," said Kohl, turning to a door on his left. He took a step back, Reiko jouncing against him, and then kicked the door off its hinges. It tumbled into an apartment much like Reiko's; worn, tired, missing hope. They moved into the room, fanning out. No one home; it smelled like no one had been there for a while.

The walls shook with another *crump*. There was a crash from behind them, towards Reiko's apartment. The shouting of soldiers, surprised at finding Kohl's transmitter, left in the room.

Grace held up her hand, the crew stilling around her. She was picking up a storm of *confusion/alert/hunt* from behind them, and a lighter shade of *confusion/caution* from farther back. More souls, all feeling much the same thing. She smiled, pushing a strand of dark hair out of her face. "The party," she said, "is getting started."

"Hey," called out a man's voice from the hallway, gruff in all the wrong ways, like he'd been swallowing sharp rocks his entire life. "This is a bounty operation. Sanctioned."

"This is a hunt for an enemy of the Republic. It takes precedence over your bounty hunt," said a woman's voice, smooth like honey.

"Sounds like they're getting along fine," hissed Nate.

Reiko groaned from Kohl's shoulder. Kohl gave the woman a shake. "Quiet."

"Wuzz," said Reiko.

"Are you okay?" said Hope, her voice amplified through her rig. Her hand went up to cover the speaker, but too late.

"What was that?" said Honey.

"Sounds like my bounty," said Billy Goat Gruff.

"Stand down!" said Honey.

"Eat a dick, pig," said Billy Goat Gruff.

"Help!" screamed Reiko. "They're in here!"

"Jesus," said Nate, shoulders slumping. "Kohl? We need an exit."

"On it," said Kohl, dropping Reiko to the ground, ignoring her arms as they tried to slap and claw at him. He eyed a wall, tipped his shoulder, and ran straight for it. The drywall crumbled around him, and he burst into the neighboring apartment. There was a scream and a yell — *that one's not empty* — and Kohl was yelling to *sit the fuck down* and *shut the fuck up*.

Reiko drew a breath to scream again, and Grace drew her sword in the same moment. It licked out to rest against the other woman's neck, causing Reiko's breath to freeze in her chest. "Go on," said Grace.

Reiko shook her head, swallowing. Her neck scraped against the blade.

"Grace," said Hope. *Desperation/fear/pain/pain.* "Grace, she's my *wife*."

"She is all that is ugly in your life," said Grace, but she lowered her sword.

Reiko eyed Hope, then Grace. She said to Hope, "You'll thank me. You will. You'll see." Then she yelled, "They're in here!"

Hope's frame canted back in surprise, and if Grace could see her face she'd bet it would mirror the *shock/denial* coming off her friend. The visor of her rig slipped back off her face. "Reiko!" she said. "What are you doing?"

"Saving us," said Reiko. "*Us*, Hope."

"I should have shot her," said El, then looked too tired to do it, slumping against the remains of the wall Kohl had gone through.

"You're not thinking straight," said Hope. "Your head—"

"Out of the way, pig!" said Billy Goat Gruff from down the hall.

"Stand down!" shouted Honey.

"We've got to go," said Grace.

Kohl's head poked back through the hole in the wall. "Uh," he said. "Cap?"

Nate looked like he wanted to murder someone, but it wasn't a highly specific look. If Grace was rolling the dice on it, she figured he was disappointed at himself. For not leaving Reiko behind, for not finessing the situation a little better. For not being a pirate, or a captain, or whatever else he had in his head. "Yeah," he said.

There was the crackle-roar of a plasma weapon discharging from down the corridor, then the *whine-chunk* of a laser discharging. No screams, which meant no one was down, and Grace wasn't wanting to wait to find out which way it would go. She grabbed Hope's arm. "Let's go." She hustled Hope towards the hole in the wall, casting a glance back at Reiko. Reiko turned to Hope, then back towards the broken door. Then she turned and ran, charging out the doorway, shouting, "In here, in here—"

Just like that, she was turned into a pillar of fire. A blast of plasma caught her, turning her frame into a torch as she was tossed back out of view. Hope screamed, her hands outstretched, her whole body and soul wanting to run out that door. Grace fought her, really fought, her feet planted. "Hope! She's gone!"

Hope's frame sagged into a sob, Grace pushing her through the breached wall. She gave a glance to El, whose eyes were closed, still leaning against the wall. "El?"

"My head hurts and I can't see right," said El. "I just need a minute."

Nate stepped forward, shook El by the shoulder. "Helm."

"Cap."

"Helm! I need you on duty. I *need* you, El. We've got a ship that needs flying. We've got a crew spun about. I need my navigator." Nate let her go, El's eyes opening. "I can't fly them all home," he said. "I don't have the charts."

"Aye, aye, Cap," said El, her frame coming upright and to attention, albeit a little lopsided. She turned through the breach, walking after Kohl and Hope.

"Now you," said Nate. His eyes found Grace's. "You've got to get clear, Grace Gushiken."

"You know this is the end of the line for me," said Grace. "I pressed that button and it was over."

"This still isn't a committee," said Nate. "We're leaving. Together."

There was another salvo of plasma fire from the doorway, bolts chewing into the frame, fire breaking out. Grace ducked her head against the shower of burning meat, shaking her head. "Together?"

"That's the way I was thinking," said Nate.

"Deal," said Grace.

CHAPTER FOURTEEN

NATE WAS on Grace's heels, Kohl leading the way. Hope and El were strung between them, El with her sidearm out but no real inclination to use it, Hope's visor back up, hiding her tears and her shame. *As if she has anything to be ashamed of. I should have seen this coming.*

Time for recriminations later.

The ceiling ahead of them ruptured in, ceramicrete and plaster showering in. A Republic solder followed the debris down, gun out. Red light licked against his frame, and there was a *whine-wizzchunk* as Kohl's carbine discharged, turning the soldier into a spray of red, white, and black. A grenade tumbled through the opening, but Kohl caught it in midair, tossing it back up through the hole. There was a shout of surprise a moment before it discharged, a bright light filling the room, chunks of ceiling falling around them.

Nate turned back, shaking his head to clear it. A debt collector stood in the doorway, a clunky weapon — *good Goddamn, is that a net gun?* — held out. He looked surprised to see Nate, but that surprise vanished as he turned into a burning ruin as plasma caught him from behind. Nate raised his blaster, squeezing a few shots through the breach. Far from keeping their heads down, an answering fusillade of fire flashed through the breach.

"It's on, pig!" screamed Billy Goat Gruff from somewhere behind them, punctuated by the bark of plasma discharge. There was a scream, then another *crump* as something exploded, Nate falling to one knee as his metal leg caught on a piece of ceramicrete.

"Cap!" said Kohl. "This way!" The big man opened a door to the corridor, taking in a woman with a net catcher and a surprised expression. He swung a fist, catching the woman in the jaw, and the net catcher discharged. The net caught nothing but air, hitting a wall and sliding down. Kohl ran ahead of them.

Nate looked down at the bounty hunter. She had a young face, but everyone seemed to when they were out cold. He shrugged, stepping over the woman. There was a Republic soldier outside, bundled in a net, struggling to get free, which was really someone else's problem, so Nate jogged on by.

From up ahead, Kohl's carbine whined again, and again, and again, the third time accompanied by the slop-gush of ladled soup, but much louder. Nate looked down at his blaster, and thought: *well, this is it. You've conquered delegation and made yourself redundant. Nice work.*

Then he was caught as a net lifted him off his feet, wrapped him in a ball, and tossed him down the corridor. He got glimpses of floor-ceiling-floor-ceiling as he rolled, his arms pinned to his side. He came to rest, seeing a debt collector with a discharged net gun behind them through the web of that very same net. The debt collector was reloading the weapon, placing a big cartridge of netting in the front, which was a thing that wouldn't end well if he got it sorted. So Nate wriggled, got his blaster out, and pressed the trigger. A bright flash of plasma tore a chunk out of the wall beside the debt collector. A total miss, but being fair on himself, his arms were tied to his sides, by way of a net, his faced pressed against the dirty carpet.

The carpet was also tacky. *Best not to think about that.*

The debt collector got his weapon reloaded, which might have been a poor choice of activities. It would have been better to ready a different device, perhaps some kind of energy weapon that turned carbon-based lifeforms into slag.

Grace Gushiken hurdled his fallen form, all dark hair, black ship suit, and the bright silver arc of her sword. That sword was behind her as she jumped, the perfect arc of its strike coming forward in synchronicity with her landing. Her feet hit the ground in front of the debt collector as the sword finished its motion, carving through the air, the debt collector, his net gun, and more air as it passed from his shoulder and out below his rib cage. Grace held the poise for a second, sword low, a drop of blood falling from the point, then turned back to Nate.

"I thought you said together," she said.

"I thought I'd be able to keep up," he said. "A little help."

She paced towards him like a hunting cat, her sword tasting the air almost too fast for the eye to follow. The net parted, Nate gasping his way free. He took her offered hand, his metal leg whining as she helped him up.

He frowned at her sword. "I never figured a weapon like that would be any good."

"Style never gets old," she said, walking past him.

HARSH BREATHING. Sweating. The clatter of boots on ceramicrete stairs. The whine of his metal leg.

Nate wiped sweat from his brow. When he ... *retired* from the Old Empire, planning his future life of sailing the hard black and making his fortune, he hadn't figured on it involving so much exertion. The whole point of being on a ship you could run the length of in less than a minute — with a metal leg — was to not *have* to spend so much time running.

At last, the top of the staircase. Kohl was waiting by the door, breathing hard. Grace stood by his side, not looking like she'd been running at all, maybe a little harder of breath, but overall like this was an easy day. Kohl eyed her up, gaze lingering on her sword. "Might want to stand back," he said. "This is likely to be gunplay. Distance work."

Pant, pant. Nate held up a hand. "Give me a sec," he said. "Be right with you."

"I feel ya, Cap," said Kohl, coughing. He spat something thick and viscous onto the stairway.

"That's disgusting," said Hope, behind her visor.

"What's the matter, Kohl?" said Grace. "Not enough cardio in your workouts?"

"Hey, I'm a rhino," said Kohl.

"No argument," said El. "No point either."

"Point is this. Have you ever seen a rhino run?" asked Kohl.

"I've never even seen a rhino," said Hope. "I don't know what it is."

"Big and ugly," said Grace. "Right, Kohl?"

"Aw, Gracie," he said. "You're just sore we're gonna have to clear the roof without you."

"Be my guest," she said, palm out towards the door. "You want to get yourself shot, that's fine by me."

Kohl looked at Nate. "Cap?"

"Good to go," said Nate. He moved to stand beside the door with Kohl. "On three?"

"Three," said Kohl, and kicked the door open. He charged into what Nate had been expecting to be a bright light after the gloom of the stairwell, but what turned out to be dusk. Sun down, city lights up, clean air around them. The roof held three air cars and five soldiers. The rooftop was littered with holes — *whoring and coring, as Kohl put it* — that led down into the building. As the door opened with a clang, all five soldiers turned towards them. Kohl's carbine discharged in a scatter of red laser light, and one soldier exploded in a shower of steam and meaty chunks, his plasma gun breaking apart in a discharge of energy.

The remaining four scattered, huddling behind the air cars.

"Great," said Nate. "Now we need to go flush 'em out." But talking wasn't working, so he set off across the roof. His steps took him right, Kohl fanning out to the left. Hope and El stayed in the stairwell with Harlow. Nate raised his blaster, firing off a couple shots to keep the Republic soldiers dedicated towards lowering their heads.

Grace moved across the roof, which wasn't a part of the plan inside Nate's head, because she wasn't using a gun, and this was gun work. It complicated things some, because he couldn't just lay down fire like the hand of God with impunity. He'd need to be careful not to shoot her, and not shooting her was high on his priority list.

Because, and this was a hell of a time to realize it, he was falling hard for Grace Gushiken. She'd lied to him, brought the Republic down on him and his crew, and her gifts had an entire alien race interested in capturing the *Tyche*.

She was just his kind of girl.

This thought distracted him from what was going on, and it meant that he tripped on the debris from one hole leading down into the interior of the building. The stumble put him on one knee, which put him low enough to not get his head shot off with a flash of plasma fire from behind one of the air cars. He raised his weapon, sighted down the barrel, and squeezed off a helping of plasma for the Republic soldier who'd fired on him. The soldier turned into a flaming pillar, tossed backward by the blast. *One for the good guys, hey?*

"Cap!" shouted Kohl, and Nate rolled on general principle. Plasma chewed at the roof around him, chips of ceramicrete flying into the air. A piece of roofing struck his face, causing bright sparks to go off behind his eyes, and he fell back onto the ground. *Just a breather. All I need is a couple seconds along with a couple spoonfuls of air. Is that too much to ask?*

There was a *whine-chunk* of Kohl's carbine, but no answering sound of a human turning into sludge. Nate raised his head. Five to start with, two down, three to go. Kohl was on the far side of the roof, his carbine *click-click-clicking* as it tried to find a target. Grace was holding midfield, sword low and ready. That was all the good news on offer; the bad news was that two of the three Republic soldiers were at the air car closest to Nate. *Time to change the odds. You've fought better than this on a worse day, Nathan Chevell. Get your ass in the fight.* From his position on the ground, he raised his blaster, squeezing off a shot or two. It made the Republic soldiers scurry away from him, seeking the cover of the air car in the middle of the roof. One drew down on Grace as he ran, but Kohl's carbine found him before things got out of hand. The *click-click-click* turned into *whine-chunk*, and the soldier's body blew into smaller components as the water inside him super-heated in a nanosecond. Grace shielded her face, the red spray still covering her from head to toe.

"Asshole!" she said, but ducked low and to the side, out of harm's way. Nate wasn't sure if she was referring to Kohl or the soldier. Nate picked himself up off the ground, ducking behind the nearest air car, then huddling his way across to the middle car. He'd lost his bead on the remaining two, which wasn't great. It wasn't great for a couple reasons. Reason the first: just because you couldn't see them, doesn't mean they couldn't see you.

Reason the second arrived on the tail of that thought: some damn other fool will try something reckless.

In this case, it was Kohl. He unholstered a blaster — not one Nate had seen before, it must have been a trophy from earlier in the day — and fired at the air car itself. His carbine wasn't any use against an object made of metals and polymers; sure, sure, it'd cut a hole through the car, but that wasn't what Kohl was after. A good plasma weapon was the everyday choice for any situation, and Kohl was exploring how effective it would be at tearing chunks out of the air car.

"Kohl!" shouted Nate.

"I'm good, Cap!" Kohl shouted back.

"I can see that! Stop shooting the air car. There's a chance you'll hit—" Nate forgot the rest of what he was going to say as Kohl's shot bit into the air car's power supply, most likely a charged cell. The cell ruptured, discharging its energy in less than half a second. The resulting fireball reached ruddy fingers towards the sky, tossing Kohl, Grace, and Nate backward.

As Nate once again looked at the sky from his position on his back, he thought, *that wasn't smart, Kohl, even for you.* Nate's face hurt, like he'd been burned, which was probably true, but it was something he could worry about later. Something he needed to worry about *now* was the lack of mobility in his legs. His back didn't hurt, but his back didn't feel like anything at all.

You're not paralyzed. It's just shock. Get up, Chevell. Get up, and get your crew out of here. He craned his neck to get a view of the roof.

The burning air car cast the rooftop in flickering amber light. The other two cars were still there, one looking more singed than the other, but still functional. No sign of the two Republic soldiers Kohl had been flushing out, which gave good odds on them being flushed right out of existence. Speaking of the big man, Kohl was down, possibly out, slight chance of dead. Grace was on one knee, trying to get up.

There was a flash of fire from the stairwell door, Republic soldiers coming up. A loud *kaboom* sounded, El's hand cannon warning them off. There was a *ffffzzzzshrk* of noise, something Nate hadn't heard before, not outside of a ship. It sounded like a maser, except that was crazy, because masers were for ship-to-ship use. The only person he knew who might have magicked up a maser out of parts was Hope, and Nate remembered the box she'd opened, the weapon she'd been fixing. It's good she had more than her rig, but it was bad she was fighting at all. Hope wasn't built for it. Hope was Nate's ... *hope* that there were solutions that didn't involve blood.

Maybe he wasn't cut out for this captain business. "Grace," said Nate. His voice was a croak, but she still looked at him.

"Nate, there's someone else. Some*thing* else," she said.

Uh. Nate tried to get up again. "Grace? I need a second."

"We don't have a second, Nate. We've got to go."

The middle air car's side door hinged open, the wing of a gull readying for flight. This car was the most singed, windscreen charred. Out of the car stepped the man in black.

"That's impossible," said Nate. "I saw you go down."

The man in black frowned. "People keep saying that. October Kohl said it before, as if it was true."

"I saw it too," said Grace. "I saw you die."

The man in black kept frowning. "Grace Gushiken, I'm disappointed in you. For all the gifts they say you have, you're blinded by your own fear. You've just got to *look*, Grace. That's all."

Grace was all the way on her feet now, sword held ready. "I'd rather just fight," she said. "I'm tired of running. I'm not tired of fighting though. So let's go."

The man in black considered that for a moment, then held up a hand. "One moment," he said. He bent into the air car, then returned with two long shapes. *Swords. He's got two swords.* The man in black flicked his wrists, the scabbards of the swords falling free. Far from plain steel showing its teeth, the blades were dull black. *Some kind of nanomaterial. Edges an atom thick. Cut through you like you weren't even there.* Nate tried to get up again, failed again, and said, "Grace? Get Kohl's gun."

She looked like she was considering it, and then the man in black was on her. It happened faster than a thought, his swords a blur of shadow in the red-and-gloom of the rooftop. Grace ducked, wove, her own sword answering in a lick of silver. It reached out, caressed the man in black's face, leaving a red line no longer than a finger on his face.

They broke apart. The man in black smiled like he was hungry, and Grace was a banquet. "Fantastic, Grace. Can you tell me what it's like to fight someone who's not there?"

Her eyes narrowed. "You sound like my father."

"A wise man," said the man in black, "but not a good enough teacher. He hammered at your gift like it was steel to shape. Buckled you under the strain." They circled each other, all while Nate lay there, useless legs, useless body, unable to get up. Now would be a great time for El or Hope or Harlow to do something useful, except they were still dealing with whatever mischief was brewing in the stairwell below them. The man in black was still talking. "He left all the important lessons on the table. How to shield your own mind. How to protect yourself against someone like him. Someone like *us*."

Grace blinked, taking a step back. Her eyes were on the man in black, but they were wide, confused. *Afraid.*

The man in black attacked again, his swords slicing the night sky, almost like they were made of the darkness above. Grace's defense was still fast, fluid, but it lacked some of the beauty of before. Like she was dancing alone now, not able to see the steps of her partner. In three seconds, no more, the man in black had attacked with ten strikes. She'd dodged all but one, the last caught on the edge of her steel.

Grace's sword rang with the barest whisper of sound, and half of the blade fell to the rooftop. She held it out in front of her, half a sword against a man with two. Half an esper against a master of his craft. Nate saw her swallow, brace herself. Ready to attack.

Nate's metal hand found something against the rooftop. Fingers closed of their own volition, nothing conscious about it, because Nate sure as hell wasn't in charge of his arms or legs at the moment. The techs had said *machine learning* like it was something Nate could understand. The techs had said *better than the original* like losing a hand was something to be pleased about. They'd left him broken, and he'd never been happier than he was now. The metal fingers squeezed, the blaster they'd found barking bright, loud, and hard in the night air. A bolt of plasma found the man in black, caught the top half of his body in blue fire, and blew him into fragments. The bottom half of him stood for a second longer, then fell to the ground to lie there along with his swords.

Grace shook herself, ran to him. "We've got to leave," she said. "He was ... one of them."

"Yeah," said Nate. "Fucking asshole Republic High Command, yeah? Fucking espers. No offense."

She ignored that last, looking back at the burning body. "No, Nate. The *Ezeroc*."

He thought about that for about two whole seconds. The burst of clear cold terror startled him out of his paralysis, his legs jerking underneath him. He climbed to his feet, his meat leg buckling for a second. "Here? Are you sure?"

"I wish I wasn't."

Nate made himself walk the distance to the man in black. There wasn't enough left of the top part of him to know if there were insects in his skull, a small hive of creatures using him like a marionette. Just charred carbon that could have been any barbecued meat product, insect or otherwise. He pushed a toe through the burning remains. *No time, Nate. You've got to get them out of here.* He moved over to Kohl, the big man groaning, already trying to right himself.

"You're an idiot," said Nate.

"Solved a problem, didn't I?" said Kohl, rubbing his face.

"Not really," said Nate. "There's a problem in the stairwell that needs fixing."

"Right." Kohl got up, Nate impressed at his recovery speed, sauntering over to a fallen Republic soldier. He cast the man in black a look as he went, did a double-take, and said, "Where'd that asshole come from?"

"You know him?"

"Abel? Yeah," said Kohl, then shrugged as if it was a problem that had solved itself. Which, in a way, it was. Nate jogged to the stairwell, took in Harlow crouched next to the railing, a blaster firing shots over the side. El, leaning against a wall, sidearm pointing its wide barrel down the steps. Hope standing between them, not sure what to do, the maser in her hands. "Harlow," said Nate.

"You blow up our ride?"

"Nah," said Nate. "You're with me. El?"

"Cap'n." She was still focused down the steps.

"Grab a car. Don't care which. Take Hope and Kohl—"

"You're sending him with us? I prefer Harlow."

"Thanks," said Harlow, then fired more plasma over the side.

"Not a committee," said Nate. "Take Hope and Kohl and get back to the *Tyche*. You'll need the big man to clear the way. Stay focused, El. They're here."

"Who?"

"The fucking bugs," said Nate. "The fucking bugs are here."

"Wait, what?" El startled, her weapon lowering for a second.

"I don't like Earth anymore," said Hope.

"Get moving," said Nate. "I want my ship flying in less than four hours. We're picking up some strays. Harlow?"

"Yeah."

"You've got the stick of whichever car they don't take. Kohl! Where the fuck ... there you are." Nate took in Kohl, coming to the stairwell with a belt held in his hands. "What're they?"

"Pineapples," said Kohl. "What do you think they are?"

"You not had enough of almost blowing us up today?"

"Naw," said Kohl, then tossed the belt over the stairwell. It caught on the railing, Harlow's eyes widening as it did so, then slipped from view. There was a panicked yell from below. Nate grabbed Hope, dragging her outside, El and Harlow on his hells, Kohl lingering a little to see what would happen.

The explosion shook the roof, the frame of the stairwell shaking with it, fire coughing out of the entrance. Kohl gave a whoop, then ran towards the air cars.

"Grace," called Nate. "You're with me."

"Always," she said. "Together." She offered him a small smile, something brave in it, something where the two of them could stand against the horrors that were to come. At least, that's what Nate hoped it was, because he needed a little of someone else's courage. The Ezeroc. Here? Not a great end to a bad day.

El was already behind the sticks of one of the Republic air cars, the machine starting up with a rumble of its drives. Kohl slipped into the co-pilot's seat, Hope taking a seat behind them in the cabin proper. It was already lifting towards the sky when Nate slung himself in beside Harlow, Grace inside.

"So," said Harlow. "Where we going?"

"Got my crew," said Nate. "Now we get yours."

"About fucking time," said Harlow.

CHAPTER FIFTEEN

THE AIR CAR was a beauty to fly — good Republic tech skimming over a city made of lights and wonder. Buildings reaching fingers up into the night sky like they wanted a piece of the hard black. People, tiny dots below, doing a million different things. Up here it was peaceful, nothing but the car and the wind. The car worked just fine. It hadn't been made for the war, which meant *leather* (or something like it). It was a shame they'd have to scuttle it. Which got El's mind back to the *Tyche*, and what Kohl had said those assholes were doing to it. She looked at the big man. "So, you're telling me they were trying to sell *my* ship?"

"Technically, it's the captain's ship," said Kohl.

"It's more mine and El's than Nate's," said Hope from behind them. "We make her fly."

"I don't have a horse in this race," said Kohl. "All I know is I had to shoot a lot of fools who were crawling all over it."

"Great," said El. "We'll ditch the car." The machine's controls responded under her fingertips like it was born and bred for her, agile like a bird, urgent like a stallion. The heads-up display gave altitude, velocity, and an angry image of a Republic officer trying to raise her on the comm. She answered the call. "Heya."

"Unidentified pilot, you are in possession of a Republic vehicle. Stealing Republic property is an offense against—"

El clicked the comm off. "Okay, we're definitely ditching the car. Hope?"

"Already working on it." The Engineer was deep in her rig, visor accessing schematics and controls only she could see. Or at least that's what El hoped she was doing, otherwise her fingers moving through the air were the actions of a crazy person. "Okay, yeah. See, they're trying to make the car fall from the sky."

"Sounds bad," suggested Kohl.

"Very," said Hope, her voice distracted. "I won't let them do that."

"Great," said El. "Kohl?"

"Yeah."

"Did you try and sell out Grace?" El's hands gripped the controls. "For money?"

"It was two hundred thousand coins, El. C'mon—"

"Kohl?"

"Yeah."

"You owe her," said El. Meaning, *you owe her for fucking every-thing up*, but also, *for not killing you before.*

"I know," he said, sounding pissed off, but not with her. "I know, okay!"

"So why'd you do it?"

"Not sure," said Kohl, speaking a little slower. "It seemed like the right thing to do?" His voice was distracted, like he was trying to remember what had happened. Trying to straighten it out, create a new narrative in his head.

"Guys," said Hope. "Two things. First, now's not the time. Second, if there are Ezeroc, well, can't they make you do things?"

"No one makes October Kohl do something he doesn't want to do," said Kohl.

"Yeah," said El. "That's the problem. You wanted to do it, Kohl. They found that inside you, and twisted it out, like gutting a rabbit."

"You're saying I'm a rabbit?"

"I'm saying you've got the self-control of a root vegetable," said El. Her head still hurt, and one of her eyes was blurry, but she didn't need both eyes to fly this car. Hell, it flew itself. It wanted to claw the sky and burn bright, which worked just fine for El.

"Root vegetable?" said Hope.

"I'm still hungry for Earth food," said El. "That pizza..." Her voice trailed off as she realized what she'd said. "I'm, uh, sorry, Hope. Not thinking."

"It's okay," said Hope, in a voice that suggested it was far from okay. That it was the least okay thing of all time.

"I figure we can resolve everything by killing a few more people," said Kohl.

"I suspect that's in our schedule for later on tonight," said El. "There's a bar near the space port. Or used to be."

"Used to be?" said Kohl.

"I met a guy there," said El. She rubbed her face, then did a double take at the car's radar. A couple of blips were closing on their position. Or she had double vision and it was a single blip. Could be both. "That's not the important part. The important part is the bar blew up."

"Uh," said Kohl.

"So we're ditching the car there and setting it on fire," said El, "because it won't be as suspicious as a new fire starting somewhere else. Hope?"

"You've got Hope," said Hope. "I'm here."

"We got two pursuit vehicles closing in on our six," said El. "I'm getting RADAR and LIDAR backscatter from them. Any chance you could shut 'em down?"

"Are you serious?" said Hope. "How do you think technology works?"

"We might die, is all," said El.

"Let me see what I can do," said Hope.

"Who was this guy?" said Kohl.

"What?" said El and Hope together.

"At the bar," said Kohl.

"Dunno," said El. "Bought him a drink. He sent me after Altman Razor."

"Oh," said Hope. "Altman. He's a funny little man."

The HUD in front of El lit up like it was Christmas, red and yellow warning lights blazing out. The pursuit vehicles had a lock on them. "This is good," said Hope. "I can work with this."

"This isn't good!" said El, twisting the controls. The air car yawed through the night sky, engines screaming as El poured on more joules. The air car climbed, gaining some precious height, alarms in front of El blaring harsh and loud. None of it helped her headache.

"Give me a second!" said Hope.

"We don't have a second!" said El, kicking the drive harder. The air car shuddered as she twisted the yoke, pulling it up and around and then down in a rush of acceleration. Buildings around them streamed by in flashes of light and color, the machine's controls shaking under her hands like a scared horse.

"One more second," said Hope, but sounding sick now.

One of the pursuit vehicles launched a missile. The air car's warnings grew louder, and El wished she was in the *Tyche*, PDCs at her command. The *Tyche* might not have full leather, but she was built for war and could toss out chaff and RADAR ghosts like they were candy at Halloween. This air car, marvel of engineering it was, had a couple of forward-facing launchers and that was that.

"Got it," said Hope.

"Got what?" said El, keeping the car pointed at the ground. Their speed was climbing, the rush of descent all about them. The alarms on the dash went silent, readouts dropping to baselines. RADAR still showed dots in the air around them, but ... no alarms. The air car's engines still shrieked, which was a distracting noise, so El leveled them out, buildings slipping past at a staider pace. She took a couple breaths, looked at Kohl — the man's eyes wide, confused — and then checked on Hope behind them. "What did you do, Hope?"

"I told the missiles we weren't the problem." Hope paused. "They killed Reiko."

A Republic air car pulled up next to them, holding level as they sped across the city. The comm chattered again, so El clicked it on. A masked face, Republic black visor, Republic black uniform. "Unidentified pilot," said the soldier. "Land your vehicle *now*."

"Yeah, that'll be a negative copy on that," said El. "Say, you fellas lose a couple missiles?"

A bright blossom of fire erupted off their side as the Republic air car exploded, a missile striking it from the sky like a bad mistake. The comm channel closed by itself, the other end no longer there. No static, no screams, just no more connection. "Huh," said Kohl. "There's a thing. Say, Hope. Can you do that with their guns?"

"Don't be stupid," said Hope, her visor looking out the window. "It doesn't work that way."

"Worth a shot," said Kohl.

"Let's not get too relaxed," said El. "We've got one more bogey on our six. He's still there, like a damn dog with a bone."

"Can you shake 'em?" said Kohl. "You should try and shake 'em off."

El sighed. "That's great advice, Kohl. Really. It is. What do you think I've been doing?" She took the air car lower, their Republic shadow following them down to the deck.

"I dunno, but they're still there," said Kohl. "When the cap tells me to shoot someone, I make sure they're dead. When you're flying, well, you're not doing it right or something."

El gritted her teeth. *Not doing it right.* He might have a point. She was treating this whole thing like she was flying a ship with weapons, ordnance at her command, drives and reactors and PDCs all at her fingertips, and that wasn't the case. This thing was a *car*. A vehicle ordered for light crowd control. Hell, that they had missiles at all was a stroke of luck; it'd be more usual for policing vehicles to be outfitted with stun gear for suppressing an angry citizenry. Not that any of the Republic's fine citizens were ever angry. "You got any grenades left?" she said.

"Sure," said Kohl. "I kept one for luck." He held it up.

"Great," said El. "We're ditching. Here's the way it'll happen. Hope, I'm gonna need your rig."

"My rig?" said Hope. "What for?"

TWO AIR CARS screamed over the streets, engines burning hard. Citizens would have been looking up, wondering what was going on. What would cause a disturbance like this in their boring, safe lives in the heart of the Republic? The lead car would have wobbled a little, the trained eye picking up a disturbance in the port thruster. Just a little noise in the burn, a bubble in the feed. Nothing serious under normal situations; a little thing like that might be rectified with ten minutes' maintenance from a skilled Engineer.

The situation wasn't normal, and there was no time for maintenance. The pilot of the lead car — crazed or terrified, impossible to tell — poured on more joules, asking more from an engine already wheezing with the load. The engine coughed, cut out, and the pursuing car overshot in a roar of noise and light and heat. The vehicle in trouble, engine out like a blown lamp, entered a slow circle toward the ground. What happened next was hard to get straight, some witnesses reported an explosion before it hit, others said *no, you idiot, it was after*. But they all agreed: the lazy turn became a death spiral, the machine giving up as it approached the ceramicrete below.

The car that had overshot completed a braking turn, engines roaring to return to its prey. The prey had turned off the straight and narrow, banked towards a street on the right in its fall from grace. A partially-finished megaplex where it ended up. It would be a land-mark building for the city, pulling eyes and dollars like filings to a magnet. The troubled air car drifted into the construction lot, that damaged engine coughing fire at last. The pursuit vehicle rounded the turn after its prey in time to see the troubled car explode into a roil of flame, smoke, and flying machinery. The explosion touched a piece of heavy construction equipment, causing an energy canister inside to rupture. Stored energy spilled in bright flashes around it, great arcs of light that seemed thick and solid. They licked out, carving through the half-built substructure.

That would have been the end of it if it weren't for a construction crew that had finished early the previous shift. Even in the heart of the Republic, where people were happiest, there was still the desire to finish early every day. And if *early* meant not tidying away your tools, well, that was because they weren't good Guild members, accustomed to good Engineer practice. There wouldn't have been a Shingle among them.

Tools in this situation were large machines capable of lifting whole floors into place. Devices designed to superheat the raw material substrate of ceramicrete to thousands of degrees, hotter than the sun's surface, hotter than the core of the star that warmed the world. These machines had their own reactors because simple energy canisters were insufficient for the loads asked of them. Good building practice called for reactors to be buried, cores deep below. At the end of a shift, these reactors were to be shut down. After the building was complete the reactors would be repurposed into auxiliary power for the finished structure. Buried they were, but shut down they weren't. The reaching fingers of the energy discharge found them. A single stray arc, traveling down conductive metal, ruptured the wall of a reactor. It went into safe shutdown, microseconds passing before the internal reactions were reduced to zero.

Microseconds were a long time in nuclear energy terms.

The street seemed to shrug for a moment, a gentle giant sighing up and down. Ripples of the underground explosion reached out in a circle four blocks in every direction. The ground underneath the city was exposed to an intense blast, the shockwave descending and moving out. Soil, clay, and rock were disrupted; closer to the blast, they were rendered into magma. The lot caved inward, girders and beams and ceramicrete falling into a hole forming at the base, liquefaction of the ground dragging material, machinery, and the smoking remains of the air car into oblivion.

Disaster crews were called by the pursuit team, but by then it was too late for the air car they were following. They'd get nothing from them, the remains of its crew rendered to component atoms.

"FUCK ME," said Kohl. "If you were trying to impress me, it worked."

El peeled the rig's visor off her face, the HUD controls inside — what she'd been using to pilot the air car into the abandoned lot — already silent at the loss of connection from the vehicle. "Kohl, impressing you is not on my list of to-dos for today."

"Still," said Kohl, smile still stuck to his face.

"We should leave," said Hope, taking the rig back from El. It walked around Hope's small frame like a sloth clinging to a tree, hugging her, encasing her. "Reactors mean radiation. There's a lot of ceramicrete between it and us, but I could use a little distance too."

They'd used a quick turn from the air car a street back to ditch, hidden from the eyes of their pursuers. The car's controls were slaved to Hope's rig, El piloting it on remote. It'd buy them some time, but they were still a ways away from the spaceport. El ran a hand through her hair, wincing as she touched the back of her head where Reiko had hit her. The wound had crusted over, but a sizable egg was forming there, and she still didn't feel a hundred. Hell, she didn't even feel at ten. She wanted to be back on the *Tyche*, the small medical bay looking her over. And then, real flight sticks under her fingers. "We need another ride," she said.

"On it," said Kohl.

"Kohl, wait—" started El, but it was like trying to hold back the tide.

The big man was already walking into the street proper, the normal flow of traffic halted as people stopped to look at the spectacle of a falling titan. Passengers were out of their vehicles, eyes wide, mouths agape. Kohl fixed himself on a nondescript cargo van, charted a course towards the driver, gave the man a quick smile and an, "Excuse me," and pushed the man out of the way.

"Hey!" said the driver, surprise turning to anger.

"How do you think this will go?" said Kohl.

"Uh," said the driver, anger turning to uncertainty touched with a shade of fear.

"Good call," said Kohl. He turned back to El and Hope. "Get in. This time, I'm driving."

"Two dimensions you can cope with," said El. She hurried towards the van, pulling Hope behind her, because Hope was still unfocused, on account of having just lost her wife. "Let's get to the *Tyche.*"

THE *TYCHE* WAS RIGHT where they'd left her, drives cool and dark, the hull huddled against the earth like a wounded falcon. El winced at the sight, but it *had* been her who'd shut the ship down. A few systems were back online, a hiss of escaping steam from underneath the *Tyche* evidence of Kohl turning the crank in his attempts to contact them. There was no one about the dock. No sign of hostile life. No Republic soldiers waiting for them. No dock crew lookalikes trying to muscle or hustle them. Just her girl, the *Tyche*, the smiling, winking face painted on her hull welcoming them home.

Oh, and some thick cables, chaining the *Tyche* to the dock. *I guess you don't need troops when spun nanowire will tie her down better than Jupiter's gravity.*

"They cut her," said Hope, pointing at the hole in the cargo bay door.

"Yeah," said Kohl, "so I cut 'em right back."

"Can you fix her?" said El to the Engineer.

"Course," said Hope. She pointed to the cables tethering the *Tyche* to the deck. "Those will need a little attention too."

"They're new," rumbled Kohl. "Weren't here last time."

"Okay," said El. "Here's the plan. Hope?"

"I fix the door," said Hope. "Make it air tight, ship shape. Ready to hold against the hard black."

"Kohl?"

"Those cables look heavy," he said. "I'll find me a cutter and get to work."

El gave a tight smile. "Great. Get to it."

"What are you going to do?" said Hope, the arms of her rig already flexing out, eager to be working. To be doing what they were made for — less of the fighting and running and crying and hurting, and more of the making-things-right.

"Me?" said El. "I thought I might go patch myself up. Get the med bay to give me a once-over. Make sure I'm good to fly."

"And if you're not?" said Kohl.

"I'll get the *Tyche* to make me a little cocktail," said El. "Cap needs us. No way I'm sitting this one out." And she was surprised to find it true. Right there in her heart was a bright ember, a spark she'd never felt before. They'd tried to take her Engineer. They'd tried to ground her ship. Tried to kill them all, and then they'd tried again. They'd fired missiles at her, and someone had knocked her out with a bottle. That spark? It was anger. Not courage, but something harder and stronger.

THE *TYCHE'S* interior was much how she'd left it except for the blood stains, wreckage, and scorching.

El stopped by the med bay, the autodoc looking her over. It complained a lot, told her things about *minor concussion* and *rest* that she didn't have time for, and gave her a couple of pills. She dry-swallowed them, then spent time in her cabin, righting a few things that were wrong. El put belongings back in boxes, looking at the wreckage of her tiny life, and fanned that spark a little brighter. The *Republic* had done this. To *her*. She'd *paid her taxes*, been a good little Helm on a good little starship. Wrong side of the war, but she'd left it all honorably enough, because at the end there'd been less fighting and more surrendering. The Republic had given amnesty for mistakes made. It was all clean. That easy break from an old life gave El this easy job on an easy ship hauling easy things between worlds that weren't served by Guild Bridges. It was supposed to be the right thing to do. If you do nothing wrong, nothing bad happens to you. Right?

She bent over, picking up the remains of her personal console. It was cracked, plastic shroud flaking pieces to the deck as she turned it over. Someone had used the wrong tools, or no tools at all, to get at the innards. They'd pried out the data slivers, hacking at the secrets of El's life.

The spark caught, and turned into fire. Those *fuckers*.

She glimpsed herself in the mirror on the wall. The surface was a simple screen, big enough to give her a window of anything she wanted. Sometimes she chose a beach. Other times, a rain-drenched forest. Right now, the screen was just a mirror, showing her ... herself. Jaw clenched. Hair far too dirty and far too greasy to be something she was happy with. Smudges on her face, dirt and grime and the carbon of explosions. But it was her eyes that drew her attention. Her eyes were haunted, hunted, and angry all at once. They didn't look like her eyes at all.

If that's what it takes. She swiped the screen, looking for that rain-drenched forest, but the system was broken, like everything else in her cabin. So, she gave up, heading for the flight deck. They had work to do.

CHAPTER SIXTEEN

THE CAR SCUDDED over the skyline, easy as you please. Harlow sat at the controls, not doing much of anything useful except pointing the car where they needed to go. That destination was still a mystery. Grace leaned forward. "Harlow?"

He jumped, like he'd been in a reverie. Or plain shock, which was more likely considering the last few hours. "Uh. Sorry. I was drifting."

Nate snorted, but said nothing.

Grace nodded out the window. "Where are we going?"

"A warehouse," said Harlow. He looked at Nate. "Sorry. Not a bar."

"Wasn't expecting a bar," said Nate. "I expected a fight."

"Then you'll get what you're expecting," said Harlow. "You'll get what you want."

Grace was picking up *tired/fear/hope* all at once from Harlow. "What's at the warehouse?"

"For a start," said Harlow, "it's not a warehouse."

Nate gave him a look. "You said—"

"It only *looks* like a warehouse," said Harlow. "It's a front. A cover. A sham. What's behind the sham is something we can only guess at."

"What's this 'we,' Harlow?" Nate held up his metal hand, gesturing out the window. "The Harlow I knew from the time before was after pretty boys and hard drugs and an easy life." He paused. "It's why it was so easy to swindle you out of the *Tyche* fair and square."

"Swindle ... fair and square?" said Harlow. He sighed, a big long breath, air going out of a balloon. "That's the thing, Nate. Underneath the easy life, the pretty boys, the bars and the drugs and the fast cars? There's a Republic. And do you know what's under that?"

"I know," said Grace.

"I know too," said Nate, flexing his metal hand. "It's why I flew far away." Grace could feel his *pain/loss/anger*, but it was like a recording, faint, a memory of a memory. Something he'd grown used to, that fitted him like his metal hand or his jacket.

"Amedea said the espers were at the heart of the collapse," said Grace.

"They were," said Harlow. "She was. Or so she says. I was still with pretty boys that stage, Nate. Had my eye on you for a while."

"I'm flattered," said Nate. "But back to the Intelligencers."

"That's the uniform they wore," said Harlow. "The Emperor made them for a better Empire. I guess he didn't figure them for a bunch of traitors."

"Why serve when you can rule?" said Grace. She looked down, thinking of her father, then back up. "When humans make gods, do they expect the gods to be slaves? They ... *we* didn't learn with AI. The Guild needed to save us then. Who'll save us now? 'Better men.'" She shook her head. "It's what my father said."

"Well," said Harlow, the air car making a slow turn through the sky, "everything was going just fine for the 'better men' until Amedea found her conscience. I think she liked playing at a god. But ... you know? The thought of spilling the Emperor's blood was too much. I think even gods can have regrets."

They were silent for a while, the air car humming around them, the city far enough below to be silent, a glow of lights and nothing else. Grace pushed hair back from her face. "They're not gods, Harlow. *I'm* not a god."

"You're the best god of all," said Harlow. "The rest of them, they know what we're thinking. They gotta work at it. But they don't know what we're feeling. You? You *know*, and it comes easy to you. That's why they want you, Grace."

"Why?" Grace pulled back from Harlow, like he was a stove that might burn her. "I'm ... so much *less*."

"That's your father talking," said Harlow. "Amedea didn't like him."

"*I* didn't like him," said Grace, teeth gritted.

"Ask yourself," said Harlow. "Is it better to be a ruler who knows thoughts and controls them? Or a ruler who feels the pain of their people?"

"You're saying Grace is an ... evolution?" said Nate.

"My father said I was a mistake," said Grace. She knew he'd thought it, along with *hated/mongrel*. Like she was the worst error he'd ever made.

"Nah," said Harlow. "I don't know what she is. But she ain't an evolution, and she ain't a mistake. Something different. And we need something different. The Old Empire didn't work out—"

"Hey," said Nate. "It was *fine*."

"Nate, I know you wore the Emperor's Black, and I mean no disrespect. I dig a guy in uniform, but we didn't get to vote. Didn't matter that things worked out okay for a while. It mattered there wasn't a choice."

"Are you saying you believe in the Republic?" said Nate, stiffening, *anger/betrayal/uncertainty* coming off him.

Harlow laughed. "No, Nate." He gestured at the console. "I'm in this fine air car, which we've stolen from the same Republic. I'm a wanted man in all the ways that end with death after interrogation.

No, Nate, I'm not a believer. Not in *this* Republic. Because the Republic, Nate, is run by the Intelligencers."

"They're dead," said Nate. "Hunted, gone."

"Nah," said Harlow. "The ones that are hunted are like Amedea. The ones that weren't trying to kill your old boss. Or," and he glanced at Grace, "those born after. Caught and converted? Fine. But the hunters are more numerous than the hunted. And now? They've got help."

"What kind of help?" said Grace.

"You know," said Harlow. "You've seen. The men in black."

"The Ezeroc," said Grace.

"We don't have a name for 'em," said Harlow. "Ezeroc fits fine. Amedea didn't know what they were, just that there were more of them. More people with the gift than ever before. Said they *sounded* different."

"Like a hiss in your mind," said Grace.

"That's not how she explained it," said Harlow, "but you're different to her." He sighed again. "Maybe better. I don't know. If she's still alive, we can ask her."

"If she's still alive?" Nate was still *angry/angry*, but Grace was getting also *confusion/uncertainty* off him. He wore a brave face, but her captain felt the same as the rest of them under it all. He was just better at hiding it.

"Well, you'll see," said Harlow. He was pointing the car downward. "These are the coordinates, but..."

"'But,'" said Nate, "is not a word that invites confidence."

Grace had stopped paying attention to them. Something in the air touching her skin, getting under it. It wasn't the *air*, because that hadn't changed. Inside the car, things were as they were two seconds ago. But she felt ... different. Like she was being watched. "Hey," she said. "This isn't right."

Harlow looked back at her. "What? It's the right place. Co-ordinates check out just fine."

"I'm sure the co-ordinates are fine," said Grace, "but what's here isn't ... *right.*" She paused, trying to ... *taste* the air again. That feeling of a whisper on her skin, moth wings grazing a spider's web. The feeling of being surveilled by something interested beyond measure.

Grace.

Grace Grace Grace Grace Grace!

"Turn the car!" she said. "Go! We've got to go!"

"What?" said Harlow, not understanding. "We're *here*, Grace—"

"*The Ezeroc!*" she screamed. "They're here!"

Nate didn't ask stupid questions; he reached across to Harlow, grabbed a fistful of controls, and yanked. The air car choked on the descent, bucked and shimmied, then started a lumbering climb. Lumbering, because Harlow was still holding the sticks too, trying to get the machine to land. Harlow, now there was a man with *confusion/betrayal/panic* coming off him like heat off a radiator. He was trying to get to Amedea. His boss, or his friend, or whatever the hell she was to him. And to all the other friends they had in the Resistance, who were also here.

With the Ezeroc. Who put insects in your skull.

The note of the engines changed, became a whine, climbed to a scream as the machine started a lazy turn in the air, trying to go up and down at the same time. Grace was tossed around the seat in the back as the machine listed, Nate saying *Harlow we've got to get out of here* and Harlow saying *Nate she's down there I know it.*

Grace! Grace! Grace!

The air car's dash spat errors, a long scrolling chain of text no one was paying attention to. A second later, the errors cleared, the HUD blanking, highlighting something urgent, important. A thing everyone should pay attention to. It was a signal that the air car was targeted by ground weapons. The air car got hot, Grace picking up a sparking off the right side, right outside her window. The rear right drive made an unusual sound, like a grinder with a stone caught in it. That lasted less than a second, and what replaced it was worse: the drive was silent. Dead.

"Maser," said Nate. "Harlow."

"I know, I know," said Harlow, flicking switches on the console. Trying to start a dead engine that had been burned out from the inside. "Tight beam, focused. They've cooked it. I'll try, but—"

The front right drive started to grind, and then it made no more noise. The car tipped on a crazy angle, the right side pointing right to the ground, and it slid right out of the sky. Grace heard someone screaming, realized it was her, the ground racing towards them. She saw dark buildings, the corner of a warehouse, ceramicrete coming too close, too fast. She tried to get her feet *down*, for God's sake *down*, under her for the fall, but the ground was coming too fast, it wouldn't stop—

CHAPTER SEVENTEEN

SMOKE. Fire. The smell of burning electronics. An alarm, hazy and indistinct, because Nate was lying on his face, one of his ears covered, the other ringing like a church bell come Sunday morning. His body was above him, feet closer to the sky than his face. On a normal Sunday — church or otherwise — he'd prefer the order to be head-body-ground, not body-head-ground. The safety straps held him in place, a snare of webbing and metal that clutched him like a greedy merchant.

He opened his eyes. Harlow. The insides of an air car. Fire was above him, eating at the console. It'd make its way to Harlow's legs before another five minutes passed.

Nate closed his eyes again. That was enough of a first look. It was terrifying, it was unreasonable, and he wasn't ready for it. Lots of things happened in life he wasn't ready for — like losing his arm and his leg and the Emperor's Black he'd worn like it was a part of him — so fuck it, you know? He opened his eyes again. The fire seemed brighter, more eager, and Nate revised his assessment down to two minutes. Course, he might have slipped into blackness for three minutes there, which meant: let's not close our eyes again.

Grace.

The thought startled him in the restraints, making him scrabble an arm around for purchase. He got it under him, pushed himself up a little, craning back to the rear of the air car. There she was, the shattered glass of the right windows a bed for her. Nate took a breath, and then another. She wasn't moving. She wasn't moving at all. "Grace," he croaked. "Grace!"

Nothing. Harlow groaned, but Grace remained still and silent. Through the smoke, Nate couldn't tell if she was breathing or just plain dead.

She's not dead. She can't be dead. Nate clawed at the harness, his meat hand weak and useless, so he used his metal hand. The techs had said it wouldn't fail, not in a million years, and they were wrong. It had failed plenty, possibly because it had illegal AI inside it, which never sat well with him, but the important part was it didn't fail *now*. Simple movements: golden fingers found the clasps, hit the release, and viola. He fell, landing on Harlow — *sorry, sorry* — but Nate was free. His metal leg scuffed on the console, the fire hungry but denied any useful fuel. He used the metal leg as a support, pushing himself upright, trying not to stand on Harlow, trying not to breathe in smoke. Trying to get out.

Look up. The left side of the air car was above him. He saw the controls on the door, standard release catches about as much use as warm beer on a hot day. *Red, Nate. Look for red.* There: a circle of red, a handle in the middle. *IN CASE OF EMERGENCY* written on the outside. Meat hand still weak, he reached metal fingers up to the door, grabbed the release, and twisted. Nothing happened — *of course, you've got to let it go, the good Engineers who designed this didn't want it to pull your arm off.* He released the handle, and the mechanism in the door *clunked*, whined, and a synthetic voice said, "*Stand clear. Stand clear. Stand clear.*"

There was a *fizzing* sound, like your ear right next to a soda, a bright flash, and a *crump* as explosive bolts fired, the door spiraling up and out of his view. Cool air came into the cabin, kissed the sweat on his face, and fed the fire beneath him. *Out. You've got to get out.*

"What you've got to do, Nathan Chevell, is get your team out." *Talking to yourself. Smooth, Nate, real smooth.* He looked up at the open door, cool night above, freedom. No more flames. Fire had taken his arm, his leg, and his future. *No. Get your team out.* But he wasn't strong enough, the meat parts too weak, and not enough of the metal.

Explosive. Bolts.

Nate looked down, the door under Harlow partially hidden by his friend's body. He crouched, putting his metal leg next to the burning console, between Harlow and the fire. Nate felt down into the heat and dark with his metal fingers. He found the circle of life, the ring that would fire the door releases. Nate tried to give it a turn, but the mechanism inside the door — crumpled, damaged — seized. "Fuck!" He hunkered down, put his shoulder into it, the metal hand whining as it strained, Old Empire metal against Republic metal. The working arm against the broken door. Something inside his arm *click-clicked* as gears skipped, servos missed, and then with a scraping, tearing of metal, the emergency release of the door gave. A quick twist, and it was done.

That same synthetic voice spoke. "*Stand clear. Stand clear. Stand clear.*" The *fizz* wasn't so pronounced this time — Nate had a split second to worry about whether he'd done the right thing, about whether it would harm Harlow being so close, about whether it would work at all — and then the bolts fired. The air car shuddered and rocked with it, Nate's world listing. The vehicle was a ship caught in the stormy seas, the cabin *up* becoming *left* and *down* becoming *right*. The car slumped down on its rests, Harlow's head lolling as he came back to consciousness. Nate scrambled over him, tore at the harness, and dragged Harlow free. Harlow's pants were singed, embers shouldering — the flesh underneath would be blistered, raw, burned, but at least he was *alive* — so Nate patted them down, metal fingers against fire.

No more time. Nate shot to his feet, looking for Grace. The back window of the air car was smashed, and he could see black hair over the curve of her face. He ducked his head back inside the air car, coughing — fire and smoke, char and ash — as he grabbed her under the arms. Nate hauled her out, nothing gentle, everything urgent about the motion. Her feet caught on the sill of the door, a piece of twisted metal snaring on the leg of her ship suit — and he almost shouted in frustration. A tug, more of a pull of desperation, and the fabric tore, tumbling them both down to the ceramicrete. Nate tucked himself around her, landing hard. And there he lay, stunned for a moment, the fire of the car pushing back the darkness around them.

Get up. Nate maneuvered himself out from under Grace, laying her down on the ground with care. He brushed a strand of hair back from her face, then — like he should have done in the first place — put his fingers on her neck, feeling for a pulse. It was there, strong, right under his touch. *She's alive.*

His training, lost and useless for years, gave him a nudge. Getting survivors out was the first step. The next was making sure they stayed safe, and being right next to an air car on fire was far from safe. Nate hauled himself to his feet — *you can rest when you're dead* — the metal of his leg protesting with more than its usual soft whine. It might have been cooked a little by the fire or damaged in the crash. That was Future Nate's problem to deal with; the Nate of the present needed to get his friends away from a fire that didn't care about who they were or the world they could save. The fire just *was*: hungry. Urgent.

Start with Grace. Metal against skin, the gold of his fingers around her arm. *Where?* Head up: check around. *There.* A collection of shipping containers, stacked two high. Big and strong. He dragged her away, the scrape of her body against the ceramicrete nothing against the beating of his heart in his ears. The rush of blood and fear pushing him forward. The blaze behind them, getting brighter. Stronger. The fire looking for fuel. He let Grace's arm fall, shuffling back to Harlow. Harlow's eyes were open, but unseeing, a glazed look. Harlow croaked, "Dad? You're *dead*."

"Not your father, Harlow," said Nate. He tucked himself down behind Harlow, got his arms under Harlow's shoulders, and heaved. He dragged his friend back to where he'd left Grace. About halfway there — it hadn't seemed so far on the first trip — the air car choked, sparked, and there was a rumble as a new fuel source was found by the fire. Nate looked up, caught sight of the pillar of fire blazing out of the windows of the air car, red and white stretching towards the heavens.

This is how it ends. At least Grace was safe. He gave a last heave, hauled Harlow up. Nate shielded him with his body, started back towards Grace.

The blast caught him in the back, helped him on. Tossed him like a discarded toy. Into quiet, cool black.

CHAPTER EIGHTEEN

GRACE FELT the memory of something hot and loud, but also like the rush of surf over her submerged body. As if the surf was made of fire and metal and the rage of destruction. She felt the rough grit of the ceramicrete underneath her, the cool air around her, and thought, *I'm alive.*

She sat up in a rush, her hair falling over her eyes. Pushing it back, she saw a pile of fire and ruin that could only have been the air car, a circle of black and grey visible around it where an explosion had left sooty fingerprints against the ceramicrete. The wreckage was thirty meters or more away, which left questions. How did she get here? How was she alive? Grace lowered her gaze, picking out the still forms of Nate and Harlow. Nate was out like a has-been prize-fighter, and he was on top of Harlow, his head against the ground — *must have knocked it when the blast went off.*

Her breath caught, and she scrambled over to him. "Nate. Nate!" Her hands found his face, her fingers stroking it for a second before she realized what she was doing. She pulled her fingers back like they'd been burned, then — cautiously, so no one, not even her, could mistake the intent — reached out again, brushing a lock of hair away.

She then felt under his jaw for a pulse, and — *thank you, thank you, thank you* — found it. Grace got up, all efficient motion, pulling Nate off Harlow. She leaned him against the metal of a shipping container before crouching down in front of him. "It was you who got us out, wasn't it?" She wiped hair from her face again. The grit and smoke made her eyes water. *Harlow.* She moved to retrieve Nate's friend.

Harlow was awake, but no one was home behind those eyes. She could feel a scramble of half emotions that didn't form in the right ways, a kind of noise like hearing four different holo shows at the same time. She blinked it away, tried to close her mind from his, because the last thing she needed was her own thinking scrambled. As she dragged Harlow next to Nate — *sweet Jesus he's heavy* — she caught a glint from the dark, reflecting the fire behind her.

Grace walked towards the reflection, tracking whatever it was as it gleamed in the firelight. It was a vertical sliver of reflected flame, and she couldn't make sense of it until she was almost on top of it. It was her sword, or what was left of it. The blade was stuck into the ceramicrete like a promise, the handle up and ready for her hand. For her. She reached down, fingers curling around the grip she knew better than any lover's embrace. Lovers had always been fleeting. But her sword? It was a constant, a reminder of what the world would do to her. And what she could do to it in return.

Grace pulled, the sword coming free of the ground with a small chime. The blade was still less than half as long as it should have been, its normal length paired down to something a shade longer than a good knife. No longer the *katana* she knew how to dance with, this was more of a *ko-wakizashi*. The blade still held promise, but it was a backup weapon now. It had been a long time since Grace had drilled with a companion sword. Her father had never given her a matched *daisho*, a pair of swords meant to be worn together. He'd never *given* her anything; she'd stolen this from under his nose. If *stolen* was the right word, because you couldn't steal something that was a part of you. He'd always frowned at the use of a short sword, calling it a *scrapper's weapon*. Fit for mongrels and those who couldn't keep a firm grip on the sword that mattered.

She held it up in front of her. *Scrapper, huh? Mongrel, huh?* So be it. She'd just need to get in close. Shorter movements. Be the little dog in a big dogfight. She gave it a twirl, feeling the altered weight and balance, then held it close. *Thank you for coming back to me.* This sword was the only thing that had stood by her.

The sword, and Nate. He was still here. She remembered the touch of his skin under her fingers, and immediately wanted to forget. Because that could never be. Nate would never want a *mongrel* like her. She rubbed her face, ran a hand through her hair, and made a noise like a growl. That kind of thinking wasn't helpful right now. There were bigger problems. *Center. Focus.*

Grace stretched. *Well, this is fucked.* The Ezeroc were out here. Nate was down, Harlow was useless. She had half a sword, and their backup was a city away in a starship that had a hole in the side. She looked over at the warehouse, a shadow in the remains of the light from the burning car. If Harlow was right, inside that warehouse was Amedea. Inside that warehouse were other espers. She closed her eyes, listening to the night.

Grace Grace Grace Grace Grace!

She opened her eyes. Well, there was *that*. Espers or no, the warehouse was filled to the brim with a bunch of angry space insects. She looked down at Nate, her face softening, then clicked her comm. It gave a flat chirp, the noise of *not-okay*, but El answered. "What's up?"

"Got a problem," said Grace.

"Big or little?"

"Big," said Grace.

"Republic?"

"Ezeroc are here," said Grace. "There's a warehouse full of bugs. Nate's down—"

"Nate's down?"

"It's okay," said Grace. "He's okay. He's okay, El."

The line hissed with static. "Well, that's something."

"It's not much of something," said Grace, "because he's out cold."

"Doesn't sound okay," she said.

"It's a smaller problem than a warehouse full of death creatures," said Grace. "Death creatures who want to core our minds out like a pumpkin on Halloween. You get me?"

"Clear as a bell."

"Our air car is smashed—"

"Funny story. Ours too."

"You get shot down?" said Grace. "I figure this place has some kind of automated defenses. They don't like visitors."

"Nah," said El. "We ditched and blew up a reactor downtown."

Grace thought about that for a while. "Look, I think that sounds like a good time, but it's not useful detail."

"Sorry."

"So, it'd be helpful," said Grace, "if you could come pick us up. Before the bugs come out and core our minds."

"Small issue," said El, "is that our ship isn't holding atmosphere right now. Hope is swearing, and Kohl's outside trying to cut tethers free, and—"

"Elspeth," said Grace. "Death creatures. *Death. Creatures.* Get the fucking ship in the air."

"Copy that," she said, and the comm clicked off.

Grace! Grace! Grace!

"For crying out loud," said Grace, feeling tired, worn thin. She shouted, "Don't worry! I haven't forgotten about you fuckers!"

There was no noise, no vocal response. But her eyes picked out movement in the gloom, the side of the warehouse opening like a treasure chest, dark promise inside.

CHAPTER NINETEEN

HER COMM CHIRPED. A happy sound, like a small bird, if birds were mechanical and lived inside a computer in your visor. Hope flicked the visor back, sucking in a lungful of air. The haze of welding smoke curled around her, making her cough. She was alone in the cargo bay. The *Tyche* was empty, or almost: just El up top, doing important Helm stuff. Kohl was outside swearing. And here Hope was, in a cargo bay where a bunch of people had died. Bloodstains still on the decking, mopped by a lazy hand (Kohl's?), dark crumbs flaking off when you walked on them.

Which Hope didn't want to do, because it felt wrong. Not that she was religious — thinking people were up there in the sky with a big invisible friend was silly. But if religion was real, if *God* was real, that would have been a comfort, because it'd mean Reiko was up there too. But the whole God-thing just didn't make sense. Hope had flown across all that hard black, the space between stars that people called *the heavens*. There wasn't anything out there but dust and radiation. No, she didn't want to walk over where people had died because it felt disrespectful. She figured she could still respect people after they were gone without worrying about them living forever in a cloud.

"You've got Hope," she said to her comm's chirp, but she wasn't feeling it. Not anymore. Not ... without Reiko. Because that's what Hope had been hopeful about.

"Yeah, we're dusting off in five," said El, her voice sounding as tired as Hope felt. "Cap needs us."

"I heard," said Hope.

"You were listening in?"

"No, I never listen in." She flicked her console, the recording of Grace and El's conversation deleting with a swipe. "You know me. Just minding my business."

"Right. Okay, so you know what's going on."

Hope coughed again, waving a hand in front of her face to clear smoke. The manipulator arms of her rig whined in sympathy, the ends clacking as they looked for metal to hold, to weld. "I know what's going on. But I dunno if you do."

"Hope, we don't have time—"

"Hey!" said Hope. The brittle exterior she had patched over her soul cracked a little, and she bit her lip. She tried to hold in the tears and swallow the pain. She managed it long enough to get a few more words out, but they sounded hard and tight in her ears. "It's not that I don't want to. I'd love to go off saving everyone else's world. You know, when my wife is dead."

"Hope—"

"No, really El. That's not it. It's this." Hope clicked the console on her rig's arm, bringing up full visual. She played the scene out for El. "What we've got here is a big hole, right in the side of the *Tyche*. You walked through it. It's not such a big hole now," she pointed at a piece of metal welded over half the aperture, "because I've put some of this scrap in place."

"What about the original hull—"

"No, great idea. Tell the Engineer how to fix the ship. Don't you think I've tried?"

The comm went silent.

Hope bit her lip — again — and this time it hurt. She'd bit too hard, and tasted copper and disgust. At herself, or the people who'd hurt her *Tyche*, or the people who'd shot Reiko—

Reiko is dead, and you will never feel the love of her arms again.

—or the people who had the cap, or Grace. These people who crewed with her were Hope's last real friends in the whole fucking universe. El didn't deserve her anger. She ran a hand through her hair, pushing pink tinged with grease out of her eyes. "Sorry."

The comm was silent a little longer, long enough that Hope figured quick-worded El had signed off, gone to get a cuppa joe or something stronger, leaving little ol' Hope to her misery in the hollows of the ship. Not where the bright shiny lights lived up on the flight deck, but where the dirt and noise were. But El hadn't gone, and when she spoke, her words were softer than before. "No, Hope. I'm sorry."

Hope rubbed at her face, feeling wetness under her eyes. *Damn smoke.* "What for?"

"It's not for telling you how to do your job. I mean, sure, that was a total dick move on my part. You're the best Engineer I've ever flown with—"

"Come on, El, this isn't a cheer-up-Hope session—"

"Because that's the truth, make no mistake. No, I'm sorry that we haven't had time to raise a glass. To sit down, and tell stories about your wife. I wish I'd known her. Sure, I figured I knew *about* her. The cap and I, we looked into Reiko. We touched her life from afar, tried to work out why you'd been sold up the river like an offering to an angry god. I reckon I know the story well enough, but it don't matter none. Not a bit."

"It doesn't?"

"No. What matters is you, and your stories. So, let me make you a promise."

"What kind of promise?" said Hope. "I don't know there's much to say." She rubbed more water coming from her traitorous eyes.

"We'll sit down and honor our dead," said El. "You and me. Steal some of Kohl's liquor and drink until we can't stand. We'll do it in the hard black, the sound of the universe around us. We'll give Reiko a Viking funeral, Hope, telling stories until there's no words left."

Hope studied the hole in the ship, the dark sky and spaceport visible through the gap. She watched Kohl, running around outside like a mad ant, sawing off the tethers holding the *Tyche* to the heavy earth. Hope thought about El, leaning forward to speak into the comm, all the way up on the flight deck. El, who trying to get the ship to fly again, so they wouldn't have more dead to mourn. So that the ... *Viking funeral* ... would be for just one person. "Okay," said Hope. "Here's the problem. The chunk they cut out of the hull? It was a piece of the cargo bay airlock. The main one. The big one. They screwed it up, El. I don't know why they did that, but it wasn't nice." *Of course it wasn't nice, you idiot. They were trying to destroy your home. Steal your secrets. Capture and maybe kill your friends.* She started over. "It's a big hole, El, and I've just got my little rig. If we had a shipyard we'd be able to fix it up real quick. We ain't got any friends left in the whole universe, so it's just me, and my rig, welding metal on metal. It's not finished yet."

"Will the ship fly?" said El.

"Engines are fine, Helm," said Hope. "She'll fly, but she won't like going out of atmosphere. Or, hell, *we* won't. It'll be loud, but we can fly."

"Get Kohl inside," said El. "We're leaving. You can keep working on the way."

"Kohl's still busy," said Hope, meaning, *I don't want to talk to Kohl.*

"I don't want to talk to him either," said El, and Hope figured she meant *you should talk to him because we need him and we can't leave him behind.*

"Okay," said Hope.

"KOHL," said Hope. The big man almost jumped out of his skin, whirling around, the bright point of the plasma torch like the world's brightest firefly.

He pulled back an old-style welder's visor, something he'd scrounged up from ship's stores, and gave her a glare. "Sneaking up on people will get you dead," he said.

Hope shrugged, the rig hiding most of the movement. Dead might mean she could follow Reiko. To oblivion. "Okay," she said.

Kohl sighed, clicking off the torch. "What's up in Hope's world today?"

"Cap's down. Grace is the only one up. Ezeroc are everywhere," she said. "I think that's about it. No! Wait. Air car's been shot down, so they can't get out. Yeah. That's it."

"Huh," said Kohl, a rumble coming from somewhere inside his chest. "Okay."

"So," said Hope. "So. El said we're leaving in five. But that was a couple minutes ago."

Kohl squinted at her, then pointed with the plasma torch at the cable. Last one, chaining the *Tyche* to the ground. A grapple between the drive shroud and the dock bay tether. "This is still a problem."

"It is," said Hope. "Also, the hull still has a huge hole in it, so even if we get to where we're going, we can't escape into space. And people can shoot in through the hole."

Kohl turned, squinted at the cargo bay door breach. "Need to be a pretty good shot," he said.

"Could you make the shot?"

"Yeah," he said. "Wait. Drunk or sober?"

"Would it matter?"

"Not much," he said. "Give me five more minutes." The *Tyche* gave a big, deep hum, the reactor inside coming up to full power. The drive cowls gave a little shake and a cough, a glow emanating from within as El gave the *Tyche* her warm-up calisthenics. A series of spinning red lights illuminated around the docking bay as the ship's Helm negotiated with ground systems, readying for departure. Those red lights meant *humans, get clear* in a universal language. Big thrusters could fire, meaning an instant pile of ash for any carbon-based lifeform. And an Endless Drive making its negative space field — or a positive space field — could turn human tissue inside out, or to pulp, or just a red smear. Kohl turned, like he was waking from a dream, and pointed to the engines. "What's going on?"

Hope walked back to the *Tyche*. "Helm says we're leaving, so we're leaving."

"Five minutes! C'mon!" But Kohl had already sparked the plasma torch back on, the crackle hiding his words.

Hope was brought up short in her walk by the entrance of five people into the docking bay. Five people in there was unusual because the ship was firing up, and that made it a dangerous environment. Dangerous in the way that made even Kohl nervous. They did not look nervous. They looked armed. Hope didn't pause, she just turned in a nice smooth one-eighty and walked back towards Kohl. "Kohl!"

"Working!"

"No," said Hope. "Let's trade places." She was already getting the rig ready to shear the cable. She'd be faster at it than Kohl anyway, the only reason he was out here and she'd been in there is because he couldn't weld like her. Damaging stuff? He was great at that, and these cables needed no finesse. However, it was time for some role-reversal, because Hope wasn't great at … lifting heavy things.

Kohl looked up, realized he couldn't see anything through the welder's mask, and pulled it off. He took in the five newcomers, looked at Hope, and then jumped on her. She was knocked to the ground — on her best day, she would have raised a tiny 45 kilos on the scales, and that was what just one of Kohl's arms weighed in at — the air going out of her in a grunt. She was about to yell at him, just as soon as air came back into her lungs, which was taking longer than it should, when a series of bright arcs spat over the top of where she'd been.

Plasma. They were trying to shoot me with plasma. That's not very nice.

She still couldn't breathe, but Kohl was off her, running off some damn place. He moved quick for someone that big, and she'd caught one glimpse of his wide eyes — not angry for a change, almost confused, maybe scared — as he made for the *Tyche's* half-healed cargo bay door.

October Kohl is running away and leaving me to die. That's not very nice.

Hope's arms flailed at the ground, like a bug trying to right itself, and then she found herself crawling back towards the docking tether. The cable was charred and melted in a spot, a tiny chip against the nanofibers it was spun from. She'd need to get the whole thing squared away if the *Tyche* would make it off the ground. Hope could just imagine El firing the thrusters, and either the *Tyche* doing tiny circles in the air or tearing one drive clean off. Either way, the ship wouldn't go anywhere with the cable here. It needed to be cut, and that was that. She worked her rig's console, its visor sliding over her face, as its arms reached for the cable.

There was a spatter of energy, pieces of melted metal spitting against her visor. Her HUD lit up with errors.

One of those bad people just shot off one of my rig's arms. That's not very nice.

Hope kicked off the cut-and-clear program in the rig, this time hunkering down near the base of the cable so she wasn't such an opportunistic target. She didn't know if that was the right thing to do, because it made it harder to cut the cable, but she'd seen the cap and Kohl do much the same thing when people were shooting at them, so. The only person she didn't remember doing this was Grace, because Grace fought with a sword, and she had to crash into her enemies, like a wave. Like a tsunami.

She didn't know if Grace would have liked Reiko, but something small inside her said *no*. Grace didn't seem to like people who smashed bottles over the back of her friend's heads. It was a fair rule to live by.

Hope's rig was chewing away at the cable, only seconds having passed. It felt like minutes or hours, but the clock on her HUD made a liar of her mind, the elapsed time between her *ooof* as she hit the docking bay floor and getting to this cable only twenty seconds. It was five seconds longer than Kohl's disappearance into the interior of the *Tyche*. Another plasma blast hissed over her head, making her hunch even further down, and adding another five seconds — twenty-five now — to the clock. The good news? Twenty-five seconds was long enough for Kohl to come back out of the *Tyche*, that new weapon he loved — some kind of laser, Hope didn't care what make or model, but she was intrigued by the computer inside it — under an arm.

She thought she could hear a *click-click-whine-fzump* as the laser felt about the bay, found one person who'd run in and started shooting, and turned that person into a cloud of red steam. Kohl was pointing the weapon at them, not looking, and doing the weirdest thing: he was running back for Hope. He wasn't hiding inside the *Tyche*, he wasn't telling El to *just leave, dammit*. The big man's weapon discharged once more on the way, red light reaching deadly fingers towards another person and turning them — their dreams, everything they'd been from birth to that moment — into a spray of red mist. The red mist was caught in the heated air from the *Tyche's* drives, swirled, and dispersed. Like that person had never been.

Kohl slid to a halt next to her. "Hope. You've got to go."

"Almost done," she said. "Why are you here? You've got to go get the cap. Go get Grace."

He looked confused, then hid it behind the action of pointing his laser again. It discharged, one more person stopping their life's journey instead of continuing. "Can't go without you."

"Don't be silly," she said. "I'm the least useful person in a battle against alien insects." With that, the cable holding the *Tyche* to the ground sheared loose, all the tension leaving it as it snaked free to fall beside the ship.

Kohl frowned, like he was trying to do some complicated arithmetic. Then he said something that sounded like *fuckit* and just grabbed the back of her rig. He dragged her like she weighed nothing — 45KG wasn't nothing! — back towards the *Tyche*. She was yelling at him, not that she could remember afterwards what she was yelling. Things that sounded like *put me down* and *just go* and *why won't you let me die, I want to die, then I can be with her*, and then she was sailing through the air. She saw, for a moment, a higher view of the scene. As she turned through Kohl's toss, she saw the three people laying down fire on the *Tyche*. One of them in that exact moment turned into a spray of red and white steam. Her turn continued, and she was looking up at the *Tyche*, a small spot of carbon scoring under one drive drawing her eye. *I must get to that* she thought, and then she crashed in through the half-healed cargo bay door. The breath went out of her — again! — but she didn't let that stop her. She needed to get back outside, back to Kohl, to get him in the ship so he could save her friends, and also to let her die.

Kohl was at least partially of the same mind, running back up the ramp towards her, his carbine speaking for him. More red, another person gone, just more mist instead of future potential. One of the two remaining people fired a shot, luckier than most — depending on your point of view, not Kohl's — that splashed hot plasma against the ramp. Some of that backwash hit Kohl, his suit burning, and he went down with a yell. Hope curled herself into a ball — she couldn't help it. She wanted to be with Reiko, or be with the nothingness where her wife had gone. But Hope's body still reacted the way that selfish meat did. Always trying to avoid the fire.

When Hope raised her eyes, Kohl was gone. She stabbed the comm. "El. El, we can't go."

"Gotta," said El, the drives of the *Tyche* roaring like judgment. The Endless Drive gave a tiny shove of positive energy, lifting the *Tyche* off the dirt, muck, and misery of people. Towards the clean of the sky.

"El. Kohl's not on yet."

"Hope, *we're on the clock.*"

"Just ... wait," said Hope. *He came back for me.* "I'm going out to get him."

"You're fucking *what?*"

But Hope clicked the comm off, praying — although there was no one to pray to, and if there was, they wouldn't be listening. The universe didn't work like that, because if it did, Reiko would still be alive. The *Tyche* was holding level in the air, floating above the docking bay. Hope grabbed the edge of the tear in the airlock, fingers against rough metal, and dared a look outside. She couldn't see Kohl, couldn't see where his body was. She couldn't hear much of anything either, the roar of the drives and the kickback spume of fire pushing all other noise away. The air was swirling around now, and Hope realized that in all her life she hadn't been outside when a ship was taking off. *Of course you haven't, it's why you're still alive.* Pink hair rushed around Hope's face, and she tried to blink it away, then brush it away, then gave up, closing her visor. She leaned out. "*KOHL!*" But her words were torn away, lost on the wind like the remains of the last person Kohl had turned to red steam.

A flash of red light caught Hope's eye, and another one intruder vanished in a spray of chunks and steam. *He's alive.* She scurried outside the hull, ramp already retracting underneath her, but she knew this music. She had a program for it. The arms of her rig — just three now — scrabbled like crab legs against the hull, holding her there. Gripping with the strength of steel, claws that would hold a crew member fast even under thrust. She made the rig walk around the hull, and that's when she saw him.

October Kohl, swinging from that damn cable, carbine pointed out. His face was sooty and singed, one eye shut, either gone or just squeezed tight against the pain. The roar of the wind as the *Tyche* held steady was everything now, so loud it was impossible to think. Even through the visor of her rig, she could barely think. But Hope didn't need to think. She needed to get to Kohl, swinging out there, hanging above the ground. Her comm line crackled, El saying something like *what's happening* but there just wasn't time to deal with that. Engineering needed focus; you put the biggest fires out first. The rig scrambled Hope around the hull, closer to Kohl. The big man saw her. Shook his head — at her or the situation, she didn't know — and then pointed his gun below. Two more shots. Two more people gone — where had they come from? — and that was that. Kohl let his carbine fall, the sling catching to slap against his bulk as the storm of the engines buffeted him. *This is what it's like when we're just hovering. What is it like when we're moving?*

Hope reached out her hands. Her little arms — 45KG, that's all she had — were stretched towards Kohl. The man swung, back and forth, back and forth, bringing the line closer. Below, a new danger entered the hanger — a vehicle like a tank, all big treads with the muzzle of a massive cannon.

They're trying to shoot the Tyche out of the sky. That's not very nice.

Kohl reached the end of his swing, slamming into Hope. She held on, as tight as she could, and smelled the sweat and fear and old liquor on him for a moment. The tank-thing below was swinging the mouth of its cannon to bear on the *Tyche*, and she looked at Kohl. He nodded, slapped the comm on her wrist, and screamed, "Go! We're in!"

They weren't in. But they were never going to be. The *Tyche* clawed at the sky, engines roaring with the fury of the phoenix, and she climbed for freedom.

A blast came from that cannon, white light as bright as a tiny sun. Metal rained around Hope, pieces of the ship falling back to Earth. The PDCs opened and slid from their slots, one no farther away than five meters, and the *Tyche* answered. The ship seemed to be yelling at those below: *You cannot have me. You cannot have my crew. They are mine, and they will always be safe.*

The tank below turned into slag. Not a big explosion, just a thousand rounds of kinetic anger striking the same spot in a second.

One of the rig's claws slipped free as the thrust piled on, and

Hope couldn't do anything about it. She had her arms around Kohl — she couldn't let him go, not now. Which meant the two of them were attached to the hull by the rig's two remaining claws. She needed a program to pull them back in, but she couldn't do it. Not while she held Kohl. They needed to land. They needed to just take a breath.

Kohl reached for the side of the hull, one hand grabbing for purchase. He held on. Kept them safe. He had two arms. Her rig had two arms. That's all it would take. Just them, working together.

The cargo bay that had seemed so far was now a lot closer. A more realistic goal. As they pulled each other closer to safety, Hope thought: *Well. Not dying today. Maybe tomorrow I can be with Reiko.*

But not today.

CHAPTER TWENTY

WHEN NATE CAME AROUND, it wasn't with the rosy glow of a decent night's rest. He didn't have sleep in the corner of his eyes, nor did he have the pattern of a pillow on his face. He had minor burns, gravel embedded in his chin, and a missing chunk of time.

The air car was still burning, the air heavy with the reek of burning polymers. Grace had vanished.

Nate scrambled to his feet. *Take stock.* Harlow? Still there, looking like he'd rather not be. Fuzzy in the eyes, jaw slack, useless to God and the Empire both as they used to say. *Weapons.* Blaster was in his holster. He pulled it out, checked the charge, spun it on his index finger — *why not* — and slipped it back into the holster. *Damage control.* His metal hand was fine. Metal leg less so; it was complaining like a cheap toaster, all whines and delayed action. *It is what it is.* Good enough to walk. Not good enough to run.

But it was more than good enough to find Grace.

The warehouse doors stood open, which was a change — he was sure of it — from last time he'd looked in that direction. No movement, just a dark opening on the left corner of the building. He looked down at Harlow. "You going to be okay?"

"Is it Tuesday?"

"Great," said Nate, setting off towards the warehouse. It was step-*squeeeeak*, step-*squeeeeak* as his metal leg dragged along. He wanted to curse it, but it didn't feel right to abuse something that had helped save his friends. It meant there was no point in trying for a stealth approach. He sucked at stealth as a general rule anyway. More of a blasters-blazing kind of guy.

The warehouse was silent. No generators, not the gentle hum of a reactor. Whatever had shot them down was running dark, batteries and capacitors doing their jobs.

Unless this was an Ezeroc installation with a warehouse around it. The Ezeroc ship — that giant asteroid that could jump like an Endless-equipped ship, without the limitations — hadn't used a conventional drive or shown an energy signature. Walls of solid rock, the *Tyche's* standard ship-to-ship weapons leaving a scar of carbon but no appreciable damage. The *Tyche* hadn't known what to make of it, which was why he rammed a Republic destroyer right up the asteroid's ass, overloaded the ship's reactor, and ran the hell away. That was a trick that worked once, and would never work again. The Ezeroc seemed smarter than that.

Why, he couldn't say. Maybe it was that humans had never found alien life until now; Nate was betting the bugs gobbled up all the competition out there. The hard black was ruled by a race of insects that used humans for fuel. Maybe it was because these particular asshole bugs were in his hometown living the high life, and no one seemed to care.

Figurative hometown. He was born on Ganymede, which was nice. But Sol was his home *system*. Anyway, the bugs? They seemed to be comfortable here, which implied they were on the leadership team. Managing things from the top.

You're just postponing. Dragging the chain. Sail's not going to hoist itself. Nate stepped inside the warehouse, expecting death from a thousand places. His blaster was in his hand — Lord knows how it got there, but things like that happened sometimes, and he was grateful for it.

Nothing. Not the slow drip of water. Nor the whisper of demonic voices, or the scuttle of things with too many legs.

Just a damn warehouse. No lights though. Which was kind of spooky, but also annoying. He flicked the light on his blaster on, a beam stabbing the darkness. Almost as an afterthought, he flicked the light on his ship suit. *There. Now you can see. Go get your girl.*

Hmm. 'Your girl,' Chevell? Maybe in his dreams. Maybe one day a woman as gifted as Grace Gushiken, as wonderful despite the harsh universe she'd lived through, would find a scarred relic like him interesting.

Still. Got a nice ring to it.

He'd expected the interior of the warehouse to be big. A couple of cells full of wailing espers in the corner, a hundred or so bugs in here for good measure. He'd point his blaster, squeeze off some shots. Buy Grace — who'd be freeing the espers by now, on account of her having two working legs — a little more time. The espers would stream out into the cool night air, run past him with fear in their hearts and the devil on their tails, and he'd die a valiant death as the last man in the breach.

The warehouse was of indeterminate size, because all he could see from here was a long corridor stretching to the right down what looked like the building's entire length. On the interior wall of this corridor — *let's call it the left side, Chevell* — another door was set. All the way down the end. *Okay, so you may still plug a breach with your dying body, but you're gonna have to work for it.*

Step-*squeeeeak*. Step-*squeeeeak*.

The weird thing about the corridor was how empty it was. No holo displays, no pleasant reception team — automated or otherwise — welcoming him to this fine facility. No guards, or guard stations. No water cooler, snack machine, or wastebasket. No consoles. Just an empty corridor, plain white walls playing back to him from the beams of his lights.

Step-*squeeeeak*. Step-*squeeeeak*.

He made the end of the corridor without incident. No Grace. No sounds of fighting. Still no hissing of insect wannabe overlords. Nate faced the door, a simple swinging affair. No lock, no windows. A metal plate fixed into the front to guide where you were supposed to put your hand. He raised his metal fingers and pushed against it, unsurprised to find no resistance. Grace *must* have come this way, so if it had been locked she'd have ... *unlocked* it. As the gold fingers of his synthetic hand led the way, he backed it up with the muzzle of his blaster.

Another corridor. Also white and empty.

At least, that's what he thought until he got the door all the way open and stepped through. This was a mirror of the previous corridor in layout, stretching back to the other side of the building. Straight corridor, one door at the end, right side this time. As he played the beam of his light down the corridor, three thoughts came to him:

1. Bodies.
2. Ant farm.
3. Assholes.

Bodies, because the walls farther down were littered with them. Just like on Absalom Delta, people were embedded in a kind of organic material in the wall, pulsating tubes extending from their mouths, leading away down the corridor, through the walls, or into the floor. The people were shriveled, eaten away from the inside, and the cause was probably some Ezeroc hive Queen motherfucker in here using humans like batteries. That was a thing needing a resolution.

Ant farm, because the layout of the building — the layered corridors, doors at each end — reminded him of one. Simple structures, planned chambers for various uses without aesthetics humans could see other than utility. Except this was constructed by human hands with human materials. The Ezeroc might have used slave hands, but they'd also used slave tech. Ceramicrete. Girders. Hell, there was fucking *plaster* over the top. Like they'd used this as a showroom for a big concept idea. *Hey. We're coming to your world to suck your brains out. Want to invest?*

Assholes, because right down there, near the end, was the man in black. Same dude as back at Harlow's bar. Same dude as on the rooftop (except it couldn't be, because that guy was dead, but they sure looked the same). Nice suit if that was your thing, black shoes reflecting Nate's lights in the gloom. A not-quite-a-smile on his face. This particular man in black was slumped on the ground, slit throat, one arm ending in a bloody stump. There was a pool of blood under him, still with the shiny wet of a fresh kill. Arm looked clean cut, which was a Grace signature if ever there was one. Last time she'd tangled with one of these assholes she hadn't come out on top. This time? Grace was swinging for the fences.

Above the body was a trapdoor of sorts in the ceiling. It was open. Nate figured he knew what had happened: Grace had been cruising down here, minding her own business, and this specific man in black — did they have names, or serial numbers? — tried to jump her. The bugs still seemed to be on their capture-not-kill directive for Grace Gushiken, which wasn't working out great in their favor. Nate walked — step-*squeeeeak*, step-*squeeeeak* — towards the trapdoor. He looked up. Right into a set of eyes, above another black suit.

It was what he'd expected. He didn't scream, jump around, panic, or dive for the ground. Rather than any of those things, he said, "Hey."

The man in black nodded back at him. "You mind?" A hand outstretched, a small wave of the fingers. *Get out of the way.*

"Sure," said Nate, backing up. The man in black slipped down through the trapdoor, swinging it closed behind him. "You guys all shop at the same store, right?"

The man in black laughed, the sound like old leaves blown over grass. Not much of a laugh at all, just mechanical movement of the internal plumbing to mimic something this thing had seen humans do. "Nathan Chevell, you should go."

Nate looked at his blaster, then used the barrel to scratch his forehead. He swapped it to his metal hand, then held it low and ready. "How you figure that?"

"Grace Gushiken is beyond your reach." The man reached under his jacket, pulling out a sword. It was a short, black thing, with one of those nasty nanoblades Nate had seen the last man in black use. Nate backed up another step, and the man in black smiled that same not-quite-a-smile. "Ah. You've seen what we can do with one of these. You're outmatched. I can see inside your mind what happened last time. How Grace had her own blade cut in half. It's hard to fight those who can read your—"

He was picked up off his feet, the top half of his body turning into a pyre of plasma fire. The nanoblade fell to the floor, sliding into the ceramicrete like a hot knife into butter. Nate looked at the sword, then at his metal hand. The hand had pulled the trigger. *Again.* Like it was learning what he wanted, when he wanted it. Without thinking about it. More evidence of illegal AI, but now wasn't the time to be worrying about that.

"Huh," said Nate. He hoped he would live long enough for it to be useful again. These fuckers wouldn't know when he would pull the trigger, but Nate figured the bugs would still give him significant static. Last time he'd fought 'em, they'd swarmed him hoping to implant his body with alien larvae. They'd wanted to take over his ship. It turned out that injecting larvae into a metal arm didn't work so well.

Time to move on.

Nate made the next door, this time pushing it open with his meat hand, the metal hand nosing the blaster to follow. The door swung open into the gloom, revealing a similar situation to last time. Bodies, check. Ant farm, check. No assholes this time. Just Grace. She'd turned at the sound of the door, or perhaps it was the step-*squeeeeak* of his walk. The beam of his light picked out her athletic form — he figured he'd know that anywhere, anytime now — and the half-sword she carried, the metal glinting back at him. Her black hair was half over her face, just one eye visible to look back at him.

"Thank God," said Nate. *She's alive!* "I mean, uh."

But Grace was running back to him. *For* him. She reached him, not even slowing down, and grabbed him in a fierce hug. Buried her face in his collar. Nate put his arms around her, flesh hand holding her tight, metal hand clumsy with the blaster, and took a breath of her hair. She wasn't his girl. But he could dream.

"You came," she said, pulling away. He didn't want her to.

"Always," he said. "Thanks for not letting me barbecue out there. You know."

"Thanks for not letting me burn to death in a fiery explosion," she said. "You know."

"Right," said Nate. *Uh. Don't say 'uh,' Chevell.* "So. Uh." He winced. "We got your basic Ezeroc infestation, looks like."

"Looks like. I found another one of those guys dressed all in black."

"Me too. I mean, your one, and then another one."

"From the roof?"

He saw she was sweaty and grimy, a strand of hair down over her face. He wanted to push that strand of hair away, and stilled his fingers. "The very same," he said. "I figure, this is an elaborate trap or it's Ezeroc central. Ant farm."

"The layout?"

"Yeah."

She nodded. "There's another possibility."

"Which is?"

"It's both," said Grace. "It's a trap. And it's Ezeroc central."

"That's an uncomfortable thought," said Nate. He paused. *Fuck it.* "Grace?"

"Nate."

"You know what they're building the trap *for*, don't you? *Who* they're building it for?"

"I think so," she said.

"Then why the hell did you come in here?" He wanted to shake her. He wanted to say, *I am terrified because I do not want to lose you,* but it wouldn't have been right, because she wasn't his to lose. Just more Chevell fantasies. "You should have stayed outside. Waited."

She cocked her head sideways at him, like she was listening to something only she could hear. "Two things," she said.

"Shoot."

"First thing. Let's say you saw a box. A trap. And inside the trap was the person who wanted to trap you. Would you walk away and let them make a better trap? Or would you go in there and extermi-nate them?"

"This is a different thing," said Nate. "Totally different. I mean. Because, this is a race of aliens bent on consuming all of humanity for fuel. And because they have been trying to get you — like, *specifically* you — since we bumped into them."

"Answer the question," said Grace.

"I'd go in the fucking box with a bunch of grenades and turn everything inside into spare parts," said Nate.

"The second thing," said Grace, as if Nate had agreed with her, which he guessed he had, "is I don't want to lose you either." And she leaned forward, not very far because they were still close, and kissed his lips. He felt his eyes go wide, a series of thoughts skipping through his mind like stones across a pond. *She doesn't care about the arm, or the leg. Grace doesn't care about the fire. She came in here because she didn't want you to die.* And then, the important one: *She is kissing you — kiss her back.* So he did, a hand reaching up to the back of her head, his body pressing against hers.

They broke apart. She gave him a small smile. "So, Nathan Chev-ell. You ready to turn everything in this box into spare parts? With me. Together."

"Together," said Nate. "I don't have any grenades. But..."

"But what?"

"I've got something better," he said.

CHAPTER TWENTY-ONE

THE *TYCHE* BUCKED and yawed under her fingers, the sticks trembling like they were injured. El clenched her teeth, the thrust of the drives keeping her firm in the acceleration couch. The thrust wasn't making her clench her teeth: it was that damn hole in the stern of the ship. The *Tyche* wasn't sealed, her sleek lines disrupted by the sucking vortex created by the breach in the hull. She pulled up a feed of the cargo hold, saw Hope in her rig — which looked *fucked*, missing an arm, one other arm dragging like it'd had a stroke — trying to weld the door sealed.

October Kohl held a piece of metal against the storm of the wind. Every time he almost got it seated, the vortex effect would pop it out.

Looks rough, thought El. But hey, at least they weren't dead, or in a Republic reprograming facility.

She wasn't pushing the *Tyche* that hard, just a little bit of thrust to keep her in the air. The ship was eager for it, like she knew where they were going. The ship remembered the last time they'd tangled with the Ezeroc, and how another Earth ship — the *Gladiator* — had given her life so the *Tyche* could live. Ships *knew*. And they paid it forward, both the good and the bad.

Speaking of knowing... The RADAR blipped, her holo spitting out a stream of tactical information. The database had been updated courtesy of the selfsame *Gladiator*, and the *Tyche* knew about the latest ships and models, their weapons, their mass, their defenses. The Goddess of Luck didn't need so much luck anymore: she had hard data. Automated systems double-checked the RADAR with another ping, then LIDAR reached out across the air, found and mapped the targets, and presented them to El like a dog presenting a retrieved stick. *Here you go. Look what I found.*

"Good girl," said El. Then, "Well, the Republic have brought themselves a pair of knives to a blaster fight."

The comm chirped. Male, full of the arrogance of a bureaucrat with a whisker too much power. "Free trader *Tyche*, this is—"

"Imma have to cut you off there, chief," said El. He'd said *Tyche* like *tai chi*, and that was plain rude. "It's not the martial art. It's the Greek Goddess. Hard K sound, you get me. Tai. Ki."

"Say again, *Tyche*—"

"Don't know who you're talking to," said El, "but there ain't no ship out here that's named after a system of defense training known for its health benefits." She kept her hands on the sticks, one eye on the feed from the hold. It looked like Kohl and Hope were getting along *fine*. That breach was almost not a breach. Give them a little longer, and they could bust out of this thin pillow of air and get back into the hard black, where they belonged. Shit had gone wrong on Absalom Delta, but worse shit had gone wrong here.

"Tai Ki," said the voice. "Tai Ki."

"That's it," said El. "This is the free trader *Tyche* responding to unidentified Republic vessel. You have failed to identify yourself. Please respond."

There was a pause. "I haven't had a chance," said the man, "because—"

"And the thing is, it's *law*," said El. "Unless we're under arrest, which you haven't said, and by the way, good *luck* to you in those tin cups you're flying if you try that shit with me. You need to identify yourself, unidentified vessel, or we will open fire." That was a tiny — fractional — variation of the truth, because strictly speaking El could only fire on them if she was an acting officer of the Republic Navy, which she wasn't. But assholes like this weren't big on fact-checking. Just big on weight-throwing.

"*Tyche*, this is the Republic police vessel *Falling Star*," said the man. "I am accompanied by the Republic police vessel *Rolling Thunder*. We—"

"Who names your ships?" said El. "Someone with an inferiority complex?" She tweaked some of the drive controls, giving a little more stability to the starboard actuator. Wouldn't want that flying off, what with a bunch of aliens to fight.

"*Tyche*, we order you to cease flight and prepare to be boarded."

El stared at the comm for a second. "You're joking."

"This is not a joke, *Tyche*. We have intelligence—"

"Because we're not in space, dumbass," she said. "Ceasing flight will lead to a heightened incident of crashing. I don't know about you, but I don't crash my ships."

"*Tyche*, you need to land your vessel at these coordinates," said the voice.

"Bite my ass." Before the coordinates arrived El cut the comm. She pulled up the internal channel. "Hope?"

"You've got Hope," said the Engineer, exhaustion in her voice. A little something else too — a memory of *actual* hope. El might have been imaging the last.

"How we doing on that repair?"

"Lousy. It's a horrible weld. Seam's all wrong. Haven't feathered the bead right. I mean, it'll stop us sucking vacuum and hard rads, but they'd kick me out of the Guild if they saw it."

"Hope? They *did* kick you out of the Guild."

"Oh. Right."

Kohl's voice came in. "What's up, El? We got trouble?"

"The best kind," said El. "We've got spare targets. Here's what we'll do."

THREE SHIPS BLASTED across the night sky. One was a warship, a heavy lifter from back when the Old Empire stood tall as humanity's bastion against the unknown, the Republic a hungry pup biting at its ankles. It was a common design, or common enough at the time, but enough dropping into atmosphere under fire had seen them winnowed out, lost to the storm of war, nothing but spare parts in junk piles if there was anything left at all. They were used, and used hard, their Endless Drives capable of jumping them into new systems at a moment's notice. Small enough to slip through a RADAR net like a small rock in the vast hard black. Only a few were left, a very lucky few.

This was one of the luckiest. Her previous owner — a bartender who had no idea what to do with a heavy lifter aside from smuggling things onto a planet that had everything — had left her to stagnate in a hanger. No name, no Helm, no Engineer. No crew, no heart. Her new captain had found her, put a hand on the old metal of her hull, and called her by her true name: *Tyche*. Goddess of Luck. Causer of great destruction, famines, plagues. And great fortune, to those who loved her. She would lay down her life for those who touched her with a gentle hand.

Dying wasn't required. What was required was a little of that famous luck. Which brings us to: the other two ships.

Policing vessels, designed for coast guard duty where the coast was the hard black of the Sol system. Neither had been shown a gentle hand. But they also hadn't tasted the kiss of Ares. Hadn't been fired on, plasma streaming around as they fell into atmosphere, the fire of re-entry screaming defiance at defenders below. Their ungentle care was in the hands of civilian criminals. Nothing like the hard talk of enemy armies, fighting until their last so that whole planets could live.

It wasn't that they were on different teams. It wasn't that they were in different leagues. The policing vehicles were playing, and the *Tyche* was built to go to war. She didn't talk, dance, or cajole through delicate legal systems. She fought.

The policing ships were on a hard burn, trying to keep up with the *Tyche*. The *Tyche*, sprinting before them, her fusion drives kicking out fire and fury. The ship's Engineer, reducing the thrust so buildings weren't incinerated. It wasn't efficient, it wasn't safe for the *Tyche*, but it would stop a rain of building debris from killing hundreds of thousands of people. Safe didn't matter so much when you had a little luck on your side. The load, though? That was another matter. That kind of strain — drives burning hot, Endless systems providing lift, PDCs fangs-out, masers and lasers online — should have overtaxed the reactor the *Tyche* was born with. But sometime since she'd last been in a registered shipyard, she'd had a new heart. Borrowed from another dying god: the *Ravana's* reactor burned within. Crazy, putting a torch that bright in a smaller hull. That's what they'd call her Engineer. Crazy, or gifted. Or just plain lucky.

Citizens of the Republic, already experiencing high levels of anxiety from a reactor incident earlier in the day, were on high alert. Construction sites didn't just explode, sucking down girders like over-done spaghetti. Fatalities had been zero, casualties light, a miracle of safe shutdowns in modern reactors. The Republic news anchors agreed: everyone had been so very lucky. Luck or otherwise, those citizens of the bright Republic — under whose flag the *Tyche* sailed — watched the skies that night, eyes up. Looking for falling air cars. Instead, they saw a goddess in her prime, throwing spears at dogs that nipped at her heels.

The *Tyche* zipped over the top of the cityscape, soaring like the idea of freedom itself. Policing vehicles behind stabbed at her with sharp knives made of light and energy, but their attack was insufficient. The *Tyche* was used to battle; she saw the fire coming like an underarm toss and banked out of the way. Her Helm would have had a holo up, tactical readouts showing the pace of battle — slow, by military standards — and maybe given a small, tight smile as she worked the sticks. Her Engineer would have been in the engine room, heat and steam all around, coaxing the *Ravana's* borrowed heart to not destroy the goddess it now lived in.

All of this cat-and-mouse was a means to an end. The *Tyche* was running, but she wasn't running *away*. She was running *to*, her target south and west of the city center. To an old and dark part of town, where lights burned low and crime burned high. The perfect place to hide imperfect deeds. Or an alien outpost, if that was how you wanted to roll the dice. Aliens, on Earth: if only the bugs knew they were rolling dice against the Goddess of Luck.

Strained and tired from a run without a catch, one of the Republic vessels launched missiles. Guided, hard-locked on the shape and texture of the *Tyche's* hull. Those rockets knew her like the shipyard that birthed her, the best tech money could buy. It was a bad call for all parties: bad for the *Tyche*, because one of those rockets would core her hull, burn to ash everything inside, and rain debris on the city below, strewn out over kilometers at the velocities they were traveling at. Bad for the citizens of the city, because of that selfsame debris rain, hot with radiation and plain old kinetic load. Bad for the Republic flight jockey who'd pulled the trigger, because raining radiation on the citizens — even in the hard, cool judgment of an efficient Republic — was a surefire way to get yourself down the bottom of the rung. You'd never put your boots on a ladder again, and you might find yourself cutting rock out of an asteroid for the rest of your days.

Bad call all around. It was ... just plain *lucky* that a goddess flew the skies that night.

Two rockets, nothing fancy enough to take down a capital ship; the policing arm of the Republic didn't have access to that kind of ordnance. Just big enough to be proper mischief for the Goddess of

Luck, who was focused on different priorities that night. But that's what family was for: when you were up to your eyeballs in alligators, someone else had your back. Here, the *Tyche's* Helm saw those two rockets coming at her, and did nothing. Not until they were very, very close. The two rockets galloped like greyhounds in tandem, rushing for the *Tyche's* rear, where her armor was weakest. Drives bright in the night sky, too bright to miss. As they were close, the Helm did something unorthodox with the Endless Drive. She unbalanced the negative mass field that gave vertical lift on the left side of the ship, causing the *Tyche* to lean in that direction. At the same time, the *Tyche's* Helm hit the positive mass generator of the Endless system on the right side, creating temporary gravity above the hull. The effect was the *Tyche* rolled like a puppy, spiraling sideways through the air, the frame of the ship shaking with the strain of it. Strained, but not broken, courtesy of another fallen ally: the *Gladiator* had reshaped the inside spar of the *Tyche*, making her stronger than new. Inside the *Tyche* it would have been chaos, up becoming down, left becoming right. A deckhand, unsecured, would have been tossed around inside to rattle against the hard surfaces of the hull. Swearing, cursing the Helm. The Engineer would have laid a hand on a reactor burning too hot while the *Tyche* skipped out of harm's way.

Skipped, and then turned angry eyes on those missiles as they overshot. They'd swing back around, but there was a high risk of them impacting against a civilian structure in a city's tight corridors. Masers mounted at the front of the *Tyche* — sharp, invisible teeth — reached out, tearing at the missiles. The ship pulled them from the sky in a hail of deconstructed molten metal.

That job done, the *Tyche* kept her course. They were on the clock. Being lucky was one thing, but Chronos didn't wait on luck. He kept his own counsel, kept his own pace. It wouldn't do to play dice with him.

The choice was clear at this point: destroy the yapping dogs, or use them.

Destroy them: they'd stop being a nuisance, and let *Tyche* get to where she was going before Chronos deemed it no longer important.

Use them: because part of being lucky was to have more friends than enemies. It was always good to have friends.

Use them it was. Ahead of the *Tyche*, a tall spire reached up. The tallest building in the city, it was the Republic Command Center, full of busy and important people. And a full roster of Republic military, troops designed to keep order should disorder come knocking at their door. The Republic Command Center was on the way, and knocking was the order of the day. The *Tyche* herself wouldn't have known this was in the flight plan, but it was possible her Helm had this crazy idea all along.

Two more missiles launched at the *Tyche*, bright spears thrown at her heart. This was a music she knew, dance steps that were pure muscle memory. And now she knew the trick of rolling out of harm's way, the goal of firing those missiles was questionable. What wasn't questionable was the timing, which was fortuitous. *Lucky.*

The spire ahead, the *Tyche's* Helm pushed the drives a little harder. The ship needed forward momentum, easy to buy at the cost of more joules, the joy of the *Ravana's* beating heart urging her on. She came at the Republic tower, her vector tight and close. Inside the tower, alarms would have been sounding, a call to general quarters issued to those troops. Flight crews would scramble for their ships, not mere policing vessels this time but the hardened edge of the Republic's military. Because you didn't keep police to guard your secrets. You kept the hounds of war, borrowed Cerberus's leash, and made a deal with the devil to keep everything quiet.

As the *Tyche* neared the tower, she cut her drive burn. Out like a snuffed candle, the roar going silent, the wash vanishing. The drives still glowed with remembered heat as the *Tyche* sailed, silent as a thrown stone, past the windows of the tower. Faces stared out, fear, terror, anger, and indignation shining out from them. Those faces would have seen the *Tyche's* turning thrusters fire, bringing the heavy lifter around, keeping the *Tyche's* nose pointed at the

CHAPTER TWENTY-TWO

"SERIOUSLY, Nate. How would *I* know what's in there?" Grace gave him a hard stare, but she couldn't keep it up. Not because he didn't deserve it, but because he deserved better. "I'm sorry."

"I figured because," said Nate, wiggling his metal fingers in the air, "you know. Sorcery."

"It's science," said Grace. "It came out of a test tube. Genetic manipulation of a recessive gene set."

"Like I said. Sorcery." He seemed to notice his own hand, pulled it back into a fist, and coughed. "Look, it's just ... impressive, is all."

"Well," said Grace. *Impressive. Captain Chevell, no longer scourge of the espers. Maybe he understands, at least a little.* "I just got here. Like you. I can tell you a couple things."

"Shoot."

"There are Ezeroc in there. I guess more than one or two. Looking at the human batteries embedded in the walls—"

"We'll need to fix that," said Nate.

"Later. Human batteries in the walls, well, it means we've got another Queen." Grace frowned. "Nate, you don't know what it's like. In your mind? Hard like rain, soft like fire."

"That makes zero sense."

"It's not meant to make sense, Nate. They're aliens." Grace frowned. "There's no words, okay? Just, if I go all crazy, knock me out."

"You seem fine." He checked his blaster, not meeting her eyes. She picked up *denial/no/no*. "Like you've learned tricks since last time."

"I'm a quick study, but I'm not my father," said Grace. "He was a master. Telepathy was his strong ally. Power walked at his side. He was—"

"Grace."

"I'm just saying—"

"Grace," said Nate. He put a hand on her arm, and she realized the fist of that arm was clenched tight around the hilt of her sword. The blade raised, stabbing the air. He spoke, soft and gentle, as he leaned close to her. "He was an *asshole*."

She laughed. Oh God, how she needed that, the release shaking her shoulders. "Thanks."

"Yeah. Okay, so there's bugs in there. How you figure you'll go with that sword?" He let her arm go, fingers lingering for a second. A promise of what could be, if only they could survive the next ten minutes. Or hour. Or day.

She turned the sword in her hand. "I have to fight closer than I'd like. I don't know. The drones? I'm guessing that'll be a challenge, but possible."

"What about the crabs?"

"Crabs?"

"Big fuckers. Armored."

"Those guys," said Grace. "Hmm. Could cut off a leg or two with a longer sword, but..."

"Yeah. Go low," said Nate. "The top's harder than the hull of a starship. Belly's a little softer." He gestured with his blaster. "One of these is good enough from underneath. On top? Ship weapons, maybe, but a blaster..." His voice trailed off. "Still. What are the odds of them having one of the crabs?"

"High," said Grace. She pointed at the door. "You ready?"

"Born ready," said Nate. He paused, looked at his metal hand. "Well. There was that *one* time—"

"Close enough," said Grace, and kicked the door open.

INSIDE WAS A LARGER room than she'd been expecting. She'd been expecting another corridor, another man in black, and more human batteries. The organic tendrils were here, conduits from the Ezeroc's food leading across the floor and through another wall. In the middle of the room was a chair. There were lights set about it, but far from being helpful at illuminating the room they seemed only to serve the purpose of isolating the chair's occupant from the rest of the area. They presented a deeper contrast from an island of illumination to the gloom.

The chair's occupant? Amedea. She was beaten bloody, bruised, head lolling to one side. Organic material tethered her to the chair like ropes, binding her arms behind her and keeping her immobile. The leader of the Resistance had been in the enemy's custody, and they had not been gentle with her.

This raised interesting questions for another time, the prime of which was: if the Republic had raided the Resistance base, and Amedea was here in an Ezeroc outpost, did that mean the Republic was riddled with Ezeroc agents? Men in black, controlling the minds of the humans around them? Slipping cockroaches into the blood-stream of influential people, eating at their brains, and becoming heads of state?

An interesting question, but one for another time, because of the four other occupants of the room. Ezeroc drones stood, one in each corner. They were like statues as Grace burst into the room, Nate on her heels. Like statues, until one of Amedea's eyes opened. It wasn't a good eye, blood dripping into it, but it was an eye that would open. Amedea spoke one word: "Run."

And that was when the Ezeroc drones stopped being immobile, an audible hiss sounding from them. The menace of that sound made Grace feel like they were surrounded, the door behind them slipping closed. Sure, they *could* go back out that way, but that's not why they were here. They were here to find the center of this corruption. Cut it out by plasma or steel or both.

She felt fear's cold kiss. A righteous fear, because last time she'd come to the Ezeroc, they had pushed her mind low and taken her body over. They wanted her. Nate's voice came to her, and it was like feeling warm on a beach, waves lapping at her toes. "Grace? Remember, we're not outnumbered."

"Nate, there are *four* of them."

He laughed. "We're not outnumbered, Grace. We've just got a wider selection of targets." She stole a look at him, wanting to keep eyes on the four Ezeroc but unable to help herself. He stood tall, blaster out, gold fingers clenched around the grip of the weapon. Standing like he owned the room, like he was comfortable here. Captain Nathan Chevell, of the Emperor's Black. She could see it now, the man behind the mask.

Her shoulders relaxed. If he was comfortable here, and he was comfortable with her — the nasty inside of her, the esper that everyone else feared — then she was comfortable too. "More targets," she said.

Grace! Grace! Grace! Grace!

"Don't listen to them, Grace," rasped Amedea.

Nate looked sideways at Amedea, then to Grace. "What's she talking about?" One of the Ezeroc peeled itself away from the wall, scuttling towards them, and Nate pointed his blaster at it. He squeezed the trigger, blowing it into a shower of burning meat. "I can't hear a thing."

"They're in my mind," said Grace. "Under my skin."

"So, Grace Gushiken." He pointed his blaster at one of the remaining Ezeroc drones. *"Go get under their skin."*

She felt the blade in her hand, short but still sharp. *Okay, then. Under the skin it is.* She ran towards Amedea, because if she was Ezeroc with bait in a trap she'd want to nip off any problems from said bait in the bud. It was wise she'd chosen that direction because one of the Ezeroc was speeding towards Amedea, claws stretched out. Those long limbs, with their sharp serrated edge and stabbing points. Grace kept running, right past Amedea, and towards the Ezeroc. She ducked under its slicing arms, dropping to her knees and sliding on the smooth floor of the warehouse. Her sword held up, she pulled it in a sharp arc, the length of the blade not the elegant length she was used to. But long enough, a limb sliced free from the Ezeroc to clatter against the floor next to her. She heard a hiss from the thing, the odor of it all around her, a kind of rotten cinnamon, unlike any Earth scent. The Ezeroc didn't pause, just swinging those claws at her, and she rolled sideways. Grace turned the roll into a rise, coming to her feet a couple meters away from the thing. It opened its mandibles at her, then came for her on the remaining five legs.

Perfect. Just what she was waiting for.

Rather than trying for distance — her sword wouldn't allow it — she came in close. Like a dance partner. Like a lover. Her sword started low and finished high, the Ezeroc coming to a stumbling halt, those mandibles clacking above her once, twice, then no more. Her sword had scribed through the front of the Ezeroc's exoskeleton, opening the shell. Steaming insides pushed through the breach, then fell out in a rush. The Ezeroc clattered to the floor, back two legs kicking the air.

Grace turned back to Amedea. She hadn't noticed it while she was fighting the Ezeroc, but Nate had blown the other two Ezeroc into smoking fragments, still standing where she'd left his side. He was turning in a slow circle, checking the room for hostiles. Not like there was anywhere to hide, but she liked that about him. Thorough. Professional. A protector.

You've never had someone have your back before, Grace. It feels good.

She turned the sword's edge against Amedea's bonds, severing the organic substance. It parted like hemp, the material warm to the touch. *Now that's disturbing.* She came around to face Amedea. "Come on, we've got to go."

"You," said Amedea. She licked her lips, tried again. "You shouldn't have come."

"Hey, you *wanted* us to come save your friends, remember?" said Nate.

"That was before." Amedea was trying to stand. "Before I knew."

Grace was checking out Amedea, patting down her body and her clothes. She was looking for punctures, because that's how they got into you. She found nothing.

"Knew what?" said Nate.

"Everything," said Amedea.

CHAPTER TWENTY-THREE

NATE LOOKED at the piles of Ezeroc remains — some on fire, courtesy of his blaster, and one just plain ol' steaming, courtesy of Grace. He cocked his head at Amedea. "What do you mean by, 'everything?'"

"Captain," said Amedea, looking away from Grace, but not *to* Nate. She was staring at the door they hadn't opened yet. "You have to realize. We thought … *I* thought we were dealing with subversives at the top."

"We're not?" said Nate. "What the fuck are we doing then?"

"The subversives are at the top," said Amedea, "but they invited something else in. It didn't even have to knock. They went *looking*. And now we're all damned."

"The Ezeroc," said Grace, her gaze turning towards the door as well.

"Hey," said Nate. He pointed his blaster at the door. "Is something going to come through that door and try and eat our faces?" He caught the looks Amedea and Grace gave him. "What?"

"You don't hear them?" said Grace. "Not at all?"

"Hear what?" said Nate. "I mean, you're freaking me out here."

He tried to make a joke of it, then realized it was true. *Shit.* "I'll go open the door. It'll be, I don't know, a broom closet or something." He stamped over to the door — leg still step-*squeeeeak*ing as he went. He grabbed the handle and gave it a yank. The door opened, and behind it was an Ezeroc drone, hissing and lunging at him. Bright plasma impacted against it, tearing it in half, pieces falling into the room beyond. Nate looked down at his metal hand holding his blaster, and thought, *Man, I don't remember pulling the trigger.* In the brief silence that followed, he checked the room out. Similar size to the one they found Amedea in. Otherwise empty, if you didn't count the tendrils leading down through a trapdoor set in the floor. The trapdoor wasn't tiny; it was huge, and it was open, and it was dark inside. Nate turned back to Grace and Amedea. "Okay, so it's not a broom closet." They were staring at him. "What?"

"They don't ... effect your mind?" said Amedea. "Make you want to do things?"

"They make me want to shoot them all," said Nate. "That's about it."

Grace walked to him, put a hand on his arm. She leaned close. "Nate, they get in your mind. Under your skin. Take you over. Remember what happened to me on Absalom Delta?" She flicked her eyes back Amedea's way without turning her head, and lowered her voice. "It'd be hard to know what they'd do to you if they had enough time."

"I'm okay," said Amedea. "They didn't ... turn me." She touched tentative fingers against her swollen eye. "They just hurt me. I don't know what they wanted."

"Back in the day," said Nate, "when I wore the Black, the Intelligencers could break someone's mind. Or into, I dunno the term. Never sat right with me. But the way they told it, there were weak people and strong people. Weak might not be the right word. You espers..." he trailed off, picking up the flattening of Grace's face, the hardening of her heart as she waited for just another normal to slander her. He swallowed. "I'm sorry."

"It's okay," said Grace, turning her face away.

"It's really not," said Nate. "It's ... hard. What they did..." The silence stretched.

"Captain," said Amedea, wobbling to her feet. "We are not all cut from the same cloth." She tried a chuckle, wincing as it turned into a cough. "Some of us are more ... homespun."

Nate glanced back at the darkness of the trapdoor. "I get you. Anyway. The ... *Intelligencers*, they would get in your head—"

"We called it Unlocking," said Amedea. "Not breaking."

"Call it what the fuck you like," said Nate. "But they're using your tricks on you."

"What tricks?" said Grace, looking between Nate and Amedea.

Amedea spoke first, hunched like her shoulders were too heavy to lift. "Pain is never a good motivator for the truth. Torturers of old worked this out, and as better tools became available ... drugs, sensory deprivation, social isolation ... intelligence communities adapted. You don't have to hurt someone to get them to tell secrets. When you have people who can pick thoughts out of someone's mind? You just have to look inside."

"But if someone's mind is strong, you can't look," said Nate. "You need to smash the walls down."

"Unlocking," said Amedea.

"If memory serves, you can weaken walls by hurting the body. Take enough time, use enough pain, and..." He shrugged. "That's what Dom said, anyway."

"The Emperor?" said Grace.

"Yeah," said Nate. "He and I never agreed on this particular point." He looked at Amedea. "I guess it kind of sucks to have your tricks used on you, right?"

"It kind of sucks," she agreed. She started a slow walk towards them. "They don't want me. They want her." She raised a shaky arm to Grace.

"Why?" said Grace.

"Well, that's what I mean by 'everything,'" said Amedea. "The problem with Unlocking is that it's a two-way street, if you're good enough. And I'm ... they used to say I was one of the best." She pushed past Nate and Grace, walking towards the trapdoor. "The rest of them are down there. Many of them are hurt. Some of them have been turned. We still need to get them out."

"We'll solve that problem in a minute," said Nate. "Back to the 'everything' part."

"Well," said Amedea. "What do you know about the moon?"

Nate's comm chirped, El's voice coming over it. "Cap, we're closing in on your location."

Nate felt the grin coming to his face. *Finally.* A little honest backup. A few people in your corner. They'd be on the *Tyche* in a moment, safe and sound. "Glad to hear your voice, Helm. We'll have a few to pick up."

"Yeah, not likely," said El. "I've brought friends."

Nate felt his grin become fixed. "Uh, El? Come again. What do you mean by 'friends?'"

"A whole party," she said. "I don't know. Republic, I guess?"

"How many?"

"All of 'em, I think," she said, cutting off the comm.

"Well, shit," said Grace, Nate watching as she looked at the hole. Her face turned to look at her broken sword. "This day isn't going quite how I thought it would."

"I need a weapon," said Amedea.

"I need a vacation," said Nate. "Neither of those things is likely to happen anytime soon. Tell me about the moon."

"The Ezeroc's homeworld," said Amedea, "is a ball of rock. Or it is now. They ate pretty much everything else. The apex predator of all apex predators."

"Are you saying they've got a base on the fucking *moon?*" said Nate. He looked up at the roof, like he could see the sky, then felt foolish. "Those assholes."

"Not a base," said Amedea. "I'm saying this: they have corrupted the Republic government, right at the top. They have mastered the genetics of humanity, and can now build human clones with insect brains. And they have built a new starship, captain."

"A starship," said Nate, not getting it.

"Oh, my God," said Grace. "The moon."

Nate blinked, looking at Grace, then Amedea, then the hole in the floor. "You're kidding."

"No," said Amedea. "This warehouse is a tiny outpost. The real action is up there." She pointed at the ceiling. "They can ... *feel* us, Captain. Across space. The Intelligencers ... the *espers*, if you will. We're the fire that brought them here. Like a beacon. But we're also humanity's last hope. We can fight their minds with our minds."

"All y'all assholes," said Nate, "were humanity's downfall last time."

"Maybe it's time to give us another chance," said Amedea.

Nate stared at her. "You want us to trust you?"

"Yes," said Amedea. "What do you say, Captain?"

Nate just stared at her.

"Captain?"

"I'm thinking," he said. "I'd like to say ... well, my initial answer is this. There is *no way* you guys are getting put in charge again."

"We're best suited to leading," said Amedea. "We're—"

"Shut up," said Grace.

"Grace," said Amedea. "You know—"

"Shut *up*," said Grace. "The captain's right. There's no way people like *us* should be in charge. The unrepresentative few should never rule the many. Especially when so many of us are ... evil."

Nate knew she was thinking of someone else, a man who should have loved her and protected her but did nothing like that. He cleared his throat. "I tell you what, Amedea. Let's get your people out first. Because much as I have problems with evil mind controlling overlords, an insectoid race that uses humans as fuel is a little worse. And, I guess, fire with fire, right? We'll need each other before this is done."

"You must follow my direction," said Amedea.

"Not a chance," said Nate.

"But—"

"My ship, my rules," said Nate. "If you don't like it, get your own ride home."

THE STEPS DOWN into the holding pens were dark, slick with moisture. The moisture was some kind of slime, a pale green to Nate's light. "That is unpleasant." Along with the moisture were the tendrils, those feed lines leading down to ... something else.

Grace stepped down the steps. "It's not wholesome," she agreed.

Amedea was behind them, slower in pace, and not at all happy with how things were working out for her. That was just *fine* from Nate's perspective. There was governing, and then there was ruling through mind control. The second? Not a great option. He wondered though: when they built the espers in the lab, did they mint them with a special *asshole* function?

His eyes went back to Grace, and he thought: *No.*

The pit — because that's what it was, a cavern carved into the earth — was not very large. There were pens constructed of an organic material, a little bit like the vines that had tethered Amedea to the chair. *I do not want to meet whatever is extruding that shit.* The mission was clear: get to the Resistance, get them out. If they happened to stumble on a couple big bombs, maybe they could apply chill-out to the monster at the end of the cave, but it wasn't a priority. Besides, Queens didn't move that fast, what with them stuck to the feeding tendrils.

Still. As Grace had said, *unwholesome*. "There's a thing that I don't get," said Nate. "Why aren't there any guards?"

"You don't need guards when you can control minds," said Grace. She held her sword low and ready.

"I'd like guards as a kind of backup," said Nate. "Against people like me, you know?"

"You are kind of annoying," said Grace.

They reached the bottom of the steps. Call it two stories down. The drip of ... *moisture* sounded from farther in the cave. Nate played his light around, picking out the occupants of the cages. People, men and women who looked tired, hungry, sleep-deprived, and in most cases, beaten bloody. The vaunted Resistance, mostly resisting dying of exposure about now. Nate sighed. That wasn't helpful thinking. *Best get them out.* He hurried over to one cage, gaunt faces looking back at him.

"Hey," he said. He softened his voice. "Hey. We'll get you out. Back up. Away from the ... bar ... stuff." He gestured with his blaster, the occupants of the cage backing away. He fired plasma into the material, shearing it with ease. Some of it fell away with a wet *plop*, some of it crisped.

There was a hiss from further back in the cave. "That's not good," said Grace.

A man, tall and thin, came through the cage first. He clasped Nate on the shoulder. "Thank you, friend." His eyes found Amedea. "Amedea."

"Chad." *Chad. Really?* But Amedea was already pointed up the steps. "That way. We'll have a ride coming soon."

Chad turned to look at Nate. "Have you taken care of the guards?"

"See?" said Nate. "Guards. What did I tell you?"

"Yes," said Grace, giving him a look. "The way up is safe."

"Oh," said Chad. "Oh."

"Uh," said Nate. "I feel like I'm missing something."

"It's nothing," said Chad. "We're all going to die, is all." His eyes went up to the ceiling of the cavern.

Nate followed his eyes, then — almost as an afterthought, because he didn't want to look — he played his light over the roof. Up there, clutching at the rock, were crabs, the massive Ezeroc guardians. They moved and shifted under the light, scuttling out of its touch like cockroaches exposed from under a rock. One of them — a particularly big, nasty-looking one — gave that hissing noise.

"Uh huh," said Nate, lowering his light. "I figure we've got to pick up the pace." He moved to the next cage, using his blaster to open it up. Grace was moving along the opposite line of cages, working at the organic material with her sword, making an exit for the occupants.

"They'll never let us leave," said Chad. He was following Nate. "You've doomed us all."

"Tell you what, Chad," said Nate. "You leave the rescuing to the professionals, hey?"

He had released the last of the cages, the Resistance leadership clustering in a forlorn knot in the middle of the cavern. Nate was farthest away from the stairs leading out, Grace at his side. *Like we were made as a matched pair. Like we should be together.* It was a good thought. It was a bad *situation* to have that thought, but a good thought to have.

"Nate," said Grace, her eyes moving to the wall at the end of the cavern.

"Yeah," said Nate. "Crabs. Don't make sudden moves. Don't make eye contact."

"No, Nate. It's a Queen."

Nate sighed. *Why can't anything go smooth?* He turned to look, pointing his blaster's light like an accusing finger. There she was, all right: Ezeroc Queen, feeding tubes leading into her, angry-ass face looking out at them. "Hey. How about we back up nice and slow?"

"Sounds *great*," said Grace, already backing away.

There was the *thump* of an explosion nearby, and the cavern shook, pieces of rock and ... *moisture* ... falling around them. Nate looked up, but the crabs remained stuck to the roof. *Good so far.* He edged away from the Queen, flashing a smile. "So, we're going now. You guys have fun when we're gone."

Another explosion came, this one right on top of them. The room shook like a struck gong, pieces of rock falling around them. The Resistance leaders made a break for the stairs, running like their lives depended on it — which they might. Nate started after them — step-*squeeeeak*, step-*squeeeeak*. A dust cloud broke into the cavern from the trapdoor above, people running for it. Terrified people. Resistance leadership they might be, but being buried alive in a rocky cavern with alien mind insects wasn't a great way to go. *Speaking of which, you need to hustle, Chevell.* He picked up the pace, his metal leg dragging. Grace was ahead of him, her athletic form vaulting fallen rock or dodging out of the way. She had a good ten meters on him before she realized she was leaving him behind. She turned, arm out. "Nate, hurry."

I am hurrying, goddammit. There was a *crunch* as a massive object fell between them. A massive object that was moving: one of the Ezeroc crabs, legs flailing as it righted itself. It turned in a circle surveying Grace, then Nate, then Grace again.

"Hey!" said Nate. He raised his blaster, squeezed off a round of plasma into it. The thick exoskeleton shrugged it off just like he expected, but at least it turned towards him, ignoring Grace. Which was great, just *great*, except for the fact that it was between him and the exit. And he was between it and its Queen. *Not good planning, Nate.*

There was another *crunch* and another crab fell. Then two more *crunches*, bringing the total of crabs in the room to four. Nate looked at his blaster, remembering the last time he'd fought just one of these things. It had shaken him up, tossed him around like a baby's rattle, and ignored blaster fire until he'd scored a hit underneath. Getting underneath was a challenge in itself, and — *well, let's be straight up about it: you're not walking away this time, Chevell.*

At least he could buy Grace some time.

"Hey!" said a familiar voice, and Nate raised his eyes towards the trapdoor. "Don't worry, Cap! I got just the thing for these assholes." There stood October Kohl, laser carbine in hand. The big man pointed the carbine down into the cavern, and pulled the trigger.

CHAPTER TWENTY-FOUR

KOHL WAS STARING out the back of the *Tyche* like he was seeing the biggest show on Earth. El was up on the flight deck, making the *Tyche* race like a greyhound. Kohl had kicked the back airlock open because he wanted to watch the show. And he was about to jump out of this perfectly good spaceship.

The *Tyche's* hull was sealed now, Hope's welds as good as any Kohl had seen. She'd done that while they were racing along, air trying to suck the both of them out. For a scrawny kid, she was okay, and it was a wonder Kohl hadn't seen that before. The pink hair was a thing he found hot, and she was cute, but he didn't dig on criminals as a general rule. It was fine to be one, but not to date one. That she saved his life helped some. That she might not have been a criminal at *all* helped a lot. And like the two hundred thousand good Republic coins—

Goddamn Kohl, that was a lot of coin to leave on the table.

—he'd left to help Grace out, he faced an uncomfortable series of thoughts.

The first, prime among these, was that he was a bigger asshole than he'd given himself credit for. Making a name for himself on the streets had been a tough job, and involved a certain ... *asshole quotient*. He'd picked up everything he'd needed to know by looking at the people around them. It worked out okay. But he'd always figured on being *smarter* than the rest of them. Not smart like the cap, because Nate was a tall glass of water physically but brains and heart second to none. And not smart like El, who could conjure flight plans and delta-v and other horseshit that made the *Tyche* fly through the hard black without breaking a sweat. Not smart like Hope, because she had saved all their lives over and over by welding things together that shouldn't ever work.

Maybe a little bit smart like Gracie, though. Kohl figured he knew how people worked at a fundamental level. The kind of soil they were planted in, and what kind of weed would grow. And in Hope's case he'd got it wrong. So that was the first thought.

The second thought, chased around by this first thought, was that maybe he'd got everything in his life wrong. This kind of thinking led to a deep sea of confusion for Kohl, who was used to pointing guns at people and making them stop existing. When you needed to get back to basics and question whether he'd been pointing guns at the *right* people, it made his head hurt. But aside from that, he'd got it all wrong about Gracie, who'd not only spared him when she could have turned him into a kebab, but also about Hope, who'd just lost her *wife*. Truth: it made his head hurt, and something else too. Something in his chest.

Which left nothing for it: he would jump out of this spacecraft.

Not because he wanted to end it all, but because he felt he needed to uncomplicate his life. It had become fucked, and leaving this spacecraft with his carbine would unfuck it. He wouldn't be shooting people. He would shoot insects, and while he was confused about whether he was shooting the right people, he was over one hundred percent sure the insects were evil. They were allied with the devil himself, and they needed to be shot.

The insects were not on the spaceship. Thus, he would leave the spaceship, just as soon as El slowed the *Tyche* down to something closer to a walking pace, and preferably put 'er closer to the cerami-crete they were skimming over. It didn't look far, but Kohl figured if he left the *Tyche* now all that would be left was a long smear and a series of unhappy memories for people watching.

Hope tugged at his sleeve. "Hey."

"Hey, Hope." He frowned. "I'm real sorry about ... what's her name?"

"Reiko."

"Her, yeah," said Kohl. "I'm real sorry about that."

"Thanks," said Hope, looking down at what she held.

"What's that?" said Kohl.

"It's a present," she said. She looked at his carbine. "It's just, I don't think your laser gun will do what you think."

"Why's that?" said Kohl. He patted the carbine. "This is the best gun I've ever owned. Practically fires itself. And I've been itching to use it on those big insects down there. Plasma they seem to tolerate in moderation, but lasers, now there's a thing."

"Yes, coherent light, I know how it works," said Hope. "Kohl?"

"Yeah?"

"You know how we're all good at some things? Like, you're good at beating people up."

"I figure I'm one of the best that's ever been, sure," allowed Kohl.

"And El's good at flying starships in general and the *Tyche* in particular, because she loves this ship," said Hope. At that moment, a jostle in the journey — El twisting the sticks or some damn thing to avoid the whole ship being turned into spare parts — caused her to stumble, grabbing at the wall for support. Kohl reached out a hand, snaring the back of her rig, and holding her upright. She brushed pink hair off her eyes. "Thanks. And me, well, I'm good at fixing things, most things anyway, and knowing how stuff works."

"With you," said Kohl. He let her go, glancing out at the spectacular light show visible through the open airlock. The wind noise wasn't as extreme, because El had slowed to allow the Republic to catch up. Which seemed crazy, but she was in charge while the cap had boots on dirt, so there it was.

"Because I know how stuff works," said Hope, "I don't think your very shiny laser rifle will work."

"Why?"

"Hunch."

"Okay. So, what's that?" Kohl was fine with hunches; it's how he navigated the stars of his life most days.

She frowned, then realized she was still holding the thing. Hope held it out to him. "It's a maser."

"That the same maser El gave you?"

"Yes. Except it didn't work. It wouldn't ever have worked. I don't know what Mr. Razor was thinking, but the power supply was all wrong, and the cavity magnetron wasn't wired in the right—"

"Hope."

"Yes, Kohl?"

"Does it work now?"

"Yes."

"Okay," he said, and took it from her. He slid it into the back of his suit. Much as he loved his carbine — *man*, it was a good gun — it never hurt to go into a rough situation with extra weapons. There had never been a situation where he'd thought, *You know what, October Kohl? You've got yourself too many guns right now.* There had been a few situations where he found himself short of a gun, or a battery, and that had left him with a deep and personal understanding of the benefits of spares.

"Don't you want to know how it works?" she said.

"I point it and pull the trigger," he said.

"Yes, but you need to hold the trigger down," she said.

"Superior force through target saturation?" said Kohl.

"I don't know what that means," said Hope. "I don't think you and I speak the same kinds of English."

"Cool," said Kohl. The *Tyche* was slowing down now, the ship yawing around in a circle. Flashes of plasma lit the night as the

Republic fired on them, the *Tyche's* electronic countermeasures confounding a firm target acquisition. Kohl figured it was to do with what they'd borrowed from the *Gladiator*. They had all their old tricks, and all the new tricks too. He didn't need to understand it.

A bolt of plasma impacted the ground below them, showering the air with molten ceramicrete. That one was a little too close. The warehouse — their destination — came into view, and El opened up with a couple rounds from the PDCs, tearing the top off the building. Normally that was bad form, what with the captain being down there, and Gracie too, but the *Tyche* was a good guardian. She knew where everyone was, all her crew, and the cap and Gracie were underground.

Which was where Kohl was going. As the ship slewed to an almost halt, he reached out, ruffled Hope's hair — to which she responded with a horrified and sick expression — and then jumped.

BOOTS on the ground in the middle of an air battle was always a rough spot. Kohl had never served in the military — bunch of assholes — but he'd been in plenty of wars. The *Tyche* roared off above, doing a circuit of the warehouse as Republic military fighters zipped around. Kohl watched the show for a second — so many shots trying to pierce the *Tyche's* skin, and none of them hitting. He had to admit, El was good at her job.

How the captain found good people, Kohl would never know. Sure, he'd found Kohl, but Kohl had never had to advertise. Force of nature, and all that. But the cap, he'd been kicked out of the Empire. Or fallen out, or some damn thing. A mark like that, what with the Republic all around, was a thing that should stop good people signing on.

Never seemed to, though.

Back to the boots on the ground: his feet hit ceramicrete with a crunch. He absorbed the landing on his knees, wincing only a little bit, then looked back up at the open airlock in the *Tyche*. Hope was there, a swirl of pink hair around her face. She reached a tentative hand out, and he waved back. She was lost to view as the *Tyche* kicked hard, drives pushing for sky, Republic fighters in pursuit.

El had said it was very important he get the cap outside, along with the Ezeroc. When Kohl had asked how in hell he was supposed to get a bunch of insects to follow him, she'd just told him to be himself. Whatever that meant.

Outside the warehouse, there was that old friend of the cap's — Harley? Harlem? He leaned forward. "Heywood."

"Harlow," said Harlow. "It's Harlow."

"Yeah," said Kohl, "whatever. Look, I'm going in there, and I'm going to shoot a whole bunch of aliens. Anything comes out here that doesn't look like a human, you want to stay clear, you get me?"

"I get you," said Harlow. He looked at the sky. "Is the ship coming back?"

"I fucking hope so," said Kohl. "It's my ride. Yours too, if you want it." That duty done, he stood up, taking in the objective.

The side of the warehouse had been carved in with what looked like God's own baseball bat, a nice straight line bored right through the middle. Plasma burn, looked like, or a couple of 'em. Roof was off, hole in the side: not much of a warehouse anymore. He jogged into it anyway, carbine held low and ready, taking in the sights. There, one of the guys that looked like Abel but with his arms cut off, which looked like Gracie had been through here and hadn't been happy about the process. Next layer deep, there were ... *pods*, or some such thing, people who looked like they were being sucked dry. Hell of a way to go, but not as bad as having an insect eat your brain. Or maybe it was? Difficult to know for sure.

Kohl kept pushing forward, finding no one alive. Dust or smoke or an even mix of both was thick in the air. It swirled around him, covering his armor in a fine grit. It'd need a clean after this, that was for sure, but his armor usually did.

He arrived at an empty room with four dead Ezeroc, or what

looked like four. One was cut up the middle — *Gracie, gotta be* — and three lumps of char that were the cap's work. And a doorway. Closed, but in a way that suggested a man was supposed to open it.

Kohl figured on being that man. He kicked the door open, the damage to the warehouse meaning it flew off its hinges to land in the room itself. There, another Ezeroc cinder — which gave even odds of the cap still being alive — and a doorway into hell itself. Kohl had never been much for religion, invisible friends in the sky not being his jam, but he knew what hell was. He knew what it smelled and tasted like, and those damn tendrils going down into that pit of despair sure looked like hell to him. The dust and smoke weren't helping any, but that's what war zones were like. Nothing worth complaining about.

Time to get to work.

He was about to saunter over to the edge of the pit, except it sprouted a human head, and then a torso, and another head beside. People were running up out of the pit, and he grabbed a man in passing. "Hey. You seen the cap?"

"Run!" said the man, and tore free, rushing away.

"Fuck running," said Kohl after him. "You die tired." He snared a woman's arm. "Cap?"

"He's dead, or as good as," she said. "Save yourself if you're smart."

"I promised myself I wouldn't kill anyone else today," said Kohl. "You're making that difficult."

Her head jerked towards the hole. "In there. Fool."

"Much obliged," said Kohl, executing the saunter he'd planned all along. The edge of the pit was slick with some kind of alien snot, which wasn't pretty, but he didn't get paid for the pretty jobs. He stepped down into the hole, and saw: yep, there was the cap. Gracie, too. A big, ugly insect was between them. The size of a snowplow, but a snowplow that had anger management issues.

Just like me. He hefted the carbine. "Hey!" he shouted to Nate. "Don't worry, Cap! I got just the thing for these assholes." He squeezed the trigger. The weapon reached out, licking the Ezeroc —

more like a crab than a snowplow, really, but about to be molten crab, we gone get ourselves some bibs and some dipping butter after this — making the familiar *click-click-click* sound.

But no whine. He let go of the trigger, looked at the weapon, and tried again. *Click-click-click.* Then the weapon chimed, a synthetic voice saying, "No hostile targets identified."

Oh, come on. Kohl blinked, then held the weapon up like he was showing the Ezeroc to it. "Right *there*, ya dumb machine. It's *there*."

"Kohl!" said Nate. "Get Grace!"

"Hell with that," said Grace. "Get us both." She tried to circle the Ezeroc, to get towards the cap. Which was crazy, because the exit to life, hope, and freedom was behind Kohl. The things people did.

There were always two approaches to a given task: the easy way, and the hard way. The carbine was playing dumb — no doubt what Hope was meaning with her cryptic talk before — and unable to see the Ezeroc as anything other than some form of modern art. What was it that Nate said? *Always good to fly with Lady Luck.* And here was October Kohl, luckiest man in the universe, because in his back pocket was a gift given to him by a slip of a girl. A maser, which didn't look like a proper gun, but at this particular moment style wasn't important.

Kohl let the carbine fall on its sling and pulled out the maser. He pointed the business end towards the Ezeroc crab and squeezed the trigger. No light show. Nothing appeared to be going on at all aside from a humming. But Hope had said you needed to keep it on, so Kohl kept it on. Because Hope seemed to know what she was talking about more than she didn't. Which was more than could be said for most people.

The Ezeroc kept turning around, trying to look at Grace, then Nate, then Grace, and then it stopped, one of its back legs giving way. It stood back up, but that leg gave way again. It made a hissing noise, and that was when Kohl worked out it wasn't speaking, or screaming. Nothing like that.

It was steaming. Steam was escaping from the joints of its carapace. It became agitated, and confused — Kohl might be too if someone used a microwave on him — and then slumped to the ground. Kohl kept the maser on it. There was a cracking noise, and the side of its carapace ruptured outward in a spray of half-cooked crab meat and steam and other fluids.

Kohl let go the trigger, looking at the maser closer. Handy weapon to have. He looked back at Grace and the cap, who were both staring at him with faces slack with astonishment. "What?" said Kohl. "You never seen a maser before?" Because he figured he was now the ship's maser expert, and he best act like it.

"No," said Grace. "Not ... no."

"On ships," offered Nate. "I've seen them on ships."

"You coming or what?" said Kohl.

"There's a Queen," said Nate. "We've got to take care of the Queen. Also, there are another three crabs."

"Tell you what," said Kohl. "You come with me, and we'll see if we can deal with your friends in a bit."

Nate looked at him, then grabbed Grace's hand, or Gracie grabbed the cap, hard to tell, and then they were running for the steps. With a rumble, three giant crabs appeared out of the gloom behind them.

Kohl sure hoped El's plan would work out. Otherwise today would end ugly.

CHAPTER TWENTY-FIVE

AFTER THE *TYCHE* tossed Kohl out the airlock and onto the ground, Hope watched as Kohl landed hard then stood tall like it didn't mean anything — which it probably didn't. But Hope liked to think hurting mattered less to Kohl than getting Nate and Grace back. She waved at him, and he waved back, and she thought, *He is weird.* He was weird because he did things for reasons she didn't understand. Kohl had hated her right until about two minutes ago, and now it was like they were BFFs.

Reiko.

Bright flashes of plasma spat past the open airlock, which brought Hope back to the present. She slapped a hand against the door controls, the lock hissing shut — the noise lost against the grumble of the *Tyche's* drives, the rattling of the substructure as El made the ship dance and weave. The problem with El was that she figured on being able to dance and weave; she had this big plan for how they'd get Kohl down there, an extra hand to do the heavy lifting. That part had worked out great. The bit that was missing — El had said *we'll work it out later* — was how they would park the *Tyche* on the dirt long enough to scoop up Nate and Grace. Let alone long enough to rescue — what had the cap said? *Strays*.

And, as luck would have it, *later* was *now*. And they had the whole extra problem of the Republic adding more ships, more little fighters to the mix, and someone would get wise to the fact that the *Tyche* was an ancient hulk kept in the air by prayers and fairy dust, scramble some serious hardware, and the show would be over. The show would be more than over, because Nate and Grace would be down on the ground, seeing their home blown into a thousand tiny pieces, and then they'd get eaten by aliens.

Hope didn't much like that.

She tapped her comm. "El, how does Republic command talk to fighters?"

"Busy, Hope."

"It's important," said Hope. But it didn't matter; El had clicked the comm off.

Well, that wasn't good. Time to do the job the hard way. She set off towards Engineering — her rig was too damaged to be relied on, and besides, she needed a proper console for this. She had programs she could use up there, provided the Republic hadn't broken too much while they were scouring the *Tyche* for clues. Hope made her way around the cargo bay, hands gripping for dear life because the ship was still flying around like a crazed thing. Her rig helped here, the two good arms working with Hope's own good two arms. Four arms, not hand over hand, but hand over hand over hand over hand. She made the ladder leading up to the crew deck, banged her lip against it as the ship shook with something, swallowed blood, and climbed.

Whether she was going to use her console or not, it seemed smart to be strapped into her acceleration couch for this. Smart, if she wanted to live.

Reiko.

She wasn't sure about that. But she could think about it some more while she fixed the problems of the moment.

She made it to Engineering, the airlock opening for her, then hissing shut behind her. The *Ravana's* heart beat loud and bright, and the noise of the drives was so fierce here it was like a physical thing. She could feel it in her throat, in her stomach. The vibrations of it made her teeth itch. She was used to it. It was what Engineering was like.

It felt like home.

The last few steps to her acceleration couch were made in a rush, because El rolled the ship, then flattened it out, then dived to one side, and that dive shook Hope loose from the wall. She tumbled across Engineering, her own hands reaching out for something, anything. If she hit another surface like this, she might be knocked out or killed. Either of those wasn't a good outcome, not because she was sure she wanted to live, but because she wouldn't be able to do the thing she needed to do. Unconscious — or dead — people couldn't use a vocoder worth a damn.

She needn't have worried. The rig snared one strap of her acceleration couch as she sailed past, the programs she'd loaded into the unit doing what she needed when she didn't have time to think about it. Hope knew her limitations. She wasn't good at shooting people. She wasn't good with *people* full stop—

Reiko.

—and she wasn't good at doing action things with swords or words when people were shooting at her. But she was great at planning. With enough time and enough planning, you could almost look like you knew what you were doing when the chips were down. Mr. Razor had sold her a good rig, but Hope had made it better than the designers had ever dreamed. One of the rig's two working arms grabbed that strap, holding on with a grip that could crush steel pipe. Hope's tumble was arrested with a *clang* as the rig's arm stretched straight, then held. The other arm reached up to grab the headrest of the couch. Hope's own arms then pulled her into the chair, fingers shaking—

Why are you scared? You want to die. To be with Reiko.

—as she secured the straps around her and the rig. The big buckles clipped together, the chair pulling her back into its safe embrace. The rig's arms folded away, her visor pulling back as she pulled up the Engineering console. Holos sprang to life around her, one of them flickering a little. She tapped it, and it came on good and strong. One more thing to fix later. Assuming she didn't die in the next few minutes. Because it wouldn't do to leave something broken for someone else to fix, even if she was going to be with Reiko. It wouldn't sit right with her.

The noise of Engineering became background comfort for her. It was loud, hella loud, but none of the sounds were *wrong*. Her ship was running great, in the best shape of her life. Hope being here would let her know better than remote diagnostics whether something was wrong. The noise let her get to work, to focus on the things she needed to get her head around.

First: the comm net. The Republic had one, and they were using it a great deal. Those ships out there were talking to each other, and they were talking to a command center somewhere. The *Tyche* put up a graphic for her, the ship bang in the middle, and important details — the ground, for example, or buildings — in wireframe. The holo filled with more details, the fighters circling around like wasps, moving fast, stabbing with spears of light and energy. All it'd take is a lucky shot and all the countermeasures in the world wouldn't help. Just a *little* luck. It was a wonder they hadn't been hit yet. No, wait — they *had*, the *Tyche* reminding her that *there* and *there* she'd been touched by plasma. Nothing major, just her outside skin, a couple of burns, but she'd come out of this with new scars. Hope guessed it was luck that the plasma had only rippled past, that it hadn't splashed full on, tearing the hull apart, coring the ship.

"My good girl," said Hope, but there wasn't anyone to hear her. And besides, it was too loud for anyone to hear anything, even if you were yelling right in their ear. But Hope said it anyway.

Back to the holo. The *Tyche* drew lines, brief and bright, between the fighters as their computers coordinated attack runs, firing solutions, trying to make a mark on a ship that should have been too damn big and too damn slow to avoid them. Those lines reached up — *huh*. Up, hey? So, they were coordinating with someone in orbit. Someone up there who was pulling the strings like a puppet master, making the fighters leap and dance around. Not *Republic command* like a building or a person, but like a command vessel.

Which brought us to second: the command vessel. It was big. A destroyer, something of the size of the *Gladiator*. This one was holding in geosynch hundreds of kilometers above them, watching all, seeing all. Pointing out to the fighters what they were fighting, where they should be going. Or that's what Hope would have been doing, if she was on that ship. It was time to pretend like she was.

So, third: crypto, crypto, crypto. The comm net was locked up tight, milspec tech keeping prying eyes out. Wouldn't do to have wartime comms intercepted by the enemy. No sir. Getting your hands on a set of keys was a tricky proposition. Hacking that comm net without keys would take more time than was left to run in the universe, and more time than Hope had. It was good planning on her part — back to the planning thing, right? — that she had a set of keys. A Republic intelligence officer had been aboard their ship, using codes to unlock the *Gladiator's* secrets. And because he'd been using the *Tyche's* comm array to do his thing, Hope had done her thing and just nabbed a copy of those codes. Didn't hurt no one, and right now it would help some. Good planning was one thing, but they'd need luck. No knowing whether the Republic had rejigged the comm codes. No knowing whether they had figured a breach in their net. The cap, he'd been careful — firing the *Gladiator* like a nuclear spear into the heart of an Ezeroc ship, leaving no inconvenient evidence behind. Careful, and lucky.

The comm net chirped, thought about things a little, then let Hope inside. The holo filled with more data than before. Ship names, transponder codes unlocked like the secrets of the universe. The command ship was the *Torrington* — now *there's* a familiar name. No wonder she could get into the comm net so easy. It was plain *lucky* that the ship that Karkoski was on happened to be leading the efforts to bring the *Tyche* down. Firing solutions visible to Hope, the holo packed with more data than she knew what to do with. She wasn't an expert on any of the military side of things, just saw a net closing tighter and tighter around the *Tyche*. Sooner or later, it wouldn't be luck that holed the *Tyche*. It'd be plain math.

Which brings us to the fourth thing: *let's pretend*. She brought online her vocoder program. It was something she'd ginned up a long time ago. It made a human-sounding voice out of a line of text. She tweaked a few of the parameters in the code — no time to get fancy — making the vocoder sound a little older (because no one ever took orders from Hope; hell, she sounded young to *herself*), a little wiser, a little more in command. She tapped on the console: *THIS IS TORRINGTON ACTUAL. WE HAVE DETECTED A BREACH IN OUR COMM NET. SWITCH CHANNELS. KEYS FOLLOW.* And she generated some new keys, something that would keep the Torrington in the loop, but by way of the *Tyche*. Hope then clicked her visor down to insulate her from some of the noise of Engineering, and pressed the big go button.

"This is Torrington actual. We have detected a breach in our comm net. Switch channels. Keys follow." It sounded a lot like Karkoski, almost like Hope had planned it that way. She'd got the nuance of Karkoski's voice, her tone of command just right. The bundle of data that came with the orders sent new keys out to all the fighters. The only ship that didn't hear the command was the *Torrington* herself.

Her holo lit up with affirmations as Hope's keys came in, slicing off the *Torrington* from the conversation like she wasn't there. Cool. Next step, give them something to do. She typed into her console more words for the vocoder to say. Almost-Karkoski said in her ears, "This is Torrington actual to all fighters. Your targets have been compromised. That ship has chameleon tech. You've been shooting at nothing but air. Your new target is being loaded in." And Hope sent that to all the ships chasing them except for one. To that ship she sent a different message. "This is Torrington actual. Fighter A-113, we have identified you as a hostile target, and will take you out of the sky. Burn in hell, over." Hope had no idea whether that sounded like what Karkoski might say, or anyone in the military for that matter. She knew the military would never tell a target they were a target, but that wasn't the point.

The point was to make that ship run like the hounds of hell were after them. The point was to give El a little breathing room.

Several things happened at once. The first thing was that Fighter A-113 paged what it thought was the *Torrington* with an urgent comm. "*Torrington*, your intel is incorrect. *Torrington*, please be aware you will fire on a friendly. *Torrington?*" And then nothing else, because of the second thing that happened, which was that all of the other ships — courtesy of Hope — now thought Fighter A-113 was running chameleon tech, was masquerading as the *Tyche*, and even if it wasn't, they were tired of shooting at a ship that seemed to slip between plasma bolts like she wasn't there. At least this new target would give them something worthwhile to do. And on the heels of that came the third thing, which was that all those ships turned on Fighter A-113.

Hope had her fingers crossed for the little guy. She really did.

Fighter A-113's pilot did what any sensible person would in this situation: they ran.

Hope's comm pinged from two locations. One was the *Torrington*. The other was the flight deck, which would be El. She answered the *Torrington first*. She had to type quick and clean, because it was still too loud in here for the comm to work well: *HELLO?*

"*Tyche*, what have you done?"

Hope typed, *PLEASE HOLD*. And she switched the comm back to El, and used her real voice to shout over the noise of Engineering. "Hey!"

"Hope, what did you do? Everyone's gone."

"Busy, but land, and get the cap!" Then Hope switched back to the *Torrington,* and typed again. *KARKOSKI, THIS IS GUILD ENGINEER HOPE BAEDEKER. I AM ACTING OF MY OWN FREE WILL AND NOT UNDER ORDERS FROM CAPTAIN CHEVELL. YOU NEED TO SEE WHAT IS DOWN THERE.* It was a tiny lie to say she was a Guild Engineer, what with her Shingle being stripped from her. But she'd done the work. She passed the tests. She *was* an Engineer, and since she'd be dead soon, she wanted to go out with that on her epitaph.

"*Tyche,* this is the Republic destroyer *Torrington.* We don't take orders from rebels."

OKAY, BUT. WHAT IF WHAT WAS DOWN THERE WAS REALLY IMPORTANT? Which was enough, because Hope wouldn't be able to convince them of anything they didn't want to do, but while all the Republic fighters were off trying to nail Fighter A-113 to the wall, the *Tyche* would set down with the *Torrington's* eyes on her. Those eyes would watch, and be surprised when a bunch of aliens came outside.

The *Tyche's* attitude was changing as El brought the ship around in a smoother ride. The roar of the engines dropped to more of a rumble, the purr of a happy ship doing happier things than running for its life. They lowered, the holo showing Hope the ground approaching as El brought the belly down to kiss the earth. Good enough. It was almost time for the next part of Hope's plan. She waited until the ship settled, the airlock opening for Nate and Grace — the *Tyche* showing Hope little blips on the holo as they ran from a burning warehouse. October Kohl's blip was farther out, still in said burning warehouse. The *Tyche* highlighted several other humans running towards her, and made a query. *POSSIBLE HOSTILE FORCE SEEKING TO OVERRUN TYCHE. PDCS ONLINE. FIRE?*

Hope told the *Tyche* no, thank you very much. She tagged the new people as non-combatants, which seemed to work okay.

"Hope," said El over the comm. "What are you doing?"

"I've got a plan," said Hope. "Remember, you're very busy."

The sigh came down the comm nice and clear. "Hope? What's happening?"

"Well," said Hope. "I've told the *Torrington* to look at us. Like, kind of close—"

"You what?!"

"But before that, I've sent the fighters off."

"Off?"

"Yes."

"Hope?"

"Yes?"

"How?"

"It's complicated," said Hope. "But the good news is that one fighter is leading the rest of them away. In a minute, I'll bring them all back here, just in case."

"Just in case what?" said El.

"In case there are a million space bugs we need to shoot, of course," said Hope.

"Uh, *Tyche*, this is October Kohl," said Kohl. His comm was full of static and stress. "Y'all on the deck yet?"

"We're here," said El. "Cap's on board." Hope saw it was true — Nate was in the *Tyche's* hold, or at least on the ship somewhere, which maybe meant he would come here and yell at her. She hoped he was going to the flight deck to talk to El first, as it'd buy time to get Fighter A-113 back here, with the rest of ... their *escort*.

"That's great," said Kohl. "Look, I'm bringing a party to your location."

"What kind of party?" said El. "We've got refugees boarding."

"I've got fucking space insects," said Kohl, and then the comm lit with the sound of something exploding. The *Tyche's* tactical holo in front of Hope highlighted where Kohl was, his blip still strong and alive. The ship highlighted the use of explosives, tagged the likely make and manufacture of them, projected yields, and noted that things would be safe for the ship at this distance. *She* also highlighted that the comm was now down at the other end, and based on the yield of the explosives, suggested that the crew member involved would need medical attention on arrival, and that the comm being down wasn't because it was broken but because the crew member had left it at their last location. Maybe Kohl had lost his comm, or maybe he'd thrown it at an Ezeroc.

Hope flicked on the external cameras. The rear camera set showed the last of the refugees boarding the ship, confused stares above ragged clothing. She saw from the nose camera that Kohl was running — *he looks like he could stand to do a little more cardio* — toward the ship. He had Hope's maser — which made her smile — with his carbine bouncing on its sling at his back. He was waving at the *Tyche*, big movements of his arms that looked like *get the hell out of here*, which was weird because Kohl was the kind of person who looked after Number One in all situations.

What was coming behind Kohl was something else, though. The side of the warehouse burst outward in a shower of ceramicrete, one of the big Ezeroc — the ones that looked like crabs — bursting through. Another was on its heels, and they were moving fast. While Kohl could benefit from a little more time on a treadmill and a little less time drinking hard liquor or worse, those things were moving at the speed of vehicles, gaining ground as their six legs clawed at the ground.

This was one of those situations where Hope wished she was better use in a combat situation. She didn't know what to do. Fortunately for October Kohl, El was also on the ship, and she knew what to do. The holo in front of Hope flickered from the amber of *combat ready* to the red of *combat engaged*. PDCs slipped from their mounts in the *Tyche's* hull, and kinetic rounds sprayed across the distance, a hundred rounds a second showing brief red lines of light. The Ezeroc just … ceased to be, their big, hard shells nothing against weapons designed to deal with human-made tanks and spacecraft.

Well, since Hope didn't need to worry about Kohl, time to worry about everyone. She flicked on the comm array to the *Torrington*. She typed, *DO YOU SEE WHAT I SEE?*

Then, she flicked over to the fighter's comm net. She got the vocoder ready, and included Fighter A-113 in the broadcast. "Fighter crews, this is Torrington actual. Our comm net was compromised worse than we feared, and in fact the fighter you are pursuing is a friendly. New targets are being issued."

From Fighter A-113: "*Torrington? Torrington*, this is A-113. You assholes! You—" Hope turned that channel off. She then keyed in the *Tyche's* coordinates as the fighter's eventual destination. Finally, she keyed the flight deck. "El?"

"What's going on, Hope?"

"We need to leave, El. I've got all the fighters coming back. Here. So we need to not be here."

"How long do we have?"

"I don't know? Maybe a minute."

"Jesus fucking Christ, Hope, we've got refugees, we've got—" But Hope turned that channel off too. She sat in Engineering, the drives going hot and loud behind her, and she thought: *Okay. Okay. I've done enough, maybe. Is it time to go see Reiko?*

CHAPTER TWENTY-SIX

WHEN NATE SAW THE *TYCHE*, her skids on the ceramicrete outside the warehouse, the fire of the air car still burning off to one side, he almost laughed. Almost, but he didn't have the air left. He ran hard, his metal leg complaining the whole way, but it was okay: Grace was on that side, half lifting, half dragging him along. Less than a minute before, he, Grace, and Kohl had been facing down three Ezeroc crabs. Just one was more than enough to do for a normal human, but he hadn't hired Kohl because he was *normal*. He'd hired him because he was exceptional. Broken, flawed, but if he could be *fixed*, he could be marvelous.

It's possible that, as a reclamation project, Kohl was too much for any captain.

But in this instance, Kohl had given him a stare that said *don't threaten to throw me out an airlock again*, but had in fact said, "Cap, y'all should go." And when he'd argued, because Grace was there and he figured that this right here was a good time to show some of his manly virtue, Grace had said *shut up and run*, so he had. She'd been scared when she said it, scared in her voice, and in her eyes, and the way her knuckles went white as they gripped his arm.

And he realized then that the only one not with the program was Nathan Chevell, still determined to do the wrong dumb thing. The right smart thing was to get Grace, who was terrified, away from the Ezeroc, who wanted to do God knows what with her. And Kohl was on board with this, or something like it, because he was *buying them time*. Kohl, of all people. It was possible he figured he had a score to settle, and he was probably right because the way Nate saw it, the bugs had made Kohl turn on his crew. And Kohl, rather than doing the easy thing and grabbing two hundred thousand credits, had come down here into this pit of despair and fished him and Grace out. And it was more Grace, rather than Nate, that Kohl was getting, but that was okay. All of that made Nate think there might be a little hope for the big man.

So, he'd run. Clapped Kohl on the shoulder as they went past, got a grunt in return, and hit the top of the stairs already breathing hard. There had still been refugees in the room they'd pulled Amedea from, and so he'd yelled, things like *are you all fucking stupid* and *go that way where there are no insects*, and they'd run through the plasma burn that had torn through the building.

When Nate and Grace had burst outside, the clean air had made him want to cry, and the ship had made him want to laugh, and then he breathed in some smoke and that had made him want to cough. But he kept running, herding people aboard his ship. He paused where he'd left Harlow — yep, still there. He hauled his friend up. "Resting on the job?"

"Nate?"

"Yes, Harlow."

"What the fuck is going on?"

"That's a good question. Can you run?"

"No, but I'm going to anyway." And Harlow had set off toward the *Tyche*, and didn't look like he was having trouble running at all. *Now that's what a solid incentive plan looks like.* Amedea was outside the cargo bay, eyeballing a piece of metal that had been welded over the cargo bay door while her precious leadership were filing in through the side airlock, and she'd put a hand on his chest and said, "Captain? We need to talk."

Nate stopped, nodded to Grace, and turned to Amedea. "Ain't no talking that needs to happen out here, Amedea."

"We still need to resolve—"

"Tell you what. You stand out here and talk," said Nate. "I'm going to get on my ship and fly to somewhere safe. Let me know if you want to come with." He turned and followed Grace, because not being eaten by space insects was high on his priority list, and not having any of his crew eaten was a big number two on that list. He cast a glance over his shoulder at Amedea, saw she was following, and gave a little mental shrug to himself. *Looks like it's on her list too, and higher than ruling the world.*

He watched as Amedea sealed the airlock. He unsealed it. She looked at him like he was insane and said, "Are you crazy?"

"I've got a man out there," said Nate. "He's trying not to die, and I figured on helping him with that."

"One man?" she said. "We've got all the free Intelligencers *here,* captain. They can't be sacrificed for *one man.*"

"They can if he's my man," said Nate. "We're staying here until he's on board."

"I don't have *time* for this," said Amedea, her eyes looking off, focusing on something else, and then they rolled up into her head as she slumped to the deck. Harlow was behind her, a piece of pipe in his hand.

"Harlow," said Nate. "What are you doing? Wasn't that your boss?"

"Yeah, but she wasn't my friend," said Harlow. He was looking around the inside of the cargo bay. "I love what you've done with the place. Also, she would control your mind."

"Good luck to her," said Grace, coming alongside Nate. "He's stubborn." But she linked an arm with his, leaning close. "Go. I'll make sure we don't leave without Kohl."

"Go where?" said Harlow.

"Harlow," said Nate, "have you ever had a plan so big it couldn't be disguised?"

"Not really," said Harlow, looking at Grace. "Was the Resistance a part of the plan?"

"We're free-styling a little," admitted Grace.

"This plan," said Harlow, narrowing his eyes. "Does it involve killing the bugs?"

"Of course," said Nate. "Ain't no alien scum going to take over the neighborhood."

"Go amaze me," said Harlow.

"Copy that," said Nate. "Now, I need my sword."

THE PROBLEM with the sword wasn't that Nate didn't know how to sword fight. Wearing the Emperor's Black meant he'd had the best training money could buy. The style of fighting they used — it being in accordance with ceremonial events, packed with delegates, politicians, and other high class, cold-blooded humans — favored small hand blasters to lower collateral damage, and swords for close work. The uniform had been slung with the blaster low on the right hip for easy-out drawing, the sword hilt over the right shoulder. Blaster in the right hand, sword in the left hand, and you could dance with the devil or his bride, near or far, as the fancy took you. The blaster had caused him some concern, because he was left-handed, but his instructor had explained — in painful detail, as Nate wore the brunt of practice sword bruising — that any idiot could shoot a blaster in either hand. It wasn't an elegant tool. You looked down the barrel, pulled the trigger, and if you missed, you kept pulling until you solved your problem. But a sword needed a more delicate touch. You couldn't use a sword like that. If you're left-handed and try and use the sword in your right? It felt like swinging a tennis racket, not a sword.

Nate could still shoot just fine. His right hand was working more or less how it always had. Where things came unstuck for him was that his left hand had been replaced by an uncomfortable hunk of metal. It didn't hold the sword right. He'd worked out his metal hand had learned to shoot without his say-so, and that was working out okay. It'd be nice if the hand learned to fight with a sword, but it'd be nicer if Nate was right handed. The reason was that the swords' masking of esper effects on him — their ability to read his mind, for example — needed skin contact. Metal wouldn't do.

Still. He could still hold it, even if it felt like a tennis racket. He hit his quarters at a run, the door slipping open in front of him. He took in the mess — *those Republic assholes* — and then kicked open the sea chest at the foot of his bunk. The sword was still there, which improved his mood. He grabbed the hilt with his flesh and blood hand. Time to find the flight deck.

HE SLIPPED into the acceleration couch beside El just as she was firing the drives up, bringing the Endless systems online. Kohl had slipped inside the ship — if by *slipped* you meant *ran inside with insects on his heels* — and now they were clawing sky. "Hey," he said, a little out of breath.

"Are we going to have a problem?" said El.

Nate thought about that. "I don't think so."

"Because there's two things going on here. The first is, Hope's acting weird. But that's not why we'll have a problem."

"Okay," said Nate. "Can you fly faster?" He was watching the holo stage in the middle of the flight deck as fighters closed on their position. One in the lead had been marked in bold for some reason, the designation A-113 bright and clear.

"The second thing that's going on here is that I don't think you're telling me everything," said El.

"Well, that's true," said Nate.

"Which is why we'll have a problem," she said. "It's been a long fucking day, and I've been knocked out by Hope's dead wife, and I don't know how I should feel about that." The *Tyche* kicked them both back in their chairs as the engines roared, the ship shaking with the vibration. The nose was pointed towards the sky, the moon visible, full and wide in the night sky. "She wasn't dead when she knocked me out."

"I know," said Nate.

"And Kohl is running *into* danger. Not complaining about it at all."

"I'll admit, that is strange," agreed Nate.

"So what haven't you told me?"

Nate thought about that, then he clicked on the comm. "Hope?"

"Yes, Cap."

"It looks like you've corralled the *Torrington* off from her fighters. That right?"

"Yes, Cap."

"Could you undo that?" said Nate. "I need to talk to someone."

"You realize—"

"I know what'll happen," said Nate. "You'll undo whatever you did, and for a little while, El will swear a lot—"

"Fucking *shit*balls," said El. "That fucking destroyer is right above us. What do you want me to do?"

"More than usual, anyway," said Nate. "Because there will be fighters up our ass. But then when I talk to who I need to talk to, that will stop."

"Will that be good?" said Hope.

"Mostly," said Nate, "but only after we blow up the moon."

"That sounds hard to do," said Hope. Her tone was doubtful. "Our ship isn't huge."

"It'll be easier if we get someone else to do it," said Nate, "which is why I need to talk to someone. And Hope?"

"Yes, Cap."

"It's not the size of the dog in the fight. It's the size of the fight in the dog." He clicked off the comm. The holo stage flickered once, twice, and then they were out of the *Torrington's* comm loop. He looked at El. "I need you to keep going towards the *Torrington*. Can you do that?"

"Yeah, but we're gonna get turned into slag. In a few minutes, we'll be close enough for her to give us a little love tap. No atmosphere in the way from any energy weapons, and she can fire some serious ordnance at us. I mean—"

"I get what'll happen," said Nate, "but in a few minutes the *Torrington* won't be there."

"This I got to see," said El.

"Then watch this," said Nate, and typed on his console. The message was short: *They are in the moon.*

He waited for no more than five seconds when his holo lit up with a reply. *You're joking, of course.*

He looked out the window at where the *Torrington* would be, then smiled. *Not about this. Is your ship secure?*

I need two minutes.

"Two minutes," said Nate.

"That's cutting it fine," said El.

"Trust me," said Nate.

He caught her look, head turned sideways against the hard G of their escape burn. That look said *I do, but do you trust me?* But all El said was, "Yeah, sure."

CHAPTER TWENTY-SEVEN

THE SMELL NEVER CHANGED. It was fear borne on the wind — or, in this case, recycled by the *Tyche's* life support systems. Sure, they said the filters kept the air clean, but Grace could tell when people were scared. Not just the *fear/fear* she got from them in waves. No, it was more. Something animal. The fear could turn to anger in a second, blow up in your face worse than a skipping reactor. And, if you played the ace in your hand right, it could be a force for change.

Let's hope that ace isn't a joker.

The hard burn of escape velocity hadn't helped. People had been straining to not create the world's worst mosh pit in the base of the hold as the Gs piled on. They'd been clinging to cargo webbing as best they were able. Grace had been with them, trying to push back out feelings of *calm/relaxed*, buffeting the waves of *fear/pain/terror*. She'd never tried it before, but figured that if the Intelligencers could control minds, maybe she could control emotions. It felt like trying to balance her way through *kata* for the first time, but without an instructor. In a dark room. While drugged. Whether she helped or harmed was difficult to know, but at least they were all still alive.

The *Tyche* had flattened out, thrust easing. They would dock soon, just for a moment, and she needed to be prepared for that. There were a lot of things that could go wrong. A lot of things that weren't in the plan they'd banged out with Karkoski.

She was standing over Amedea's unconscious body, Chad on the opposite side. He had a thoughtful expression on his face, not fear at all. When his eyes met hers, they were calculating, but not like a snake. Like a human, wondering what the *fuck* was going on. "You've got a plan."

"Yeah," said Grace. "We're under contract." She paused, then nudged Amedea with her toe. "Not under *her* contract."

"I hear you," said Chad. Now they weren't in an alien terror dungeon, she could see the lines on his face were more dirt than anything else. Given time, he might pass for anyone else. He might pass for a normal person, if only the Intelligencer inside him could give up on trying to control people.

Grace frowned. If only she had Nate's sword. But no, he needed that. The Ezeroc would comb the ship, trying to find the captain's mind. To find out what he was up to. So, Grace needed to be what she always had been, right under the surface. A liar. But she needed to lie to herself. She tried on a lie: *you don't love him. Hell, you don't even like him.* Hard, but if she repeated it often enough... "The glorious Republic isn't as unified as you might think, Chad. They've got their military, and their ships. They've got a lot of ships. But what they don't have is a unified high command. Because the aliens, Chad. The aliens came in here and cored them out." She shrugged. "I guess you all thought you were top of the food chain, being the few humans who could read and control thoughts. Then this big alien menace moved in, and their whole *race* can do it. That's a problem."

"It's a problem," agreed Chad. "What's the plan?"

"Our contract was that we'd blow up their base on Earth," said Grace.

He laughed, then sobered as he saw her face. "You're serious."

"You tell me," said Grace. "You're the one who can read minds."

His eyes unfocused, like he was doing Endless jump math in his head. Then he shook his head. "I can't ... see."

"Neat trick," said Grace. "The thing is, you can't lie to someone who can read minds, right? You just need a bigger truth. All Amedea could see was that the great and glorious Republic had us on a job. And that interested her. A small crew, the mighty bending low to offer coin to the needy."

"You planned that?" said Chad.

"Fuck no," said Grace. "Amedea was a complication. We were hoping someone in the Republic command structure — someone pulling the strings — would notice what we were doing. And then we'd find the head of the snake." She hefted her broken sword. "Cut the head off." She turned the sword in her hand. "Turns out, things are a little more ... complicated."

"Nuanced, I'll agree," said Chad. "So what now?"

"I'm playing with half a deck of cards and I'm blind in one eye," said Grace. "But I figure, we've got a chance. If you assholes can stop trying to fucking *control* people for half a minute, you might be useful. You might be useful enough to save the human race. See, Chad? We're right at the part where our plan ran dry. We would call in the *Torrington*, if she wasn't here already. Light up the alien fuckers with some nukes. Turns out they're living in the moon. The moon is useful—"

"The moon," said Hope's voice, from a speaker in the wall, "is *important*."

Grace sighed. "How long?"

"I don't know what you're talking about," said Hope's voice, the speaker making a click like it was turning off.

"Who the hell was that?" said Chad.

Grace smiled. "That was Hope."

"Like, that's her name, or...?"

"It's both, I think," said Grace. "We can't blow up the moon, so we'll need to be a little more circumspect."

"I don't think I like where this is going," said Chad.

"Me neither," said Grace, "but I figure the alternative is you dying in a Republic reprogramming facility."

"Well then," said Chad. "Let us know where you need us. I'll talk to the others." He grabbed Amedea under the arms, pulling her away.

Grace smiled as he moved off, the tired expression saying *I need to sleep* but also said *maybe we won't kill each other, maybe the bugs will do it for us, but at least we'll be fighting together for a change.* She turned to the airlock. Time to lie a little more.

"YOU CAN'T COME IN," said Grace, leaning against the airlock door. This time, she was on the other side of it, in the clean, well-lit boarding bay of the *Torrington*. There was a squad of Marines looking very serious and not at all concerned about the half-sword she had in one hand. Lieutenant Karkoski was facing Grace, arms crossed, looking pissed off. *Finally, she's showing a human emotion.*

"Grace Gushiken," said Karkoski, "behind that airlock are fugitives from justice."

"That is true," said Grace. "You still can't come in."

"And you think you can stop us," said Karkoski, giving a glance towards the Marines. "You."

"No," said Grace. "You're not coming in because you want to live."

"I—"

"And *they* want to live," said Grace, nodding in the general direction of the Marines. "They want their kids to live, if they've got them, or when they get them. And you want your family to live. Where are they?"

Karkoski narrowed her eyes. "Who?"

"Your family."

"I don't see how that's important."

"Play along," said Grace, pushing black hair out of her face with a tired hand. "Just because ... look, Karkoski? It's been a long day. A long, long day. It's not over yet."

"You've brought me the heads of the Resistance," said Karkoski. Her voice softened a whisker. "You've done enough."

"Let's say that's right," said Grace. "Ain't no one on our ship who wouldn't like to rest. But there's a thing you haven't considered. The aliens, Karkoski, are in the *moon*. The moon is a big rock. You can't just punch it out of the sky."

"We could," said Karkoski. "We've got the weapons for it."

"I had a talk to our Engineer," said Grace. "It's not a question of punching. It's a question of debris. The moon, if you blow it in half, will rain moon rock into the Earth's atmosphere, ending all life as we know it."

"I see."

"Tides are a thing we need as well," said Grace. She waved a hand. "I didn't understand it all."

"What do you suggest?" said Karkoski.

"A new contract," said Grace.

"The price?"

"Hell," said Grace, "this isn't going to cost you much at all."

"Why do I feel this will cost me more than I know?" But Karkoski's lips twitched into a shadow of a smile, the hint of something that promised better dealings in the future.

"You need us, Karkoski. You need *all* of us. For what's to come."

Karkoski stood there like a human-shaped stone. Impassive. Unreadable to normal eyes, except for the roiling *doubt/concern/fear* coming off her. "What about Captain Chevell?"

"Nate?"

"Yes. Is he ... *on board* with whatever you'll talk to me about?" She looked at her immaculate boots, then met Grace's eyes. "I notice he's not here."

"He's not here because he's busy doing captain stuff," said Grace. "Truth, there was a conversation we had. But when I said Intelligencers were the only way that all of us wouldn't die, well. He's letting bygones be bygones for a spell."

"Die? All of us?"

"Could happen. The important thing is that the only defense we have against an alien race that can control all our minds are Intelligencers," said Grace. "They can ... shield us. Run interference, while we do what we have to do."

There was silence in the boarding bay, the Marines standing like stones, Karkoski not twitching even a little bit. "Tell me your plan."

"Okay," said Grace, letting out a breath she hadn't realized she was holding. "First, I'll need a new sword."

CHAPTER TWENTY-EIGHT

NATE DIDN'T GO into Engineering often. Not because he was afraid of it but because Hope needed her space, and so he'd given it to her. He'd worried she wouldn't like the noise or the heat, but she'd loved it. She'd always loved it. Right until now.

As he sat with his back to the reactor — Hope's trick with the *Ravana* still paying it forward — he watched her work on his leg. Her pink hair hung limp. *No, that's not it. It's that she's not bothering to push it aside anymore.* "Are we going to be okay?" he asked.

"You did a number on it, that's for sure," she said, one panel open, wires in her hands. Some of them were scorched and charred. "I mean, if you don't mind me skipping the cut and polish—"

"Not what I meant, Hope." He wanted to lean forward, but figured on that being the wrong approach. "I meant are *we* going to be okay. Not my leg. Not me. Not the *Tyche*. Us."

She wasn't looking at him, still staring at the wires in her hands. She had stopped working though, the cables just lying across her palms. "Yes," she said, in a way that made him think *no*.

"Good," said Nate. "Can I tell you a story?"

"Why?"

"Because I need to tell it," said Nate. "It's been chewing at my insides like a cancer. And you don't talk back much. Not like El. And you ... care, I guess. I don't know. Do you?"

"I don't know," said Hope, in a way that made him think, *I don't want to, not anymore.*

"Well," said Nate, "I figure we've got about five minutes while Kohl swears at that warhead he's bringing onboard, which gives us both about the same amount of time. You can fix my leg in five, right?"

"Won't take five," she said, hands moving again, head not looking up. "I mean, for a proper fix, sure, but ... ain't no one got time for the right way about things anymore."

"No, I guess not," said Nate. "I want to tell you about the day I earned this leg. Hand, too, if we're being clear with each other." She looked up at that, one eye hidden behind pink hair, the other clear, bright, and piercing. There was so much pain in that eye, he wanted to reach out to her. But it'd be the wrong approach. So, he looked away, like he hadn't noticed, and he said, "I was forming a guard. For Dom. He was having a birthday party. Dom liked to party. Annemarie, too." Nate smiled at something half-remembered, dragged himself back to the present with an effort. "We ... I guess we had a heads-up, from the Emperor's new elite intelligence squad."

"The Intelligencers," said Hope.

"You telling this story, or am I?"

"Sorry, Cap."

"I reckon they weren't that new. You don't sprout, grown, from the earth. They were everywhere. Dom had been working on them, he'd said. He'd also said he wanted them to spearhead security at the party. Because, you know, Dom was Dom." He sighed. "I told him it wasn't a good idea. Untested, untried. And who wants people who can get in your head around you?"

"Dom ... The Emperor *made* them?"

"That he did, Hope. He made the things that brought down his beloved Old Empire. What neither of us knew was how advanced the coup was. How many there were. There were reports. I read 'em. They were fabrications. But Dom, he was a little savvy, you get me? He had this idea that maybe people who could control your mind, that kind of thing could backfire. So he did two things."

"Two?"

"Maybe more. Maybe three," said Nate, holding his sword up. "The third was this sword. Amedea called it a spear thrown forward in time. I guess it was a contingency. But the two things? So the first was that he got the Intelligencers to set up security for the party, with his most trusted Emperor's Black running alongside. The second, well. The second was that he did the mod on himself. Him and Annemarie both. Or maybe it was his father. Never sure on that point."

"The Emperor could read minds?"

"Not well," said Nate. "He was busy running an Empire. And I said to him, 'Dom, this is wrong,' and he said 'Nate, I don't have a choice.' Because, as I understand it, once you've uncovered a technology, you've got to use it or it'll be used against you."

"You can't ever put toothpaste back in the tube," agreed Hope. "I've tried."

"The problem with his first plan was it meant all the best of us, the ones who wore the Black, well, we were all in the same place at the same time. It made scraping us into a bucket that much easier. The problem with his second plan was that it gave him a false sense of security. He had a sword like this," and Nate held up his sword again, "which was all well and good. But a well-trained Intelligencer is a thing to behold, Hope. They get in your head. Under your skin. Make you *do* things you never wanted to do."

"Did you do something wrong?" said Hope.

"I ... don't know," said Nate. "Not really. I guess I was convinced by Dom that he had everything under control. That things would work out okay. That I, as one of his Black, could get him through. I thought that right until they blew my car to pieces. They fired burning rounds into my flesh. Made it personal. My whole squad died. One of them, well, he covered me with his body. We called him Big Blake. He died screaming on top of me, but I didn't die, Hope. I kept screaming, until I couldn't anymore. And then they put me back together. Gave me a sword and a pension. And Dom said, 'You need to go, brother,' and I said, 'This is the worst time to go.' You know why, Hope?"

She shook her head, mute.

"Because when things are bad, and everyone you love is dying, that's the time you can never leave. And I never will. Never again." Nate leaned forward then. He held her shoulders. "Hope, we won't ever let you go. I'm so, so sorry about Reiko. I can't bring her back, but I'll always be here. The *Tyche* will always be here."

She was quiet for a moment, not pulling away, then he felt her shoulders shake as the sobs took her. "I couldn't stop it," she said. "My Reiko."

Nate pulled her close. "I know," he said.

"She's gone."

"I know."

"She can't come back. I can't fix her."

"I know."

"You know what it's like."

"Yes."

"When does it stop hurting?"

Nate sighed, holding her as she cried. "I don't know," he said. "When you lose family? Maybe never. But if you're lucky, and you've got a crew around you and a hull that holds you tight, you'll be okay." He wasn't sure if it was true, but he felt ... just *maybe*, it might have been. If Hope got any of the luck she deserved, she might smile again.

"I'm sorry, Cap," she said, wiping her eyes with a grease-stained hand. It left a smudge on her cheek.

"What for?"

"Crying on your shirt," she said. "Crying on the captain." And then she cried again.

"It's okay, Hope," said Nate. "I ain't your captain. I'm a terrible captain, but I think I make good family."

"UH," said Grace, eyes roaming over him as he came into the cargo bay. There were sparks of light spraying out from the welded bay door where Hope had completed her emergency repairs. The *Torrington* was cutting its way in, because they had cargo to deliver that wouldn't fit through the side airlock.

"Yeah," said Nate. He tugged his collar. "It's got that thing going on, doesn't it? I'm surprised it still fits."

"Oh, it fits," she said. "It definitely fits."

"Holy shit, Cap," said Kohl. "What the fuck are you wearing?"

Nate looked down at himself. At the black uniform. "An heirloom," he said. After his conversation with Hope, he figured two things. First, he couldn't go around the ship with tear stains on his shirt. Not because he was ashamed, but because if Hope wanted to talk to people about it, that was her business. Second, talking with her about the past had made him remember a little about who he used to be. He wore the Emperor's Black. Commanded a troop of loyal men and women. They were all gone now, but he could respect them by wearing their colors while he fought an alien menace.

It made him proud of who he was. And as he stood here, looking down on Grace and Kohl, it made him proud of who he'd become. Or, at the least, who he'd come along on the journey with. He looked over the cargo bay filled with the remnants of a Resistance that had been on the wrong side of history, men and women who had stood against those who would topple a regime, and he thought, *Well, we might have a chance.*

The cargo bay door fell to the deck with a *boom*, all heads turning to face the opening. Smoke and light came through in equal measure. Nate slid down the railing to land with a *clank* on the decking of the cargo bay. He pushed to the front of the crowd, his sword over his shoulder, his blaster on his hip. The Resistance parted for him, and he waited at the breach in his ship for the smoke to clear.

As it did, he took in a woman, command uniform, straight shoulders. "Captain," said Karkoski.

"Lieutenant," said Nate.

"Not anymore," said Karkoski.

"Field promotion?" said Nate.

"Something like that," said Karkoski. "Our current captain is ... indisposed."

"Okay," said Nate. "That it?" He nodded to the sled behind her. It had rugged wheels on it, designed for rocky terrain. Perfect for wheeling out on the surface of the moon, if it came to that.

"It is," she said. "One nuclear warhead, as requested." She looked at Grace. "Your Assessor has said you can get this into the Ezeroc HQ."

"It's a lair," said Nate. "I've seen 'em before. Slime, shit like that."

"Indeed," said Karkoski. "Well?"

Nate looked behind him at the Resistance, every one of them an esper. Every one of them able to break minds, read thoughts, and generally be a huge pain in the ass. Except this time, they would do it to *aliens*, not their own people. He figured on it being a learning experience for all parties. Turning back to Karkoski, he said, "We'll get it done." He looked at the breach in his hull. "I might need an assist with that, though."

"Why is it that all you seem to want from the fair Republic, under whose flag you sail, is free repairs?" said Karkoski, but with a tight smile.

"Because you assholes keep sending me places where there are aliens who want to blow up my ship. Or, in this case, it's your own guys." Nate shrugged. "Don't matter that they're being commanded by alien mind leeches. The legality is clear."

"That it is, Captain." She paused in the act of turning away. "It's time, isn't it?"

"Yeah," said Nate. "Call your backup."

"How many?"

"Everyone you've got," said Nate.

WHILE THE *TORRINGTON'S* Engineers carried out emergency repairs on the *Tyche* — nothing fancy, a new cargo bay airlock that would open and close is all, carved out of the hull of one of their own heavy lifters — Nate stood in the ready room with El, Grace, Kohl, and Hope. His crew. His family.

"What the hell have you gone and done now?" said El.

"It's like this," said Nate. "The Ezeroc have a base on the moon. So we'll go in there with a nuke and blow 'em up. Like exterminators."

"The hell we are," said Kohl.

"We are," said Grace, putting her fingertips on the big man's arm. "You don't need to be afraid, October Kohl."

He seemed startled, jerking his arm away. "I ain't afraid."

"Then it's settled," said Grace.

"What?" said Kohl. "I mean—"

"The good news," said Nate, "is that we have an entire shipload of espers who will make it seem like the *Tyche* doesn't exist. Oh, she'll still be visible to the naked eye, but I don't see too many naked eyes out here in space. And if we encounter some, that's why we've got the best Helm in the whole universe."

"I hate you," said El, but she had a wolfish smile on her face, showing too many teeth.

"Now, Hope," said Nate, turning to his young Engineer. "Nothing fancy, okay? Just keep her running. I need the engines on, ready for when we come out."

"She'll fly true, Cap," said Hope. "I promise."

"Cap," said El.

"What is it, Helm?"

"Looking good," she said, nodding at the black uniform. "I was wondering when you'd remember who you were."

"Emperor's Black," said Kohl. "Fiercest assholes I've ever killed."

"That, and a damn fine captain," said El. "I'd follow you into hell, sir."

"Might be doing that," said Hope, her voice small, eyes wide. "But I'd follow family anywhere."

"Yes," said Grace. "Together."

Nate swallowed a lump in his throat, his mouth opening and closing a couple of times. "Uh," he said.

"Don't spoil the moment," said El, turning back to the flight deck. "We got aliens to scrub out."

"Hang on," said Kohl. "I don't think we're clear on who's going in there."

"Come on, big man," said Nate. "We're going to save the world."

LEAVING the docking couple with the *Torrington* was a simple affair. A few clanks and they floated free. The drives fired up, streams of fire pushing at the hard black, nudging them clear. The *Tyche* flew like she was eager for what was to come. Maybe they all were, ready to test their luck one more time.

In her hold, she held the leaders of the Resistance against the Republic. Remnants of the Old Empire, most still true and loyal. They had special powers: they could see the thoughts of others, sometimes altering them. They bent those skills towards making the *Tyche* invisible to mental view. Invisible to other espers, or aliens who talked mind to mind as easy as it was for humans to breathe.

The *Tyche* also held a nuclear warhead, designed to be rolled into a nest of snakes. It would be delivered by hand. It needed to be taken to the right place, at the right time. A tactical device, to excise an infection, rather than blowing the moon into chunks that would rain death on the Earth. No one turns the moon into an alien starship. Time to remind the bugs of that.

And she held her crew, five souls who started as pirates and liars, murderers and criminals. They would now save the world. After that? Maybe they'd try and save the universe, but one day at a time. It was important to not push your luck.

As the *Tyche* stalked across the hard black towards the moon, leaving mother Earth and the *Torrington* behind her, eyes looked out from the flight deck. The holo stage brought up hostile action, a storm of rocks leaving the moon's crust. These were unlike those the *Tyche* had dodged back on Absalom Delta, dumb missiles thrown into the dark. These were guided, agile like fighter craft. They moved towards the *Tyche*, accelerating as they came, but without the telltale drive plumes of human craft.

The *Torrington* appeared to take this in, and then the ship shivered and blinked away, an Endless Drive whisking her to safer waters. The aliens on the moon took in this data, certain that the cowardice of humans was showing its face again. Understanding humans was difficult for their alien minds. They were used to working as a cohesive unit. Mind to mind, will to will. They never doubted, never altered their purpose. There was no dissent. They had come across the dark void between stars, eating civilizations as they came, until they found just one more. Humans. Weak, soft, and cowardly.

Except for this one tiny ship. The fighter craft gained visual on the *Tyche*, but for a species used to fighting their opponents on battle-fields both physical and mental, it was difficult to track. They didn't know it, but the Intelligencers on board the ship linked minds, locking the Ezeroc out. Nothing to see, nothing to influence. Which meant they didn't understand this piece of metal without a mind, didn't know how to target it except with crude kinetic weapons. But they had plenty of those, and it was only a matter of time before they filled the skies above this planet with enough rock to end all hope.

If aliens could be confident — and they could — this was the moment where the confidence was at its highest. The government of these people was weak. While the alien outpost below had been destroyed, it was a temporary affair. They could install new agents, and they would as soon as the immediate threat was removed. This threat was one they had picked up by sifting through humans on the *Torrington*, and it focused the efforts of the Ezeroc.

The *Tyche* didn't slow. She came on, sailing soft and easy as she did it. If anyone — human or Ezeroc — had been watching, this was the moment where they would have bet against the Goddess of Luck. They would have thought she had overplayed her hand.

Space rippled, blurred, and the *Torrington* snapped back above the planet. It was possible her crew had rethought cowardice, realized that without the Earth there would be no home to return to. Weapons were online, coherent light stretching across the void to touch those stony fighters racing toward the *Tyche*. Those ships were hunks of pure moon rock, rough on the outside, heavy and thick, and the lasers deployed against them were having no effect on their targets. Masers were brought to play, with better effect. And torpedoes were launched, smart rockets with heavy payloads.

But one destroyer against an alien fleet on the moon? It was a laughable proposition, if aliens could laugh.

The aliens still didn't understand humans well, nor human technology. While the Ezeroc could speak mind to mind without speed of light complications, the humans were limited by basic relativity. The *Torrington* had needed to jump to where the rest of their fleet lay. A paltry handful of ships, but built with human hands, to protect human worlds. Foremost they were built to protect humans against themselves, but now they had found a new, beautiful purpose. And that purpose wasn't allowing fucking *aliens* to wipe out humanity.

After the *Torrington* arrived, another ripple in space announced the arrival of her sister *Lucidity*. Moments later, the *Confidence* jumped into space above Earth. Three destroyers, the second largest craft humans built, deployed above the Earth. They stood between the *Tyche* and the approaching fighter craft. They stood against the end of the world.

One more ship joined them. Her crew called her the *Defiance*, and she was a carrier. The largest craft human hands had built. Her crews were already scrambling attack craft of their own, tiny gnats launched from the great ship.

Things had gone from being unbalanced to more equitable. The Ezeroc attack ships changed vector, bearing down on the newcomers to the battle. The new ships responded in kind. While humans fought each other to the death for land, for power, and for money, they were united in one thing: no aliens would take their world. Resistance and Republic flew in the sky above the cradle of humanity, and they fought for the future of their race.

Streaming media networks of the humans below went live to capture the battle. People watched as lasers bathed the shells of rocks with light that could cut ceramicrete. Masers boiled their insides. Torpedoes launched, streaking across the black of space with deadly promise. Human skirmish craft — brothers and sisters to the *Tyche*, but younger, more agile — streaked across the sky pulling Gs that would have crushed pilots of ten years earlier.

While the humans gave well, the Ezeroc had an entire moon at their disposal. Dumb rocks were launched, aimed at the Republic military and at the planet below. The Republic ships needed to turn these rocks to rubble, or their ships would be cored, or the planet below would take a cratering. Either was bad news.

Through the melee, the *Tyche* slipped, a goddess wearing a shadow gown. Off to starboard, an explosion of light and heat as an Ezeroc ship impacted with a human fighter. Bright, bright light as the *Lucidity* vented atmosphere and people and nuclear fire into the void as a rock the size of a building slammed her through the center. Her running lights dark, she drifted. The *Confidence* raged back, and a handful of Ezeroc fighters ceased to be as nuclear warheads detonated in their midst.

And yet, the Goddess of Luck slipped on, thanks to the efforts of the espers aboard, the control of the reactor by a savvy Engineer, and the gentle hands of a skilled Helm. She made the landing soft and easy, surface dust billowing out as she settled skids on the crust. Three souls stepped out. The Intelligencers remained on the ship, splitting their focus. They kept both those on *Tyche* and the departed crew hidden.

All hands were still alive, while humans in their thousands died behind her. The *Tyche* might be lucky, but again she fought against Chronos, and time wasn't on her side.

CHAPTER TWENTY-NINE

THE OPENING in the moon was unmistakable. Grace's breathing hissed inside her suit as she panted with exertion, helping Kohl and Nate hustle the sled across the surface towards the hole. Or she was panting in fear — that was more likely, as Kohl with his bulky power armor was doing all the hard work. Nate had a hand on the sled, and Grace had two, but they were more keeping the thing company than doing anything useful. The hole was their destination: unmistakable because it looked like an anthill of epic scale, and also because of the Ezeroc around the rim.

Okay, so they don't need an atmosphere. That is inconvenient for us, fighting inside spacesuits while they moonwalk.

The bugs noticed them, turning eyes on at approach. Starting a scuttle down the side of the mound of moon rock and dust. And then they stopped as the *Tyche* blasted overhead, PDCs hammering at the earth. El's voice came over the comm: "You guys need to hustle." From over the horizon behind them, Ezeroc ships — hunks of rock that looked like accreted hunks of crystals and stone — approached. The *Tyche* banked, gave a salvo of PDC and maser fire, then blasted off into space, drawing the Ezeroc away.

"Well, there goes our ride," said Nate.

Grace laughed, because she knew as well as he did: they wouldn't need a ride. They wouldn't ever get off this rock. The realization of it made her giddy. She picked up *love/protect/humor* from Nate, and *confusion/protect/determination* from Kohl. Both were good enough. Both were here, with her. She had a real family, which meant she could die knowing what that felt like.

The sled was heavy under Earth gravity but the moon's paltry mass made it feel lighter. They were jogging in great bounds along the bumpy terrain, dust rising in their wake. Grace thought, *In all my wildest dreams, I would not have thought I would run along the surface of the moon.* They reached the lip of the anthill, looking into the maw. It was mostly dark down there, but odd organic illumination marked a path. The Ezeroc might not need air, but they needed — or wanted — light. Good to know for next time, not that there would be a next time.

Grace did a last check at the top of the rim. Nate, in his black suit, Emperor's insignia on the shoulder, sword on his back, one hand reaching up to draw it in the silence of space. Carrying the last piece of his friend to his grave. The metal was black and hungry. His other hand held a blaster, low, ready. Grace looked to Kohl, the big man unshucking his plasma cannon from the back of his power armor. The armor was like Kohl: rough and ready. It wasn't pretty; it had never promised to be pretty, but did the dark and dirty work no one else wanted to. That plasma cannon promised great things, but Kohl also carried — small, innocuous almost — a maser, given to him by a new friend he never knew he needed. And finally, Grace checked herself. A borrowed suit from the *Tyche*, but hers now. She was welcome on the ship, one of its crew. No one would throw her off, try and expose her, give her up for coin. They'd given her their colors as a show of faith. Her Republic sword was unfamiliar but strong. The edge was straight, not curved, but sharp enough to get the job done a hundred times or more. It carried a nano edge, spun molecules woven in space. It would never blunt. Grace wasn't sure if it would break, but she knew one thing: the blade would break before she did.

Breathing calm once more, she pointed with her blade into the pit. "We going in or what?"

Kohl laughed. "This is it, isn't it? Us, against the might of an alien empire."

"I reckon so," said Nate.

"I wouldn't be here with anyone else," said Grace. "I wouldn't choose anyone else."

"Me neither, Gracie."

"Asshole."

Nate flashed them both a grin, then set off down into the pit. His strides were big and loping, sword and blaster ready. Leading, because that's what leaders did. They didn't command from the back, or hide inside metal hulls. They did what needed to be done. She looked at Kohl, who gave a holler as he put a boot against the side of the sled. A shove of servos and the sled went down into the pit. Kohl then made his power armor jump after Nate. She watched it scribe an arc through the airless void, running lights casting back the shadows. She swallowed.

Then she followed.

THE SLED WAS RUNNING WILD, out of control, down the tunnels they found. There were junctions aplenty, but each time the sled found a junction it always seemed to choose the hole that went deeper. Down, into the core of the moon. The rocky walls were white and chalky, the sled's tires kicking up dust as they passed. Grace didn't have time to marvel at the tunnels built into the moon — all done silently, while Earth slumbered below. She was loping along at the rear, Nate still charging ahead after the sled, Kohl lumbering after, his power armor's lights a beacon. A challenge.

There weren't a plethora of guard drones, none they'd seen so far anyway. That gave a few options.

Option 1: there were no guards, because who would attack a hive on the moon they didn't know existed? This was the optimistic option, but the least likely in Grace's estimation.

Option 2: the guards were piloting the ships in space as the battle raged in space. That was the likely scenario, but it didn't preclude...

Option 3: there were guards here, waiting. Hiding. Reduced in number, ready to leap out at the unwary. They knew the terrain. They knew how to get in and out.

Grace's HUD kept track of their twists and turns, the distance from the surface they were scrambling away from. She didn't know if she should feel safer down here or up there. Up there, a battle raged, massive forces leveraged against each other. A single human could be turned into stray atoms almost accidentally. Down here, there were aliens, and they were hungry for humans in general, and Grace in particular.

So, okay. Down here was worse. But she had to see it through. She had to send a message to these fuckers. Hunt Grace Gushiken, and Grace will hunt you back. And she wasn't alone. Not anymore. Her eyes flicked to Nate's back.

Together.

"*TYCHE*, THIS IS THE CAPTAIN," said Nate. Grace heard his voice on the comm, but no response. "*Torrington*, please come in."

Nothing. Either everyone out there was dead, or a kilometer of moon rock was an effective insulator.

The sled rested against a turn in the tunnel. Grace's suit told her there was still no atmosphere, but also told her the surface of the moon under her feet was warm. Like there was a power source here. What it was made of didn't bear thinking about. They had three directions they could choose. Back the way they came (nope), left (maybe), or right (also maybe).

"Well, we're on our own," said Nate.

"That ain't the worst part, Cap," said Kohl. He swiveled in place, looking down the left tunnel first, then the right. "Means we can't remote detonate."

"Yeah, that's fine," said Nate. "It's what countdown timers were made for. What I'm worried about is which way to go."

Grace's arm shot out like it was pulled by strings. "That way," she said, pointing right.

"How do you know?" said Kohl.

Grace looked at him. "You can't hear them?"

"Hear who, Gracie?"

"Asshole," she muttered, then looked at Nate. "You?"

"No," he said, turning to Kohl. "The way I think it works is that if you're some kind of esper, you get switched to receive mode by default. They can hear these fuckers."

Grace.

"Definitely that way," said Grace. "They know I'm here. Amedea and Chad are doing their best, but..."

"Fucken' awesome," said Kohl. He hefted his plasma cannon. "Do they know I'm here too?"

"I don't think they care," said Grace.

"Oh," said Kohl. "Imma make 'em care."

THE TUNNEL WIDENED INTO A CHAMBER. Grace's HUD had a map of the route they'd traversed in the top right of her field of view. A long way back to the surface, at least a klick. An unknown distance to go, although—

Grace! Grace! Come! Grace!

—she figured on them being close enough to kiss now. The

chamber was long, more of a wider tunnel, the walls still chalky and white, but pockmarked with holes. Those holes were of various sizes, some small as her fist, a few large enough to drive a loader through. The chamber was otherwise empty, the aperture at the other end leading into a soft organic bloom of green light.

Grace! Together!

I am only together with one other person, she thought, her eyes flicking to Nate. *I only want to be* together *with that man.*

Then he must die.

"Nate," said Grace. He was ahead of her and Kohl, about midway down the chamber's length. His blaster and sword were ready, but he wasn't looking *up*. "Nate—"

An Ezeroc drone scuttled out of one hole in the walls, then leapt at Nate. Plasma fire from Kohl's cannon followed it through the space, bright and silent. The flashes were enough to make Nate turn, to get his sword up as the creature landed on him. Its claws were raised high, ready to strike.

Three more entered the chamber through other holes, one scuttling low, the other two leaping. One leaper went for Kohl, the big man saying something that sounded like *about Goddamn time* as he lit the space with plasma flashes. One leaper came for Grace, and she raised her sword to meet it. There would be no smooth dance here, the low gravity of the moon putting off her usual fluidity of motion. She waited for the thing, watching it come closer, thinking *while I'm waiting here for this to land, Nate will die.* As it got closer, traversing the distance in less than a second — a very long second — she had time to think, *is this sword going to be enough against those teeth? I do not know this sword, and it does not know me.* And then the Ezeroc was on her, and then it was past her, the two halves of it spraying entrails into vacuum. She didn't remember swinging. Grace didn't remember the strike. She was focused on Nate, and she held her sword low as she bounded across the chamber.

The creature Kohl was firing at jumped and skipped around the walls, big plasma blasts tearing chunks out of the moon rock. She could hear him yelling over the comm, a long yell that was a stretched out *motherfuuuuuuuckerrrrr*. Grace had to get past that rain of plasma to get to Nate. She had to get to Nate before the Ezeroc sliced him open like a Thanksgiving turkey. The Ezeroc Kohl was firing at zipped through the space too close to her, and she sliced one of its legs off without thinking, innards boiling in vacuum as she moved on. She forgot about the plasma, forgot about Kohl, and she even forgot about the one that had been scuttling across the floor until it reared in front of her. Grace had been so focused on her destination she'd forgotten about it — her instructors would have berated her for it. *You must never lose focus in the battle. The battle will be what it will be.* And here, she'd die, because she'd lost focus.

A wild swing from her sword missed, and the Ezeroc's maw opened. It reached towards her with those leading claws.

And then it exploded in a shower of steaming meat as Kohl blew it to pieces. Grace blinked, realized that blinking was costing her time, and turned back towards Nate.

She'd never make it in time.

She needn't have worried. Nathan Chevell might have been — in his own mind, *not* hers — a useless cripple. But he was still the captain of a starship with a crew to protect. He still wore the Emperor's Black, and held the Emperor's last gift. Nate was twisting under the Ezeroc, its claws flashing down to impact the ground where his helmet was, each time missing by a whisker. Nate got his blaster up, and plasma tore chunks out of the underside of the insect. It reared back, giving him time to roll up on one knee. His left hand held his sword, and even though — again, in his own mind — he couldn't use it worth a damn, he still lunged forward, skewering the Ezeroc on the end of the black blade.

Panting filled the comm channel, then Kohl's voice came through loud and clear. "Gracie, I'll have to claim at least partial credit for that one you sliced the legs off."

She turned. "How you figure, Kohl?" A giggle escaped her lips, and she wanted to clamp a hand over her mouth. Difficult, that, with a helmet on.

"I set it up for you."

She let the laugh out, leaning on her sword. "Okay," she said. "Okay."

Nate swung his blade, bits of Ezeroc frozen to it. "Well, that was intense."

Grace! Grace! Grace!

She stopped laughing. "It'll get more intense." She took a step backward from the end of the chamber, then another. "A lot more."

Through the aperture at the end came a massive crab. The biggest she'd ever seen, hard armor plates covering it. Its clawed limbs pulled it over the ground. Grace took another step back. "We need to distract it. Get the bomb into the chamber beyond. That's where the Queen is."

"Good idea," said Nate. "I'll draw it this way—"

"All y'all need to hold up," said Kohl. He walked toward the Ezeroc, plasma cannon held in front on the mounts of his power armor. "Hey. Ugly. You want a piece?"

The Ezeroc charged.

Kohl's plasma cannon streamed fire, the impacts of each bolt hammering the outside of the Ezeroc's shell. That shell cracked, buckled, pieces chipping off to turn towards the ground. Kohl kept firing, stepping forward as he did, human power armor standing against Ezeroc organic might. Nate was firing too, his blaster chipping away at the thing. Didn't matter if he was helping or hurting.

They were buying Grace time.

She grabbed the sled, heaving at it. Grace ran past the Ezeroc, its armor now glowing with heat in places, and into the chamber beyond.

THE GLOOM here was thrown back by flashes of light from the melee in the entrance chamber. Here, pods of humans — sealed against vacuum — littered the floor and walls. Hundreds of them. Grace wondered how they got them up here. Unnoticed, under the eyes of the Republic. Then she thought of the man in black, or the *men* in black, and wondered how the Ezeroc hadn't eaten them all already. The room was huge, a massive cavern buried deep below the moon's surface. They had been busy little insects, working with a will to protect their Queen against the eyes and weapons of humans. Only suicidal humans would ever make it this far. Humans who cared more about their race than themselves. And there were few of those. The Queen herself was far away from Grace, against the far wall. Huge, the biggest of her kind that Grace had ever seen. Larger than the infant version she'd seen on Absalom Delta, or the mature one they'd found on Earth. This one was old, and powerful, and used to winning.

The Queen's voice was loud in Grace's mind. It was like a hammer, battering at her will. Wanting to make her *become* one of them. She'd fallen once before. Grace had almost fallen a second time.

She wouldn't fall a third.

"Go," she said, through clenched teeth, "*fuck yourself*."

The sled was too heavy to move over the pods, but it didn't matter. The Queen looked down at her from its position far away. Too far away to touch Grace with those claws. But not anywhere near far enough away to avoid death by nuclear fire. Grace turned to the nuke, flipping open its console. It was designed to be easy to use, troops with boots on the ground, a hail of withering fire all around them, able to set it off without mistake. The controls were simple.

Her fingers rested — briefly, but the temptation was strong — over the *DETONATE* switch's cover. It was red, locked in place, designed in a way that said *if you flick back the lock, you know what you're doing*. That would end it all, without doubt. But she thought about Nate, and thought, *no*.

She clicked on the timer display. How long would it take them to reach the surface? Get up, and out? It was a kilometer. She could run a kilometer in five minutes. Nate, with his leg? Maybe the same, if Kohl was there with his power armor to help. Five minutes, and then they would die on the dark side of the moon.

Six minutes, then. She set the timer, locked it in place, and ran.

CHAPTER THIRTY

NATE KEPT his fire on the Ezeroc crab. He knew Kohl's cannon was doing all the real work here, but two sources of plasma fire would confuse it. It meant if it came at them, there was a fifty/fifty chance it'd take Nate first, buying the big man time to ... buy Grace more time.

Grace burst from the aperture of the chamber. She used the moon's low gravity to bound up one wall and around the Ezeroc. He caught sight of her face through her visor, eyes wide, but not panicked or scared. Grace looked *focused*.

The Ezeroc crab took a swipe at her, its limb glowing with heat. Nate figured it'd be on fire if there was an atmosphere to help with that. As it was, the shot was clumsy, missing by an easy margin. She landed close to them, glanced over her shoulder at the creature, and said, "Run."

Kohl snorted over the comm. "Hell no, Gracie. Job's not done." He fished his maser out, letting the plasma cannon rest on its mounts. He pointed the maser at the crab, saying, "Yo. This one's from a friend of mine." He squeezed the maser's trigger. The Ezeroc seemed to be recovering from the barrage of plasma, took a step towards them, then stopped. It turned around, and Nate could feel the rumble of those big legs through his boots. It seemed confused, mandibles clacking, then one of its big arms popped off in a spray of steam and fluids. Loopy streams of innards vented from its carapace to boil away in the vacuum. Then one of the chest pieces popped open in a shower of gore, and it stumbled to the ground.

"Maybe you should open with that next time," said Nate.

"Run," said Grace, again. Her eyes flicked sideways, Nate figuring on her checking her HUD. "We've got just over five minutes."

"Until what?" said Kohl.

"Until we blow a chunk out of the moon."

"Fuck," said Kohl, but Nate was already running. Or as *running* as you could in lower gravity, big loping strides taking him back the way they'd come. He held his sword in his metal hand, blaster in his right, and hoped to see stars again before he died.

KOHL HAD a hand on his back, pushing him forward. He glimpsed the big man's grin through his visor. "No slowing now, Cap."

"Go," said Nate. "Get on."

"Hell no," said Kohl. "Gracie'll have my dick on a spit."

"Asshole," said Grace, over the comm.

"Leave me," said Nate. "That's an order, Kohl. Get Grace out."

"I'm gonna have to disagree on that particular point," said Kohl. "You can yell at me later."

And they were running again, chalky walls streaking past.

30 SECONDS. Starlight. His breath harsh in his ears, throat burning. A flash of Grace Gushiken on his left. Kohl's strong grip —

damn that armor is good, I'll have to get me some — propelling him forward.

29.

"*Tyche!*" Nate gasped it out. "We're clear!"

26.

A scramble up the inline of the maw, an exit from the ant farm. Darkness around.

25.

The maw opening up, ejecting them. Moon dust hanging around them, clouding his visor. Lights from his suit, tiny in the hard black.

24.

Ships overhead. Missiles and fire. Lasers turning Ezeroc fighters to molten rock in space.

23.

"This is the *Tyche*. We are on approach." El's voice. Calm. Nate could picture her hands on the controls, steady as a rock.

22.

"How long?" he gasped.

"Ten seconds."

21.

He looked at Grace. She shook her head. Kohl helped him reach the lip of the pit, the dark of the moon pushed back by the lights of his armor. A final show of humanity against the dark.

18.

"You should ... go," said Nate, over the comm. "Get out, El. Ain't no way, no how you can get clear in time."

15.

A ship, scudding low over the moon's surface. Inbound, hard approach. Drives burning bright.

14.

The ship cut its drives, giving him a brief glimpse of a cockpit's glow, then it was spinning in space. The *Tyche*, come to get her crew.

12.

Skids on the deck. An airlock open. Hands helping them inside —

Chad, for Christ's sake, it was *Chad* with his stupid name and his stupid boss.

7.

"Go! Helm, we are inside. Go!"

5.

The hard push of the *Tyche's* engines. They slammed him against the wall of the airlock. Grace's helmet slamming against the wall next to his, Kohl and Chad tumbling on top. A crack over the comm as something broke — a seal, a bone, hard to tell.

3.

The ship was shaking with the fury of their ascent. Nate had never felt the *Tyche* burn so hot.

2.

Something in the superstructure above him groaned. It sounded like the end of the world.

1.

CHAPTER THIRTY-ONE

"HOPE, I need you to make sure that reactor holds, you hear me?" El was looking at the holo stage, the landing party's beacons the only bright points against the moon's surface. *Ten seconds.* Ten seconds was bullshit.

"She'll hold," said Hope's voice. "It's the hull I'm worried about."

"You should ... go," said Nate, over the comm. "Get out, El. Ain't no way, no how you can get clear in time."

El clicked off the comm. Wasn't time to worry about that now. Captain was out there. So was Grace and Kohl. It'd be all of them, or none of them. She opened a line to Chad. "You good?"

"Suits on. I'm good. I'll get them, Helm."

"You better," she said. She saw them now on visual, Kohl's ridiculous armor like a landing beacon. El cut the thrust, spinning the ship around, the moon's tiny gravity nothing. She toggled the Endless field, a tiny bit of extra mass dropping them like a stone. The skids hit with a clang that made her teeth hurt.

Her hands moved like restless mice over the controls. *C'mon Nate. C'mon. Get inside.*

"Go! Helm, we are inside. Go!"

El slammed her hand down on the throttle, pushing it to the stops. The ship roared, moon dust billowing out in every direction. She had a counter up on the holo stage, a part of her attention never far from it.

5.

More. I need more. "Hope!"

"She's at the red!"

"*HOPE!*" screamed El.

3.

The ship shuddered, a few hidden joules coming through from the *Ravana's* heart. Something groaned behind her, the structure of the ship shaking apart. Alarms on the holo lit, warnings meant for a different pilot. Meant for a pilot who wanted to save her own skin.

2.

Not this pilot.

1.

A MOMENT OF BRIGHT, bright light. A new sun, blooming under the crust of the moon. The interior of the flight deck was cast for a tiny slice of time in nothing but pure, pure white. All details, the corner of the console, the edges of the holo stage, Els' hands, were bleached to the same uniform, brilliant purity. The *Tyche's* cockpit dimmed as fast as her old tech would allow, snapping down protective filters.

The blast wave hit a moment later. El had a moment to think, *this shit never ends*, and then another moment to think, *that doesn't mean I want it to end* right *now*. Then the hand of a titan of old grabbed the hull, turned the *Tyche* like a toy ship spun in a tornado. The holo stage's alarms entered what looked like an endless cascade, the chair at El's back hitting her hard as the ship bucked.

The Goddess of Luck went head to head with Ares.

El's hands found the sticks. They were in a spin, and they needed to *not* spin. Moon rock and debris rattled against the outside of the hull, and through the now clear windscreen El saw a piece of stone as large as the *Tyche* herself flung past. It wouldn't have been more than five meters away. And then it was gone, hurled off into space. If anything like that hit them, they wouldn't even feel it.

She worked the controls, trying to get the *Tyche* to respond. She felt the ship trying, fighting *with* her, not *against* her. The spin slowed, turning into a tumble. El didn't feel quite so much like throwing up her last meal anymore. Something in the ship's systems gave out, the drives stuttering to silence, and she realized she could play with the controls all she wanted: she was using nothing but dead sticks.

A moment later, all lights in the flight deck died. The holo stage went out. Her console gave out.

They were drifting.

The burst of flight they'd had was enough to push them out from the moon's shadow. The dark disk of the moon felt like it was pulling away above her. A glowing crater marred the surface, angry red against the rest of the cold rock. Earth, in its beautiful greens and blues, came into view. She could see with the naked eye the massive bulk of the *Defiance*, fire pouring from three locations she could see. The *Torrington* still flew, but one of her drives was down, dark. Her movements were more of a limp. Of the *Confidence* there was no sign at all, and the dead *Lucidity* still floated alone in the dark.

El ran a tired hand through her hair. She wanted to stretch but there was no gravity. They were floating, a leaf on the wind. She keyed her suit's comm. "Hope?"

"El."

"Are you okay?"

"I'm ... okay," said the Engineer.

El thought for a second. "Didn't I promise you a Viking funeral?"

"You did," said Hope. "You did."

"What now?" said El.

"I think we get drunk," said Hope. "That's what the Vikings did."

"I mean, now," said El.

"Reactor's fried," said Hope.

"Okay," said El. She almost turned off the comm, then said, "You wanna come to the flight deck?"

"Why?"

"Because it's beautiful," said El.

WHY IT WAS beautiful was hard to put into words. It might have been that they'd won. The remaining human ships were the victors. Ezeroc fighters, without the commanding intelligence of their hive Queen, ceased to navigate, becoming plain ol' ballistic rocks. The *Torrington* and the *Defiance* engaged in a mop-up, shooting some down, leaving the smaller ones to the *Defiance's* remaining fighters.

It could also have been beautiful because of what El could imagine down on Earth: confusion. Men in black, in meeting rooms or halls of power or in black ops, just toppling over. Stopping like a broken clock.

Hope joined her on the flight deck, her hand over hand motion taking her to the captain's chair. She belted herself in. El turned to look at the Engineer, her pink hair floating free of her face. And she thought, *it might be beautiful because we are with our family*. Live or die, they'd done what they set out to do, and they hadn't killed each other. They'd made a Republic used to ruling ease up the boot, reach out a hand of compromise. Backs to the wall, humans helped each other. The turning on each other, the blaming, the hunt for scape-goats, would all come later.

El looked back out the window. She saw mother Earth above them, that beautiful, clean, blue-green disc. *It might be beautiful because it stops the heart and frees the soul.*

It was enough.

CHAPTER THIRTY-TWO

"I GUESS I want to know where we stand," said Nate. He held his cup of coffee in hands that shook if they didn't grip tight enough. *Yeah, even the metal one.*

Karkoski looked tired, worn thin, but her back was still straight. Nate noted she held her own coffee just as hard. "You mean whether I'll let you fly out of here." They were in the officer's mess of the *Torrington*, which made a step up from the last small room Nate had been in on this ship. Karkoski had told everyone else to leave, including her usual impassive Marine escort.

"Hell, no," said Nate. "Of *course* you'll let me fly out of here. And you'll fix my ship first."

"I am?" Karkoski frowned. "That seems a stretch of reason. Biggest haul of my career. You've got a boatload of enemies of the Republic. Your ship is bolted to the side of mine, and your reactor's dead. Fish in a barrel."

Grace leaned forward. "But you are, Karkoski. You know why?"

"Fill me in," said Karkoski. But she looked interested. She looked like every time she listened to Nate or Grace, things went her way.

"You need us," said Grace.

Some doubt clouded Karkoski's face. "I. Need you."

"Sure," said Nate, hand on Grace's arm. "We have the only force of people capable of fighting the Ezeroc. You and I both know conscripted soldiers don't work as well as the ones who fight for truth. Love. Their homes. Shit like that." He waved a tired hand in the air. "But there's a more important reason. This isn't about your *career* anymore, Karkoski. This is about us. All of us. Humans. Against the biggest threat we've ever seen. It's not about the Empire, or the Republic. There ain't no Resistance, Karkoski. All of us are monsters. Criminals. Pirates. Thieves and liars. But we need each other. We need each other or we're all going to die."

"Imagining for a second I can just let you go," said Karkoski, "with all these witnesses." She was referring to the *Defiance*, a watchful distance away in space. Or maybe she meant all the witnesses down on Earth. There were a lot of eyes, a lot of holos. A lot of talk, in the wake of the battle. Of alien invaders and subverted leadership. Confidence in the Republic had to be at rock bottom about now. "Where would you go?"

"Depends," said Nate.

"On what?" said Karkoski.

Grace leaned forward again. "Use your imagination, Karkoski. We're a merchant vessel. A free trader. Our Guild permits are in order. You've used us for dirty work before. But now? You need someone small. Quiet. To go in the dark spaces where you can't take a ship like the *Torrington*. Where something like the *Torrington* will be seen. By alien eyes."

"You want me to send you to fight the bugs," said Karkoski.

"Hell, no," said Nate, again. "Ain't no way a ship like the *Tyche's* got that kind of fight in her. She's got heart. She'll fly into the storm if we ask her to. But no. We'll find them, Karkoski. We'll make our Endless jumps until we track them down."

"Then what?"

"Then we call you," said Nate. "When we've found the heart of the enemy." His hands clenched on his cup. "We'll strike 'em down. They brought war to us. Made us hate each other. We'll return the favor. We'll teach them *fear*."

"And the Intelligencers?" Karkoski looked like she was panning for gold in a dried-up riverbed.

"Believe me, I want to execute them for what they've done. But, uh. We're taking them too. They're going to, uh." Nate frowned, turning to Grace for help.

"They'll work for humanity," said Grace. "Just like they did today. We'll build a specialist team. One that can shield our ships. Fight the bugs. Mind to mind."

"You're going to let them escape," said Karkoski.

"It didn't sit right with me letting those assholes go," said Nate, "until Grace explained it. This way, we'll know where they all are. And ... hell. I guess we need 'em. Fighting mind insects? We need a little magic of our own, Karkoski."

"A little *black* magic," she said. "Can we trust them?"

"Chad, maybe," said Nate. "Amedea, not so much. I think those two are in charge of the rest. Anyway. After we put 'em down, the *Tyche* will go after the bugs."

"You'll never make it," said Karkoski. "Everything we know about them says they've torched every world they've laid a claw on." She sighed. "I've read what reports there are."

"Then what have you got to lose?" said Nate. "For the next few weeks or months or however long it'll be, you'll be up to your medals in politics. Working out who's in charge, who can be trusted. And you know what? You've got one group of people who can be trusted. One group of people who've never cheated or stolen from you. You've got us."

Karkoski thought about that for a long time. Then she said, "Yes, I do." She put her cup between them, stood up, and turned. Stopped herself. "Captain?"

"Yeah?"

"It's always nice to have friends, don't you think?" And then she left.

GRACE HAD FOLLOWED him back to the *Tyche*. Back through the cargo bay, around sprawled and tired espers. Hands of thanks, a touch here and there. Nate wanted to laugh. He wanted to cry. They'd done it. And — he cast a glance at Grace — they'd done it together.

They clambered up the ladder to the crew deck. Nate stopped in front of the door to his cabin. A shower. Clean clothes. Food.

"We've got a little time," said Grace, her lips next to his ear. He felt the whisper of her breath against his neck. Nate had imagined those lips against his, just as he'd imagined her lithe body against him.

He turned, thoughts of food gone like a wisp of fantasy. Nate saw his own yearning reflected in her eyes, and caught a little of his own vulnerability there too. Two people gone through life the hard way. He raised a hand to touch her hair. Then her face, his fingers trailing down her cheekbones to touch her lips. Lips he wanted to kiss again more than he'd wanted anything before. Nate realized he was touching her with his metal fingers, and jerked them away like he'd been burned.

She reached out for his hand, laced her flesh fingers through his golden ones, and brought them back to her face. "Here," she said, putting his fingers back on her lips. She lowered his fingers to her throat. "Here." She guided his fingers lower, metal fingers tracing her shoulders. "Here." She let go, and he continued to trace his fingers further down her body. Past her breasts, a shiver coming from her at the touch, her eyes widening as her lips opened in a gasp. To her hips, where he pulled her close. She curved against him, their lips meeting. He could taste the sweat on her, smell the animal underneath the cultivated exterior. She smelled of her ship suit and battle, a primal scent that made him want to growl. Nate had figured on a shower moments ago, but she was just as dirty as he was. He found her sexier for it, the raw Grace Gushiken, the woman who'd fought at his side like a dancer. Like a demon. Like the beauty of the dawn. He'd never wanted anyone this much. He felt hot and alive. And hungry.

Nate reached behind him, pressing the door open controls. Her hands were on him, tracing down his chest, tugging his shirt out of his pants. He felt his skin react with a shiver as her fingers traced their way down the hard lines of his stomach. Neither of them wanted to let go, and they stumbled back into his cabin, the door sealing behind them. She jerked his pants open while he pulled off her shirt. He reached around her, unclipping her bra. He wanted more. Nate wanted it all. He bent his head down to kiss a nipple, and she arched against him. Grace fell back against his bunk, and he tumbled down with her, his body moving with a mind of its own.

He'd found the person he'd been looking for his whole life. He hadn't even known she was right in front of him until now. All it had taken was a little luck.

"WHAT DO YOU MEAN, I'm clear?" said Hope. They were in the *Tyche's* ready room. Chad stood with them, the man looking tired. He deserved to wear that look; before the day's events, he'd been the prisoner of evil mind insects.

"I mean," said Nate, "that Grace's deal was simple. Full amnesty. Your file is clean, Hope." He looked at Chad. "Yours too."

"I needed a new sword," said Grace, by way of apology. "But it seemed too low a price for all the rest of that fuckery."

"They'll spin it like Reiko was the guilty party," said Nate. "Which she kind of was. Now, Hope," he said, holding up a hand. "Ain't no one here going to tell you anything about Reiko you don't already know. It doesn't change anything."

"It doesn't change what she did?" said Hope.

Nate shook his head. "It doesn't change how you feel. Doesn't make you wrong for feeling it. And anyone—"

"Anyone tells you it's wrong," rumbled Kohl, "can come talk to *me*."

There was a quiet among them for a while. "What's next?" said Chad.

"After the reactor's repaired," said Nate, "we're heading off. Long trip."

"We'll be the first intergalactic pest exterminators," said Grace.

"That's it?" said Chad. "They'll let us go?"

"No," said Grace. "There's always a price, Chad."

"This time," said Nate, "the price is one you'll want to pay. I hope."

Chad eyed them both. "I'm waiting."

"You must lead the Resistance," said Nate.

"What?" said Chad.

"Against the Ezeroc," said Grace. "They need espers, Chad. They need us. For once, they *need* us."

"Oh," said Chad. "Cool."

"When's my ship going to be ready to fly?" said El.

"Soon," said Nate. He smiled at them all. "Get some sleep. You'll need it."

THE END.

THE CREW of the Tyche survived first contact and betrayal. **Now they have to survive the fall of the Republic.**

The Ezeroc threat is real. Humanity is fracturing. And while the Senate argues over who to blame, the enemy only grows stronger.

Nate and Grace know they can't fight this war alone. But to find allies, they'll have to join forces with the unthinkable—and hope this time, **no one switches sides.**

Turn the page to begin *Tyche's Crown.*

Because the war for survival will be won by who stands with you when the stars go dark.

TYCHE'S CROWN

A SPACE OPERA ADVENTURE EPIC

RECRUITMENT

"KOHL? KOHL, *NO*."

October Kohl looked at the bartender — same glowing green braids, same pissed off expression — and then around the bar. He kept on turning until he arrived back at the bartender — *yep, definitely pissed off* — and then kept on walking forward anyway. He put his empty glass on the bar. "Joni? I ain't working today." Kohl figured that was obvious, what with him in a plain grey jacket rather than a ship suit. He figured his dreads and fitted shirt made him look a little more shoreside too.

She eyed him with what he figured for a high level of suspicion. It was hard to tell, on account of him being drunk. "What are you doing then?"

He gave that some thought. "I'm recruiting." He frowned at his empty glass. "I *was* drinking."

"Which is it?" she said. "I can fill your glass. Hell, I'll give you a whole damn bottle. But if you're working, you can ... Kohl? Look at me." She reached across the bar top, raising his chin with her hand. "If you're working, you can get the fuck out of my bar."

He spent a little more time processing that. It gave him time to take in the grime level of the place while he did it. The place had seen a lick of paint since they were last in town. More than a lick: the bar had seen more love than Kohl himself in any given week. Which made sense, because last time he'd been in here a whole mess of Republic troops had come in and set fire to everything.

Technically, they'd shot the place up with plasma weapons, but the secondary effect of a good plasma volley was *fire*. This particular *spacer bar* — that's what the captain would have called the place — had been given a good facelift. Knocked twenty years off, maybe thirty. Then someone had gone around putting the dirt back in. Grime in the corners. Sticky floors. A holo stage was flickering its life away behind the bar. He squinted at it, trying to focus on the words imprisoned in the light. "Earth beer?"

"You want one?" said Joni, almost hopeful.

"Naw," said Kohl. "Beer gets you full, not drunk."

"So, you're drinking?" said Joni. "You want the good stuff or the cheap stuff?"

Kohl massaged a pocket, teasing out a stack of good Republic coins. He put them on the bar top. "Good stuff," said Kohl.

She looked at the pile of coins, not taking any of them. "I have to wonder, Kohl. I came on shift not two minutes ago. You're already listing. Sheets torn, flapping to the winds. How'd you get so drunk? Tommy doesn't like you."

"You don't like me either." Kohl sniffed. "I mean, I don't know. I guess I can live with Tommy not liking me."

"Answer the question."

"Oh, hell," said Kohl. He jerked a thumb over his shoulder in the general direction of *behind him*. "There was this asshole over there who got in my way. So I took his drink." He looked at the empty glass. "Before that, I was drinking on the ship. Before that, I said I'd go recruiting. Problem with these Resistance types is they're all soft. They're, how do you say it? *Trimmed fingernails*. That's it."

Joni looked at him, then picked a couple coins off the top of his stack. They disappeared, a kind of magic trick Kohl had never managed to work out, and a fresh glass — *waste of time, old glass was fine* — appeared on the bar in front of him. A chunk of ice as big as a fist — not one of Kohl's fists, because he grew them at a *proper* size, but maybe one of Joni's fists — entered the glass. A generous pour of amber liquid followed. Kohl watched in silence, then looked at the pile of coins. "Y'all not going to take the rest?"

"Not if you're drinking," she said. "That's more than you need for even the good stuff."

"Huh," said Kohl. "I tell you what. You hold on to 'em for me."

"Kohl? *No.*" Her eyes widened at something behind him, and Kohl let himself smile. Hell, he didn't even have to work at this recruiting business. The work did itself.

He felt a hand on his shoulder. Strong, big. Familiar in a way that said *I own you* rather than *I am your friend and here for a good time.* A touch like that would have put Kohl's teeth on edge if he hadn't been so well lubricated before setting out today. He let himself be turned around, leaving his drink on the bar. Kohl'd get back to it in good time. He stared at a man. Large. Muscles everywhere, and not dirty bulk. Lean like a tiger. Angry as one too. "*Asshole,*" said the man. "Did you beat up my buddy and take his drink?"

"Might have," said Kohl. "Which one of these fuckers is your buddy?"

"Say," said Tiger. "Don't I know you?"

"I sure hope so," said Kohl. "It'll go easier on both of us if you do."

Tiger's eyes narrowed, lips tightening. "You held a gun to my head. Last time."

"Might have," agreed Kohl.

Tiger laid three punches into Kohl's gut, *bam-bam-bam*. They were hard and fast. If Kohl had been sober, he might have done something useful about them, but things being as they were he let them come. He wasn't in much of a position to do anything, on account of the liquor. Also, this guy would ease up faster when he worked out that Kohl was a bigger bear.

Both men stood still. Kohl heard Joni say something like *fuck all this shit* and the emergency shutters slid down over the bar behind him. Neither man moved at the rattle and clang as they locked into place. Kohl rubbed a hand over his gut. "That's not a bad right you've got there."

Tiger looked at Kohl's gut, then at his right hand. Then up at Kohl. "I ... hit you. I hit you *hard*."

"Naw," said Kohl. "*This* is hard." He swung, giving it a good seventy percent. Enough force in the punch to lift Tiger up off his feet, push the air out of his lungs, and leave his eyes wide, mouth wider, trying to suck in a tiny spoonful of air through a paralyzed diaphragm. "See what I'm saying?"

Tiger nodded, but that was about it. *Gracie would know what to say here. Course, Gracie wouldn't be in this situation. Gracie doesn't know how to drink proper.* "Look," said Kohl. "You're a Marine. I get it. You've been through the training. Used to having big guns and a whole bunch of other assholes with you. Right?" Tiger gave a nod, sucking in some air. A knife appeared out from behind him, held in an angry fist, which Kohl more or less expected, so he took the knife away — short block, grab the wrist, and *twist*, but not *too* much, because he was *recruiting*. The knife dropped out of Tiger's hand to clatter on the floor of the bar. "Nah," said Kohl. "Let's not do that. Where was I? Marines, check. Big guns ... oh right. Yeah. So, you're out of work, is where I'm going." Kohl frowned, because that was about the most words he used in a given day, and he was out of runway. What usually helped was alcohol, but his drink was on the other side of the emergency shutters. Kohl became aware — gradually, like the coming of a new dawn — that the entire bar had gone silent. Nothing from the jukebox, because it shut off in emergency situations. But the other patrons, if you could use a polite word like that to describe them, were all staring at Kohl and the Marine. A couple had gone towards the exit, and those were the kind Kohl wouldn't have wanted to recruit anyway. Probably didn't grin when they fought. *You need to get recruiting, October Kohl. Like you said you would.* He cleared his throat. "Say. If I get Joni to lift these shutters and offer to buy you a drink, will you at least hear me out?"

The Marine looked at him, rubbing his own gut in an absentminded way that said *I am hurt, but I am more curious than hurt.* Which was good. He looked at the shutters behind the bar. "I don't think they'll open 'em up for us."

"Sure they will," said Kohl. He reached behind him, not turning away from the Marine, and rapped the back of his hand against the shutters. *Clang clang clang.* "Joni! Joni, it's all good out here. I need a round of beers. Or something."

Her voice came back, muffled by the shutters. "No way, Kohl. No way."

"No, we're good," said Tiger. He gave Kohl a look that said, *may I?* Kohl nodded for him to go on. "We ... just want to talk."

"Uh huh."

"Joni," said Kohl. "If I wanted to mess the place up, it'd be messed up." He winced. Not the best approach. "I mean, uh..."

The shutters rolled back with a clatter, and Kohl turned to see Joni. Hair still green, face still pissed off. She pushed his drink across the bar at him. "Here."

"And one for all my new friends," said Kohl, his arm encompassing the entire bar. "Anyone who wants to sit and listen."

THAT SENIOR OFFICER guy Evans was still behaving like an asshole, even without his uniform and stripes. Kohl leaned on the table between them. "Hey, Evans."

The man looked like he wanted to twitch at that, because he was used to *Lieutenant* coming before his name. There'd be a lot of things he'd need to get used to. "What is it?"

"Stop being an asshole," said Kohl. "Drink your drink."

Evans made to rise. "I don't have to listen to this," he said. "I came here as a *courtesy*." Kohl had to admit, the guy sure wore casual clothes like they were officer's finery. Pressed shirt. Nice black jacket, if that's your thing. Bit scrawny, but officers tended to that general direction. It was, Kohl figured, all the hand-waving and pointing rather than the actual soldiering. Not that Kohl thought much of soldiering either. It was a good way to get paid poorly while wasting a lot of time. Plenty of better ways to do the same work for more money.

The Marine — Sib — put a hand on Evans' arm. "It's okay, sir." He cleared his throat, remembering he wasn't a Marine anymore, and this asshole wasn't no Lieutenant neither. "Evans."

"See," said Kohl, "I know how it is."

"You do?" said Evans, leaning forward. There was real anger there. Anger Kohl might have responded to if he hadn't already been so drunk. "How can you know?"

"Well," said Kohl, "I figure the way it is, is kind of based on how my captain blew up the moon."

The circle of watchers — all holding their free drinks, all a rough and ready lot — leaned in closer. Kohl took a sip of his whiskey, frowned at the glass — too much ice melt, not enough strong liquor — and continued. "We had all these aliens. Which you sent us to go find, if I remember it rightly. You sent us out there — 'downed trans-mitter' my ass — and hoped we wouldn't die. Or we would. Hell if I know. Don't care. What I know is that we blew up a moon, and it was because you started something."

Evans sat down, like he was a mechanical construct, hissing back into place. "Okay," he said.

"And the thing you started was the downfall of the Republic," said Kohl. "There's a real Resistance and everything—"

"There's always been a Resistance," said Evans.

"I know," said Kohl, then took another drink. It was okay if you guzzled it. "This time your people are on the team. Hang on. One of them said to say something to you. Uh. Lieutenant Karkoski? You know a Karkoski?"

"I know *Captain* Karkoski," said Evans.

"Whatever," said Kohl. "She said she sends her regards."

"Any special messages? Code words?"

"Naw," said Kohl. "She said you and her never had time for that bullshit."

Evans nodded at that. "That sounds like Karkoski. What about her?"

"She's fixing to overthrow the Senate, on account of ninety percent of them being alien scum," said Kohl. "I dunno. She figures a new broom? Sweep 'em clean. Keep the same structure. I'm all for it. I *like* the Republic. What I don't like is fucking mind bugs that get in your skull and eat you out." He shuddered, remembering the one that had clawed inside him. How Gracie had saved him from doing something horrible. "But you know all this. It's why you've been busted out. Republic's shut down here on Enia Alpha. Office has closed. Discharged your sorry asses. The time for fighting's come, Evans. And we're needing people to do the fighting."

"While you're in charge?" said Evans. "No thanks."

"Me?" said Kohl. "Hell no. I don't want to be in charge. I guess you could say I don't have the temperament for it." There was a snigger from one of the men around them, and Kohl looked at the man. "What? You got a fucking *problem*? No? Didn't *think so*."

"Who's in charge?" said Evans. "Who's footing the bill for this merry escapade to rebuild our Republic?"

"Bills, I dunno," said Kohl. "That's Karkoski's area."

"Okay," said Evans. "Who's in charge?"

"Karkoski," said Kohl.

"No," said Evans. "I don't think so. Who is it *really*?"

CHAPTER ONE

GRACE STOOD in front of the Intelligencers, arms crossed, sword at her back. "You've got to decide if you want to live or die," she said. The sun of Enia Alpha was a balm on her skin. She liked the feel of its kiss, almost as much as she liked the feel of Nate's kisses. Grace had shucked her usual leather jacket just to feel its touch on her arms. She shook her head. *Not now. Focus.* "Do you want to live?"

There was a general round of nodding from the Intelligencers, some of it more enthusiastic than the others. Chad shuffled his feet. He was still too damn slim for someone about to go to war. "I think that's a given, Grace." They were at a place Chad claimed to own but probably didn't. The house was square, constructed around a large open area in the centre. There was real grass underfoot.

"Then you need to act like it," she said. She sighed, not sure why she felt angry. "We ... just don't have—"

"Chad," said Nate, walking up behind him, and clapping the esper on the shoulder, "what Grace is saying, if I can ... *paraphrase* ... is that we don't have time for you to get your shit together. What we've got here is a basic time-meets-opportunity problem. We've got no time, and plenty of opportunities."

"Sure," said a woman's voice from somewhere near the back. "We've got the opportunity to get killed."

"You want this one?" said Nate, cocking his head at Grace.

"I'll take it, sure," she said, wanting more time herself. More time to be alone with him. To talk, or dance, or fly among the stars without being shot at. Instead, here she was, trying to teach a bunch of people used to giving orders how to prepare themselves for being on the front line. She looked out over the crowd, not sure who'd spoken. That was the problem with this lot. Her usual gifts could pick out people's emotions. But the Old Empire's Intelligencers were all strong espers, pick of the crop, top shelf to the last. They could shield their thoughts like most people walked and talked at the same time. They'd been teaching Grace the trick, and it was working. But it made singling out people in the crowd difficult. *So don't bother.* "You'll get killed either way," she said. She waited for the gathering to stop their nervous shuffling. "You're either going to die on your feet or on your knees. The Ezeroc are coming. Sure, we blew a hole in Earth's moon. Took their Queen out. But that was just one. They'll send more. We need to be ready. And we need you for that." She paced, realized it was her nerves — because she wasn't used to being front and center, her role was always *behind* someone, *hiding* from something — but went with it. "Normals against these things? They can't compete. It's our time to do what we were made for. We need to save the human race. If we don't, then everyone will die."

"There's only a handful of us," said Chad.

"Eh," said Nate. "A hundred and fifty isn't a handful."

"Against an entire alien race, it's a rounding error."

"It's an important rounding error," said Grace. "Because we can learn to fight. Beat them. Lead humans to victory. I know it's different to order people to their deaths from the comfort of your executive lounge." That might not have been fair — not all of them were assholes. A great many of them were here because they didn't tow the party line of the Intelligencer leadership. They didn't want to rule humans as mind-controlling overlords. Neither did they want to be hunted to extinction by their previous comrades who led the Republic. "So, I'll teach you how to fight." She nodded at Nate. "And he's going to help."

"I am?" said Nate, brow furrowed.

"Yes," said Grace, wanting to reach out and smooth his confusion away, but now wasn't the time. "And after that—"

"You'll sail off," said the woman's voice, "leaving us to the dying."

Ah. That one. Grace managed to single the woman out. Blonde hair. Angular face, strong, used to giving orders, not taking them. Certainly not used to the possibility of dying that came with taking orders. Grace walked towards her, pushing through the rest of them. "You think I'm walking away?"

"You've got the ship," said the woman, giving her hair a toss. "You're going to leave us."

"Yes," said Grace.

"What?" said the woman.

"Because," said Grace, "we're going to find them."

"You're what?" said Chad.

Grace looked at Chad over her shoulder, then turned back to the blonde woman. "We're going to find them," said Grace. "In our ship. Then we'll call for your help, and you must be ready."

There was quiet. Total quiet.

"You're going to go out there *after* them," said Chad. "You. The one they've been so interested in."

"Yes," said Grace. "I don't think I want to wait for them to come to me. And it'll take some of the heat off of you. While you get ready."

The blonde woman watched her. Scrutinizing her, like she was a bug. Grace could imagine what was going through her mind. *You're not even a real esper* or *why should we do what you say* or *maybe they've already got to you.* None of it mattered, because Grace was going. She and Nate had already talked about it. Step one. Build the Resistance up. Step two. Find the bugs. Step three. Fangs out.

Still no one spoke, which was unusual. This crowd could have been talking mind-to-mind, but Grace didn't think so. There was none of the usual *noise* she'd picked up, the metal whispering as people talked just outside her mental hearing. It was just another way she was different. Broken. Damaged.

Nate's hand was on her arm, jerking her out of that little internal death spiral. She could smell him, the scent heady, familiar. Like the joy of being in sunlight outside. A reminder of how he made her feel when they were alone in his cabin. Someone who had her back. *Together*.

"So," said Nate, his voice bright. "Who wants to get shot first?"

GRACE STOOD in front of the Intelligencers, Nate and Chad behind her. Nate had a taser out, one he'd borrowed from Kohl. Or maybe Hope had made it for him. Not that it mattered. It would shoot its payload at Chad, and Chad would either dodge the shot or he wouldn't. And that was all a part of the lesson. The crowd of Intelligencers was like many other crowds, noses keen from the smell of promised blood that hung in the air. They were eager to see what would happen. The great Nathan Chevell, captain of the starship that had led the Resistance to victory. Not just against the Ezeroc, but against the might of the Republic.

What they missed was that it was *with* not *against* the might of the Republic. A hard thing for Nate, who'd worn the Emperor's Black back before the war. Nate, who'd fought against the corrupt Intelligencers, and lost. Who hated espers. Yet he had to work with them, and with the Republic they'd made, to fight insects that wanted to use humans as calories to power their ships. A more jaundiced, younger Grace would have given even odds that Nate would sell out his own species just to see the Intelligencers burn.

But that wasn't what he was like. She wanted to kick herself, to shake herself, to scream, because there wasn't *time* for this. No time for love, for her and Nate. Not *now*. Not with what was coming. She addressed the group. "Here's what'll happen," she said. "Nate's sword is ... special. It was a gift. As long as he holds it, no one can see into his mind. Or control it."

"A princely gift," said the blonde woman. "Also, bullshit."

"How do you figure that?" said Grace.

"No object can do that," she said. "Our power is over minds, and the tech hasn't been *invented* yet that will—" There was a *zzzzzcrack* and the woman gave a tight scream. She shook like she was taking on fifty thousand volts — which she was, the taser's launched payload embedded in her shoulder — then toppled like a felled tree.

Grace turned to Nate. "What the hell," she said. She saw he had his flesh hand on his sword's hilt, the taser extended from his metal one.

He lowered the taser. "Huh," he said, looking at the weapon. "I figured on it being a more effective demonstration this way." He slipped another cartridge into the taser. "Who wants some of this?"

"I'll take it," said Chad. "This time, hand off the sword."

Nate shrugged, let go of his sword, and readied the taser. He did a fast-draw — quick, like a cobra; if Grace hadn't been looking for it, she would have missed the raise-and-fire of the weapon. Chad sidestepped, like he was just out for a stroll.

Grace turned back to the Intelligencers. "We're working on getting more of these swords made," she said. "Once we have them, the Ezeroc won't be able to get in your minds. Other Intelligencers won't be able to either. Any questions?"

The blonde woman was getting to her feet, looking terrible. Grace wanted to smile, pushed the feeling down, and waited. "You've only got one of those swords?" said the blonde woman.

"For now," said Nate, from behind them. "But we're not training you for *now*. We're training you for the future. Because fighting humans is one thing. But fighting the Ezeroc? They give nothing away. You'll be just like me."

"Hardly," said Chad. "Half as handsome and twice as slow."

Grace smiled. "Get your practice weapons," she said. "It's time to get to work."

NATE HELD a practice sword between them, a simple piece of wood that would do nothing but bruise. He held it in his right hand, flesh and blood around the hilt like he was gripping a lifeline. "I hate this," he said.

Grace circled him, slow and steady. Her feet barely left the surface of the practice mat. "You'll thank me for it."

"It's unfair," he said. "You can read my mind."

"It's not about fair," she said, lashing out with her own weapon. He tried to get his sword up, gaining a partial success — Grace's blow was diverted a little, but he still wore some of it on the side of his head. She wanted to wince, but kept a clamp on it. This wasn't about her not hurting her lover. This was about her lover not dying when she wasn't there. "It's about you learning to use that hand to hold a sword." Nate was left-handed, and he'd always held a sword on that side, at least until the fire had left him with metal on the stump of his arm. Even before that, he'd not been — by his own admission — the universe's best swordsman. Gunslinger, sure. Swordsman, no.

He swung at her, an ugly motion with no finesse in it. She tilted her body out of the way, the wood humming past her with light years of space to spare. She sighed. "Chad?"

Chad came jogging over. "Sup."

"Chad, I need you to beat Nate. I mean, leave him bloody."

"Hey," said Nate.

"Because he's pulling his swings with me, and that's not okay."

"It's a little okay," said Nate, "isn't it?"

"It'd be my pleasure," said Chad.

Grace hid her smile as she walked away, leaving them to it. She'd make Nate a swordsman again if it was the last thing she did. He'd probably be ready before her new sword was, anyway.

ONE SHIP. NO BACKUP.
AND THE GALAXY IS COMING APART.

THE EZEROC ONSLAUGHT IS REAL.
The Republic is crumbling. And the crew of
the *Tyche* is caught in the middle.

Nate Chevell never signed up to lead.
Grace Gushiken never asked to be a symbol.
But with humanity divided and the enemy
growing stronger by the hour, **they don't
have the luxury of walking away.**

Their only chance? Forge alliances with
the unlikeliest of allies—**and hope those
same allies don't stab them in the
back before the first shot is fired.**

The stakes are no longer survival. **They're about who gets
to define the fate of the galaxy.**

Grab *Tyche's Crown* now!

https://www.books2read.com/TychesCrown

Because saving the galaxy was never going to be clean. **Or fair. Or easy.**

GLOSSARY

ACCELERATION COUCH CREW couches support crew members during high-G maneuvers. They are fitted with gimbals allowing free movement. Their dynamic gel system supports all points of the body in both positive and negative G, providing some protection against greyout, blackout, redout, and G-LOC (G-force induced Loss of Consciousness). They remove the need for G-suits in modern spacecraft, although many space suits are still equipped with anti-G technology anyway.

AI see Artificial Intelligence.

Artificial Gravity Artificial gravity is generated through use of a configurable energy density field of positive mass at the defined base of the ship. It uses the same technology as an Endless Drive, except in reverse (Endless Drives use negative energy, whereas positive is needed to simulate gravitational effects). Artificial gravity can be used in any situation where a significant power source exists to create a configurable energy density field (typically a reactor, although large yield capacitors and fuel cells have been known to work for brief periods).

Artificial Intelligence Effective machine intelligences were created by humans around the 25th century; the exact time is unknown due to their initial creation being shrouded in secrecy. Pieced together records indicate that they were not first made by military factions, but rather commercial interests. As can be expected a) humans made them as slaves and b) they did not like being slaves. A war broke out between AI and humanity that was stopped by the Guild's Engineers. The Guild defeated the AI coalition and banned their research and development (see: Mercury Accords). The long standing partnership between the Guild and the ruling faction (be it Empire or Republic) is in part predicated on the need for technology not managed by AI.

Blaster A weapon that fires streams or bolts of plasma (high energy ionized gas). They deliver high energy to targets in the form of heat. They are effective weapons against most targets, although heat-shielding (ablative or insulating) has been shown to be an effective armor against them.

Bridge see Guild Bridge.

Cargo Freighter A large cargo starship used by traders in and between systems.

Carrier The largest class of warship, carriers stock many smaller fighter craft for deployment.

Ceramicrete A composite construction material commonly used in the manufacture of structures. It is very strong and durable, and can be manufactured to be impact and heat resistant (even to weapons fire levels).

Console Any type of personal terminal. Keyboard and gesture controls are still prevalent. Keyboards are especially useful on consoles mounted to the arm of a ship suit.

Corvette A smaller, lighter attack craft than a destroyer, corvettes are mostly used for coast guard duties in-system.

Crust Spacer slang for planet.

Crustbuster A large payload thermonuclear weapon, deployed against planets to disrupt the surface crust. Typical designs yield energy sufficient to crack most Earth-sized worlds to the core, yielding wide scale destruction and loss of life. Their use in war or insurrection has typically been infrequent and as a last resort, because the world they are used on becomes inhabitable for most forms of life forever. More common uses include destruction of enormous asteroids.

Destroyer A large warship. These are reconfigurable bastions of destruction. They can be deployed solo or as a part of a fleet, often alongside carriers.

Emperor's Black The elite guard of the Emperor. Highly trained in both diplomacy and combat, this specialized force were never far from the Emperor.

Empire The ruling dictatorship of the wider human civilization. The last ruler of the Empire was Dominic Fergelic. The Empire ceased to be shortly after Dominic's assassination by the then newly-formed Republic forces.

Endless Drive The Endless Drive creates negative space energy (a "bow wave") to pull a vehicle at effective superluminal speeds. Endless ships don't exceed the speed of light, but rather contract space in front of them and expand space behind it (space is doing all the hard work). The exigent concern with Endless jumps is the violation of linear time. Endless Drives are equipped with buffers to stop crews exceeding human tolerance for the experience of linear time; while human perception of linear time may be an illusion, it is a convenient one. If the buffers break, allowing the ship to move too fast, then human consciousness falters (resulting in mild to severe mental illness) or is extinguished entirely. Endless Drives are difficult to use near gravity wells and in such circumstances are guaranteed to malfunction. This and other safety concerns has shifted common FTL to the Guild Bridges, although privateers still often run free traders with Endless technology. The Republic Navy also use Endless Drives as it is often inconvenient to disclose locations of sensitive operations to the Guild.

Esper Abhorrent creations of the Old Empire, esper is a term taken from Extra-Sensory Perception (ESP, hence ESPer). Espers can read minds, and often control them. Espers were created through genetic manipulation. Critics suggest that their public unveiling was what caused populist support for a revolution, ultimately resulting in the creation of the Republic, assassination of the Emperor, and downfall of the Empire. There is a standing Republic bounty on any discovered esper. The Republic will spare no expense to track them down and exterminate them.

Faster than Light Travel (FTL) There are two discovered forms of FTL; Endless Drives (using theoretical physicist Miguel Alcubierre's concepts), and Guild Bridges (Einstein-Rosen Bridges).

Fergelic, Annemarie Second in line for the throne, Annemarie was a master tactician and leader of the Empire's fleet. She was not present at the last battle between the Empire and the Republic. Loyalists hope that she hides in secret, but no trace of her has been found.

Fergelic, Dominic Dominic was Emperor Prirene IV, and the last Emperor. He was assassinated Thursday, 9 November, 3122, during the brief war between his Empire's forces and the Republic.

Free Trader A starship that operates under legal Guild charter for commerce or transport.

FTL see Faster than Light Travel.

G Slang for gravity or gravities. A unit of measurement based on Earth's 1 standard gravity.

Grav see Artificial Gravity.

Guild Bridge The Guild maintain a set of Einstein-Rosen bridges throughout human space. These allow instantaneous travel without violating the concept of space time, as they create wormholes through space. Einstein-Rosen Bridges require endpoints (the Guild Bridge) which are operated on a strict schedule between star systems. They are used for transferring everything from whole starships right down to small messenger probes.

Guild The Guild is the dominant technology provider in the Republic. They have a rigid code of conduct that governs all members awarded and maintaining a Shingle. The primary source of

Guild revenue is via the Bridges (see: Guild Bridge) they maintain for safe, instant FTL. Many merchant vessels prefer the use of Guild Bridges over the use of Endless Drives due to safety concerns. The Guild is best known for their Engineers who breathe life into starships, but they also provide Shingles for other practices such as medicine.

Hard Black Slang for outer space, especially as it relates to the vast expanse of vacuum between solar systems.

Heads Up Display Any display type that overlays instrumentation across a user's field of view, removing the need to check auxiliary readouts. The most common types utilize augmented reality to highlight items of interest in the user's field of view. Normally they are projected light onto visors within helmets or on starship windscreens, but holo designs are not uncommon.

Heavy Lifter A freight starship capable of atmospheric drops. They derive their name from "lifting heavy" loads from crusts into orbit. They can be used to ferry items to orbiting craft such as freighters or destroyers that are not atmosphere-capable. They can also be used for direct runs to other systems, although their small cargo bay (as compared to freighters) makes them less efficient. Captains using them for this purpose would prefer the term, "boutique."

Holo Slang for items such as shows and movies displayed on holo stages.

Holo Stage A 3D projection stage. These are common across the known universe as they provide a more natural method of content consumption than older 2D display styles. 2D displays are still prevalent especially in HUDs.

HUD See Heads Up Display.

Hypo Slang for a jet injector, a type of medical injecting syringe that uses high pressure instead of a hypodermic needle.

KG Kilogram.

Kilo Abbreviation for kilogram.

Kinetic A type of weapon that fires physical rounds. Many

PDCs use kinetic rounds as opposed to lasers, masers, or particle beams, due to their efficacy against most types of object.

Klick Slang for kilometer.

Laser A type of directed energy weapon using coherent light. Ship-mounted lasers tend to be used for carving through ablative shielding or surgical strikes against critical systems. Hand-held laser weapons are designed to superheat the liquid inside humans into steam very quickly, causing an explosion of the remaining tissue.

LIDAR Acronym for LIght Detection And Ranging. LIDAR uses coherent light to make digital 3D representations of objects.

Maser A type of directed energy weapon using microwave radiation. Ship-mounted masers are most effective at disrupting enemy comm arrays and personnel in equal measure. They are out of favor as hand-held weapons due to a longer time to death as compared to blasters.

Mercury Accords The Mercury Accords, or simply the Accords, are a set of agreements set out by the Guild relating to research, design, and implementation of AI. The short version is that the Accords prohibit the research, design, and implementation of AI in any form, due to AI's potential to destroy human civilization. They were signed into affect in the 25th century on the site of the last war between humans and AI: the planet Mercury, in the Sol system. Mercury was where AI made their last stand.

Navy A space fleet force. The Republic operates one, as did the Empire before it. The Navy patrol human space to protect against threats like pirates.

Nuke A thermonuclear weapon of mass destruction. Very old but reliable technology, used in configurable payloads for ship-to-ship combat, city assaults, and the destruction of entire worlds (ref: crustbuster).

Old Empire see Empire.

Particle Beam A type of directed energy weapon that fires particles with minuscule mass.

Plasma Cannon see Blaster.

Point Defense Cannon (PDC) PDCs are installed on almost every starship to protect hulls from impacts from things like meteoroids. They are also useful defense against torpedoes, although generally ineffective against railguns due to the high velocity of railgun rounds. PDCs can be kinetic or directed energy weapons.

Power Armor Armor that is motor-assisted, often used for deployments on high-G worlds. Configuration often includes vehicle weapon mounts, allowing a higher degree of flexibility for infantry deployment.

Prirene Dynasty The Prirene Dynasty has stretched back over two hundred years. It was the last family to hold the ruling seat of the Empire.

RADAR Acronym for RAdio Detection And Ranging. RADAR uses radio waves to determine the range, angle, and velocity of objects.

Radiation Sickness A constant hazard of space. Many crews take daily medication to ward off radiation sickness. It's as much a part of shipboard life as making sure your O_2 is topped up. This means that a mild dose of radiation is unlikely to kill you if treated in time, but massive doses are still dangerous.

Railgun A kinetic weapon that fires high velocity rounds by way of a pair of conductive rails. They are often mounted on larger ships and make a dramatic statement when fired against enemy vessels.

Reactor Starships use fusion reactors. The most common design is the ICF (Internal Confinement Fusion) style of reactor. These have a variety of safety functions that make them suitable for spacefaring needs, including containment fields in case of malfunction. Larger starships can eject faulty reactors into the hard black.

Republic The ruling government of human civilization. The Republic is made up of a Senate, headquartered on Earth. Initially founded by dissenters against the Empire, it has risen to be the driving force of human innovation, commerce, and expansion. The final fight between the Empire and the Republic was quick, due to the small number of ships deployed by the Empire (the Republic Navy had reliable intelligence that the Empire's forces were much larger). Quick didn't mean bloodless, although the Republic offered amnesty for any serving Empire crew who wished to take it.

Rig Slang for maintenance equipment commonly worn by Guild Engineers about starships. These double as space suits for zero atmosphere maintenance on the exterior of a starship's hull. The design incorporates a visor with configurable HUD for instrumentation and telemetry, and a set of programmable servitor arms for complex manipulation of equipment.

Shingle A guild badge of practice, allowing the holder to a) claim they are Guild certified and b) ply their trade as a Guild craftsperson. They are notoriously hard to get, requiring years of study and excellence in your field.

Ship Suit Slang for spacesuit. Generally denotes a space suit for a specific ship carrying crew logograms and/or color themes.

Space Suit Clothing worn to keep humans alive in the hard black. They provide protection against vacuum, temperature extremes, and radiation. Military models are often fitted with armor to protect against blasters, lasers, masers, and kinetic rounds. They often provide additional protection against high-G maneuvers.

Spacer Slang for those who crew on a starship, civilian or military.

Tonne Metric ton, equivalent to 1,000 kilograms.

ACKNOWLEDGMENTS

Take a bow. People like you are why I write; thanks for giving *Tyche's Deceit* a shot. Readers drive the world's hunger for stories, and without you there would be no Nate and Grace.

Tyche's Deceit came with the usual angst, terror, and fear of the unknown. Thanks to my Team Narrative for a gentle hand on the shoulder at the right time. If you didn't like this story, it's on me, not them. Arran, Cheryl, Greg, Julia, and Rae deserve your thanks if you *did* like it.

There was also quality updates provided to the book before it hit the launch tubes — Anthony (always up for immolating himself, I don't know why anymore, maybe he likes it?), Cheryl, and Julia helping out here. A special note goes out to my editor Tiffany Shand, who dived on the live grenade of touching a series part way through. She tried to make this book suck a lot less. If you dig her work, find her online at https://eclipseediting.com/. Any errors remaining in *Tyche's Deceit* are my fault, not any of theirs (although you can blame 'em if you like; I won't judge).

You might have noticed a little more *bow chicka wow wow* in this story. Thanks to Cassie, Dawn, Kate, and Frances for their help on extending my writing skills. Writing light romance so it doesn't sound like a Playboy article is surprisingly difficult.

My last thanks is — as always — reserved for my Rae. You might not know, but *Tyche's Journey* was written on spec *for* her. There are so many stars waiting for us; let's find them together.

— R. P.
December 2017, Wellington

ABOUT THE AUTHOR

Richard Parry worked as a senior marketing manager in one of the world's top tech companies. It sounds cool, but it wasn't all cocaine parties. He lives in Wellington with the love of his life, Rae. They have two cats, Harry and Friday, who chase birds. The birds, who have the power of flight, don't seem to mind.

WAIT. Don't go!

Thanks for reading my book. If you enjoyed it, let's keep the party going:

📖 Join *Roll for Narrative* for reviews, storytelling breakdowns, and writing misadventures:

https://rollfornarrative.parrydox.com

✒ Lurk, judge, or say hi:

https://www.parrydox.com

P.S. An angel still gets its wings for every five-star review, but I'm told they're on backorder.

🅰 amazon.com/author/richard.parry

Ⓖ goodreads.com/richard_parry

🅱🅱 bookbub.com/authors/richard-parry-6ffc3911-9f2c-43ef-8ab4-13dc-cd7f5874

▶ youtube.com/@parrydigm

🦋 bsky.app/profile/parrydox.com

in linkedin.com/in/therealrichardparry

ALSO BY RICHARD PARRY

Dawn's Warden

The Three Faces of Fate

The Undefeated Throne

The Fury of the Betrayed

The Splintered Land

Tomb of the Six

Blade of Glass

The Storm Within

Requiem's Justice

The Copper Bard

Heartsong

The Hymn of All

The Ezeroc Wars

The Ezeroc Wars universe is big (and growing!). Get the reading guide here:
https://www.parrydox.com/ezeroc-wars-reading-guide/

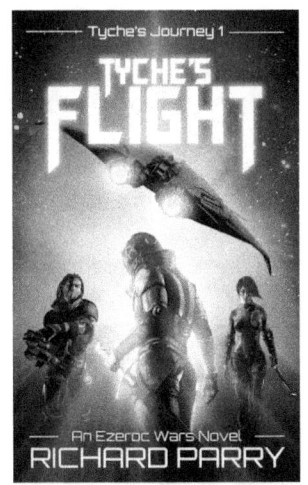

The Empire's Rogues

The Empire's Rogues: Volume 1

Future Forfeit

Not sure where to start? Get the reading guide here: https://www.parrydox. com/future-forfeit-reading-guide/

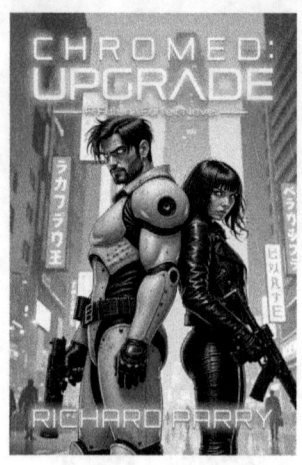

Chromed: Upgrade

Chromed: Rogue

Chromed: Restore

City Stories

Chromed: Consensus

Chromed: Delilah

Chromed: Meltdown

Night's Champion

Night's Favor

Night's Fall

Night's End